"Hi there!" a tall, gawky man booms out as he strides into the room. He appears to be in his thirties. He has large, intensely blue eyes and dirty blond, curly hair so long it lies in a floppy Afro. His face is ruggedly handsome, even though it is thin. He is shirtless but wears Levi's cut off just above his knees and white tennis shoes. The air charges up when he enters the room, and instantly he has everyone's undivided attention.

. . . . Then suddenly, he spins around, looks directly at me, and asks, "How old are you?"

I'm taken aback by his lightning-quick move and personal question, and I snap as if I've been attacked, on the edge, as I was in Carol City. "Fifteen. *Why*?"

"Mm, mm, mmp. *Too bad*!" He grabs his chest dramatically and acts disappointed.

"What?" I'm thrown off guard, then instantly incensed.

John smiles wider than I ever thought anyone could and winks a big blue eye at me. "Too young!" Again he turns on his heel and pushes through the screen door, roaring laughter to the night sky and all the way to his cottage.

"What . . . a . . . creep!" I say with disgust, wanting to scream at him. "He has no idea. Young, my ass," I add, fiercely blushing.

"Uh-oh, Dawn." Terry sounds worried.

"What?" I snap, not sure why I am so upset.

"He *likes* you."

I blush even harder.

Dawn Schiller

THE ROAD THROUGH WONDERLAND

SURVIVING John Holmes

MEDALLION
P R E S S

Medallion Press, Inc.
Printed in USA

"Dawn has survived. This book is a testimony to her will to overcome. As we wrote, shot, and cut *Wonderland*, she allowed us absolute transparency on a darkness few ever experience. She understood hers was a story that had to be told, not just as a cautionary tale against the horrors of violence and abuse, but as a beacon leading others in her predicament out of peril. This book is her triumph, but the narrative weaved within these pages is a true nightmare that will haunt you, as it did me, for years."

—James Cox, director and cowriter of *Wonderland*

"When I got an advance copy of *The Road Through Wonderland*, I thought I already knew the story. I picked it up casually, and then I could not put it down. I was up till 3 a.m. reading it. The power of Dawn Schiller's writing is that within a few pages, you are so drawn into her harrowing, roller-coaster life with her fractured family and then with porn star John Holmes, that you almost become her while reading it. There is not much separation between writer and reader. Schiller draws an unforgettable portrait of a lost, drug-addled corner of late 1970s Los Angeles and what it was like to be a lonely girl targeted by a predator in that world. The most mesmerizing memoir since Jeannette Walls' *The Glass Castle*, this whole book is one long, chilling money shot."

—Dana Kennedy, correspondent and journalist,
AOL News, *The New York Times, People, Time*

"Dawn Schiller's chilling account of her youth as the underage mistress of legendary porn star John Holmes is infused with the goodness and humanity that ultimately delivered her from her abusive ordeals. A classic story of an innocent young woman's descent and self-redemption, *The Road Through Wonderland* is gritty and starkly honest; it is at once a horror tale and a story of triumph."

—Mike Sager, writer at large, *Esquire*; author of
Scary Monsters and *Super Freaks*

"Dawn Schiller's harrowing account, *The Road Through Wonderland*, is a must read for everyone but especially professionals trained to identify and respond to horrible abuses such as those Dawn endured during her years with John Holmes and others around him. As I read, I wondered what we as a community can do to allow kids like Dawn to reach out for help rather than face death at the hands of their abusers on a daily basis. Unfortunately, in Dawn's case, by the time the abuse came to the attention of the police, she was already eighteen. Though very incapable of caring for herself, she was legally seen as an adult. And though visibly battered by Holmes, she was returned to his 'care' by police. I am thankful that our response to intimate partner violence and the exploitation of children and especially our 'throwaway teens' has improved over the last thirty years. However, we have a lot more work to do before people understand how predators like Holmes target vulnerable children and that these troubled children are worth saving."

—Sgt. Joanne Archambault, San Diego Police Department, retired;
executive director of End Violence Against Women International;
coeditor of *Sexual Assault Report*

"Courageous. Not only will Schiller's haunting story stay with you, but her beautifully descriptive writing will as well. This book is for anyone who has ever wondered why and how adults—or, for that matter, society—could turn their back on abused children. Schiller's painful insights help us begin to understand how these horrible things might happen. A haunting story in beautiful form. . . . Dawn Schiller manages to write so beautifully about something so shatteringly repulsive. Her picturesque descriptions [demonstrate] her ability to somehow connect with the beauty of the natural world while being neglected, exploited, and abused by the human world. The thing to take away from *The Road Through Wonderland* is not that it is a bizarre or extreme story, but that it is a girl's true story and gives us a rare and haunting look into what *surviving* takes. This important book illustrates the complexity of the victimization of children. For too many youth, victimization is not a single event but a process or even a state of being."

—Mitru Ciarlante, Youth Initiative Director,
National Center for Victims of Crime

DEDICATION

To my daughter, Jade,
my greatest blessing, who deserves the truth.

To the throwaways who have been battered and
robbed of their voice.

Published 2010 by Medallion Press, Inc.

The MEDALLION PRESS LOGO
is a registered trademark of Medallion Press, Inc.

Typeset in Adobe Garamond Pro
Printed in the United States of America

ISBN: 978-160542083-7

10 9 8 7 6 5 4 3 2 1
First Edition

CONTENTS

FOREWORD

A WORD FROM VAL KILMER

When I met Dawn Schiller on the set of *Wonderland*, I was amazed at her happy, warm smile and her loving attention to her young daughter. Nothing I saw in her even hinted at the terrible torture I knew she had endured with John Holmes. I liked her instantly. It was a very challenging role, playing someone so lost and destructive, and desperate. As I prepared to portray a man who caused her so much pain, she consistently proved that love heals all wounds—ALL. DAWN was and is an inspiration to me, as she will be to you. There is nothing in this world we cannot overcome, if we trust in love. Dawn bravely watched each scene with nods of approval for both Kate Bosworth and myself. Bravo, Dawn, for your courage and grace to share your story with the world. It's a healing message for all the women and girls in the world who have not yet found their strength. It's there, and Dawn's story proves it. Her story is a miracle. She is a miracle. I am proud to know her.

—Val Kilmer

A WORD FROM KATE BOSWORTH

I was nineteen years old when we embarked on the cinematic journey of *Wonderland*. I didn't really know what to expect from Dawn Schiller when we first met, but I assumed she would carry an obvious pain about her. She had been four years younger than I was at the time when she first met John Holmes and fell prey to his severe manipulation and abuse. I could not imagine how someone so young could be involved in such a horrifying situation as she had been and remain intact.

But broken she was not. Wise. Knowing. But certainly not a fragile victim. I was immediately struck by a certain purity about her. Her clear blue eyes shone at me with such clarity, warmth, and openness. We spoke for hours on end and in detail about her experience in *Wonderland*. Although she admitted how difficult it was, I was awed at the strength it took to confront these horrifying memories. The sort of thoughts one desperately tries to lock away and forget, never looking back.

The story of the Wonderland murders is remembered by most as a dark, drug-fueled tragedy. A moment in time which marked the screeching halt to an excessive, out-of-control high most thought would never end. In 1981, four people were found murdered, beaten to death with lead pipes in their home late at night on a long, twisting road called Wonderland Avenue. As news began to trickle in, there was immediate mention of drugs. Shots of bloodied sheets over bodies wheeled out on gurneys in the early morning Los Angeles light. Then whispers of the club owner Eddie Nash. And then, stranger still, of the infamous porn star named John Holmes.

As I immersed myself in the depths of this film, I began to realize we were not only retelling a story filled with incomprehensible evil but one of hope. Of overcoming the darkest of circumstances and surviving. This is her story.

Dawn, I thank you for sharing your story not only with me, but with the many people who will now take strength from your brutal honesty. And who will be encouraged to not only survive but, like you, to thrive.

—Kate Bosworth

We will not regret the past nor wish to shut the door on it.
We will comprehend the word *serenity* and we will know peace.

"The AA Promises"

You can't give it away unless you've got it, and
You can't keep it unless you give it away.

—Dawn

PROLOGUE

My name is Dawn Schiller. Some of you know me as the girl played by Kate Bosworth in the 2003 film *Wonderland*. I am not that girl.

When James Cox, the director, told me he'd cut the scene from the movie in which John beat me after selling me off to Eddie Nash for drugs, I felt as if John were choking the air out of me again.

Why would James do this? He was honest with me: It was because the audience couldn't handle seeing John hit me. They wouldn't "like" John or be sympathetic toward him.

I went home after the premiere and listened. I waited to hear comments from my family and friends. Mostly, no one said anything, which told me a lot.

And my family? Well, in general, they just nodded and said, "That's not what I remember." Buried in their memory was the fear of losing me—their daughter, sister, aunt, and niece. Of never seeing me again. Of finding out I had been beaten and raped, devastated by drugs, or sliced up on the streets because John had control of me.

They remember a very different John.

Where was the story of how I had escaped with my life from a man who was so self-seeking and ravaged?

I never wanted to tell this story . . . about my past with John . . . about my "secrets." It took a private investigator who found me some sixteen years after the murders to convince me to tell my tale. This was the catalyst for me to dredge up so much pain.

Ultimately, it was my voice—my essence—that John stole from me, and I wanted it back. These many long years after John, I have my voice again.

John did a lot of things to me—broke my bones, my heart, my innocence, my skin—but in the end, from where I stand today, he did a lot more. Through his name, *the king* unknowingly gave me the power to use my voice—to speak out and raise hope for many other thrown away and abused young women and girls.

If you thought you knew the story of Wonderland—if you thought you knew who John Holmes was—think again. I am here to tell you the story of those dark years in Hollywood behind the legends that others have tried to tell. This is the story of someone real who was there. This is my story, written for my daughter, Jade, and revealed to give a voice to those who were silenced and will never have the chance to be heard.

> I pray for the angels who have gone before me,
> For the broken ones still waiting to sing.
> I honor their names, their places on earth.
> May they soar in heaven on golden wings.
>
> —*Dawn*

CHAPTER ONE
Fireflies

Before you met me, I was a fairy princess
I caught frogs and called them prince
And made myself a queen
Before you knew me, I traveled
'round the world
I slept in castles and fell in love
Because I was taught to dream . . .
I found mayonnaise bottles and
Poked holes on top
To capture Tinkerbell
And they were just fireflies to the
Untrained eye
But I could always tell . . .
I believe in fairy tales and dreamers' dreams
Like bedsheet sails
And I believe in Peter Pan and miracles
Anything I can to get by
And fireflies

Lori McKenna, "Fireflies"

Times are tough in Carol City. Our neighborhood is going to shit. Blacks and Cubans are in a constant battle for superiority. Everything is a reason to fight. It sucks being white in this neighborhood. We are the minority and the excuse for any black or Cuban to start a war. Here, only one thing is certain: the constant feeling of no hope.

We rebel, us whites. We are actually a mix of everything other than black or Cuban. Smoking pot helps take us out of the reality of this place, and ditching school seems the only way to avoid a daily ass-kicking. On a lucky night, we might score an illegal downer or two from a girlfriend's older brother. At least we *think* this makes us lucky. Neighborhood rivals lie in wait for our lunch money and anything else we have in our pockets, so for protection, we pick a different street corner where we can hang out together each night.

The dark notes and doomed lyrics of bands like Black Sabbath, Led Zeppelin, and Deep Purple become our leaders. We understand each other.

Dad probably never thought he was leaving us in one of the worst neighborhoods in Florida, but Mom is bitter. "Et seems like et's happening overnight," she keeps saying in her sharp German accent. "Efferyone just starts moving out in vun year. Et's going from a nice neighborhood to dis," she daily repeats with disbelief.

Mom is losing her children to the cruel streets of this impoverished inland Miami City, and she feels helpless. Maybe if I knew this, I would be more compassionate.

But I doubt it.

At fifteen, I'm trying to survive, and I blame Mom for everything.

Mom works three waitress jobs just to keep up the payments on our house, because Dad isn't keeping his promise to send money. When she comes home at night, Mom is tired, angry, and sometimes, on scary nights, vicious and ready to snap.

After Vietnam, Dad took off in 1969 for a job with AT&T in

Iran. "Laying cable in the desert will bring us quick riches," he pledged. But his luck has changed, and the only thing he sends in seven years is one sad, lonely letter. The words on the rough-textured and stained paper taped crudely together tell us he is in a Thai jail, his passport has been stolen, and he needs us to send *him* some money.

Mom scrapes together what little she can from her hidden tip jar and sends Dad a MoneyGram, hoping this will be enough to help him come home. But there is no response from that far side of the world, and the one spark of hope she has kindled is silenced for another endless stretch of time.

In the evenings, before I can fall asleep, I ritually listen to Mom's muffled weeping seep out from beneath her bedroom door. I listen because it is my way of making sure all is in order and she hasn't left us too. But it's on those random nights, when Mom's pain is so great, that I hear her cry out to God, "Why?" It is on those nights that my heart breaks with hers, and our voices and tears blend into one long, pitiful wail, rising up into the splintered, hollow walls of our house. She can't believe her dream for a better life in America has deteriorated to this—working so brutally hard and watching her children be consumed by the streets. Mom fears that we are damned, and this terrifies me.

❧

Mom gets the call one April morning in 1976. Dad is not only in the States, but he is in Florida, not far from us, and is coming home this afternoon.

When I first hear that Dad is coming back, I think the world will begin to turn in our direction again. The way I see it, life can now be something to look forward to, not to cower from. Somehow, in my desperate need to find hope, I create an image of my father, the man who abandoned us to this hopeless place, as my hero.

My mind reels. I flash on the idea of "normalcy," something we can have again. I yearn for my life to be like the happy family television shows I spend my afternoons escaping into. Maybe we can have a family like the Waltons. I'd even take the Bradys. I don't care. I do care that we be like them: supportive, compassionate, and never experiencing a problem that can't be worked out. They are perfect families. The fantasy makes me feel warm and tingly with anticipation. Can all the wrong or missing things in our lives suddenly be whole because Dad is coming back? Can we be a family again?

We are thrilled. My brother, sister, and I race around the house, screaming at the top of our lungs, running in and out of each other's rooms, frantically attempting to straighten up for Dad's arrival.

Mom gets caught up in our enthusiasm at times, but a strained, nervous look never really leaves her face. She sees that we are quick to forgive. There is no way we can really understand her burden of raising us alone these past seven years.

"Vee'll see," she mumbles and tries not to dampen our spirits. Perhaps she foresees how easy it will be for Dad to win us over, that his absence will make him seem kinder to us when he arrives.

I can sense how much she hopes it won't happen.

It does anyway.

❧

Wayne William Schiller. An all-American, blue-suede-shoes kind of guy: That is my father.

In 1957, he sneaks out to make a short hop to Philadelphia from New Jersey with his older cousin, Lash, to stand in line at ABC-TV. At sixteen, he is chosen as one of the first *American*

Bandstand dancers, but back home, he gets a beating from his father for disobeying—and he never returns.

My dad is a very bright man who likes being hip with his hair combed back in a cool "duck's ass" and wearing his peg-leg pants. Accused of being "incorrigible" by his mother during his parents' divorce, he is rescued by my great-grandmother, who thinks boys can do no wrong and is passionate about bailing her grandson out of everything.

Awed by the art of savoir faire, Dad fancies himself a master. He can always find a way to get out of an uncomfortable situation and look like the good guy. His grandma has taught him that.

The world is his oyster as he strikes out on his own at a young age.

Soon he is an Army man stationed in Germany, where he meets Mom.

⚜

In a bar in 1959 on base in Amberg, Dad dances with Edda Therese Ilnseher, a dark-haired, dark-eyed beauty. Mom's a babe, and it doesn't take Dad long to swoop in with his charm.

Standing five feet tall and looking awkward next to my dad's six-foot-two stature, Mom, like many other German women, is looking for a better life, away from the hard times she grew up with in postwar Germany.

Born on a farm in Bavaria in 1939, she and her brothers and sisters were displaced war refugees, Old World survivors. Dad calls them Gypsies, and I think of her family living in caravans, wearing turbans, and reading fortunes on the side of the road. They were orphaned when my grandmother, whom I never met, died on a meager farm in the country. Mom was eight years old and the youngest of six children.

A few years after World War II, Mom was shipped to a Catholic orphanage, where she remembers the nuns being strict and cruel. She lived in one of Munich's cold, crumbling brick nunneries for several years, until her older sister raised enough money to bring her and her brothers and sisters back together again.

There, in that bar in Amberg, it is my parents' night out to dance.

Mom thinks the streets are paved in gold in America, and she is feeling pretty lucky that the American GI smiling at her is also very handsome. When Dad speaks perfect German to her, she takes it as a sign that God has answered her prayers. She knows very little English and innocently trusts that he will guide and protect her in the New World.

On December 2, 1959, they are married at the city hall in Munich, Germany. It is a simple wedding with a justice of the peace and two witnesses, who are friends of Dad's from the base and strangers to Mom. A few months later, he is stationed back in the States near his home in Toms River, New Jersey. Happy and in love, Mom and Dad take off for America.

We live at 718 Main Street in the big house my great-grandfather built. Since his passing, my great-grandmother, Cora Hilbert, has lived in the house and now lets us live with her and her sister, Great-Aunt Ella.

"Grandma," as we call Cora, is a thin-faced woman with broad hips and tight, gray, bobby-pin curls pinned painfully close to her scalp.

Aunt Ella, barely five feet tall, wears her white hair in tight curls too. She is a very round woman with a matching circular, soft face, and one of her legs is a good six inches shorter than the other. My grandma tells us the story of how, when Aunt Ella was a baby, she was so small their mother used a shoe box for her cradle. I think shoe boxes were big back then.

Grandma and Aunt Ella speak High German and wear plain housedresses, aprons, and black lace-up boots six days a week. Sundays, they dress up in their customary church-day attire, complete with hats and gloves.

Aunt Ella's one boot has a higher sole on it, and she uses a cane so she can walk properly. She is, we are told, an "old maid." She never married, and everyone in the family takes care of her. To me, Aunt Ella is the sweetest, kindest lady, always soft-spoken and polite, ever prepared with a hard candy in the pocket of her housedress or apron. When we children are being scolded, she often stands up for us, stepping into the middle of Mom's cross words or wild backhand swings or rage as she drags us upstairs to "get the belt."

"Now, Edda, what has the child done?" Aunt Ella asks. As quickly as she can, she stands and then wedges her lame leg between Mom and me. Anchoring herself with her cane, she distracts Mom and buys me time to hide. Aunt Ella knows if she questions long enough, Mom's temper will subside. It works—sometimes.

But most times it doesn't.

Still, many sweet childhood memories are made here in the big house on Main Street. Grandma does the cooking, and Aunt Ella always bakes. Crumb cake is my favorite: cinnamon, buttery crumb cake. In the pantry every Sunday morning is a large bowl of sweet dough, the ingredients mixed from scratch. Aunt Ella's faintly lavender-and-stale-rose-scented black sweater drapes tightly over the bowl's edges, and the yeast, thick and rich, fills the air in the warm pantry closet.

"Keep the door closed," Aunt Ella says, "so the dough will rise."

It always rises mysteriously.

Downstairs, at night, it is customary for Grandma to sit in her favorite rocking chair facing the darkened mouth of the massive red-brick fireplace. Tilting to and fro, the old, worn, knotty-wood rocker creaks when I sit in it, pretending I am grandma, gray and wise.

On many an evening I discover Grandma snoring loudly in her chair, head leaning forward on her chest, arms crossed tightly around her waist in a hug.

"Grandma, Grandma, wake up," I whisper one time, gently shaking her arm after watching her snore awhile longer. I ponder how odd and different she looks while asleep in the low living room lamplight.

"Oh, did I fall asleep?" she mumbles, her voice sweet and sleepy.

I quietly guide her up the polished oak stairs to her bedroom.

Grandma and Aunt Ella share a large bedroom on the second floor, and before bedtime each night, we children ritually appear to unlace their boots and to say our "Now I lay me down to sleep" prayers together, blessing everyone we know afterward.

One winter evening, after saying my prayers with Grandma and Aunt Ella, I turn to leave their room and see through the window the year's first snow gently and silently fall. I lean against the radiator at the window and excitedly call out the snow's arrival.

"How lovely," my grandma says, too tired to get up and look.

They let me stay for a while in their room as I watch the shadowy street and trees become blanketed in white. The streetlamp below the window illuminates the quickly falling flakes and bathes everything in a pale blue light.

I love them—Grandma and Aunt Ella. Filled with the magic of an angelic moment, I feel so much love for them that particular night. After a while, I say my good nights and kiss each again.

It is a perfect moment that will be etched into my memory forever.

***

Aunt Ella and Grandma are religious. They are Lutheran by birth, but it seems Grandma wears the Bible on her dress. On her bad days, she has a tendency to call on the devil and offer to send us to him should we "not mind." Of course, she does this with God's permission and always asks us, "Is that what you want? To go to hell and the devil?"

"No, Grandma!" we cry. "We're sorry. We don't want to go to hell and the devil."

I don't know what *hell and the devil* is, but one thing's for sure: It isn't good.

When Grandma says this, it seems we are going there even if we don't want to. Sometimes at night, when unlacing my aunt Ella's boots, I ask her worriedly if that's where I'm going—to the devil. I worry mostly because of the memories of my uncle visiting my room at night, those nights when I felt blank inside, like a dirty rag doll. She never answers, but instead casts a disapproving sideways glance in my grandmother's direction. Grandma then purses her lips, making them thinner than ever, and says a short, sharp "good night," turning over in a huff without reciting her prayers. I never really know if I'm going to the "bad place" or not, but I feel terrible that she won't pray with me.

Still, the best and most fun hours we children spend are outside in our sprawling yard. Filled with wild honeysuckle, it is home to big, funny, flowering trees good for climbing. Behind our clothesline is the little garden patch, where we grow radishes and carrots. Farther back still, behind the garage, is a never-ending cluster of woods, as big as the whole world.

Here, we find box turtles, and we keep them as pets until Grandma or Mom makes us let them go. (Aunt Ella always lets us keep them.)

Here, too, we pick wild strawberries. Then we dash into the house for a bowl and sugar and scurry back out into the afternoon sun to sit and eat our prize picks.

Dr. Bricker, our neighbor to the left, owns a large portion of tangled woods that melds into ours. We pick dogwood blossoms from the short, gnarled trees in his part of the back woods and bring them in as presents for my mother, grandma, and Aunt Ella. Sitting out on our large, green lawn, my brother, sister, and I gather dandelions, playing the game where we hold them under each other's chin to see if we like butter. I always like butter.

The best thing about this time in New Jersey is the wonder of summer twilight, when the fireflies come to show their luminous, green flashes. They are magical, sweet remnants of my fairy-tale dreams. While I sip tea with my royal court of dolls under our climbing tree, the fireflies protect me as they soar above. I am their queen, and they love me.

Warm days lazily turn into nights. The eastern sky blazes purple and pink at the peak of the fireflies' evening arrival. Their little lights blink randomly, floating on the thick, honeysuckle air.

Sometimes near, sometimes far, the fireflies dare us to believe in them. When they grace us with their presence, my heart knows they come out to enchant us and remind us of their existence.

I try to stop my brother, who, to my horror, only wants to catch their glowing bodies. "Maybe they're fairies," I tell him.

When he catches them anyway and puts them in jars, revealing their insect nature, I am still convinced they are magical beings that simply change when caught. Insisting that the glass prisons will kill their magic, I free every firefly my brother gathers. Soon he believes in them too.

❧

I arrived the firstborn of three children. Mom was pregnant with me soon after coming to the States with my father. Born in a neighboring coastal town called Point Pleasant on December 29, 1960, I had golden curls and crystal blue-green eyes exactly like my father's. In fact, it is said among family that, aside from being a girl, I was the spitting image of my dad.

Dad calls me his little princess, and I shine whenever he gives me attention. It means everything to me when I hear him say how beautiful and smart I am.

When Dad comes home at night in his fatigues and Army boots, I run to greet him at the door. Sometimes, after he settles into his armchair, I unlace his tall, black boots and then bring him a frosty stein of beer.

"Ahhh. Now, that's my princess," he praises. "That's a good girl."

I am special, and he loves me because I take care of him. I am proud of myself for making him happy.

Thirteen months younger, my sister, Terry, was hairless for the first three years of her life. Freckle-faced, she is bigger boned than I am—a fact our parents repeatedly announce, to Terry's dismay. Even though I am older, we appear to be the same size.

My mother likes to dress us girls in similar clothes, only in different colors. (We hate this.) I always get blue; Terry always gets pink. We learn to dislike these colors.

Terry's eyes are the purest green-yellow, reminding me of cats' eyes with their glow-in-the-dark quality. They are a cross between my mother's and father's: not blue-green, not hazel-brown, but spooky green.

I forever wish for her color of eyes.

My brother, Wayne Jr., is just shy of four years younger than me. He is the first boy and the baby of the family. Named after my father, Wayne is, in my grandmother's opinion, like a missing link in our family chain. How she hoped for another male to be in charge!

Wayne has dark brown hair, and his hazel-brown eyes sparkle with mischief. His chubby cheeks stay with him into his teens, and Terry and I tease him mercilessly for resembling a chipmunk, giving him plenty of excuses to torture us in return.

To Grandma's chagrin, however, my brother doesn't much look like my father. He looks more like my mother than anyone else in the family does. But Grandma will overlook his dark features because, after all, he is a *boy*!

<hr />

In 1965, Dad signs up for Vietnam. Then in 1966, he re-ups! In the Army's Aviation Brigade, Dad becomes a helicopter door gunner stationed at Camp Holloway in Pleiku with the 119th Assault Helicopter Company, aka the Gators, or the Flying Dragons.

At the time, I don't understand just how much danger he is in. A door gunner's average life expectancy is only seven days. Every day, we wait for the mailman to arrive. It's a relief to see a letter from Dad and not from Army headquarters. It means he is still alive.

Dad's letters tell us how much he misses us and can't wait to come home. He says Vietnam is hell and that he cries when he sees our pictures. He sends photos of the young Vietnamese children picking through garbage piles for food and of him hanging out the side of a helicopter, his band of ammunition draped over his shoulder as he aims his machine gun at the camera.

These are tearful times. Mom, Grandma, and Aunt Ella are never without a handkerchief, dabbing their eyes, avoiding our stares. They speak German to each other so as not to scare us with news of the war. They know our young eyes and ears record everything, seeking some hint of news. In the three years Dad is in Vietnam, I understand only that he is a good guy fighting the bad guys and he is in danger.

Being the oldest, I am allowed to stay up late and help pack boxes with blankets, peanut butter, and canned food that will survive the rains and humid weather of southeast Asia. The women bicker over what is best to place in the care packages, while I stand, somberly watching. I know they're arguing because they are scared too. Even with all their commotion, the package is wrapped carefully so as not to break on the long journey to Dad. As the final seal is placed on the box, Grandma turns away and hides her tears while Aunt Ella says an audible prayer.

In 1967, the day arrives when Dad comes home from the war.

It is the last part of winter, and several feet of snow still blanket our town. Looking out an upstairs window, I see the sun's harsh glare off the snow-packed front yard.

Then I hear the doorbell.

"He's here!"

I run down the stairs, crashing into Mom's leg. She holds me back at her side as she opens the door. Decorated in metal stars, colored bars, and oak leaf clusters, Dad stands there in full uniform, legs apart and hands behind his back. Almost in slow motion, he smiles and looks at us.

The next thing I know, Mom and I are squeezing him hard. Dad pauses, takes a minute, and then embraces us back. After holding Mom again for a long time, he picks me up and spins me in the air.

"How is my little princess?" he asks. "Have you been a good

girl for your mother?"

I realize I must've said, "Yes," because suddenly he is crying and hugging me tight, while my brother and sister cling like little monkeys on his legs.

Dabbing handkerchiefs at their eyes and noses, Grandma and Aunt Ella have appeared to welcome him too, and Dad sets me down to greet them.

❧

Home again, but still in the service, my father is stationed in different parts of the US, and we're along for the ride, first to Fort Hood, Texas, then to Barstow, California. Dad is working his way through the sergeant stages of the military and is very proud. I am proud of him too.

Mom tries hard to be the perfect military wife, ever ready to move with a change of orders, always having Dad's dinner on the table when he comes home at night. Sometimes she works odd jobs around the base to earn extra money for Christmas, but her English still sounds like German, and this makes her very uncomfortable in public.

A couple years later, when Dad finishes his enlistment with the Army, we head back to Toms River.

❧

It isn't long before Dad starts to go stir-crazy as a civilian. His moods become wild, and he is gone a lot.

I don't remember Dad being like this before, but Grandma says it's because of Vietnam. According to Mom, though, it's because he's a liar and a cheat. I think it's because he is angry at Mom.

Mom and Dad yell a lot.

Dad is angry at us a lot now too.

Being settled down is not Dad's thing, and New Jersey doesn't have the best jobs to suit his qualifications—so he says. Of course, Dad deserves better than this; he is a *vet*! He has walked through hell and back!

Believing different states will offer opportunities better than any "this place" has to offer, Dad goes out to find them. He constantly tells us he wants nothing but the best for his children, and, though there seems to be something much meaner about him now, we always believe him.

Aunt Ella dies in May 1968 before Dad gets back from his job search. A series of small strokes paralyze her, and she needs twenty-four-hour professional care. She has trouble remembering who we are.

The day they take her to the nursing home on a stretcher, I cry. Before they carry her out the front door for the last time, she lifts her arm in what appears to be an effort to hold one of our hands.

The ambulance drivers are moving too fast, and I can't reach her in time.

We visit her only a few times in the nursing home before she dies in her sleep. She has horrific bedsores and doesn't know anyone in the end, I'm told, but I can't believe it, and I miss her terribly.

Things only seem to get worse from here.

While searching for a job in Florida, Dad secures a position with Southern Bell as a telephone communications technician: a "telephone man." He returns to New Jersey to talk my great-grandmother into selling her beautiful home and moving to Carol City, a middle-class suburb of Miami. He says he can be happy in the warmer climate, and he promises to never leave her alone again.

My great-grandma says yes. After all, he *is* the man, and everything he says and does is right.

She will live to regret her decision and never speak much about it in the end.

⚜

Grandma sells her house to Dr. Bricker next door for a pittance. He is ever so pleased that Dad wants out fast and the house can be had at a steal. He tells us his intentions are to turn it into a retirement home for the elderly. Whether he does or not, I never find out; but later, in our big backyard, a pool takes the place of our beautiful climbing trees.

Our new house in Carol City, Florida, is nothing like the hand-built one we left in New Jersey. The yard is much smaller. The house, built of cinder blocks instead of wood, has metal awnings to protect the windows from the seasonal hurricanes.

Quickly, we kids comb our new home for things familiar. In the backyard is a kumquat tree and a lime tree, and in the front, a royal palm. All are much smaller than the trees we are used to, and we instantly disapprove.

Sporting the décor of the 1970s, the house is an aqua color. The walls have wood paneling, and the floor is covered in green shag carpet. "It's da latest ting," Mom informs us while we make frowning faces.

Roaming our yard are frogs and giant toads that foam poison when we come near. The creatures have the sad, terminal habit of sleeping on the cool road at night, and their slimy webbed feet aren't fast enough to jump out of the way of oncoming cars. So in the mornings, we always find at least two freshly splattered ones on the street out front. It's disgusting.

Mostly it is hot, hot, hot! So hot we can't sleep at night. Although we've adapted to different climates in the past, the dense humidity of this miserable place is too much to bear. I get up in the middle of the night to rip off my clothes because I can't stand it.

On the stifling nights when I can't sleep, I trudge to the bathroom to search for water to cool off. When I switch on the light, masses of loud, scurrying cockroaches dash to their hiding places. Screaming for our mother becomes a nighttime practice for us children, until Mom contracts an exterminator and installs air-conditioning in our swamplike Florida home.

❧

My first job at our new house is to clean the yard. The royal palm tree in front needs its dying fronds peeled away and put in something called a trash pile.

Trash pile? What's a trash pile? I think.

I don't know, but everyone has one.

I am grudgingly yanking off branches when suddenly something slimy jumps out and glues itself to my face. Screaming and in a panic, I run in circles, yelling for help, and my brother and sister run out to see what's happening.

Wayne, not afraid of creepy things, simply pulls the creature from my face, looks at it, and laughs. A little tree frog's sucker fingers have stuck to my skin so hard they've left tiny round marks on my forehead and cheeks.

I cry hard.

My mother tells me I am stupid.

But I know why the tears are there. My sadness has risen too high, and like an awkward, toppling stack from the roadside trash pile, I can hold it in no longer.

Everything is too different, and no one is happy.

Mom always screams, and Dad is mad.

Dad even starts to take the belt to us when we are bad, just as Mom has always done. He calls it "the snake," and he is strong.

Dad doesn't call me princess anymore, and my heart is broken.

I just want everything to be like it was before. I want to go back home to New Jersey. Before, we could always go back. This time is different, though. We are stuck here, in this awful place; here, where they have things like *trash piles*; here, where it is always summertime; here, where, no matter how hard I look, there is never any magic—and never, ever any fireflies.

Dad goes to work at the phone company right away, but he isn't happy there, either.

School starts, and I begin the third grade at Carol City Elementary. I am eight years old, my sister is seven, my brother is four, and my great-grandma is eighty-two. Mom and Dad, in their thirties, are ageless in my eyes.

In no time, Dad is restless again and decides to find work elsewhere. This time, overseas is "where the real money is," and he's determined to tap into it "for the family."

Putting our faith in him again, we say good-bye as he leaves to seek out our fortune in far-off countries. He has been with us in Florida for only six months.

As the years roll by without Dad in Carol City, we struggle, waiting for him to return. Trouble begins within a year of our arrival. Things get bad fast. Really bad.

In the schools, angry students plant bombs and stab teachers; on the streets, robbers target the elderly.

Grandma makes friends with our next-door neighbor, Owello, a Cuban man in his eighties who speaks through a hole in his throat. One day, after walking into town to cash his Social Security check, he staggers home with a fresh stab wound in his hand. Punk thieves hid in an alley waiting for him to walk the few blocks home with his meager monthly cash folded neatly in his pocket next to his freshly smoked cigar.

Owello's arms flail wildly as he explains, without a voice, how he bravely fought the robbers at first. Then his shoulders slump, and he shakes his head as he describes how he was overpowered. Tears run down his leathery cheeks, and with broken nods, he agrees to let Grandma bandage his hand.

Afterward, the two of them sit on his porch, numbly looking out at our lost neighborhood and in at our deteriorating lives.

My first fight is on our street in front of an entire block of kids. While I am out walking our dog, a girl jumps me. I am ten, and she, a girl who used to play with me, is twelve. Taking a beating, I am devastated.

Being small for my age and still a child, I am terrified to walk down the streets again. But in order to prove myself and not be marked as an easy target, I have to learn to throw a punch and challenge the girl who jumped me to another fight. This time I'm prepared, and she loses a tooth. Staggering home, my only injury a hole in my knuckle, I am oddly triumphant yet scared out of my mind that I might have to fight again.

I do.

Once the ball begins to roll, gang activity in my community escalates faster than lightning speed. For me, school is becoming the worst place to be: a place where a person can get killed.

In fact, going anywhere alone in Carol City or the surrounding towns is becoming very dangerous.

My brother, sister, and I have to grow up fast. My childlike demeanor, the innocence of my age, is now stuffed into the deepest recesses of my psyche, hidden and safe. I keep my guard up and feel protected only in moments of absolute privacy. All too soon, my childhood has turned upside down forever, leaving my mind focused every waking moment on survival: *How do I avoid a confrontation? Where do I go to be safe? How do I protect myself?* Like a mantra, an internal prayer, these questions chant constantly in my mind, keeping me ever vigilant.

One day, knowing a big black girl wants to beat me up, I skip a seventh-grade class. Instead, I walk to a local convenience store to buy a Coke and waste time till my next class. I hang out aimlessly on the cement curb out front as the hot Florida sun beats down on my head. A carload of Cuban men approaches me, gang members who threaten to throw me into their car and rape me. In a split-second decision, I break the cool Coke bottle against the curb, point it at the closest man, and shout defiantly, using my toughest street voice: "Fuck you! Go ahead! You may be able to take me, but I swear, I'll kill one of you." Screaming at the top of my lungs I scan the area and hope to bring attention to myself.

The gang members sneer.

"So which one will it be?" I continue. "Which one of you is going to die? You?" I lunge my jagged weapon forward. The leader stops, lifts his brow thinking, and nervously backs away from the sharp point of my bottle and the wild fury of my voice.

The four men fumble into their car, hissing poisonous threats of revenge. "You wait, little *gringa*," they scream, anger raging in their eyes. "We come back! You not gonna be so tough all the time!" But the ploy works, and not turning their backs, they burn a trail of rubber behind them. I am almost thirteen and have now gained the reputation of a "fighting crazy." They are right. I calculated the situation correctly. Sheer terror and panic bring out a side of me that holds no punches when being backed into a corner. To the death—a tough title to hold, but to me, it's one way to get some desperately needed reprieve. Little do I know I am learning the life skills to do just that in the short years to come—save my life.

Heavy-duty thieves find our house an easy target, and Mom is also forced into dangerous confrontations. After a double shift at work, Mom drags home from her waitress job and accidentally walks in on the toughest criminal of the neighborhood. "Cleveland" is a dangerous, nineteen-year-old black boy, with scars so thick along his head, his hair no longer grows on most of his skull. He is well-known as mean and deadly for starting fights with baseball bats at neighborhood parks, and there he is in our kitchen, raiding our refrigerator.

"Vhaaat is dis?" Mom screams with all her five feet one German might, furious with the intruder. "You get out of my house, you son of a bitch! You take food from my childrrren! You, you, I call da poliiiice! Get out!" She backs the now-frightened thug out of our house, pointing her finger and threatening to kill him if she ever sees him near her family again. Neighbors crawl out of the woodwork like gnats to a streetlight to watch, gaping, as the woman in the white shirt and black waitress skirt backs the toughest guy in the neighborhood out of her house with only her finger. It isn't hard for anyone to see who I imitate.

Mom, Terry, Wayne, and I get tougher and tougher in our attitudes, and Grandma grows more and more weary. She is very elderly now. As the built-in babysitter while Mom works her many jobs, it's tiring for her to deal with us children and our rebellion at the growing hostility of our neighborhood. Mom not only takes her rage out on us children, but on Grandma too. As far as I know, she only threatens to hit her, never really making contact with her fists.

We lose Grandma to pneumonia in January of 1976, just a few months before Dad makes it back. She has waited loyally for him to return—almost seven years. I watch her as she rocks in that same rocking chair from New Jersey, Bible in hand, crying daily until the end. What a horrible feeling it gives me to watch her wither away, sad and abandoned, disappointed by the one she loves the most.

Some weeks before her death, near Christmastime, I have a succession of terrifying dreams that Grandma will leave us: three dreams in a row that frighten me down to my bones. I become hysterical. Mom tells me everything's all right, but I know better. I pay attention to my dreams anyway, and those last weeks that Grandma is alive I am extra nice, offering to help her do her chores and cook the meals. I do kind things again for her and share happy thoughts about Aunt Ella and the snow in New Jersey, like it was before we got here, before the hardness. I remember sitting out on the backyard patio, she in a green and white lawn chair, my head in her lap. She strokes my long sun-kissed hair with her bony, wrinkled hand and I tell her I love her, hoping she loves me back.

"Grandma," I ask, "am I a good girl?"

"Yes," she replies, "you are a good girl, Dawn. You are a *good* girl," and she pats my head softly. I am taking in every ounce of her that I can—her touch, her smell, her look, not wanting the moment to end. She smells of faint lavender and mold from the hand-rinsed Ace bandage I help her wrap around her varicose-veined leg. I wish she wasn't so tired anymore and that I had been nicer to her in the past. I want her to be happy. She deserves to be happy.

On the third day, after her death, I see her one last time. She walks through the house floating in a cloud of pink. At first, I think it's my sister wearing her favorite pink pajamas. But when I hear Terry's voice at the other end of the house, I know it can't be her. Grandma's hair is a fuzzy gray, and a warm glow surrounds her. Her presence seems soft as she passes by my side and glides toward the back bedrooms. I jump up to follow her through the house, desperately willing her to stay, as the delicate pink figure disappears at the end of the hallway. Grandma's gray hair and pink outline slowly dim to nothing and I stand in amazement, staring at the blank brown paneling, feeling only the sense that she has come to say good-bye and that she knows she is loved.

With Grandma gone, there is less money for the household bills, and Mom is under much more stress to make ends meet. I am the oldest. Mom reminds me of this constantly, especially during her rages. I need to help the family, help my brother and sister. It is my responsibility. I think I have found the perfect solution: a job through a work program at school allows me to work half days and get credits at the same time. This means money for Mom and the house and less time at a school I dread.

I am proud the day I land a cashier job at a Burger King a few blocks away. I love wearing the orange and yellow polyester bell-bottoms and puffy patch cap. I get a free Whopper meal each day and memorize the "Have It Your Way" rules at the back table, right where Grandma used to take us out to eat for a hamburger on her Social Security payday. *Mom will be happier now. Not worry so much,* I tell myself. But that doesn't happen.

She dislocates my jaw on a morning that I am late for work. It is a few days after my first paycheck. I have given her money for food and the house and bought her a gold necklace as a belated birthday present. Three charms hang from a real 14 karat chain, silhouettes of the profile of two girls and a boy. On each of them is engraved "Dawn," "Terry," and "Wayne." The morning she attacks me, I try to rip the necklace off her neck, but she protects it as she throws wild punches with her strong right fist. I scramble off the utility room floor and out the back door, limping and crying the four blocks to work.

My uniform, my pride and joy, is torn at my chest. I am bruised, swollen, and hysterical as my day-shift manager tries to console me. I tell him it is my mother; she does this all the time. I thought she wouldn't be this way if I was working and helping with the bills. I thought she would stop. It is always the money that makes her so angry, or that's what I believe. But Mom still needs to let me know that she is boss, and now I know that I will never make her happy, that she will not love me more even if I'm working and trying to help her out. I give up. My manager offers to help and find me a safe place to stay, but I am too embarrassed.

Eventually I lose my job. I stop showing up. I stop showing up for school too. Instead, I hang around with the outcasts of my neighborhood. They are my new family now. I stay at various friends' houses for days and sometimes don't even call home to tell Mom where I am. On the streets at night, I listen to heavy metal, get high, and hate life.

⁂

The time draws near to Dad's expected arrival. Two hours before he is supposed to show up, we are dressed in our best, keeping vigil at the windows. I wear my coolest clothes: magenta elephant bell-bottoms, beige midriff top, and desert boots. I fling an oversized, green Army jacket with a smiley face patch on the front pocket over my shoulder. (It is too hot in Florida to actually wear such a jacket.) My down-to-my-waist, light brown hair is parted in the middle and pulled behind my ears to keep it out of my face and a pale splattering of freckles dust my nose. At fifteen I want to show my father how cool I am and how much I love him . . . still.

Terry dresses in similar clothes. She also wears elephant bells and some kind of fashionable knit top. She paces anxiously, jumping at the sound of each passing car. Her hair parts down the middle and is a bit darker and shorter than mine, and her face is covered in more of the family freckles. Her cat-green eyes are lined with worry that Dad will be devastated at the news of Grandma's death a few months earlier, and so we decide to let Mom break it to him.

Wayne keeps a silent seat crouched behind the heavy drapes at the dining room window facing the front of the house. He wears no shoes, cutoff shorts, and a tattered T-shirt. His sun-streaked blond hair badly needs cutting and hangs raggedly into his large chocolate eyes. The eight-foot-long body of his favorite boa constrictor is wrapped around him, and he holds its head close to his face. "Queen," his prize possession and guardian, is the one thing he can't wait to proudly share with Dad.

Mom shocks us all when she emerges in a full-length red negligee and matching see-through robe. *That's so gross,* I think to myself as she poises herself at the front door, blocking my sister and me from being first to open it.

"Go over derr," she directs, her German accent still thick after all these years. "I vahnt to open da doorr vehn he gets herr," she announces. She is determined to see her husband again and show him exactly what he has been missing all these years. Mom knows she is still a babe, damn it, and she is still in love with him.

Like a recurring dream, Dad's car pulls up in front of the house. There is no snow on the ground as there was in New Jersey when he came home from Vietnam, but there is a strange sense of déjà vu in the air. Time is motionless until he finally steps out of the car, a long-haired stranger wearing bell-bottoms, a tie-dyed shirt, and sandals. "Dad's a hippie. Cool!" Tentatively, my father's oddly familiar shape walks toward the house. Beside ourselves with excitement, the three of us kids simultaneously race to the front door, fling it open, and fight for first position, squeezing Mom unceremoniously out of the way. Dad cracks a small smile at our reaction to his arrival, pretends not to notice, and continues up the walk. I see a tiny opening and take it. In an instant I manage to break free and dash out and away from the others, run with all my might, and jump into his arms. I hug him tight, not believing this moment is real. I don't say anything, only a few mumbles that are supposed to convey how glad I am that he is home. My brother, sister, and mother follow right behind me, crying and hugging him too.

Mom and Dad head into their bedroom after only a short while in the house. My impression that things aren't going as Mom planned comes from the tearful face and the change of clothes she wears when they emerge only a few minutes later. Dad comes out and sits with us in the living room as Mom storms silently into the kitchen to make sandwiches for dinner. I can hear her crying through the clinking of mayonnaise jars and knives as the refrigerator opens and closes. Finishing, she places the platter on the dining room table and disappears into her room, leaving Dad, Terry, Wayne, and me to eat the light meal together at the heavy octagon table. We feel the awkwardness and tension of their re-union, and even with a thousand things to say, we find it difficult to make any conversation.

"How's school?" Dad asks.

"Fine," we lie, and an uneasy silence again fills the air.

"Sorry to hear about Grandma," he adds, embarrassed and looking genuinely saddened.

We nod and hang our heads. There is more silence as we watch time pass. The setting sun casts its shadow through the curtains of the sliding glass door, and before the light disappears completely, Mom, eyes swollen and red, comes out with a handful of blankets and a pillow. She lays them on the couch without say-ing a word and returns to her room. We still say nothing.

The next day it is announced to us that Mom and Dad are

divorcing. From what we witnessed the night before it doesn't really surprise us, but the news is still depressing. This isn't what any of us expected. I feel desperate, thinking this might mean that we will lose Dad again. Angry with Mom, I blame her again for him wanting to leave. Dad is "cool"; Mom is mean and doesn't understand us. There is a bitter, heavy silence in the house for the next few days after their announcement, a silence louder than any explosion can be to a child. It is the end of the family we long ago briefly knew and had spent most of our lives hoping and fantasizing to be once again. The fireflies are gone forever. *What now?* I wonder. *What will happen to us now?*

CHAPTER TWO
The Man in the Box

In the days that follow, Dad gets up early, sits at the dining room table, lights a menthol, and shuffles his deck of cards. *Frrrruuuttth, click, click. Frrrruuuuttthhh, click, click, click.* The cards smack the table with a sharp snap.

"You drink coffee, Dawn?" he asks me, as I stand watching.

"No, but I can make some."

"Ahh . . . yeah," he says as if he is drooling. "Cool, man."

I shuffle into the kitchen and pull out the instant coffee that has been hidden in the cabinet for a forgotten number of years, boil some water, and mix a strong, black cup.

"Two sugars," he calls, hearing me stir the heady brew. Carefully, I walk the hot cup out to him and place it on the table. "Sit down," he says, not looking up from his cards. Pleased to be near him, yet nervous that he might notice that I don't know what he is playing, I do as I'm told. "Do you play solitaire?" he asks, already knowing the game is lost to my understanding.

"No. I don't think so. What is it?"

"Ahhh! Never mind! You'll find out about it later," he teases, waving his arm and dismissing me. I stand, unwilling to leave. Dad ignores my hovering, continuing his game and chain-smoking. I begin to feel bored, but I'm curious about him, so I

28

dash to my room and return with my macramé. I am making a roach clip and it is going to be a nice one. Suddenly, the corner of Dad's eye lifts. "What's that?" he asks with a pleased, curious lilt to his voice.

"What's it look like?" I answer, smiling at the fact that he's showing some interest. A tingle of excitement sits me up straight and quickly I want to sound like I know what being cool is all about.

"Don't mess with me, Dawn," he says, shaking his head. "You *know* what I mean."

"Yeah, I know what you mean," I tease. I had sensed it all along.

"Well? You got any?"

There is a long pause before I decide to answer. Is my father asking me for a joint? I can't believe my luck. Man, he is cool. This is *soooo* cool! I dart back to my room and pull out my box of stash from under my bed. An old cigar box, torn and dirty along the edges, holds a couple packs of Zig-Zag rolling papers, several books of matches, and a plastic bag with a few roaches, ash, seeds, and a sprinkling of sticky yellow leaves. I race back to the table and proceed to roll up my best Jamaican Gold bud. Dad's eyes light up, and he is smiling big.

Thick smoke fills the air, and we are stoned before we are half-way through. I am what my friends call a lightweight, and never really inhale more than two tokes at a sitting. The rest I fake, but I am playing tough so I can hang with Dad, and instead finish sucking back the entire joint with him.

"Oh shit"—*pop*— "a seed, look out!" We both giggle stupidly, snorting while holding our breath.

"Ah, I knew you were cool, Dawn, the minute I saw you," Dad says with a half grin as his eyes glaze over.

"I knew you were cool too, Dad, as soon as you got out of the car," I ramble, and my body gets heavier as my high kicks in.

"Groovy, man." He nods and takes another long pull from the joint.

29

Damn, I am stoned. I have trouble holding my head up, and the air in the room makes a weird whirring noise in my ears, but I am determined to hang. I send a glazed look over toward Dad, who doesn't look like he is feeling high at all and I worry that he will think I can't handle my pot. My thoughts mellow, and I relax when he asks, "You got any tunes?" Relieved to break the silence, I pull out my favorite Led Zeppelin album, and we drift off on the band's haunting version of "Stairway to Heaven."

So pass the days with my father while he waits for Mom to initiate the divorce proceedings. Every day I roll Dad a joint before I go to school, and get stoned with him afterward. By the time Mom comes home from work, we make sure the house is aired out and everything is put back in its place. Mom does not approve, and if the house isn't straightened up before she gets here, she will hit the roof, and neither of us wants that kind of interrogation. Dad and I are getting acquainted with each other, and pot is our median; it helps ease the tension of all the unanswered questions that lie between us. We crack jokes and listen to the latest Cheech & Chong record that leaves us rolling in tears of laughter. Man, this is far out! None of my friends can believe how cool he is, and they all want to come over to meet the dad who smokes pot with his daughter.

Slowly Dad begins to talk about where he has been all these years while we waited for him in Carol City. He unravels exotic stories of Bangkok, India, and Kathmandu that captivate me. He talks about backpacking his way through Asia "on a shoestring," and the times he spent as a monk in northern Thailand, begging for alms every morning before sunrise with a shaved head and eyebrows. He tells me the story of being in Bangkok when Jimi Hendrix and Janis Joplin died. The Thais, he says, were so upset that they staged a mock funeral procession down Sukhumvit, a major road in the large, tangled city.

He speaks to me about Thai culture, making it very clear that

I understand the head is the highest part of the body and it must be given absolute respect. The foot is without a doubt the lowest part of the body, and never, never should the foot come near the head in any way, at any time, *ever*. This is considered the greatest of insults, especially if done intentionally. He speaks Thai to me and teaches me the words I inquire about. "You got a good ear, Dawn," he compliments, and I feel good about myself. Not once do I ask him why he didn't come back to us or stay in touch instead of traveling the world. Not once do I hold him responsible for leading Grandma to believe he would come back before she died. He seems kicked back and mellow, and he gives the impression he has no responsibilities—and I don't see it either.

But Dad has a few secrets. One in particular is a mysterious form of meditation he practices in the early morning hours. Daily he sends me to the local store to purchase candles, fresh flowers, and incense. He picks cumquats and limes from the backyard and takes them discreetly into the bedroom. On the dresser in Mom's room, after she has left for work, Dad ritually positions a small box, then the candles, fruits, flowers, and incense we have gathered, in a specific pattern. Some of the time he places next to the box a small shot glass of whiskey or Scotch from the cabinets where Mom has stashed it away for special occasions. Dad is very protective of the contents of his little box, and he keeps its mystery hidden—so of course I am very, very curious.

I am not only curious; I am fascinated, but I get no response from Dad when I ask prying questions about his secret treasure. I keep my eyes on Dad, hoping some clue will be revealed, and on a morning after he has slipped into the bedroom for his "meditation," I seize an opportunity to stand at the door. Pressing my face close to the threshold for what seems like over an hour, I strain to listen inside. I hear nothing for a long, tense time except my own slowed breathing. The smell of incense drifting up from the bottom of the door is the only evidence of any movement. Then something happens. I hear a muffled voice, low in tone and in a language I recently learned was Thai. It sounds like a kind of conversation. *Is that two different voices?* I wonder. I press harder into the door, my ear at the jamb, trying to hear more. Suddenly, the voices stop, and I am overcome with the distinct, uneasy feeling that it is known that I am listening. Scared of getting caught, I pull carefully back from the door and race into the living room. With my heart pounding, I pick up my macramé and shakily try to thread a bead. Dad emerges a few minutes later. He seems distressed, not like his usual mellow self. He says nothing that day or for the next several days, and I feel miserable. I don't want to blow our newfound friendship, but I am driven and want to know what he is up to, so I wait it out.

To my relief, it takes only a few days before Dad opens the subject. "So . . . what did you hear, Dawn?" he asks matter-of-factly as he shuffles his deck of cards.

"What, when?" I put on my best blank look.

"You *know*!" His tone is sharp this time.

"A—a—at the door the other day?" I stammer. "It sounded like you were in there with someone; speaking Thai."

He gives me a long, hard stare, scaring me even more, and then looks down into my eyes. "You can't tell anyone!" he says seriously. "You have to promise!"

"I . . . I promise, Dad. What was it?"

Concern furrows his brow, and he repeats, "You understand? No one!"

"I promise!"

Dad seems satisfied, nods to himself, and slowly leans back into his chair. He takes a few moments, breathes in deep, and begins. "Several years ago, in Bangkok, I met a lady. Her name is Pen Ci. When my passport was stolen and I was thrown in jail, she helped get me out by bribing the police and the judge. After my papers were miraculously recovered"—Dad's hand sweeps the air as if he is waving a magic wand—"she took me to the northern part of Thailand to live with her in her village."

Her name is, I think, making a mental note of Dad's curious use of the present tense.

Dad catches his breath and continues. "She's considered a holy woman in her village, and she helped me out of a, well, er, a bad spot. We spent a lot of time together, and, uh, you know, we fell in love." He keeps his gaze focused on the heavy red drapes, avoiding my shocked expression.

"What happened?" I press him.

"Well, that's when I did the monk thing I told you about. To prove, you know, my love for her, I, um, had to become a Buddhist monk." Dad begins to fidget. "I needed to respect their religion and gain merits with the Buddha. Eventually, we got married."

"Got married!"

"Yeah, it's not legal as far as the States are concerned, but it's legal in Thailand," he says, still averting my surprised gaze.

What about Mom? I think. *And what does this have to do with the talking box in the bedroom?*

"We had a son," he pushes on.

Now I am numb. This is a wilder story than I imagined. *Does this mean I have a new brother?*

"His name is Jack, and, uh, they're waiting for me to send for them."

I can't stand it. "Where are they?" I find myself blurting out.

With an intense flash of his light blue eyes, Dad finally looks at me directly. "In a village in the north of Thailand." His arm points up as if to indicate north. "As soon as this divorce thing is over with, I'm gonna send for them and meet them in California."

I stay silent for what seems an eternity. I have so many more questions. Surging emotions threaten to explode in ebbs and flows of both fear and rage, and I want to scream, "What about us?" But instead I am quiet. My head hangs low and my shoulders are slumped at the years of rejection. I want to burst into a flood of tears. I am immobile and struggle to find some hope. Then I begin to understand that Dad trusts me with his truth. As messed up as it is, it is his truth, and our continuing relationship hinges on how I will react.

"It's just the way things happened, Dawn," Dad speaks up, acutely aware of the long silence and my pain. "After Vietnam, things were just different between your mother and me. I was—I *am* different . . . ," he continues. "Things can never be the same again between us. I mean, I love you and Terry and Wayne, but it's all just different." He is rambling, explaining his side of things awkwardly, unable to find the right words.

"So, you're moving to California?" I ask shyly, still not looking up and scared to death that he is going away again.

"Well . . . that's the plan." Dad breathes a heavy sigh, then shuts down. "Why don't you roll us a joint, Dawn, and let's toke one?" I get up to retrieve my stash box and roll a fatty. My fingers are shaking and it takes me a while, but I finally manage to piece together a loose "pregnant" one and light it up. Dad and I take a few turns pulling drags from the joint before it starts to fall apart and he drops it in an ashtray. For a long moment we both sit and stare at the brown walnut finish of the dining room table.

"What about the box in the bedroom, Dad?" I remind him, and realize my stomach is churning. "What's in there?" I am overwhelmed and anxious with all this latest information, but very aware he hasn't finished explaining everything.

"Ahhhh, yes . . . the box in the bedroom." He leans slightly into me; his tone is low, mysterious. "Well, now here's the story about that."

My eyes widen with excitement, and I manage to settle my hands in my lap and listen intently.

"Up country, in northern Thailand," Dad begins, "me and this other guy, a Thai guy, were planting rice in the paddy fields when we hit something in the dirt with our plow. We thought we broke it and were pissed off. So we pulled the dirt back to clear it out and saw a, uh, kind of a faint green light coming out of the ground."

"Far out!" My mouth drops open, and I nearly jump from my seat, but Dad refuses to be interrupted.

"We went to check it out and found these two round stones lying in the hole, green light all around them." Again, Dad gestures wildly. "We pulled them out and a guy, or well, uh, what looked like a guy, really old looking . . . you know, with the long white beard and hair thing, and he kinda came glowing out of the stones and spoke to me and my friend." Dad's hair falls into his face as he stops, avoiding my gaping expression, but I catch him steal a glance my way from the corner of his eye.

"What did he say?" I ask in absolute amazement. My body is stiff and my hands clench tight as I hang on his every word.

"You ready for this?" Dad turns to look me straight in the eye.

"Yeah." Now I'm holding my breath.

"He said he was a spirit who lived a long time ago. He said he had been hidden for many years. He said we were lucky, that he was a gift to those who found him—and now, we could speak to him whenever we wanted, that he would guide us." After a long pause he adds, "Then he told us our future." Dad hangs his head lower and glances from side to side before continuing. "He told me how I would find my fortune and that coming back here to the States was where I would find it. It's something I had to do. At first we didn't believe it, but he told us that the stones, one for each of us, couldn't be destroyed. He dared us to try and break them."

I take a deep, trembling breath and try to absorb the phenomenal unraveling of the green stones. Dad sees my reaction and waits a few beats for me to catch up.

"Pen Ci and I took my stone to all kinds of places to see if it really could be destroyed. We tried everything—smashing it, running it over, and banging it with anything we could find—but not a scratch. We even took it to a shooting range, but the bullets just ricocheted off—no mark, nothing." Dad went on, "Nobody could believe it. It was written about in the local Thai papers and everyone considered it to be this big spiritual thing. Then . . . it got scary." His voice was hushed now.

"Scary? Why scary?" I'm even more worried now.

"Well, there was too much publicity. We were afraid people would want to steal it, and if they wanted to steal it, they wouldn't care if they hurt or killed us for it."

"So . . . so what did you do?"

"We had to leave the village and go to Bangkok to stay with some of her family," he ends the story abruptly as if he has said enough.

"Oh," I say flatly. "And no one came after you? What about Pen Ci and Jack?" I press on anyway, wanting him to be less vague.

"Yeah . . . uh . . . I . . . uh," he stammers and his feet begin to shuffle under the table. "I'm . . . uh . . . working on that."

I don't answer. I have already figured out that Dad speaks only when he is ready to speak. I'm confused about his ultimate intentions and after a few minutes of silence and trying to sound as nonthreatening as I can, I ask, "Working on it? I thought you were going to meet them in California?" Then in a soft voice, still not wanting to piss him off, I come straight to the point. "When are you going to do that?"

"Gotta have a plan, Dawn, gotta have a plan," he replies with a half smirk almost to himself. Still not looking up from his cards, in an "I dare you to question *me* about life" way, he turns, looks deep into my eyes, and asks, "Don't *you* got a plan, Dawn?" His mood changes rapidly as he shifts the questioning toward me.

"Plan?" I answer, taken off guard. *I'm fifteen, and I live under my mother's roof in a neighborhood going nowhere,* I think. I don't believe I even have any choices, much less the ability to *plan* anything. I stammer on, "Uh . . . I . . . uh."

"Awww, come on. Don't give me that." His voice sharply accuses me of lying. "Everyone's got a *plan*!"

Well, I don't! my mind screams. Dad's mood swing has shocked me, and I stay silent, afraid that he is getting mad. He continues playing his solitaire hand, slapping the cards down hard, making it uncomfortable to sit next to him. Finally, I can stand the tension no longer, and while Jethro Tull's *Aqualung* plays menacingly in the background, I make a gesture of peace. "Wanna smoke another doobie, Dad?"

"Yeah!" he says, sounding lighter again. "Why don't you roll us another one, babe." His mood is sweet. As if he is sorry he had sounded harsh, he cracks a smile and it immediately melts the tension.

"Snot is running down his nose," ring the lyrics from the cabinet encased stereo. I look up at him and smile.

Dad's relationship with my brother and sister is quite different from mine. With Terry it is hit-and-miss. Sometimes she seems friendly and sometimes not. She has her own agenda and friends—and she keeps them hidden. She is only a little more than a year younger than me, but it makes all the difference in the world. At times she sits at the table with Dad and me, taking tokes from a joint and watching him make his plans as he studies his playing cards. Consumed with the constant worry of surviving in our neighborhood, Terry doesn't seem much interested in the stories Dad tells. Some of his adventures catch her attention, but mostly she is relieved that his presence takes the pressure off of Mom's angry control over her.

She is always on guard, concerned about who will try to fight her next. She is also proud of her strength. One afternoon, while Dad sits playing solitaire at the dining room table, we happen to glance out the window. There looms Terry facing two Cuban girls from the block. Quickly Dad and I stand at the glass to watch and although we can't hear what they are saying, we can tell it is a confrontation. In an instant, she throws a hard punch that lands right between the eyes of one girl's face. I race to the front door, swing it open with a bang against the wall, and run to help my sister. I can hear Dad pound on the window yelling for them to knock it off, but when I arrive, it is only in time to see them scramble out from under Terry's flying punches. Heart pumping and fists balled tight, I barely have time to pick up a rock and throw it after the fleeing girls warning them not to ever come back. I look at my sister, her face and arms red as she tries to catch her breath, and shake my head in disbelief.

"Damn, Terry! How the hell did you do that?"

"I don't know," she replies, huffing and puffing for air. "I just fucking did it." I can see the waves of adrenaline wash over her face. Dad quickly appears.

"Niiice," he says admiringly, rubbing her shoulder. "Now that's a Schiller for ya. That's a Schiller. They'll think twice before trying that again, eh, Ter?"

Terry stands, swollen with pride, and comes down from the rush. She answers with a threat, "They'd better, Dad!" At fourteen she is the toughest girl on the block. That day she is also the proudest.

My brother, Wayne, is never around. He is a typical boy who loves spiders and snakes, exploring, and setting things on fire. (Well, maybe he's not so typical.) He likes fishing in the local canals and comes home with mud puppies as the "catch of the day." "You can't eat those—they don't have any eyes!" my sister and I shriek as he chases us around the house trying to touch us with their slimy skin.

Wayne doesn't know what to say to a father who has been gone since he was four. He is eleven now and has only vague memories of Dad. Still believing Mom's interpretation of things, he is cautious and spends his time getting to know Dad in a shy, subtle way. He pops his head in at the table from time to time watching Dad's habitual card playing with uncertain interest, but he gets bored easily. He isn't into smoking pot and doesn't like seeing me get high. Bothered by Dad's lack of attention to him, he likes to slip out of sight without a word, get his snake, "Queen," from his room, sneak back in, and egg her up my leg from under the table.

"Quit it!" I squeal, annoyed at his prank.

"No," he dares and tries to get Dad to notice his pet snake. He makes a face at me to poke fun of my smoking pot like I'm cool.

"Come on now . . . let's not play around," Dad tells him. "What do you got there?"

Slowly, Wayne pops his head up from under the table and brings Queen into the light. "Let me see. What's that?" Dad asks, feigning interest. Wayne is thrilled that he has his father's attention, and he hands him the snake with a big grin.

"It's a boa constrictor," Wayne explains excitedly. "And they live around here. They'll squeeze you to death!"

"Cool. Uh. That's nice, Wayne." Dad smiles approvingly.

Wayne beams and dashes from the room to gather the rest of his reptile collection. Dad holds on to Queen awkwardly, and to his dismay Wayne returns to show off all of the slithery friends that he has hidden throughout the house. From that point on my brother spends most of his time catching bigger and creepier pets to display for Dad's approval, always getting the same dull interest from Dad and relishing every bit of it.

Dad wants to keep everything as even-keeled as possible. He wants out of his marriage with Mom and figures that the less he says, the better off he is. Although he trusts me with bits and pieces of his past, and feels pretty good that I am his one captive audience, he still seems nervous that I might go to Mom with his secrets. He knows how hard it is for her to accept the divorce. She believes they should stay together, at least for us children, but now that the split up is inevitable, all she can do is hide her feelings of failure and try to seem friendly. She doesn't want to be the bad guy, even though it looks like she will take the blame anyway. Dad knows this too.

The divorce process, once the terms are agreed on, takes about six weeks. In the days after initially filing the papers, Mom and Dad sit down with us children. "We have something serious we need to talk to you about," my father announces.

The three of us line up in front of the couch, silent and not making eye contact.

"Well, you know that your mom and I are divorcing, right?"

"Uh-huh," we mumble.

"Well, the thing is . . . Well, um, you kids are going to have to choose which one of us you want to go with, uh, as your guardian," he explains clumsily.

Wow! I haven't thought of that. I haven't thought at all that I would have any say in the direction of my life. Dad is definitely cool. He is mellow and doesn't like to fight. He has traveled all over Asia and has been on great adventures. He understands how I feel and likes the things I do. He is teaching me new things about faraway and exotic lands, and I want to see the beautiful places he talks about. He lets me make my own decisions, and just as my mother suspects, he looks like a good guy to me. I never blame him for leaving us and not coming back. Instead, I believe his stories of being unjustly thrown in a Thai jail and am impressed with his survival of the ordeal. I am in awe of all the things he has done and look up to him with the unconditional love of a daughter.

It doesn't take me long to pick Dad. It doesn't take long for my sister to pick Dad too. My mother's heart sinks. The look in her eyes is that of deep hurt and pain, but her face quickly changes to an angered mask. I don't understand her reaction. *She will be happy to not have us as a burden anymore,* I say to myself, and with Dad's help, I chalk up her attitude to her bad-tempered personality.

"Vell," she snaps, "vat about you, Vayne?"

"I . . . uh . . . I." My brother's head hangs down. He is obviously uncomfortable with the spotlight. "I . . . don't know," he answers in a barely audible voice. He sounds small and confused.

He wants to connect with his dad, the other man in the family, but at the same time, embarrassingly, he is still young enough to want his mom. As tough as we all think we are, he is only eleven years old. I feel bad for him. I can see it is tearing him apart, and I want to hug him and convince him to come with us.

"Vell, who do you pick, Vayne?" Mom insists, "Me or your fater?"

His face turns red. Backed into an emotional corner he quickly responds, "You, Mom, you!" A flood of tears streams down his face, and he bursts down the hallway to his room. The door slams shut behind him, shaking the decorative plates that hang from the paneled walls. Dad cringes, slips his hands into his pockets, and turns away to glance out of the dining room window while Mom puffs up her small frame, looking strangely triumphant. She gives my sister and I each an icy stare, turns on her heel, and storms out of the house. *Bam!* She slams the door louder than my young brother's earlier attempt, enough to make the cement walls quake, and wordlessly declares herself the unsuccessful winner of our family's pain.

So Dad *has* been in the process of formulating a plan, and now I know I am a part of it. *At least for the next three years until I am eighteen,* I think. Now it is safe for him to reveal to Terry that he is headed for California and we are going with him. The house is quiet. No sound comes from the back bedrooms, and I guess that Wayne has slipped through the window with Queen or one of his other reptilian friends. Terry disappeared earlier, and there is no more movement from Mom.

"I wasn't sure you wanted to go with me when I talked to you before, Dawn," Dad admits with a shy smile, his gaze still focused through the glass.

"What? Hell, yes, I want to go with you, Dad." I almost jump from my seat. I can't believe it. Am I really going to get out of this place? Questions swirl through my mind, and I can't contain myself. "Dad? Where are we going to stay? Am I gonna meet Pen Ci and Jack? When are they coming to the States?"

"Now, hang on, Dawn," Dad says, motioning his hand downward for me to calm myself. "Let's take this slow." Suddenly, his face lights up, and he puts his finger up in the air as if to gesture that he has an idea.

"What?" I'm curious now about the excitement on his face.

"Ah-haaaaaa!" he says slowly and points his finger toward the sky like a lightbulb has gone off. "I know. We'll ask the cards."

"What? Read our fortune?"

"We'll do it over here."

Dad leads me into the living room, moving the coffee table out of the way and grabbing his deck of cards. We both sit cross-legged on the living room floor. He picks out a red queen, lays it in the center of the floor, and explains that she represents me. He hands me the cards and I begin to shuffle. "Place all your thoughts into them while you shuffle, Dawn," Dad instructs. He sits with his legs crossed directly opposite me and is very still. I get the sense that he has done this many times and imagine this is how he speaks to the man from the stone.

I close my eyes, pressing the cards hard between my palms, and begin to shuffle. Carefully, so as to not break the train of thought, I give them back to Dad. He holds them in his palms and mumbles a prayer under his breath. Slowly, he places each card down in a star pattern, then circles it with more cards, and finally places one facedown on the red queen. He takes a deep breath. "Ahhh. That's a good one, Dawn. Ahhh. Now, let's see."

At that moment, Terry comes storming into the house banging the door behind her. "Hey!" She sounds out of breath and heads in our direction. "What are you guys doing?"

"Shhh," Dad tells her, trying to keep his concentration. "Sit down."

Terry approaches like an oncoming train, stepping directly over the cards to find a seat on the couch against the wall.

"Aww, God damn it!" Dad yells, flinging down the remaining cards. "You can't do that!"

"What? What happened?" Terry asks, wide-eyed and frozen.

"Aww, shit!" Dad moans, "Son of a bitch!" He reaches down with more grunts and groans of disgust and scoops up the spread of cards.

"Wait," I cry. "What are you doing?"

"I can't read these cards. They're all wrong now."

"Wrong? What do you mean, wrong?" I'm in a panic. "Can't you make it right?"

"Ahh, there's nothing I can do, Dawn. She put the bottom of her foot over your head. Over your head! Here . . . ," he says, pointing to the red queen.

"What . . . what did I do?" Terry whimpers. "I didn't mean to."

"You ruined my reading!"

"It's not good," Dad says as he gets up from the floor. "It's not good." He shakes his head and walks away.

I am bummed. The silence is thick between my sister and me as we both sit, stunned. We are already nervous about all the changes that are happening. Deep in my heart I hope this is not a premonition of the days to come.

Time drags by at an exaggeratedly slow pace as the school year ends. I can't wait for us to be out of here. Dad passes his time predictably. He wakes early in the morning, sits at the table with his coffee, and reads the paper. When he is done, he faithfully pulls out his cards and begins endless games of solitaire while he mentally makes more of his "plans." Once summer arrives and school gets out, I sit with Dad and drink coffee, reading the parts of the paper he has just finished. I have my own deck of cards and have fun practicing my shuffling. Dad watches from the corner of his eye, smiling.

So go the remainder of our days—most of them, anyway. My excitement is high; the divorce will be final very soon, and we can be on our way. But then comes one odd morning at the end of June. I drag my feet into the kitchen as usual, annoyed at the harsh Florida sun flooding the house, and find that Dad is not in his regular spot at the table. *This is odd,* I think, but I am not alarmed. I tiptoe into Grandma's room, where Dad sleeps, and stand next to his bed. Dad is curled in a ball with the covers over his head, moaning in pain.

"What's the matter, Dad?"

"I don't feel good," he groans weakly.

"Why?"

"My head! It hurts!"

"Do you want some aspirin?"

His voice is a childlike whimper. "'Kay."

I wait for him to say something else, but he says nothing. *This isn't right,* I think, strongly sensing the presence of something serious. I run to retrieve the pills. Dad downs a double dose of the aspirin and after a while comes to the table to check the paper's headlines. He's feeling a bit better but wants to go back to bed.

"Where does it hurt, Dad?"

"Right here," he says, pointing to the space between his eyes. The spot looks angry and red as if he has been poked. I dismiss it as only a migraine that will get better soon. (I've never associated the constant small pimple on the side of his nose with this terrible headache. After all, it is "just a pimple.") Dad doesn't stay up very long; he says that the pain is getting worse, not better, and he goes to bed early.

Mom stays quiet through all of this and keeps her distance.

The next morning is as bright as the day before. Dad doesn't come to the table again, so I worry and go to check on him.

"Dad, are you all right?" I call out softly.

He is again curled in the fetal position and sounds like he is barely breathing. He mumbles something I can't understand.

"What?" I ask, beginning to panic.

He lets out a long, low groan that sounds as if it comes from a wounded animal. I can't understand him and reach out to touch his shoulder.

"Dad! Are you all right?"

With great effort, he rolls over and pulls the covers off his head. Trying to block the light with his arm, he looks up at me.

"Oh my God!" I'm shocked at the sight of his face. "Dad, you've got a big lump between your eyes where that red spot was yesterday!" I gush. It is too late to try to sound calm.

Dad looks panicked, and he touches the spot. "Yeah, I thought I felt something. Is it bad?" He looks me over carefully to check my expression.

"You gotta go to the doctor."

His voice is barely audible. "Yeah, I think you are right, babe. Go call your mother."

Mom races home after my panicked call and takes Dad to the hospital while the three of us children wait nervously at the house for any news of what's wrong. Already stressed about the divorce and getting the house ready to close escrow, Mom is afraid to reach out emotionally again, but she can never turn down anyone who needs help in such a desperate way, not even if that person is the husband who is soon to be her ex. She waits patiently at the hospital until the doctors are able to diagnose his condition.

It takes only a few hours before we hear that the news is not good. It appears, to the best of the doctor's knowledge, that Dad has cancer. The only puzzling thing is that they have never seen any kind of cancer like this before. What they know is that the lump on Dad's face is definitely a tumor and it is growing fast. Immediate surgery is the only hope.

When Mom calls, she tells us they are signing permission papers scheduling Dad for radical surgery first thing in the morning. The tumor, we are told, is growing so rapidly that they have to cut off his entire nose.

"Oh my God!" I scream, putting the phone back on the hook. "This is terrible!" Then I remember the date. "But . . . but . . . it's his birthday tomorrow," I sob. I've been planning to give him the macramé necklace I just finished working on, the one he shyly mentioned that he liked, the one with the roach clip on it.

We are all in tears.

Mom comes home in silent shock and quietly readies us for the hospital in the morning. In the blink of an eye, the relationship I've been developing with my father has changed, and again the uncertainty of the future is frightening.

Dad is out of surgery sooner than they had anticipated. We stand anxiously as they wheel him into the ICU recovery room, where we see that his entire face is bandaged. The doctors explain to us that the tumor does not appear to be malignant at this point but that its rate of growth is alarming. "Tumors that grow like that can easily turn malignant, and this one could have suffocated him quickly if it had gotten any bigger. Apparently, he used to mix batches of Agent Orange in Vietnam. This may very well be the cause of this type of cancer, but it's too early to tell. We made the best decision in removing the nose," the doctors confirm.

It all makes sense, of course, but damn this is harsh.

When Dad begins to wake, the nurses call us in, knowing we are eager to visit and support him.

I walk quickly to the edge of his bed and softly call out to him, "Hi, Dad . . . how ya feeling?"

His eyes flutter open, and he tries to focus. He raises his hand to fumble at his bandaged face. "Umph," he mumbles wearily, and closes his eyes tight as if trying to wish the whole nightmare away.

I take his hand and struggle to find healing words but fall painfully short. My eyes wander over the room, across the white square-tiled floor, and up the mint green–colored wall next to the head of the bed. A calendar advertising a local insurance agency reads *July* in bold letters. I remember today is Dad's birthday.

Excited, I blurt out, "Happy birthday, Dad!"

It is *not* the best thing to say. The look he gives me could kill a large animal. I feel awful and kick myself for saying it. I shrink back, appalled at myself, and let my brother and sister take their turns visiting. I clench my fists and hope they will find better words of comfort.

Then it is Mom's turn. "Vell, do you need anyting?" Mom asks coldly, her accent sharper than usual. Now that she knows he is going to live for a while, she feels put out. There is a strange vindictive tone to her voice that makes me uncomfortable. Mom has a habit of speaking her mind and damn the consequences. Unfortunately, she doesn't seem to care that Dad is so vulnerable right now. She puffs herself up like a cobra ready to strike and, to my dismay, lets all of her pent-up anger fly. "Vell, maybe you should have thought about all those things you did to us, Vayne. Dis never vould have happened. Da vay you left Grandma vaiting for you! She died vaiting for you!" She stops abruptly, her eyes shoot accusing daggers, suggesting that this tumor is God's retribution on him.

Terry, Wayne, and I back into the corner of the curtain in the ICU cubicle.

How could she?

Dad's eyes light up through the fog of the anesthesia, and he glares at her. "You . . . you wished this on me, didn't you, Edda?" His voice cracks, and he throws a desperate stab of guilt at her. Mom stands still in her tracks. In shock and horror, her eyes and mouth drop open. Dad's brief moment of strength fades quickly, and he falls back onto his pillow. "Go home," he says, dismissing her with a weak wave.

"Come on, kids!" Mom orders as she turns on her heel and walks out.

Somehow, I guess, the little green man with the long white beard in Dad's stone has lied.

CHAPTER THREE
From Sea to Shining Sea

Where's Terry?" Dad demands, walking into the air-conditioned house from the hospital. He has heard from Mom that she ran away.

He looks awful. Like a heavyweight boxer after a title fight, he has dark, heavy bruising under his eyes from the radical scraping of sinuses, and his voice is raspy. It has been two weeks since the surgery, and his face is still heavily bandaged at the nose area, the gauze strips wrapping around his head.

Much less laid-back and more serious now than he was before the surgery, Dad is now barking orders. Dealing with a life-threatening illness, he has little patience. He's not messing around. "Where is she?"

I stand up and answer matter-of-factly, "Nobody knows, Dad."

"Aw, *now* what? What is it, Dawn? What's the deal?"

"She ran away."

"Aw, come on. What was she thinking? That I wasn't coming back?"

"I don't know, but I think I know where to find her." I don't tell him this, but I have heard a rumor that she took off with her boyfriend.

"Then go find her!" His tone is filled with disgust. "Let's get this shit over with."

My sister, Terry, is very mixed up. As the middle child, she seems to find it difficult to feel favor from either Mom or Dad. She took a huge step of uncertainty in choosing our father to be her legal guardian. At this point in her fourteen years of life, though, she trusts only the streets. With Dad so suddenly at the hospital for a surgery with unsure results, Terry's best reaction was to bail. When the familiar streets called, she ran to them for comfort.

Terry's boyfriend—Juan, a Cuban boy she clings to as her solace—also hangs out on the streets. Older than Terry by four years, Juan protects her from most of the Cuban aggression she seems to naturally attract. He also helps get her into lots of trouble. Juan, a grown kid from the streets of Carol City, fancies himself a smooth con man. He stands five foot two inches tall and has pockmarked skin, dark eyes that shine mischievously, and a crooked smile. He is the one Terry is with when she is often nowhere to be found. Rumor on the street has it that they are shacking up at a friend's house near Collins Avenue on Haulover Beach, where we often hitchhike when we skip school.

Dad isn't in the mood to mess around. He wants to get this show on the road. The divorce is final, the house is sold, and he is in a lot of pain. We have only a couple of days before we have to vacate our home.

"Go get her," he orders again, knowing I will handle things.

"Where's Terry? We're looking for Terry." Scouring our neighborhood, I leave the message with my best sources on the street. I am eager to help Dad, and I puff myself up with the importance of the role. When I receive the address where she is staying, I head back home with the news.

"Let me see that!" Dad impatiently snatches the paper from my hand. "Okay. What do you have to tell me about this, Dawn? What is this place? What's their deal?"

"I don't know. Sounds like a gang place, Dad."

"Awww, shit! Let's go get her!" He grabs the car keys from the wall and heads out the door. I follow close behind, and as I slip into the passenger seat, I silently ready myself for a hostile confrontation.

It is an unusually windy day. The tallest palm fronds sway wildly, threatening to drop their heavy coconuts. We pull up to a pale yellow house on a block of stucco homes, each one a different desert color. Dad walks up to the front door with an air of command. Then he stops, slowly looks from side to side, and rings the doorbell.

The house is silent. I see a side window curtain pull back. The door squeaks open, a safety chain clinks across the gap, and a pair of dark eyes peek out. "Is Terry here?" Dad is polite, but firm.

"Why?" The eyes behind the door are suspicious.

"She's fourteen, and I'm her father. She needs to come with me!"

The eyes glare at us for a few minutes longer; then in a sudden decisive move, we hear the chain rattle and the door opens. "She's back there asleep." We step in and scan the room. A young Hispanic girl peeks out from behind the door. "Terry told us her parents were dead and she had no place to go," the girl explains to my father, her accent thick. "She's in the back room to the right."

"Go get her, Dawn," Dad instructs, holding his head down and away so the girl won't stare at his bandaged face. "Tell her to hurry!"

I scoot past them, hurry down the hall, and barge through the door. Terry is under a pile of blankets. Her foot sticks out from under the covers, bearing a macramé anklet I made for her last birthday.

"Terry! Terry!" I bend to feverishly shake her bare foot.

"Ump, whaaattt?"

"Terry. It's Dawn. Dad's waiting for you in the front room. You gotta go. Now!"

"What?" Terry sits bolt upright. "He's here?"

"Yes! Now let's go!"

"No! I'm not going!" Her hair wild, she scans the room. "Where's Juan?"

"I don't know, and I don't care. Now let's go before Dad gets real mad."

"Is he mad?"

"Not yet, but don't push it. He's in a lot of pain, and this is the last thing he wants to do today. You *know* we're leaving for California in a couple days. We gotta be ready!"

"He doesn't want me to go with him, Dawn." Her voice is a whimper, and I know she is feeling insecure. "Besides, I love Juan!"

"Oh my God, Terry, you do not! Let's go. Now!" Terry lets out a few audible groans and slowly gets up. She stalls for time, rummaging through her things, stuffing a large, plastic garbage bag full. "Come on!" I'm getting antsy. Things are too quiet, and Dad's been waiting too long.

Giving in, Terry picks up her bulging trash bag and follows me out to face Dad. He is standing with his hands in his pockets, jiggling his change, and nervously looking out the window. The Hispanic girl fidgets at the door as she watches us come out. Dad avoids our eyes. "You got everything, Terry?"

Terry stands still, eyes filled with horror. She hasn't seen Dad since the day of his surgery, and the gruesome evidence of the missing piece of his face stops her cold. "Yeah." She looks down and brushes a tear from her cheek.

"Then let's go."

I stop to thank the girl and her family for taking care of my sister, and then I fall in to follow Dad to the car.

"Tell Juan I'll call him later, and let him know where I am, okay?" Terry calls out to the girl from the backseat window.

Dad presses down on the gas.

We drive back to Carol City in silence. Terry sits by herself hugging her plastic bag and looking despondently out the window.

We arrive at the house in time to see Mom and Wayne packing boxes and small pieces of furniture into her car. I try to catch a glimpse of Wayne's eyes, but he averts my gaze. His long, stringy, sun-streaked hair hangs in his face, and his shoulders sag like a tattered dog toy. He briefly looks my way long enough for me to see that his eyes are red and swollen and his cheeks are streaked with tears. He is taking the breakup of our already broken family really hard, and I am going to miss him just as much as I know he will miss me.

Terry makes a beeline for the house, not looking at Mom or Wayne, while I stand in the front yard, immortalizing the images of what I called home for the last seven and a half years. It is time to close things up and say good-bye to the shapes, smells, and shadows of a difficult part of my childhood. I stare at the cherry hedges on the side of the house. I gaze at the royal palm by the mailbox, noting how much it has grown. Then I think about Grandma.

The presence of Mom is everywhere also. I memorize the multicolored bushes that rest just under her bedroom window and recall with a strange attachment the sadness that lives there. I stare at the sidewalk in front of the house, where I roller-skated on a Christmas morning in my new faux fur and Naugahyde jacket that Mom worked so hard to be able to afford, and I smile. *What is a* nauga *anyway, and how many did it take to make this jacket?* I wonder and laugh. Even with her many jobs, Mom always tried to make Christmas special. I know that despite all the rage between us, I am going to miss her. I picture how we might have been closer, and my heart hopes that all the hurt between us could somehow be instantly fixed.

"Are you coming in, Dawn?" Dad's voice snaps me out of my daydream.

I figure Dad probably wants me to roll him a joint, and I answer, "Yeah, be right there." It is becoming twilight, and everyone has already gone in. I walk past Mom's car, loaded to the brim with the precious treasures of our home, and I brush a tear from my eye.

Why does it have to be this way?

It is so hard here. If we stay I will probably end up dead, like a lot of the other kids I grew up with. Drowned in a canal like the girl I sang with in the choir before Grandma died; wiped out in a car wreck from a midnight race; shot down for whatever might be in my pocket. I know this. I want a better life, but why does it have to be so hard?

The next day Mom and Wayne are gone early. They are busy renting an apartment in North Miami. Dad and Mom have made arrangements to split the proceeds from the house, and Mom is very fair. As long as she can help it, she will never let her children go without, and in her own way, she wants to make sure her two girls have enough.

Dad is busy packing all his medicines and bandages together for the trip when he focuses on Terry and me. "Pack only the things you really need," he says, counting his rolls of gauze.

"Dad, I gotta talk to you," Terry insists, pulling him off to the side of the room.

"What, Terry?" He sounds annoyed at what he knows she is about to say.

"I'm not going without Juan!"

Dad looks up at her, then challenges, "You're not *what?*"

"I love him, Dad, and I just can't leave without him!"

"Do you know what you're saying, Terry?"

"Yes," she says, her voice shaking.

"And where am I going to put him? We don't have enough room."

Seeing a possibility that Juan can come with us, she shoots back a response. "Yes, we do, Dad. I'm only bringing a little bit, and he doesn't have much stuff, either," she rationalizes.

Dad thinks for a moment. "What's he got, Terry?"

Terry stands, looking blankly at him for a minute, then asks, "What . . . what do you mean?"

"What's he got?" Dad repeats. "Money . . . pot . . . you know. What's he got to contribute? To bring with him?"

Terry smiles as she comprehends Dad's meaning, knowing she has good news. "He's got money, Dad, *and* pot."

"Yeah? Really?" He perks up with interest. "Well, where is he?"

As if on cue, Terry runs to the phone to call Juan, and in only minutes he is knocking at the door.

"What the hell? Were you waiting around the corner or what?" Dad asks, amused at the comedy of Juan's appearance. "Come in; come in." He welcomes him in with a wave and a smirk.

Juan is grinning from ear to ear and sits down at the dining room table, ready to strike a deal. He pulls out a bag of Jamaican bud, promising to pay his own way and Terry's too.

This makes Dad very happy. "Go get your stuff ready. We leave in the morning."

After a sleepless night, I watch the sun rise on our final day in Florida. "Do you have the map, Dawn?" Dad asks for the third time, making a final run through the details.

"Yeah," I mutter, distracted by the way Mom and my brother will not look at me, even though they have come to say good-bye. Although I am excited to leave, my heart is heavy. I try to make myself believe it will only be for a short time and we will see each other again soon. Dad has promised Mom he will keep in close touch with her, and she reminds us that if we don't like the arrangements, we should let her know and she will work something out for us to come back.

"I promise you, Edda," Dad swears uncomfortably, "they'll be fine. Now let's say our good-byes; we gotta go."

I reach out to Mom first and hug her hard. Her body is stiff, and she is softly crying. "I love you, Mom," I tell her, and I begin to cry also.

"I luff you too, Dawn," she says, hugging me close, her German accent thicker through the tears. "If you need anyting, call me. Your fater knows da number."

I walk over to my brother next. "Hey," I whisper. There is a long pause. "Are you going to be okay . . . you know . . . with Mom and everything?" I keep my tone light.

"Yeah, I guess so." He sniffs, obviously holding back tears. He looks dejected.

"I love you, Wayne." I reach out to give him a hug. He melts into my arms, fitting into my body like a well-worn glove. We hug, sweetly, only the way a baby brother and big sister can, and then he lets loose with deep, heavy sobs.

"I love you too, Dawn," he says through his flood of tears. We hold each other tight one last time, then pull away again, wiping our faces dry.

As he looks down, my thoughts search for just the right words, but what can I say? "Be good, Wayne . . . and don't worry. We'll see each other soon." I try to reassure him, but my stomach churns with uncertainty. I turn away quickly, before I can stand no more, and walk out to our car, packed to the gills the night before. I get in and stare out the window. I'm not in the mood to watch everyone's good-byes. I am anxious to flee, to get on the road.

The more I dwell on it, the more of a downer it all is. It doesn't help that I think Juan is another downer, but I will go along with it anyway; after all, Dad is the one in charge.

We pick up Juan around the corner, where he is waiting with an army green duffel bag and his mirror shades. He thinks he is so cool, and it makes me laugh. Terry shoots me a glance that says, *Knock it off, Dawn,* but I laugh again anyway, kicking back in my seat up front.

Everything looks so run down around our old streets as we cruise through the neighborhood, and I am glad to be getting out. On the left is the old Kwik Check, where we shopped for groceries with Grandma. It is completely dilapidated now, badly needing a paint job, broken shopping carts lying strewn about in the parking lot. On the right we pass the local 7-Eleven, where I hung out with my girlfriends and spent nights sitting in our guy friends' souped-up GTO, trying to act tough and cool. At the intersection comes Burger King, the site of my first job. The bright orange and yellow building obnoxiously marks the on-ramp onto the Palmetto Expressway, the highway out of this hell.

The Florida Turnpike is only a short distance off the expressway, giving us a straight shot north past the Everglades on our left, Lake Okeechobee on the right, and miles and miles of rolling hills with lots of orange trees in between.

Juan keeps the joints burning, wanting to maintain the party spirit and to show off for Dad. This eases Dad's pain and makes him happy. I do my "fake inhale" act, which I have long since perfected, trying to keep up with Juan's excess, and it works well after the first couple of good tokes. I want to be cool too yet still maintain enough sobriety to avoid falling over immobile and completely stoned.

Eventually, Terry and Juan fall asleep on the extra sleeping bags stuffed between them in the backseat, and the smoky air clears up a bit. Through a glassy-eyed haze, I watch the Suwannee River buzz past. Dad keeps to the west, staying in the Florida panhandle through Tallahassee, and by dinner we stop at an overnight campsite in the Seminole State Park.

Camping outside in the warm, tropical summer weather seems

to me the perfect way to say good-bye to my old life. I stare at the stars, bright even with the waning light of dusk at their backs, and I eat my bologna sandwich.

Facing a western horizon and my future, I fall asleep wrapped in the warm colors of sunset.

⁂

Oklahoma is where we will camp next. We pass through Alabama, Mississippi, and Arkansas as quickly as we can. In an area where he has heard a lot of racism exists, Juan is getting nervous about being a Hispanic man with a bag of pot down his pants.

We are all a bit nervous, but Dad and I still have fun teasing him as we head out of these states. "Hey, Juan! Get down—quick! There's a cop!"

Juan's brown face turns pale, and he falls quickly onto the backseat. He stays down low until we start to laugh.

"Quit it, you guys," Terry scolds. "That's not funny." But the tears stream down our cheeks, and our sides ache from the joke.

The pot keeps our laughter strong as we enter into the boring safety of the country's plains. Miles and miles of wheat and flatlands make the afternoon sun unbearable. We have no air-conditioning, and it doesn't help that Juan is running out of grass.

The radio plays the same top-ten hits over and over. Even though we are glad Oklahoma plays more rock 'n' roll than the rest of the Southern states, we are slow to jump into our enthusiastic "air guitar" motions when Lynyrd Skynyrd's "Free Bird" takes its turn. We are tired of singing, "really love your peaches, wanna shake your tree," the best line in the Steve Miller Band's song "Joker," and we get grumpy.

I can tell Dad is weary of being at the wheel for so long, and I am pissed off too that Juan has lied about having a driver's license. He lies about how much pot and money he has as well, telling Dad he is about to run out only after we are well on our way. *No wonder he's so scared,* I think.

We find another cheap campground in the western part of Oklahoma, and for dinner we load up on bread, lunch meat, and sodas. I am glad to be close to the Texas border, hoping its scenery will be more exciting, and I settle down to go to sleep. Again, the summer sky is beautiful. Purples and pinks, yellows and magentas blaze vividly as we watch, mesmerized by the colors fading into darkness on the huge curve of the Oklahoma horizon.

⚜

The landscape in the northern tip of Texas is just as dreary, and the music much worse. Country music plays on every radio station, but Dad says this is to be expected here in the cowboy capital of the country. It is 1976, our country's bicentennial: two hundred years since the Declaration of Independence was signed. This is a special year. We all know we won't be alive to see another celebration of history like this one, so we focus on this moment in time, even if the music is a drag.

The mood in the car is still uptight, though. It's obvious that Dad's face is causing him a lot of pain, and it frustrates him to have to change the bandages every day while on the road. To top it off, we smoked our last joint in Oklahoma, and everyone is feeling ridden hard and bummed.

Terry and Juan are crashed in the backseat, drooling and snoring loudly. Sleep seems to me the best way to get through Texas, so I try to doze off, but Dad doesn't want me to.

"You asleep, Dawn?" he teases whenever he sees me nod off.

"Hmm? No, I'm awake," I lie, my neck sore from snapping to

attention. "Hey, look! Right on! There's New Mexico!" I finally announce, making the border call loud enough to wake both Terry and Juan.

"Far out! Finally!" Their heads pop up from the backseat.

New Mexico is much better. Once we are in the state awhile, the scenery is overwhelming. Massive multicolored rock formations appear out of nowhere and seem to follow us for miles along the highway. We gawk out of the windows as we travel through the most amazing state parks.

The music gets better too, thank God! Radio stations now play rock 'n' roll again with some groovy new tunes that send our "air guitar'" strings flying wild again. Our spirits are lifted as we cruise on Interstate 40 and head for Albuquerque, then continue west through the southwestern part of New Mexico.

We are relieved that the monotony of Middle America is behind us, and when Arizona's border call is made, we are all hoots and hollers. "California, here we come!" we chant, laughing at the cliché.

Flower power, peace, and love are everywhere. Dad especially relates to these emotions because of Vietnam, he tells us. Hitch-hikers flash us the letter *V* with their fingers as peace signs to prove, "Hey, it's cool, man," even if we don't stop to pick them up.

Some of them look desperately needy, and out of sympathy, I ask Dad why we can't give one a ride.

"Ehhh," he says, shrugging it off, "it's too much trouble."

He's probably right, I think.

Then, as if he's had a second thought, Dad asks, "Why? You think any of them have weed?"

"Hey! That's a good idea!" I perk up. "I'm not sure. Maybe . . . We'd have to check 'em out to see." I point to an approaching hitch-hiker. "Look, there's one!"

"Ooooh, let's take a look at him." Dad sits up in his seat. "What do you think? Quick—does he got any?"

I wait until the car gets closer, and then I lean toward the window to look at our prospective passenger. "Uhhhh, nawww, nope!" we conclude simultaneously as our car whisks past a strait-laced-looking young man.

"He looked like metro," I tell him, using a Florida term for the police. "Did you see his hair? Too short."

Dad agrees. We keep the search going for many miles into Arizona and eventually turn it into a driving game.

"What about him? Nawwww, nope!" We excuse each prospect for various reasons, driving by too quickly to stop anyway. Sometimes it is just because the hitchhiker doesn't look "cool" or looks too dirty, creepy, or crazy. Or they look like they might want to smoke *our* pot! "No way!" we shout, insulted at the idea.

Dad keeps driving on Interstate 40 through Flagstaff. We eat sparingly in the car. Except for bathroom breaks, he doesn't like to stop much. He insists repeatedly there isn't the time or money to do any sightseeing, even though we don't have anywhere in particular to stay once we get to California. "We'll figure it out," he tells us, not leaving room for me to ask the obvious questions about Pen Ci and Jack.

Finally, when we realize we are close to the Grand Canyon, we can't resist pleading with him to take the short detour north. "For just a minute?" we beg. "Please!"

We win. Dad is just as curious to see such an amazing natural beauty, and he gives in. "Besides," he rationalizes, "we need a bathroom break."

❧

"Whoa! Is that it?" we yell, crooking our necks out the windows to get the first look.

"Yeah! I think so. Over there!"

This was it.

"Wow! It's beautiful!" we whisper in wonder as we get closer.

Dad pulls up to an open parking space and shuts off the engine. Paper and cans spill out as we open the doors to scramble to the edge of the roped-off canyon and gawk with the rest of the tourists.

It takes our breath away. Standing there speechless, I realize time is nothing; it slips by without notice. We listen to the sound of the wind whistling through the miles of ominous levels below.

"All right." Dad breaks the silence after only a short time. "Let's get going. We gotta head out. We wanna get to the border tonight, remember?"

Reluctantly, we peel ourselves away from the spectacular view and wait in line for the john.

By the time Terry, Juan, and I get to the car, Dad is putting away his bandage kit and quickly presses down the ends of the tape that hold the gauze to his face. He doesn't want to clean his wound in the bathroom here because of all the people; he always wants privacy when he faces the horror of his uncovered image.

"Is it okay to come in, Dad?" I ask respectfully, so as not to embarrass him. "Are you done?"

"Yeah, yeah, I'm done." He turns away and secures the bandage a final time. "Get in," he says, signaling the "all clear."

Protective and sensitive to my father's pain, I feel deeply sad watching him suffer such a disfiguring ordeal. Although he doesn't ask, I try to help in any way I can, even if it is only making sure he has his space, time to himself with his affliction. What else can I do?

On the way out of the Grand Canyon, we pass many more tourist outlooks, but Dad refuses to stop and we don't press it. It is obvious he is hurting quite a bit. We remain quiet as the car winds back down to Interstate 40 and out of Arizona. Dad finally breaks the uncomfortable silence and begins the hitchhiker game again.

"Hey! Does he got any?" he says, straining to sound lighthearted.

Everyone's mood lifts, happy that Dad seems to be in better spirits.

"Well, maybe," I tease back.

"Nawww! No," chime Terry and Juan.

"Well . . . maybe?" Terry changes her mind as we quickly pass by, smiling and waving.

"Well, I hope someone looks good soon," Juan pipes in, "'cause I need to smoke a joint!"

In fits of laughter, we agree, and not much farther down the highway, we see him. "Oh! Oh! What about him?" Terry and I shout, pointing at the road ahead.

"He looks like *he's* got some!" We're excited as we spy the groovy-looking blond guy with his thumb sticking out. Dad slows the car.

"Wait. Wait," Dad warns. Then suddenly he makes up his mind and urges us, "Quick! Quick! Yes or no? Yes or no?"

"Yes. *Yes!*" It's unanimous. "He's *definitely* got some. He's carrying a bag. Look!"

"Okay! Okay! Here we go." In one fast move, Dad pulls off the road while Terry, Juan, and I stick our heads out of the windows, smiling and waving him over.

He runs toward us, clutching his suede, fringed shoulder bag close to his side, and a bad feeling suddenly comes over me. Catching up to the car, he stops at my window and in a breathless voice says, "Hey, man. How far you going?"

"California," I reply, trying to keep my cool.

"So am I. Where in California?"

"Ah, don't know."

I look toward Dad.

"Get in, man," Dad offers hurriedly from behind me.

"Are you going as far as LA?"

"Yeah, sure, man. Get in." Dad waves for him to come on board and not hold us up. Smiling big, the blond guy climbs in.

His name is Marty. He is from Los Angeles and returning from a trip to Colorado, where he was visiting an old girlfriend. When his car broke down, he decided to hitchhike home, stopping to see the sights along the way. He has long, sandy blond hair with a lighter blond moustache, and he wears a button-down shirt, white pin-striped elephant bells, and a headband that hides the beginnings of baldness. He is older than I first think, around Dad's age, and not as cute. Draped across his shoulder is an overstuffed leather bag decorated with different-colored beads tied on the fringes, and there is a sleeping bag strapped to his back.

"I'm Wayne. This is Terry, my daughter, and her boyfriend, Juan." Dad makes the rounds through the backseat. "And this is Dawn, my oldest daughter."

"Hi," I say shyly. I feel a little awkward at his stare, and uncomfortable at having to sit between him and my dad.

Marty looks at my dad as if he is lying and then sits up in his seat, winks at me, and smiles. "Right on."

Ewwww, I think and flash my sister in the back a long look that says, *Don't say a word.*

"So, we'd, uh, smoke a doobie with ya, but we ran out back in Oklahoma, man," Dad says, fishing to see if we were right about this guy.

Marty's head shoots up. "I got some!" he offers enthusiastically.

It is music to my father's ears. You can see the excitement rise in Dad's body; his legs begin to bounce. "Right on, man. Right on."

Like a pro, Marty rolls a joint on his lap and lights up. "Man, I wasn't sure it would be cool, uh, with your daughters in the car, you know."

"Aww, no, no, man, it's cool," Dad assures him, trying to act laid-back and casual when Marty hands him the joint.

Hours have passed, and I am stoned and uncomfortable. Marty's head keeps falling onto my shoulder as he struggles to stay awake. It is getting dark, and Dad wants to stop. The road signs tell us we are almost to California, and we decide we will sleep at the border on the Colorado River.

Marty stretches his legs. "So, where are you going, exactly?"

"California. Somewhere." Dad lets out a short laugh.

"No. Really, man. I mean, where in California?"

"Not really sure. We're kinda looking for a place to, you know, get on our feet. I've just had this operation, uh, on my face. Cancer. They took the whole nose a couple weeks ago," he explains, a bit shy about his appearance, "and I was in the middle of a divorce from Dawn and Terry's mother, when, uh, it all came down."

"Bad scene, man." Marty shakes his head. Nobody speaks, and the air is uncomfortable. Then, as if he has struck gold, Marty calls out, "Hey, maybe you can ask this chick I'm gonna stay with if you can crash there for a few days."

"Aww, naw, man . . . Really? Do you think that would be cool?" Dad perks up. He was hoping Marty might be able to help us. What luck.

"Yeah, we're together now and then, you know, man. Nothing serious, but she'd like it to be." He raises his eyebrows, and they start laughing together as if it's a private joke.

"I know what you mean, man. I know what you mean." Dad snickers.

"Her name is Harriet—she's kind of a Jewish princess. She lives in Glendale."

"Where's that?" I ask, wary of his story and this place: Glendale.

"It's a suburb of LA."

"Right on, man," Dad says. "Just point the way. We 'preciate that, man. 'Preciate that," he mumbles. Turning up the tunes, he is feeling pretty good. I, on the other hand, am feeling sick inside. I have been hoping Dad knows what he's doing for us. I mean, he is the one who always talked about a "plan." But now it is clear we will have to rely on luck . . . and a woman named Harriet.

"Right on, man." Marty reaches into his leather bag and lights up another doobie in celebration.

༄

We make camp that night on the California side of the Colorado River. We are here! California! Too tired to get really excited, we focus on eating dinner. We are right in the middle of the Mojave Desert; the wind blows viciously on our small campsite, flinging sand everywhere, making it hard to even breathe.

We call it an early night, and Marty, Terry, and Juan lay out sleeping bags at the side of the car, which serves to block the sand and wind. Dad and I sleep in the car, he in the front seat and I in the back.

What a luxury, I think, happy to be out of the blowing sand. As I settle down for the night, the wind howls mournfully. I toss and turn, covering my head with my pillow, trying to drown out the eerie noise.

Something lets the wind and sand blast into the car. Marty is trying to climb into the backseat with me.

"What are you doing?" I ask, shocked that he would try to lie down with me.

"Shhh, it's okay. Let me in," he insists.

"No! Get out of here!" My voice is getting louder. "I'll wake my dad, and I mean it!"

His eyes turn angry and glare at me.

I think about the weather outside and feel a twinge of guilt, but I don't want him sleeping draped over me, even if that's all he wanted.

"*Okay! Whatever,* man," he hisses and backs out of the car.

I stay awake for most of the night listening to the sounds of the sad howl of the wind and worrying that Marty might creep in on me again. For the first time since we left Florida, reality strikes and the sad pangs of the permanence of the separation from my mother and brother sink in. They were always there, somewhere near me, for all of the fifteen years of my life. Now the safety of their constant nearness is gone, and I miss them. Aware of the distance and weary from traveling, I suddenly feel very lost in this vast California desert. Holding myself tightly to block out the wind and the loneliness, I finally fall asleep.

The hot desert morning sun shines down on my face, waking me. I realize I have slept in. *Ugh,* I think. *Everything's so dried out. I need something to drink.*

Everyone is already up and milling about, so I forage through the backpacks for some water. We take our routine turns at the bathroom and pack the car quickly before it gets too hot. Marty avoids my gaze, and that is just fine with me. I don't want to mess up our chance for a place to stay in California, so I let the whole thing slide.

Dad kind of picks up on the awkwardness between Marty and me. He's obviously suspicious but doesn't say a word.

In no time, we are back on Highway 40 heading west again, driving straight through Needles and lots more desert. *I hope this isn't what LA is like,* I think as we connect to Interstate 15 in Barstow. Then it is one long road after another as we approach Glendale.

"Are there always this many highways?" I am curious.

"They're called freeways in California," Marty informs me dryly.

"Oh." I take in this new word and spend the rest of the drive absorbing the sights, making note of the differences between the East and the West.

"This is the famous Ventura Freeway," Marty announces to us on our final leg of the trip. "More people travel this freeway than any other in the US."

Wow! I think. *That's a lot of cars.*

We enter Glendale at dusk, as the colors in the sky begin to fade. *It gets cold here at night,* I notice uncomfortably, *even in summer.*

We turn onto Acacia Avenue from Adams and park the car in front of two rows of pale aqua cottages separated by a small, tree-lined courtyard. In the center of the courtyard is a row of baby trees and bushes that run the length of the cottages back to the garages. The front left cottage is 1010-A East Acacia, and the lights are on.

Marty jumps out of the car first. "Cool, she's home!" He sounds enthused. "Park over there so the manager doesn't ask you to move," he instructs, making sure we don't block anyone. "Let me go in first and tell her I have company. Don't worry. She's cool, man. It'll be cool." He throws his leather pouch over the shoulder of his patched jacket and bounds across the street.

Terry, Juan, and I stiffly get out, stretch our legs, and scope out the neighborhood.

"Hand me my sweater," I ask Terry. "I'm freezing."

There is a light mist in the air that you can see under each streetlamp when you look up and down the block. A heady, perfumed scent wafts from the flowers of the giant trees, and their shadows line the darkened street. It reminds me of the honeysuckle in our New Jersey backyard, and compared to Florida's streets, this one is quiet except for the noisy chirping of the crickets. *Night is different here too,* I think, shivering, as Terry and I venture a few houses down the block.

"Come on," Dad calls out, waving us back. Terry and I race to catch up with Dad and Juan. Dad checks his bandages, and I comb my hair before we walk up to Harriet's cottage together.

Marty is at the front door. "Come in," he invites us.

We walk single file past Marty into the living room of the small, one-bedroom cottage.

Harriet, a short, mousy-haired woman in her early thirties, gets up from the couch to greet us. Her brown eyes sit close together over her sharp nose, and they are very red. The room smells of pot as she says with a dry mouth, "Hello." It seems Marty has smoked one with her while we waited outside. Leaning on the fireplace mantel so she won't lose her balance, Harriet says, "So, Marty tells me you guys need a place to stay for a while."

"Uh, yeah," Dad answers. "Uh, for a couple weeks, maybe. Just till we get on our feet."

She seems to study us for a long time, especially Dad, and in the haze of her high, she finally smiles at him and says, "Well, I guess some of you can sleep on the floor. The couch *is* a sleeper," she adds, slurring her words and losing her grip on the mantel. She grabs at it again awkwardly. "But I gotta clear it with the manager first."

"Oh. Yeah. Right, that's cool," Dad says. His hands are in his pockets, and he's looking away so she can't stare at his face too long.

"It will take just a minute," she says, walking over to the phone and dialing with difficulty. We hear her ask someone on the other line to come over, that she wants to talk, that it is important. "No, you gotta come over," she insists. "Bye." She turns to us, grinning, and says, "He'll be right over."

"Right over?" Dad is nervous. He is tired and dirty after the long drive and not prepared for an official meeting with the manager.

"Yeah, he lives just across the courtyard."

Knock, knock, knock. We hear three sharp raps on the door. Harriet wobbles over to answer, already knowing who she'll find. "Come in," she says with a mischievous smile, standing back to let the manager inside.

"Hi there!" a tall, gawky man booms out as he strides into the room. He appears to be in his thirties. He has large, intensely blue eyes and dirty blond, curly hair so long it lies in a floppy Afro. His face is ruggedly handsome, even though it is thin. He is shirtless but wears Levi's cut off just above his knees and white tennis shoes. The air charges up when he enters the room, and instantly he has everyone's undivided attention.

Harriet introduces us. "Hi, John! This is Wayne, his daughters, Dawn and Terry, and Terry's boyfriend, Juan. And, of course, you know Marty." Then, addressing us, she says, "This is John. The manager." She sounds slightly goofy with her slurred formalness.

In two long steps, John walks straight over to my father with his hand extended. "How you doing there, Wayne?" he says with a bit of a cowboy lilt to his voice. He looks Dad directly in the eyes, never once flinching at his appearance.

"Hi." Dad shakes his hand, and I can feel his unease.

"Hey, Marty." John nods in his direction.

Marty returns the nod.

I wait for John to acknowledge the presence of Terry, Juan, and me, but he avoids our eyes and scans the room without a comment. *How rude!* I think to myself.

"Uh, can I see you in the bedroom please, John?" Harriet asks, distracting me from my mounting dislike for her manager.

"Yeah, sure," he answers quickly, heading for the room in the back.

"Come on, Wayne. You too, Marty," Harriet says, and they disappear down the hallway, leaving us wondering what will happen, and me still smarting at how rudely we have been ignored.

After a half an hour or so, John comes stumbling out of the bedroom laughing and exaggeratedly falling into the walls. "I'll see you later," he calls out behind him, rolling with laughter. "If you need anything, just let me know. You got my number!" He turns toward the living room with a big, short-toothed grin on his face and then walks directly past us into the kitchen, again without acknowledging our presence.

At the sink I hear the clanking of a glass, then water coming from the tap, and I think, *What a jerk!* Terry and I turn our backs to the kitchen, as if to say, *We don't care about you either.* We stand facing each other by the mantel where Harriet had retrieved her balance.

Still laughing boldly, John heads for the front door to leave. Then suddenly, he spins around, looks directly at me, and asks, "How old are you?"

I'm taken aback by his lightning-quick move and personal question, and I snap as if I've been attacked, on the edge, as I was in Carol City. "Fifteen. *Why?*"

"Mm, mm, mmp. *Too bad!*" He grabs his chest dramatically

and acts disappointed.

"What?" I'm taken off guard, then instantly incensed.

John smiles wider than I ever thought anyone could and winks a big blue eye at me. "Too young!" Again he turns on his heel and pushes through the screen door, roaring laughter to the night sky and all the way to his cottage.

"What . . . a . . . creep!" I say with disgust, wanting to scream at him. "He has no idea. Young, my ass," I add, fiercely blushing.

"Uh-oh, Dawn." Terry sounds worried.

"What?" I snap, not sure why I am so upset.

"He *likes* you."

I blush even harder.

CHAPTER FOUR
Too Young

Sun filters through the blinds, lighting the hardwood floor of the cottage at 1010-A East Acacia Avenue. Lazily, I open my eyes and scan the room. Sleep blurs my vision as I stretch and remember Harriet's cottage . . . and John. *What nerve,* I think, reminding myself that I am angry. A huge, unfamiliar green lump lies at the threshold of the front door. I stare mindlessly at the sunlight that moves up and down the green surface for a while, wonder what it is, then notice a stringy brown something that resembles hair. It must be Juan and Terry in their sleeping bag; I am happy I didn't have to sleep on the floor. I roll over and stretch again, feeling my bones appreciate even the lumpiness of the mattress beneath me. I roll onto my side to see Dad sleeping next to me on the pullout couch, his bandages intact. *He must have stayed up late to party,* I think.

I suddenly have to pee. In my oversized T-shirt and under-wear, I scope out the area for the bathroom and tiptoe quietly around the slumbering green lump and the various sofa cushions strewn about on the floor.

I linger in the bathroom; the pink and black tiles feel cool against my feet and the fifties-style sink dispenses a stream of cold water that I splash on my face. Towels and clothing I recognize as Marty's and Harriet's litter the small space, and the heavy smell of their muskiness permeates. Softly I tiptoe back to the couch and pull on my pants.

"You up?" Dad murmurs.

"Yeah."

Dad is silent again, then says, "Wish we had some coffee."

"Yeah, me too," I answer, studying the room around me. "Maybe we can find a store."

"Yeah! Why don't you and Terry go?" His voice is slightly pleading. "Harriet told you about a little market around the corner last night, remember?"

"I remember."

Through the filtered light I notice several gigantic houseplants loom from hooks at the windows, making it hard for me to tell the position of the sun. Massive fronds cling to the curtains and walls, threatening to take over the house.

I reach over and tap on the green cocoon with hair. "Terry," I whisper. "Terry, you 'wake?"

"Uhhhhhhhhmph," she groans, "nooooooo."

"Yes, you are," I prod. "Come on. Get up. Let's find a store."

Terry is slipping in and out of sleep. "Give me a minute." Slowly she rises, releasing pained grunts and groans. "This floor sucks," she complains, pulling on her clothes.

"Thanks, Ter," Dad calls from the other side of the sofa bed.

"Welcome," she answers grumpily. "All right, Dawn. Let's go."

We stumble out into the bright afternoon sun of Southern California, and I realize we have slept in late. We walk down the center courtyard past several cottages and out onto the street, following the directions from the night before and making our way to the corner liquor store for some instant coffee and juice. Our walk back is leisurely, as we take in the different styles of houses and types of trees. The blue sky is clear, with none of the characteristic smog Marty warned us about. The air is warm and dry, not humid as it is in Florida. I'm not sure I like it, and Terry and I complain that our noses are scratchy and irritated.

"Purple trees!" I shriek. "Look, Terry, they have purple trees!"

"Cool! Are they real?"

The ground, covered with blankets of colored blooms from jacaranda trees, beckon us to gather up heady handfuls and breathe in their curious smell. "Mmmmm." We are delighted and squeal some more. Spiky balls from the western sycamores mingle with the blooms on the sidewalk, making the walk back to Harriet's awkward and uneven.

As we turn the corner to the cottages and arrive with the coffee, John is there. He is in the kitchen under the sink, clinking and banging at the pipes. Dad and Juan are folding the mattress back into the couch and straightening up our things, piling them in a corner on the wooden floor.

"Wait. Look out!" Dad's voice is panicked. A massive, hairy dog comes running toward us at the door. I brace myself for attack. Harriet, who is leaning against the doorframe between the living room and kitchen in a slightly odd, seductive way, jumps up to grab her dog's collar.

"Wolf! Halt!" she commands. The dog freezes. "He's okay, girls. Let me get him back into the bedroom. He's a pureblood collie. Do you want to pet him?"

Terry and I fall to our knees to pet the classic-looking dog. "Wow!" I tell her. "He is beautiful." It is true. His coat is long and tangle-free, silky and warm like a winter fur. A long, sharp nose leads to sweet brown eyes adoring Harriet, and I wonder at the depth of her kindness.

Harriet beams and guides the dog proudly to the back room. Quickly she returns, heading back to the kitchen and her conversation with John.

"Can you hand me that wrench, honey?" I hear him gruff from under the sink.

"Shhuure, John," Harriet answers, syrupy sweet.

I walk into the kitchen, place the bag on the table, and purposely turn my head away from his voice, ignoring him.

"Would you like some coffee, Harriet?" I offer, opening the bag.

The clanking of the pipes stops. There is a thick silence. And then it starts up again.

"Okay," she answers swiftly. She gives me a look that says she noticed John's brief attentive silence.

Abruptly, the long, skinny legs that sprawl out from under the sink curl, and John shoots to his feet. I'm startled; he has my attention. In an instant, our eyes fix intensely; and just as quickly, John pulls away. I look down. Both of us blush, embarrassed. As much as I don't want to acknowledge John, I can't turn away from his gaze; and he can't turn away from mine.

"All fixed, Harriet," John declares as he breaks away from my transfixed stare and grins from ear to ear.

Oh my God! I think to myself, now focusing on the coffee in the bag. *What was that?* my brain screams, and I feel frozen to the spot.

"Thanks, John. Thanks," Harriet hurriedly answers. She is tense now, uncomfortable with the obvious energy John is directing toward me, and she walks over to open the door for him to leave. "Can I call you later, after I talk to them?"

"Uh, yeah, sure," he stammers and gathers his things. "Looking forward to it." John flashes a charming smile across the room and sends another glance in my direction before closing the cottage door.

The room is silent and awkward. Dad and Terry are going through the bag of Dad's pills on the coffee table, and Juan has just come from the shower and is combing his hair with a giant wire pick.

"So, guess what?" Harriet announces.

"What?" Terry has been sitting next to Dad on the couch.

"Well, if you want to earn some extra cash, there's some work around the courts. John and his wife, Sharon, are willing to pay you for gardening and stuff like that."

Wife! my mind cries with shock. *He sure is acting weird if he has a wife.* I attempt to dismiss any kind of feeling I might have about him. *This guy is strange,* I tell myself, blowing him off, trying to forget his gaze.

"Oh, uh, yeah, sure," Juan, Terry, and I answer intermittently.

"To help you get on your feet." Harriet sounds caring, warmhearted.

We thank her.

For a moment, I see us through her eyes and feel pity. *We must look pretty bad.* I picture how ragged we must appear to a stranger. But I shrug it off and replace the image with us as a family simply starting out in a new place.

"Cool, man. Thanks a lot," I mumble.

"Good. I'll call John and Sharon and set it up right away," she tells us, smiling proudly. Dad sips his coffee and digs in his duffel bag for his deck of cards.

The morning is already blinding and hot as Terry and I walk over to John and his wife's cottage at the opposite side of the court-yard. The rows of identical pale aqua stucco and white-trimmed single-story cottages are bland. But the manager's unit, the second cottage from the front, has a small wire-fenced space between it and the front unit.

Dad, Marty, and Harriet stayed up late the night before getting high in Harriet's bedroom while we crashed together on the pullout couch. Juan slept alone on the floor, complaining that I wouldn't let him sleep between Terry and me. Marty was gone early, having told Harriet he needed to "check in" on a job for a while, but having confided to my father that he was going "to see another chick."

As we approach the red stone steps of the porch, a little black-and-white brindle dog with bulging eyes and flat face races toward us at the fence, ferociously barking and snorting so hard that it's back legs lift off the ground with every snarling breath.

"Oh my God, Terry, look at that dog! That's the ugliest thing I've ever seen!"

"What kind is it?"

"Shhhhhh," I say, lowering my voice and giggling. "He'll hear you."

Somehow, the little dog understands we are laughing at him and his barking fades. Holding our bellies, we gather our composure and knock. We hear a few loud steps before John opens the door. He greets us curtly, looking serious and businesslike compared to his demeanor the night before.

"I'll meet you down at the garages," he says, searching the room for his keys.

"Sure. Thanks."

We walk down through the courtyard, this time with no barking dog to alert the neighbors, and stand in front of the garage door. John's light blue Chevy van sits parked next to an old magnolia tree.

"Terry. Look at the license plate. That's weird. What does that mean?"

"I don't know."

"W-A-D-D." The letters on the California plates are large and bold. We don't understand it. We hear John walking down the courtyard clanking a huge ring of keys, and we nudge each other to be quiet. He rounds the tree and smiles at us. I get the feeling he has heard our comments, and I mouth to my sister a silent, "Shhhh." He comes at us with long strides, his gestures expressive and dramatic. He runs his hands through his hair and rubs sweat off of his brow, as if he is posing because he knows we are watching. In the outside light, in his cutoff jeans and white T-shirt, he is taller and skinnier than I remember.

"Oh no," Terry says suddenly, turning away. "His shoes!"

My eyes scan the ground. John is wearing the loudest, red, white, and blue, stars and stripes tennis shoes we have ever seen. They are obnoxious!

What a geek! I think, feeling my face burn red. This guy is definitely strange, and I'm so embarrassed for him.

John walks past us, still fumbling with the keys, and unlocks the garage. Avoiding our eye, he gathers hoes, gloves, and hand rakes. "Where's Juan?" he asks, his voice husky and his back toward us.

"He's coming," Terry nervously answers, trying to cover for the other half of the green lump back on the cottage floor.

"He's still sleeping," I mumble under my breath and roll my eyes.

Terry nudges me hard in the side, stopping me from saying more. John pauses, glances my way, and smiles. Slowly I turn away, my back to him, and smile too.

"Come on." John changes the mood with his booming, serious voice. "I'll show you where to start." John leads us to the back cottage. The overgrown weeds are thick and tangled. It looks as if no one has tended to the yard for many seasons. The sun, already hot, blares fully onto the side of the cottages. "You'd better get working, girls, before it gets too hot." John heads down to Harriet's to get Juan.

"I hope he's up, Terry," I say doubtfully.

"Me too."

John returns with Juan in tow, leading him farther down the courtyard to work on pruning a large tree. Terry and I labor silently in the heat, pulling weeds and digging up their roots. Hours seem to go by. We are getting tired and thirsty when, suddenly, John appears next to us.

Without a word, John is down on his knees pulling weeds and digging deep into the soil next to me. The sun turns to hot noon as he wipes the sweat from his brow, leans back to squint at the sky, and announces, "Let's have lunch." John leads us single file back to his cottage. I like the idea of straggling behind, still connected to the earth, not quite willing to be in the static conversation among John, Terry, and Juan.

"Sit down," he offers as we enter the coolness of his living room. "And don't mind the dogs. They only bite a little." He laughs at his own joke.

The room is a menagerie of knickknacks and charm. Half of the living room is covered from floor to ceiling in numerous homemade shelves. Looking at each shelf, I see an animal figurine, an exotic shell, a brass lion, and a candy dish. The walls are giant puzzles, with every square inch adorned with hats from around the world, curious framed costume jewelry, antique meat hooks, and various antique weapons. Patchworks of different-colored carpet samples, pieced together by hand, cover the floor, and in the corner by the front window, the most beautiful gold desk with a glass-mirrored top and lion's head drawer handles leans under a billowing curtain.

The ugly dog is back and barking at our heels, blowing snot as we take a seat on the couch.

"John L," John shouts, smiling and pretending to sound harsh, "you be nice!"

As John disappears into the kitchen, a miniature dachshund comes waddling out of the back room barking blindly into the air.

"That's Buttons," John calls from the kitchen between whirring noises. "She's the grandma and blind as a bat."

John L jumps up on the couch, loudly sniffing each of us in turn. Buttons nudges my leg lightly, relying completely on her sense of hearing and smell. I reach down to hold out my hand, talking to her softly.

The dogs quickly converge on John as he walks out of the kitchen with a tray full of food and drinks. Setting the tray down on the small coffee table, he pulls up a footstool and grins. "Dig in!" On the tray is a log of sausage, a wheel of the oddest-smelling cheese, a loaf of French bread, mustards, olives, other unopened jars, and a pitcher full of frothy pink stuff. John grabs the glasses and starts pouring.

"This is my own invention," he proclaims proudly. "I call it fruit frappé."

"Yum, thanks." I gulp the smooth, sweet, thirst-quenching liquid.

As we savor our cool drinks, John starts dishing out food. He pulls out a huge Buck Knife, skillfully unfolds it with a sharp *snap* into the air, and slices the sausage.

"This is summer sausage. The best!" He cuts off hunks and throws one to each of the begging dogs at his heels. "And this is Camembert." He spreads thick, greasy globs onto pieces of torn French bread, one for each of us. "Mm, mm." His eyes roll into the back of his head. "Have you ever smelled anything better than that?" he asks, smiling and putting the cheese up to our noses.

"Ewww!" Terry says, faking a gag.

"Not bad." Juan sounds like he wants to show off.

"It's okay, I guess," I answer. It does smell good, but I'm still carrying a grudge and don't want to agree with John too much.

John gives me a quick look and a smirk as if to say, *I know what you're thinking.*

This infuriates me. *God, he always acts like he can see right through me. He doesn't know anything about me!* my mind screams as I sit chewing my food in silence.

John eats facing the bookshelves, away from the table, staring, as if in deep thought.

"What's that?" Terry asks, breaking the reprieve and pointing at the funny-looking jar on the tray.

"Why don't you try some and see?" John says, snapping back into the conversation. John reaches for the jar and twists open the lid. He pulls out an oily-looking nugget, holds it to his mouth, and proclaims, "Frog legs!" before swallowing it whole.

"No way!" I cry. "That's disgusting!"

"I'll try one," Juan pipes up, laughing at me.

"Yeah?" John says. "How about you, Terry?"

"No, thank you."

"That's the sickest thing I've ever seen. You have no idea how many squished frogs we saw every day in Florida," I interrupt, letting down my guard and revealing a bit about myself.

"Really? Well, we can just put them away then." John smiles.

"No wait," Juan cries, wanting to meet his challenge. "Hey, Terry, you have to try some too!"

Trying to be revolting, Juan gulps down three of the slimy legs; Terry is brave and tries one small piece as a dare. John doesn't eat any more and downplays the game. I get the feeling he is taking my side suddenly.

We clean up and then head back out to finish the yard work, feeling relaxed from the food and more secure about earning our keep from the manager. At dusk we lock the tools in the garage, and John gives us decent pay. Dirty and tired, we head back to Harriet's to shower and have some dinner.

Harriet clangs in the kitchen making her famous cheese potatoes and meat loaf while Dad stands next to her at the stove praising her skills. She is glowing. To me, they look really stoned, and they're acting giddy.

After my shower, I find a quiet spot behind various huge potted plants at the kitchen table to scan over my poetry. So much has happened to us in such a short time, and we have met so many people that I feel I need to write. Cat Stevens' "Wild World" plays on the stereo in the living room and, like the message of the song, I hope I will be all right on our new adventure in this crazy world. I am in a reflective mood. Poetry is my solace: the one thing that belongs to me and no one else.

"Whatcha doing?" Dad asks, peeking his head over the plants.

"Aw, you know," I answer shyly.

"Oh, that stuff again?" Dad remarks, seeing me in a familiar mode of writing. "Company's here and dinner's ready. Come and eat."

In the living room, Harriet is introducing a guy in his twenties to Juan and Terry. "Oh, hey, Mike. This is Dawn," Harriet says, pointing in my direction as I enter the room.

"Hey," I say, thinking there is something dull about this guy even though he looks kinda cute.

"Hey," Mike responds, his eyes growing large as he looks up at me, causing me to step back a bit.

"Mike lives next door," Harriet informs us with a smile. There is a brief silence before Harriet offers him to join us for dinner.

"Sure thing!"

Everyone sits where they can find a spot. Mike and I end up sitting next to one another on the floor. I sense he is feeling as shy as I am at the way Harriet keeps smiling at us, as if she is setting us up. *Ewww,* I think, embarrassed, and then dismiss the entire idea.

We quickly finish dinner, warm and delicious after all the hard work that day. Then we sit making small talk.

"Is he coming?" Mike asks.

"He said he would be here in a little while," Harriet tells him.

"Who?" I ask curiously.

"The manager." Harriet's voice is dry.

Mike smiles and rolls his eyes. "Yeah, the manager," he says, laughing to himself.

Just then there is a knock at the door. It is John. He is freshly showered, and his hair is combed loosely back. He's wearing a faded jean jacket with hand-sewn embroidery, a fresh white T-shirt, nice-fitting faded blue jeans, and heavy tan Frye boots. His presence is intense as he walks in, smiling as if he has just been introduced. "Hello!" He smells of nice cologne, and for some reason I feel a bit uncomfortable that I am sitting next to Mike.

"Oh, uh, am I interrupting anything?" John asks, overacting and feigning embarrassment for having walked in on something private. For a quick second, I think I see him flash me an almost jealous look. "Shall we go to the kitchen," he indicates to Mike, "or, uh, do you want to go next door?"

Mike gets up. "The kitchen's fine, man. Don't want to hold you up." He leads the way. John follows, then turns to scan the room again, landing the last look on me before he enters the kitchen. It is clear that Mike is going to buy some pot John is holding. When they come back into the living room, Mike is smiling and John won't look my way.

It is strange, but I don't want him to leave. He is kind of fun, sometimes, and at least entertaining. John stands in the center of the room in a way that makes me feel like he wants my attention. I keep my head down and try not to notice.

As he says his good-byes, he reaches down behind me and picks up a blossom that has dropped from one of Harriet's flowering plants. "Is this yours?"

"Oh, uh, no, but uh, thank you," I stammer, taken aback by his sudden closeness and the intensity of his eyes.

He draws in a quick breath, places the flower behind my ear, says good night again, and walks out. No one says a word.

My heart is racing. My cheeks are burning red. *Why?* I think. *Why? Knock it off,* I tell myself. *This is ridiculous.* I try to push him out of my mind.

After John leaves, Mike rolls a fatty and passes it around. Dad and Harriet sit huddled together on the couch, whispering secretively. "Why don't we go to my place?" Mike announces.

"Cool!" Terry and Juan chime as we scramble to our feet, leaving Dad and Harriet to themselves.

Mike's cottage is your typical stoner bachelor pad. A single, old, worn couch, television, and broken-down coffee table are the only evidence of habitation in the living room. "Sit down," Mike offers. "I got enough to roll one more doobie. John's gonna bring some more back in a while."

Cool, I think. *At least we will be entertained.*

Juan and Mike sit to talk about themselves. Juan's stories of survival on the streets of Carol City trump Mike's pot smoking stories, and Juan is eating up the attention.

Terry and I take a pass on the pot and kick back on the sofa to enjoy some semi-privacy. The small color television runs lines of irritating static, and we take turns getting up to play with the wire hanger rabbit ear antenna. I feel comfortable and secure sitting with my sister on a couch in front of the TV, a reminder of our old life. We fall into easy laughter at a comedy channel that finally comes in clear.

Hours have slipped by. It is getting very late, and John still hasn't returned. All television stations have signed off for the night. We can stay awake no longer, and the three of us say good night.

"He always shows up," Mike tells us on our way out. "You just never know when."

Quietly we creep back to Harriet's, tiptoeing on the hardwood floors. The lights are out.

"Dad, Dad," I whisper. There's no answer.

"He's not in here, Dawn," Terry says, examining the empty room.

"Oh, help me pull the couch down then." I am irritated that Dad is in the bedroom with Harriet.

Juan rolls out the sleeping bag and scrambles in, waiting for Terry to join him. "I'm sleeping with Dawn on the couch," she insists. "The floor's too hard."

He mumbles something in Cuban and rolls over.

Lying in bed that night, I realize I can't sleep. John is on my mind—intensely on my mind. It makes me mad. *You think you can get me,* I think angrily. *I'll show you. I'm not someone you can have that easy.* I picture an image of us together and, with a shiver, cast it out.

Hours later, I am awakened by the sound of his van pulling down the alley. I hold my breath as his footsteps walk loudly up the courtyard, hesitate, then step up to his cottage. Then I hear him

open and close his door. I fall asleep wondering about the pause
in his steps, the sense of him listening, and I can't resist the urge to
picture him, standing there, curious if someone is awake.

In the morning I decide that this is enough of the John attraction thing. No more messing around. We have just arrived in
California, and acting like this is crazy. There are tons of things
I want to do, and I am looking forward to them. Making new
friends, going to school, and starting over are at the top of my list.
This is a new start, a new beginning. We are out of the "road to
nowhere," away from Carol City. This is our new lease on life. Besides, John is in his thirties! He is much too old, and *he is married!*

Sharon Holmes rarely seems to be around. Terry, Juan, and I met
her briefly on our first day at the cottages. Just home from work,
she was walking up to her porch in her white nursing pants and top
while the three of us sat lounging on Harriet's front steps.

"Oh, uh, Sharon," Harriet called out to her, "I'd like for you to
meet my new houseguests."

Expressionless, Sharon looked at all of us. "Hi," she said curtly,
nodding after everyone was named. Her face remained stonelike,
detached, and a cold chill ran down my spine. *Scary,* I thought.
Harriet told us she was a children's nurse and very smart, but she
looked mean to me. Without any further comment, Sharon turned
quickly on her white rubber heel and stepped through her doorway,
leaving us to question whether she approved of us or not.

Five days a week, Sharon pulls up in her blue, black-top

Chevy Malibu at around 5:30 in the evening. In her white nurse's uniform, she ritually heads for her cottage and carries a book bag full of patients' charts and Harlequin romances. She wears thick, dark-rimmed glasses, no makeup, and a different-colored curling yarn every day to tie back her long, salt-and-pepper hair. Rarely does she speak to anyone. I only see her talk to people when she receives rent checks or arranges repairs for the tenants. When she is home, an occasional eerie glimpse of her silhouette stands quietly behind her screen door. She looks much older than John, and Harriet and Mike think she acts more like his mother than his wife.

"They're not together like a couple," Mike tells us one day after Terry comments on how cold the relationship between John and Sharon appears.

"How do you know?" I ask.

"John told me and, well, just watch them," Mike answers. "They hardly even talk to each other. John goes home for dinner every night, and she does his laundry. That's what he told me. It's been like that for years now."

"That's so weird," Terry says. "Maybe she's seeing someone else."

"I know. Maybe. Everyone thinks it's weird, but no one asks them about it. It's their thing, I guess." He shrugs, as if it's no big deal.

Mike's cottage makes a great hangout and feels the most comfortable of the places we've been since we left Florida. He, it turns out, is a twenty-two-year-old struggling college student and not just a stoner. Mike slips easily into a big brother kind of friendship with Terry and me, and he and Juan become buddies.

Easygoing, Mike has a soft spot for us after learning about our trek here and Dad's sickness. He knows Harriet's place is crowded and awkward. In no time, Juan has a key to the front door and we are allowed to hang out even if Mike isn't home. Just as quickly he agrees, along with John and Sharon, that Juan and Terry can live at his place. Juan has found a job in a hamburger joint down the street on Lomita, and Mike needs help with the rent anyway.

Juan's first paycheck makes the payment on a used water bed, and the obvious spot for it is smack-dab in the middle of the living room.

"Congratulations, Ter. You're an official independent couple now." Dad pats her on the back. Terry looks away. She is not very happy about Dad's enthusiasm—and not too happy with Juan.

At first, I don't spend a lot of time at Terry and Juan's new place. I don't want to interrupt their arrangement, and I'm enjoying more time to myself. I am also happy to be away from Juan. There is a new freedom in my heart, a lightness. *The sun really shines here,* I think. *People walk down the street and don't get jumped.* I know Terry is scared, but I feel hopeful for the first time in many years.

The words to my poetry come to me like butterfly wings, happy and free and beautiful. Silly poems of gratitude and love flow like water from my pen, and I keep them like precious pieces of my soul, safely bound in my book of writings, pleased with the feeling that I have turned a corner of darkness in my life.

John continues to keep Terry and me busy with gardening during the month before school starts, but as I promised myself, my attitude toward him is cold. That doesn't stop him. He takes every opportunity to be the center of attention whenever he is around. On days when he comes to Harriet's to pay me for work or to give me instructions for gardening, he positions himself in the middle of the room, speaking with a booming voice and moving his body in animated gestures.

God, he needs so much attention, I think. Oddly, he never looks directly at me. Still, the uneasy feeling that John is really trying to attract my attention nags away at my gut, and I flinch at his quick sideways glances in my direction. I resolve to build the walls up around me even stronger—walls like the ones that kept me safe in Carol City. I'm good at that.

Dad spends time away from the cottage registering us for school, signing up for food stamps, and getting himself on the local veterans hospital list for follow-up care for his face.

While he is gone, Harriet and I begin to get close and hang out a bit. The kitchen is warm and full of good smells. She likes describing her incredible treelike plants and teaches me her secret method for making cheese potatoes. The stove sizzles hot with blintzes, a sweet Jewish pancake that is another of her passions. She enjoys teaching me the meaning of kosher foods and how to make delicious Jewish dishes, such as brisket. I am curious and ask lots of questions. I love her stories about her childhood Hanukkah traditions.

Occasionally, when Dad is gone, Harriet will call John over to check on the plumbing, the window screens, or other various things around the cottage. I think it's kind of odd that she needs the manager so much. I can swear that Harriet is about to swoon every time John knocks on the door.

There is one day, however, when I decide to ask Harriet why she flirts and acts so goofy after John has just left. "What are you doing?"

"What do you mean?" She bats her eyelashes over her glazed look.

"I mean the way you act." I make it clear that she obviously appears affected by him. "I know he and his wife aren't together, but do you like him or something?" I ask, trying to figure out a reason for her silliness.

"Like *him!*" she shoots back. "Don't you know who *he* is?" she says excitedly, her face coming in close to mine.

Completely repulsed at her change of character, I glare back. "Nooooo. Am I supposed to know who *he* is?"

Her eyes like brown saucers, large and round, stare at me with the utmost of disbelief. Suddenly, she grabs my arm. "Come here. Let me show you something." She pulls me over to her hall closet, looks over both shoulders, and with one hand firmly on my arm she opens the closet door. I am stunned. Inside, long white rolls line the back of the closet wall. It is the largest collection of posters I have ever seen.

"What are those?" I ask, impressed by the collection.

"Look!" Harriet insists, too excited to keep her voice down. She grabs a large roll of posters and begins to unravel them.

The first one has the words *Liquid Lips* splashed across it in red.

So? I think. Then I see him. There is a super large, very handsome picture of his face as he holds another woman in a deep kiss. "Is that John?" I am shocked at what I see. "Wow! He's really cute in this picture," I admit, getting excited that I know a famous actor, simple manager of cottages.

Under the title on the marquee is "John C. Holmes as Johnny Wadd." Below that, I see an *X* above the words "Adults Only."

"Ah, WADD. That's where the license plate comes from . . . and *X?"* I say out loud. The shroud of innocence lifts, and my stomach rises to my throat as the sexual tones of the posters become apparent.

"Uh-huh," she answers slyly.

Harriet uncovers another one: *The Spirit of Seventy Sex.*

Oh my God! His shoes! Those obnoxious red, white, and blue sneakers he wore the other day glared at me from this next poster. Harriet continues pulling out posters. The title on the next one is *Confessions of a Teenage Peanut Butter Freak.*

I can't take it any longer. "No! Wait! Stop!" I insist, now overwhelmed with shock and trying to hold back feelings of complete embarrassment. This is way too much information for me. I feel strange, almost violated, and I am kind of angry with Harriet for showing me any of this stuff.

"He's a movie star!" Harriet breathes. "There's lots more, and he always brings me a poster from every movie 'cause I'm such a big fan," she discloses candidly. "You've never heard of him? Really?"

"No, no, I haven't. Really," I admit in a low tone, shaking my head. "I've never seen one of those movies, and I don't know anyone who does."

"Well, it's a secret." She suddenly sounds uncomfortable, and she looks over both shoulders. "Promise you won't tell anyone about this. It's kinda my thing, you know."

"Yeah, uh, I promise," I assure her, even though I'm not feeling very loyal to *her thing*. "Don't worry." I close the closet door on Harriet's fantasy.

Inside, I am numb. *That person on the posters—who is that?* I mean, I realize it is John, but it doesn't seem like the same man I met here, the manager. This whole scene is totally bizarre and, as tough as I act on the outside, I know this is completely over my head. Now I am convinced that staying away from John emotionally is the smartest thing to do.

As I suspected, with Marty gone, Dad and Harriet are an item. It seems sure that Marty won't return, and they get hot and heavy. It doesn't make any sense to me, knowing Dad's big story about Pen Ci and Jack coming to the States. But he is obviously into his own thing, and communication with him is distant at best right now. Maybe he thinks I'll tell Harriet about them, or maybe he is afraid he'll get in trouble for being an unfit father. I don't know, but our relationship is much different than it was in Florida. *Does he know,* I wonder, *about Harriet's closet shrine to John? And if he does, does he care?*

The worst part about their new relationship is that Harriet is getting less friendly and more motherly. The closer she gets to Dad, the more she begins trying to act like a parent to Terry and me. Because I still live under her roof, she questions my whereabouts and gives me lists of chores. She and Dad stick together like glue, and I am jealous.

I only get a little of Dad's time, when Harriet is at work. All we talk about anymore is the VA hospital and how he refuses to have another operation even for cosmetic reasons. "If people don't like the way I look," he cries defiantly, "then they can look the other way!"

When Harriet gets home after work, she and Dad slip off immediately to her room to get stoned, leaving me to fend for myself. I head to Terry's next door and hang out until late at night. The next morning, as usual, Harriet questions me about where I have been most of the night and what time I got in.

"She can't tell us what to do," Terry and I insist resentfully when we are alone together. This is simply unacceptable. Nobody can just walk in and try to replace our mother. Not after what we've been through. We both miss our mom, even with all the problems we had with her. Though Dad refuses to talk about her, we write her regularly.

In truth, Harriet feels sorry for us. John feels sorry for us. Everybody feels sorry for us. We are two young teenage girls: one with an older, dubious boyfriend, and both with a disabled father. We would be homeless if Harriet weren't providing us a place to stay or if John and Sharon weren't giving their permission. Harriet knows that. Food is scarce for us. Harriet shares what she can, but it is never enough. Juan brings home extra hamburgers from work, but still we look as if we never eat. We're as scrawny as little sticks. The tenants in the courtyard agree we are a family that needs help. The few elderly renters in the middle cottages act nonchalant as they bring us extra servings of food from their dinner tables. John gives us gardening jobs, insisting to Sharon that he doesn't want to do the work himself—but in actuality, he wants to help us.

School will be starting soon, and we need an address in order to enroll. I can't wait to meet new friends my age and get some relief from the oddness of this courtyard. *At least we aren't fighting in the streets like before,* I think thankfully. But I worry I won't be able to handle the California school system after such a horrible education in Florida.

To top it all off, with Dad and Harriet definitely close, I feel as if I've lost my newest best friend. I'm jealous, but trying not to show it. I keep to myself around the two of them, especially since Harriet's been in her motherly role.

I rely hard on my poetry; it keeps me sane. Sitting in a corner on the porch or leaning up against one of the back cottages by the garages offers me a tiny place to find the quiet I need to write. Being alone and writing seem the best way for me to release my emotions and process my spinning, whirling life of change.

John often walks past me as I am writing, on his way to his van or back to his cottage. When he sees me alone, he only nods and walks by, respecting my quiet. I appreciate that he understands my need for privacy and find out later that he spends his own quiet time writing poems about his private thoughts and dreams.

John's brother and sister-in-law, David and Karen, live in a back cottage with David's stepson, Jamie. David, a tall, thin, dark-haired man with a dark goatee, is rarely seen outside; when he is, he's in his pajamas and robe and only out to get the mail. "He has epilepsy," Harriet told me once, "and can't work." Karen is a stocky woman with light blonde hair, small facial features, and thick legs. Her son, Jamie, is seven and her spitting image. Both in their late twenties, Karen works as a secretary for a temp agency in Glendale to support them while David takes care of her son at home. Sometimes, I see John go briefly in and out of David's, laughing loudly as he leaves the cottage, but never do I see any of them together outside. It seems strange to me, but I don't really give it much thought.

I am sleeping on the pullout couch by myself now, and I stay next door at Juan and Terry's until after Dad and Harriet go to bed. Late at night, I eat whatever I can find in the refrigerator by myself. Sometimes if there are leftovers from a meal Harriet has made, I sneak portions of food over to Terry through the back door.

Dad calls John the "Candy Man." He makes regular evening

pot stops at Harriet's and then at Mike's. His constant companion, a brown Samsonite briefcase, is loaded with candy bars, gum, sodas, and cigarettes for Terry and me. He knows my favorite brand of smokes is a good Marlboro Red, and he just happens to always have a pack handy. The whistling of a cheap spaghetti western tune floats through the courtyard. John bangs the door to the cottage open and stomps in, briefcase in tow. He snaps it open and pulls his corncob pipe and plastic film container from the clutter of crumpled True Blue cigarette packs and his silver flask. Dipping his finger into the container, he grabs a small bud, stuffs it into the pipe, and lights it with a *snap* and *crackle*.

Drawing deeply, he smiles and walks over to Juan first and nods as if to ask if he wants some of the sweet smoke, but he doesn't wait for a response. John turns the pipe around, puts the cob end into Juan's mouth, and blows a long, hard shotgun into his face. He walks over to Terry next, takes another deep pull that nearly chokes him, waits for her to nod, then blows out the smoke for her to inhale. He turns to face me. I feel my face burn as he bends closer. John doesn't wait for my okay. He fixes his eyes closely on mine and sends a slow stream of smoke into my mouth. My eyes roll back as I cough back my breath. John stands up, pleased with himself, and throws his things back into the briefcase. Grinning from ear to ear, he takes a sweeping look around the smoky room, laughing his way out the door.

As the weeks roll on, John gets friendlier with Dad and Harriet. They love his pot, and John likes dropping off party *treats*. "He's a nice guy," Dad tells me, and he doesn't say that about many people. I figure John, like everyone, feels sorry for Dad because of his disability and wants to help a veteran feel better. It's patriotic.

John still vies for my notice, and although I am friendly, I won't allow myself to be pulled into his intensity again. On a day when he stops by Harriet's to "shoot the shit" and drop off some weed, he asks to see if Terry and I can help out with cleaning and painting one of the empty cottages.

"It's okay with me," Dad says. "Ask them." He points to me and then in the direction of Terry's cottage.

"It's cool with me," I answer quickly, excited to be making more money. School is starting in a few days, and I need to buy some clothes.

"Yeah?" John smiles, then pulls back shyly, looks down at his feet, and mumbles, "Well, we'll need to get some supplies and, uh, I have an appointment tomorrow."

"Go get them now," Dad offers, suddenly sounding helpful. "Dawn can go with you."

A lump sticks in my throat. "Okay. Bitchin'," John says, checking his watch. "Can you go now?"

"Uh, yeah, sure."

John and I head back through the courtyard, and I suddenly feel nervous and shy. I can't help looking over toward his cottage, wondering if Sharon is watching from a window somewhere. We silently load up in the van, acting formal and stiff. John hands me a piece of paper and tells me to write down a list of things we will need for the job. My tension eases as we make the list, taking turns calling out the next thing to buy; we make it a challenge, a game, and we laugh. A quick look flashes between us that says, *Hey, we work pretty good together.*

More relaxed than we've ever been together before, we finish our errand and head back home. Looking over at John in the driver's seat, I notice how handsome he looks while driving. It is a comfortable, warm feeling. His dark blond curls fall around his face in a rugged sort of way. The blue of his eyes shines bright against his mildly tanned skin, and he moves with an air of fierce confidence that makes me feel safe. John plugs in his eight-track tape of Jim Croce and starts singing, "Bad, Bad Leroy Brown." I giggle at his dramatic, loud voice, and he looks at me, smiles, puffs himself up, and sings even louder. Giggles turn to laughter, and

I give in and try to sing with him off-key. John tries hard to keep a serious face but can't, and we both break down into bursts of hysteria.

Back on Acacia, we wipe the tears from our eyes as we unload the van. *I haven't laughed that hard in a long time,* I think.

John waves at me and walks away, booming, "Good night. See ya early tomorrow."

I smile back at him.

"And tell your sister to come to work," he calls back.

The icy tension between us has been broken, and in my heart my protective walls have been lowered. I begin to genuinely like him. I am seeing how naturally kind and funny he really is, and I completely and purposely reject the person I saw on the posters in Harriet's closet. After all, he doesn't seem like that kind of guy—from what I can tell.

The next week, the day after Labor Day, is the start of school. Early on the first day, a knock comes at the door. Sliding out from under the covers of the sofa bed, and wearing only a tank top and underwear, I sleepily answer. I see that it is John and, without thinking, open the door. "Yeah?" I say, rubbing the sleep from my eyes and pushing my long, dark hair away from my face.

John stands frozen, staring at me through the screen without a word.

"Yeah?" It takes a minute before I realize he can see my silhouette. When I do, I quickly step behind the door.

"You up?" John asks, slowly shaking his tangled curls. Then he snaps out of his daze. Nostrils flared, he looks at me hard. "Time for school," he says and turns to walk away.

"Thanks," I call out as he disappears, wondering why he seems abrupt and angry. *Maybe he's grumpy when he gets up,* I think, blowing it off. But then I wonder, *Why is he getting me up, anyway?*

CHAPTER FIVE
California

School begins in early September of 1976 for Terry and me. This is my first year in high school. *The tenth grade at Glendale High. Wow!* I think, searching out the front office, registration papers in hand. The halls are crowded with hundreds of students trying to find their classrooms. After registering, I roam the bustling corridors in search of my first period class. In my assigned room, I settle into a large, crowded group of many different-colored faces. *There are all kinds of nationalities here.* I'm happy to see that no one race outnumbers the other. When the teacher addresses us as sophomores, I get excited. *I'm a sophomore,* I think, then immediately stress. *I hope I'll fit in okay.*

California public school schedules call for an early start and early finish. I walk home alone, holding my newly issued books. While passing some students hanging out at the snack shop, I assess the scene and sense with relief, *They don't look like gang members to me. They do have some nice cars, though.* I keep a wary eye on them anyway.

It is a two-mile walk back to Harriet's cottage. Dad dropped us off in the morning, showing us the best way back to Acacia. I take in all the landmarks as I turn from Verdugo Road to Adams, passing Maple and Garfield to finally turn onto Acacia Avenue, where the cottages are third from the corner. Turning in to the courtyard, I can hear Terry and a guy's voice come through the open window of her cottage. *How did she get home before me?* I wonder. Terry started at a different school than I did this morning, Roosevelt Junior High, the ninth grade. Just as it had been in Carol City, the freshman year is held in junior high here.

I walk up to the steps and give a quick, sharp courtesy knock, open the door, and walk right in. "Hey, what are you . . . ?" My voice trails off. John is sitting on the couch, looking up and smiling. It is just he and Terry in the living room, and the two of them suspiciously stop talking as soon as I enter. "Oh, hi." I nod at John and give Terry a stare to demand to know whether she is hiding something.

"Well, I, uh, gotta go," John says and hurriedly closes his briefcase. "You and Juan let me know . . . about what we talked about. I'll be around. You in time for school this morning?" he asks me as he heads out.

"Uh, yeah. I was. Thanks." I watch his tall figure rapidly exit.

"Good. See ya." Instantly he is gone.

"What is that about?" I ask Terry. "Something fishy's going on."

"He wants to know if Juan and I want to see some of the California sights. Maybe go camping this weekend at some beach. Like Malibu or something."

"Well, are you?"

"Don't know. Gotta ask Juan when he gets home from work." She doesn't sound very enthusiastic.

"I want to go too." I find myself a little hurt that he didn't ask me.

"Oh, I'm sure *you* can go," Terry says with thick sarcasm.

"What do you mean by that?"

"He's over here a lot, Dawn, and he is *always* asking about you."

"No, he's not! Like . . . what does he say?" I'm completely blushing now and terribly curious about their secret dialogue.

"Everything! 'Where is Dawn?' 'When did she get home?'

Why, just now he asked me if you got to school on time this morning." She rolls her eyes.

"Yeah, I know. He did come over and wake me up this morning," I admit shyly. "Do you think he worries about us, Terry?"

"I think he kind of feels a little like a father to us. I mean, he always asks me if you and I have eaten, he gives us jobs all the time, and he constantly brings me frozen Snickers bars. He calls them 'Terry food.' I get so embarrassed when he says that!" She blushes, her green eyes and freckles standing out against her red skin.

"But he knows how much you *love* them, Terry." I laugh. "You'd kill for a frozen Snickers bar, and he knows it. I think that's sweet."

"I would not!" she insists and playfully tries to act indignant. "Well, maybe just a little."

I hang out until Juan comes home from work. Wearing his white cook's hat and apron, he looks greasy and tired. When he takes his hat off, his Afro is cocked to one side like a Dr. Seuss character's, making Terry and me giggle. Juan raises his finger in an effort to scold us for poking fun at him, but he loses track of the thought as his drooping eyes zero in on the water bed. He flops down hard and immediately sends a loud, fake snore into the air.

"Hey, wake up!" Terry slaps him on the ass. Juan ignores her and snores even louder into the blankets.

"I said wake up, damn it! Where's my dinner?" she demands, standing up and acting like she's going to sit on him.

"Okay, okay! I'm up! I'm up!" He rolls to the edge of the bed just out of reach of Terry's quick hand. "Over there, by the door." He points to the sagging white hamburger bag slumped on the floor.

Terry and I race for the food and frantically pull out the cold, soggy burgers and fries. "Eww," we complain. I see there is only enough for the two of them and decide it is time to give Terry and Juan their privacy and go check in at Harriet's.

"I'll see you guys in the morning. Let me know what Juan says about the beach, okay?" Without looking back, I smile to myself at the thought of sightseeing in our new home—California. I know Juan will agree to getting out and having some fun, and now as I enter the doorway to Harriet's, I take a deep breath and look forward to the days ahead.

Like clockwork, John is at my door bright and early to wake me for school. This time I know the knock is John's, and I stand modestly behind the door. We exchange brief *hellos*, and when he walks away, there is more of a friendly feeling between us.

Dad drives us to school again but informs us this is the last time; we will have to walk from now on; he just doesn't feel well enough to be getting up and driving every morning.

"It's okay, Dad. It's cool," Terry and I assure him. We are already tiptoeing around him, trying not to impose, and this is just another brick in the wall between us. We take it in stride. We know Dad will get better. It will just take time.

Class is as crowded as it was the day before, and I recognize no one. *It's early,* I tell myself, and I try to fit in the best I can. I smile at some of the students who look as lost as I feel, but I get a cold response and decide to back off. I can already see some cliques form between kids who obviously know each other from the year before. They are almost all blonde, tan, and beautiful. *These must be the jocks,* I deduce, feeling a twinge of sadness when I remember how I tried out to be a cheerleader back in Carol City, before the gang fights got out of hand. *That didn't last long. Well, I guess it's too late to get into that.* The cold looks from the students still sting. *I must not have the right look. So forget 'em!* I fling my head and put on my best tough armor as I pass students by, not allowing anyone a chance to smile.

After school, I head straight to Terry's. She is in the kitchen standing in front of the open refrigerator door. I sneak up behind her. "Whatcha got there? More 'Terry food'?"

"Ahh!" she screams, turns, and punches my arm. "Don't do that!"

"Aha! You're eating a Snickers. I knew it!"

"So . . . ? And, yes, John was here and, yes, he brought more 'Terry food.' Jealous?"

"Not of that!" I try to coax her out of the kitchen, run to the living room, and leap on the water bed. Waves of water trapped under plastic roll me from side to side. I giggle and begin to tease, "Terry, where are you?" Quiet. "Terry!" Still no answer. "Okay, fine, I'm leaving."

"No, no, wait." Her words are muffled by a mouthful of peanuts and chocolate. "I'm coming. I was just starving, Dawn. I haven't eaten all day." She plops on the water bed with me, licking the chocolate from her fingers. "Dad wouldn't answer the door today. I tried to knock. A bunch of times."

"Why is he being like that?" I ask, suddenly solemn. "You think it's 'cause he don't feel good?"

"Maybe. That's part of it, but he told me that since I was with Juan he considers me on my own, and I need to take care of myself or let Juan take care of me." She shrugs her shoulders. "I don't like asking him for anything, Dawn. I only ask if I'm really desperate . . . and then mostly I feel too shy to even ask at all."

We sit together in silence for a while, not really knowing what to think or say about Dad. "I just try to stay out of his way anymore too, Ter."

"At least John brings me something to eat, even if it is candy and he calls it 'Terry food.'" We laugh and tease-punch each other's arms, quickly trading physical pain for the tearing ache in our hearts.

My mind switches gears. *John,* I remember, feeling my stomach tighten. *He's always around, isn't he?* I don't want Terry to see the confusion inside me, to sense anything deeper than a casual observance. "Yeah, he seems like a nice guy."

Her strong gaze catches my eye. "Oh, yeah. He wants to know if we want to go shooting in the mountains tomorrow after school."

"Shooting! Who? Us? Guns? I don't want to shoot anything!"

"That's what I told him. He said target shooting, not shooting anything live."

"Oh." I mull it over for a minute. "Well, I do want to see the California mountains. We never saw any mountains in Florida; only hills. But I don't know if I want to shoot, Terry. I'm kinda scared. What about sightseeing this weekend? What did Juan say?"

"Oh, the beach is still on for this weekend." Terry half mumbles under her breath. "You couldn't stop Juan from going if you tried." She pauses. "I don't know, Dawn. Do you really want to go into the mountains with this guy and his guns?"

"I think he's okay, Terry. He's been real nice to us since we've been here, and everyone knows there's safety in numbers, right?" I don't want to blow things out of proportion. Besides, I want to go, even if shooting scares me . . . and, well, I like being around John.

"Yeah. I guess. Juan can come with us too, for protection." She rolls her eyes.

❦

The next day I can hardly wait for school to get out. I keep my nose in my books and manage to robotically make it to my classes without any major problems, except checking the clock every five minutes. *Knock it off, Dawn,* I keep telling myself. *Calm down. There's nothing to get excited about.* When the final bell rings, I race to gather up my things and head home double time. Hot and sweaty, I arrive at the cottages, my long hair clinging to my face, arms, and back. Terry and Juan look at their watches and shake their heads.

"What? Aren't we still going to the mountains?" I ask, trying to catch my breath.

Juan smirks and turns away.

"Why? You worried about something, Dawn?" Terry teases.

"Well, *am* I too late?"

"Yeah, yeah, we're still going. Calm down." Juan sees I'm about to panic.

Right then John bursts into the room. He is dressed in his usual blue jeans, jean jacket, and Frye boots. Over his shoulder is a large, heavy duffel bag that he immediately lowers to the floor. Crouching down on one knee he unzips the bag and pulls out one of many rifles: a sleek, handsome, light brown .22 caliber with a small scope. Carefully, raising the barrel up to the ceiling, he cocks back the cartridge with one swift, smooth move to make sure the chamber is clear. He lifts the .22 up to his eye after deliberately aiming it down and away, and squints as he looks through the scope to check the hairline sights. "Looks good." His nostrils flare and his veins bulge with every movement. Fresh out of a steamy shower, he smells clean, like fruit shampoo, and his hair is wet and combed back on the side. I am fascinated by the beginnings of a thin, light moustache on his upper lip as I watch his precise and agile movements with the rifle.

"You look good," he comments, glancing up at me. He nods his head toward my clothes and flashes a huge blushing grin.

"Who? Me?" I stammer, stepping back, startled as all eyes stare in my direction. I glance down at myself and notice, embarrassed. My light, thin gauze shirt is soaked through with sweat, and several damp strands of my long hair are wrapped around my braless chest. My face burns, skin deep red. I rush to hug myself tightly and run for cover in the kitchen amidst waves of shrieking laughter. Grabbing the knob to the back door, I shout, "I'll be right back!" and dash to Harriet's for a change of clothes.

⚘

Climbing the Los Padres mountains in Ventura County from Newhall, we drive slowly off the 5 Freeway, up a windy dirt road that seems endless with drying shrubs. Red hills marbled in beige-and-white limestone swirls roll like the rough seas on either side of the bumpy path. John insists that I sit in the passenger seat next to him while Juan and Terry sit on the floor of the van. White knuckles cling onto the back of my seat. In a cloud of orange dust, we come to a stop. John briskly puts the van into park, jumps out, and walks straight for a bullet-riddled tree. Scanning the area, he rips off the old tattered targets from the center of its trunk and calls out to Juan to bring him the duffel bag.

"Coming, man." Juan is eager to please, but flashes an *oh shit* look when he lifts the heavy bag.

With long strides, John crosses through the grass to rescue Juan. "Just the targets and staple gun, man," he says, amused at how easily Juan has become fatigued.

"Oh, oh, yeah, man," Juan replies. Sweat already drips from his brow.

John and Juan staple a fresh target to the tree and dash back to where Terry and I stand waiting. Out of the duffel bag John pulls two long, thin .22 caliber rifles, carefully pointing the barrels toward the sky. He loads the first one and checks the sight. John makes eye contact with each of us, thinks for a moment, then hands the gun over to Juan, who takes it readily.

I throw him a hard, distrustful stare. "Be careful, Juan."

Juan blows me off and strokes the long handle of the rifle recklessly. "Watch out, Juan!" Terry and I shout. John's head snaps up, and he immediately grabs the rifle out of his hands.

"Always, *always,* point the barrel of a gun up and away from anyone! Always!" John is severe; his expression twists on the brink of anger. "That means *never* point a gun at anyone . . . unless you plan to pull the trigger!"

Juan's head hangs low; his shoulders slump at the scolding. "Okay, man," he sighs. His cockiness fades as he timidly takes the rifle back, holding it up and away.

John eyes him hard, then walks over and finds a spot about fifty feet away. Juan follows. The rifle stock against his cheek, John takes aim and fires the weapon in rapid succession until the bullets are spent. Once again John orders Juan to keep his gun down and heads over to pull his target from the tree. I can see his smile shine from a distance. His chest is swollen, and his eyes twinkle with pride as he stomps back through the brush to show us his talent. Every shot hit the inner dark ring, and too many to count shredded the small black center into pulp.

"Wow!" We are all impressed. Juan is next. Nervously, he takes his stance and aims. When he retrieves his target, a blank target in hand, we all break out laughing, even Juan.

It is now Terry's and my turn. John calls us over and shows us how to hold the long skinny rifle, aim through the scope, and fire.

Terry instantly takes comfortable hold of the awkwardness of the weapon and steadily fires, every shot reaching somewhere on the paper target. This time John is impressed and playfully steps out of Terry's way, pretending to be frightened of her courage, strength, and skill.

"Quit it," Terry jokes, half smiling at the compliment, but still shy with the non-girlishness of her nature.

John calls me next. Hesitantly, I step over the dry sticks and leaves and take the rifle from his outstretched hands. He stands with his arms around me, holding each of my hands in the proper position, one on the barrel, the other with my finger lightly on the trigger. His hair, long since dried, is damp again with perspiration, a few curls falling randomly over the blue of his eyes. I can smell the earthiness of his skin engulfing me like a rich, soft blanket. My body shakes, and my balance is unsteady. He senses my fear and my unwillingness to let go of his grip and leans his body hard against me, supporting me like a strong oak. Gently he places his head on my shoulder and presses his face into mine; his finger curls over my shaky hand, easing down on the trigger. The gun jerks upward; then, quickly, John brings it back into range and fires off the remaining shots.

I am shaking, the ringing of the shots echoing in my ears. Relieved to be done, I let John take my hand and walk me over to the tree to check the target.

"Whoa!" he shouts. "She did it!"

Stunned, I stare at three small holes on the outer edges of the target, and then I smile.

John yanks the target off the tree and, like a proud father, walks me back to Terry and Juan, his arm around me warm. I am proud too, but not for my shooting skills. I feel a strange comfortable sensation present in me. Like a missing piece to the puzzle of me has been fit into place—a small piece, but the right piece. It feels good.

The three of them take a few more turns with the gun as I graciously decline any further shooting. John doesn't push it. I feel he understands how afraid I am of it. Instead, he shows me how to load the rifles properly.

The sun is setting, and the sky is turning its evening colors, signaling that it is almost time to go. But John is reluctant to stop. At the last minute he dives into the canvas duffel bag and pulls out two dull gray pistol cases. The first one, he explains, is a Ruger .357 caliber handgun. "There is only one reason for the existence of this gun," John tells us with gravity, "and that is to kill."

Ugh, I think with disgust as a chill runs down my spine. I don't even want to touch the thing.

"And this is a genuine Colt .45," he continues, putting on a phony, thick Western accent. This is a prettier gun than the cold menacing steel of the .357 with a smooth, glossy white handle that is polished to look like ivory. He loads both pistols, sets the .357 aside, and without inviting anyone else to shoot, grabs a pair of earplugs from the dashboard, walks to the target, and takes aim. Loud, rapid explosions pierce the air as he empties the gun into the bullet-riddled tree and returns for the Ruger. As adrenaline courses through him, his nostrils flare and his brow furrows. He spreads his legs and, with both arms extended, takes aim toward the tree, firing once again.

Earsplitting *bang*s blare repeatedly from the blue fire barrel end of the gun. I grab my ears, bury my head in my arms to block out the deafening noise. Sharp, crashing walls of sound ricochet through the dry desert air, numbing my head. Finally I look up. John walks back, his jaw clenched and pulsing as he carries the remaining shreds of the paper target.

"Damn!" Juan shouts.

The image of the vicious damage from the two powerful pistols rips and cracks every cell of my being. I have nothing to say.

John packs our things, and we follow his lead to quietly get ready to leave before our daylight is lost.

I am relieved to be almost finished with the shooting part of this excursion. My heartbeat slowly returns to normal. I settle back into the passenger seat of the van, comfortable with the hum of the engine as it slips into gear, and I admire the scenery of the mountain pass in the darkening dusk. Bouncing along the eroded dirt road, John comes to a sudden stop.

"Hey, what are you doing?" Juan asks, popping his head up from behind John's seat.

"Shhh. Just a minute," John whispers, quietly reaching for one of the .22 rifles. Juan sees him fumble and quickly reaches to help. "See that bird?"

"What bird?"

"Over there? On that branch?" Carefully he raises the barrel of the rifle—cold metal taps the glass of the half-opened window—and aims at a large oak's knotted limb.

"That tiny, little bird—way over there—on that big tree? Quit joking." I see nothing, a small speck if anything.

"Yup. Watch me shoot it from over here." His head lowers close to the sights.

"No, you're not. No, please don't, John. That's not funny. Jooohhhn!"

Blam! One piercing shot fires from the rifle.

In horror I watch as a small shape falls lifelessly through the branches to the ground. I scream, mortified and in shock. He killed it. A small, harmless creature. "No, no, no," I cry hysterically. I refuse to believe what he has done. Like a sharp slap when you least expect it, the tears sting my face and won't stop. "You weren't supposed to do that," I sob. "I didn't think you would do that!"

John gapes at me. "I, I didn't know you cared . . . would cry like this, Dawn," he says softly, reaching out to touch my arm.

"No, no, no!" I slap his hand away. "Don't touch me!"

John's face is pale; his eyes well with sadness and tears. "It's okay, Dawn. It's okay. Come here; please, come here." He reaches for my arm again, sliding over to my seat on his knees. "I'm sorry. I didn't know."

I can't look at him. I hate what he did. Exhausted and drained, face buried in my hands, I let him hold me and I heave weighty sobs into his chest.

Surprised, Terry and Juan don't know what to do. "I didn't see anything," Terry says timidly.

John cups my face in his hands to calm me. "It's okay now. See? I'll be right back. Okay?"

"Okay," I sniffle, wiping the tears from my eyes.

He jumps out of the van and walks over to the place where the bird has fallen. Rustling around the brush for a few minutes, he returns without a word, face solemn, and he starts the engine. He stares straight ahead.

"Did you bury it?" I ask with a quavering voice.

"Yes."

Fresh tears spill onto my damp and swollen cheeks. "What kind of bird was it?"

"A sparrow."

Sadness overwhelms me again, and I let the tears fall freely. John quietly reaches his hand out to hold mine, tightly, for the long drive home.

Right on time the next morning, John taps on the door to make sure I am up. His demeanor is timid, soft-spoken, more than I'd noticed before. He finds it hard to meet my gaze.

"Thanks." My tone is low, a whisper, and I feel a bit embarrassed. Through the filtered view of the screen door, I watch him turn and walk away. There is a feeling of safety, a new connection with him that I can't seem to name, but the nearness of him is comfortable for some reason: calming and strong. The night before showed me a side of John that shocked me, as well as something intimate and sweet . . . and perhaps it is in me too. *Is my tough girl gig up?* I'm not used to feeling this way. I gently close the door, gather my things, and get ready for class.

The rest of the week in school seems to drag, along with the mundane faces of my classmates. When Friday comes, I am relieved to be away from the pressure of trying to fit in and look forward to the weekend and the beach. John isn't home until well past dark that evening, keeping Terry, Juan, and me wondering if his plans have changed. With a *bang,* the door bursts open and

John barges in, flushed and smiling big. As always, our eyes meet as he scans the room. Instantly we blush.

Breaking into a soft-shoe ta-da, John slaps his Frye boots on the wooden floor and with arm extended pronounces, half joking, "Ready?"

"Ready? Ready for what? We were *ready* for bed. We'd been waiting for hours. Where are we going this late?"

John mocks us, pretending to fend off our comments as attacking blows. "Hey, hey, ouch, that hurts." He playfully falls onto the couch. "I'm sorry; I'm sorry. Tomorrow, be ready early. Have your sleeping bags and clothes packed, and I'll bring the goodies." He lifts an eyebrow.

"Tomorrow!" we cry, disappointed. "Fine."

"Good. I have a couple of errands left to do tonight. Anyone want to go?" He gets up from the couch and heads for the door.

"I'll go," Juan shoots back.

"Yeah? What about you girls?"

"I guess so." Terry sounds weary.

"Sure."

⁕

Driving through Hollywood at night is wild, mesmerizing. Excitement rolls through me like an amusement park ride. Colored lights flash FLOWERS, HAMBURGERS, and HOTELS. Massive billboards advertise the city's evening wares and busy-looking people move robotically about the streets. I love the warm evening air that blows on my face as I lean out of the van's window and reach my hand up toward the glowing neon tubes.

"Oh my God!" Terry gasps as she clutches my arm and hastily turns away from the window. My stomach flutters. I see it too. Blinking lights on an enormous marquee surround a seductive woman in a kitten costume, long tail swirling around huge pink letters that read *Pussycat Theatre.* In larger letters underneath, the words scream, *John C. Holmes XXX Double Feature: Mitchell Brothers' Autobiography of a Flea. All Night Long.*

It's him! My thoughts screech to a halt; hot and cold shivers snap through my veins. *It's really true!* My body stiffens, freezes in place; I continue to stare out the window. His name is up in lights, and it frightens me. Without missing a beat, ever so slowly, I cast an uneasy sideways glance in John's direction. He grips the steering wheel; bulging tendons in his arms move with the pulse of his veins. I know he sees my reaction. Briefly he shoots me a glance and rigidly leans over to check the passenger side mirror.

"Ladies and gentlemen, Hollywood and Vine," John announces, sounding like a tour guide.

I push the recent shock of truth out of my mind and focus out my window again. Gold-trimmed marble stars line the sidewalks of the busy street, naming past and present movie stars. Neon on black background contrasts harshly with headlights from the passing cars. Silently I take in the sights of Hollywood, trying to understand what I see. *John's movies are a big deal here?* I'm confused about how the marquees seem as large as and so close to other legitimate theaters.

With a jerk, John whips the van into a recently vacated parking space and slides it into park. "Grauman's Chinese Theatre," he says, opening his door. "Coming?"

Quickly we scurry out and run to catch up with his distancing shape. Massive, bright red and gold oriental pagodas engulf us in slow motion as we approach the sidewalk.

"Whoa," Terry exclaims. "Look at the lions. And look, here, at all the footprints of the stars."

"Far out!" Juan chimes in.

Stone lions sit regally on either side of the theater guarding its entrance; a huge dragon curls toward the front. My world is reeling. I've never seen such glamour. Eyes wide from the bombardment of my senses, I look over at John. In his light blue jean jacket and faded jeans, he stands poised over one of the cement slabs, hands in his pockets.

"What are you looking at?" I ask, walking over to stand next to him.

"John Wayne." He shifts his weight, his tone respectful. "He's my favorite."

Curious, I look down at the signature that captures his attention. I can feel his breath while we stare down at the historical movie relic.

"Over here, Dawn," Terry yells. "It's Marilyn Monroe! Come see!"

"Really?" I hurry to where she stands. "Oh. And here's Judy Garland."

"Elizabeth Taylor over here," John's voice calls back.

The game is on. We take turns finding familiar stars and making fun of the size of their hands and feet—and in some cases, a nose (Jimmy Durante's) and legs (Betty Grable's). A small, odd-looking group of people has gathered nearby and seems to be stepping toward every slab John has just finished viewing. I look into the eyes of a tall, middle-aged bald man after a few deliberate moves around the concrete autographs, and check John's reaction. He is upset. He looks at his watch and signals to me that it is time to leave.

"Come on, Terry—Juan," I yell. "Let's go." We hastily fall into step behind John walking toward the van.

"Who were those people?"

"Who? Them?" John sounds flustered.

"Yeah. They seemed kinda weird. Were they following us?"

"Uh, I don't know. Just people. It's getting late, and I want to show you guys one more thing."

"Cool!" Juan's excited.

Terry and I nod, and I instantly forget about the strange group of people we've left behind—people who still huddle and stare at us as we drive away.

We turn the corner in the direction of Glendale. *Los Feliz,* the sign reads. We come to a quiet, greener part of town where the houses are true-to-life mansions, massive and dreamlike. I gawk at the wealth of the estates that lie blanketed in the cottony light fog of the summer evening. After a prompt turn onto Fern Dell Road, we enter Griffith Park. *Observatory,* the word and the arrow on the sign guide us toward the top.

"Wait till you see this," John says excitedly.

"See what?"

"Just wait."

We drive in the darkness, climbing steadily toward the top by way of many winding roads and switchbacks. As we rise above the city, countless colored lights span far into the distance. Halfway up, John pulls the van over to the side of the road. A thin cloud of dust is visible through the headlights as we come to a sudden stop near the guardrail.

"Come on." John's mood is intensely happy as he leads us to the edge of the cliff.

Juan, Terry, and I stand in awe.

"Welcome to Hollywood!" John grandly extends both arms across the vast city lights. He is in his realm. A thin, pale line of light follows the horizon at a far distance. The bright lights below gently soften into the stars above.

"Wow! It's beautiful!"

Juan and Terry take the moment to snuggle into each other's arms and giggle. I step away and stand to the side. My arms fold across my chest—a barrier against the evening chill and an attempt to give them space for their romantic moment. John sees my distance, walks over, and stands next to me. Silently we look out at the shimmering view. Everything feels peaceful, those puzzle pieces falling into place again. A gust of wind breaks my trance, and I shiver, pulling my arms in even tighter. John instantly takes off his jacket.

"Here," he offers, softly stepping closer and wrapping his jean jacket around my shoulders.

"Thanks." I feel the closeness of his scent. *Oh God,* my thoughts quickly warn. *The marquees. Who is this guy?* My heart and mind race with mixed emotions. I stand perfectly still.

Unexpectedly John's aura changes back to the warmth of a moment ago. I relax again. Reaching down, he puts his arm around me—a strong, friendly, fatherly arm—and gently guides my body to the left. "See that?" He points out into the open, sparkling sky.

"Yeah." Paralyzed by his touch, overwhelmed at his strong but gentle hold on me, I can barely respond.

"That's the famous Hollywood Bowl," he tells me in an even, now teacherly voice.

"Oh." I have never heard of the place, but I'm interested and absorb this new information readily.

"Hey! It's getting cold," Terry unexpectedly calls from the van.

With difficulty, John and I pull away from one another.

"Hurry up," Terry snaps. She seems aware of something between us.

"We are," I call back. *Jeez. Nothing's going on,* I say to myself, irritated at her summons. Then I remember she saw the marquees too.

John and I say nothing more to each other the remainder of our trip home while Juan churns out a dozen or more tiring questions, arms flailing in all directions to make his point. John's lackluster answers tell me his mind is wandering on other things. A chill runs through me, and I hug my knees to my chest for warmth, partly expecting to see John's name again as I stare out my window at the passing lights.

John parks in his usual space beneath the giant magnolia tree next to the garages and the big main house. During the stroll up the courtyard, John is quiet again; his jawline pulsates as it always does when he's deep in thought. We move slowly, in step with each other, up the concrete walk toward the bungalows. I don't want to say good night, so I walk even slower. John does the same.

As the red painted brick of our steps approaches, John looks over at me and smiles. "Bright and early!" he reminds everyone.

"Bright and early," Juan echoes back.

Saturday morning sunlight shines through every window of the cottage. It is already beautiful and warm outside.

"This is California's Indian summer," Harriet tells me as she wanders through the living room to fetch coffee from the kitchen, her dog, Wolf, following close behind.

Knock, knock, knock. It's Juan at the door, checking to see if I'm awake.

"It's only 6:30." I yawn.

"John's already been by, wants to leave in a half an hour." Juan looks a little disheveled.

"I'll be over in a minute. I'm already packed."

I tap on Terry's door a few minutes later, and John answers, handing me a steaming cup from a Thermos lid.

"What's this?"

"Coffee. Drink. It'll wake you up." Graciously he takes my backpack and pours another cup for Terry, who is sitting on the edge of the water bed rubbing her eyes. Terry is grumpy in the mornings.

"Ugh," Terry groans, sending John into a gut-busting laugh.

"Well, uh, I'd give you a Snickers bar, Terry, but I'm all out." He tantalizes her in a low, sensual voice, knowing how the candy makes her mouth water. John is clean-shaven this morning, except for his thin, light moustache. His hair is damp, and he smells of musk and green apples.

"Quit it! I'm up. Just give me a minute," Terry snaps back. I can tell she feels embarrassed.

"We'll meet you at the van then," John says.

Loaded up and in a much happier mood, we take off down Los Feliz Boulevard again heading back into Hollywood.

"Slight detour, kids. I have to stop at my answering service, check my messages. It'll just be a minute," John informs us. Nothing looks familiar on Western Avenue so early in the morning. The streets are freshly hosed off and empty in front of the closed shopwindows; only a giant hot dog-shaped stand on the left has a line of haggard souls waiting for coffee. A casual glance to my right stings my senses again: JOHN C. HOLMES IN XXX. I quickly turn away, sink down in my seat. I don't want to think too much.

"Here we are," John says, making a turn onto Santa Monica Boulevard and into a small parking lot. "Be right back." He grins and jumps out. A tiny, square, concrete building with a large, old-fashioned, black rotary phone dial painted on one side and a giant cord and receiver on another is painted with the words *Answering Service*. Back in an instant, John flips through a stack of messages, then passes them over to me. "Put these into my briefcase for me, would ya?" he asks sweetly.

"Sure," I reply and suddenly feel special. Carefully I set the fat stack of messages on top of the scattered mess of his briefcase. "Call me, sweetie. Love, Gloria," reads the top one. I shut the briefcase. *Does he have a girlfriend?* I wonder, feeling my stomach twist. *What are you thinking, Dawn? Of course he would have a girlfriend . . . probably lots of them. He's not interested in you. He thinks you're just a kid.* I snap out of it, toughening up my spirit, and promise myself not to get too close . . . again.

Back onto Western we soon catch the 101 Freeway heading west toward the Pacific Ocean. The eight-track tapes are blasting;

John sings loud and off-key to Neil Diamond, Jim Croce, and Gordon Lightfoot, leaving us in stitches and helpless to do anything but join in. The mood is fun; we are kids, sipping coffee, singing, and giggling at our own silliness. Exiting off Kanan Dume Road we head through the mountains until we reach the Pacific Coast Highway and drive north for about another mile. *Zuma Beach,* the sign reads. We scream, and John pulls to a stop.

"This is it!" John gets out of the van to stretch his legs as the rest of us spill out into the parking lot. It is still early, and the beach is fairly empty. Pale, shiny sand goes on and on for miles with white lifeguard huts dotting the length of the coastline. Pulling down my blue cutoff shorts, I straighten the brown bikini underneath my top for the walk to the beach. My red tank top and flip-flops match the bandana I wear tied around my head as a scarf.

Terry gets out and quickly pulls me off to the side. "I don't feel right about this," she whispers.

"Why?"

"Didn't you see the signs on those movie theaters last night and today? That's John! I couldn't say anything last night or this morning because everyone was around, but I don't like this," she says in a hurried hush. "I have a feeling about him."

"I know, Ter. I saw it too. Harriet tried to show me the other day, but I didn't want to see that stuff. It's okay though. I don't think he is going to do anything."

"He's trying to get close to you, Dawn. I don't like it."

"I can handle myself, Terry. Relax. Now come on. Here they come."

Terry doesn't own a bathing suit, doesn't like the way she looks in them. Cutoff shorts and a baggy T-shirt drape her frame, leaving her real shape a mystery.

"This way," John calls, lifting the blankets and ice-laden cooler. We follow him single file toward the giant rocks at the south end of the beach.

"Where're we going?" I ask.

John keeps walking, trudging through the deep sandy beach, still heading for the rocks. At the base, he connects to a well-worn path, leading us up and over to the other side. We pass a few stragglers on the same trail, all of them fighting to keep their balance like us. I jump off the final rock onto the soft, cool sand. It takes me a minute to comprehend where we are.

"Pirate's Cove! Clothing optional." John is grinning from ear to ear.

"Oh my God!" Terry shrieks. "I'm leaving!"

"No, wait. Come on, Terry," Juan begs. "Let's stay. Please!"

Terry clutches her beach bag to her chest and reluctantly presses on. She keeps her hair in front of her face, eyes glued to the sand. I try to stay nonchalant, say nothing, and not stare at the darkly tanned sun worshippers. People seem to be middle-aged or older, I note from the glances I steal. I notice also the few fully dressed young men who cling to the rocks at the back of the cove gawking at the beach's free entertainment.

"Those are the young Catholic boys saying their rosary—getting ready to go to confession." John frowns with disgust at their hypocrisy.

John leads us to a sunny spot near the water and spreads out two large blankets for everyone to lie on. I walk over and sit near the edge trying to act casual and slip off my flip-flops. Terry and Juan find a spot on the other side of the blanket. She flashes me a worried look as John plops down next to me. Suddenly, as if to say, "Oh, well," Juan shrugs his shoulders, makes a wide, greasy grin, and proudly strips his clothes off first.

"Oh God!" Terry hides her face in her shirt.

John watches the water, transfixed for several minutes, his expression quiet, subdued. He shakes his blond curls, undresses, then quickly flips over onto his stomach and closes his eyes. Terry and I deliberately avoid looking at either of the guys directly. I decide to buckle down. I pull off my tank top and shorts, revealing my swimsuit, and apply some suntan lotion.

"You'll get tan lines." John's muffled voice rises from the blanket.

Startled, I freeze for a second. *Is he daring me?* I wonder. My sense of pride is challenged. *You can do this,* I tell myself. I gather my nerve, reach back to untie the top of my bathing suit. John springs to my side and in a gentle, nonthreatening way, helps me undo the strings. The cool morning air and sun combined feel good against my newly exposed skin. Feeling pretty courageous, I lie down and close my eyes.

"You'll get tan lines."

Sitting up, I look over at Terry. She is still clutching herself, wearing her shorts and T-shirt, refusing to "go with the flow," and throwing out death stares. Juan is facedown, asleep in the sun.

Smiling at John's second comment about tan lines, I "bite the bullet" and modestly slip off my bathing suit bottoms, fold them next to me, and fall back to enjoy the full warmth of the sun.

We lie statuelike, but soon I surrender to the waves of sleep taking me in and out of sweet puppy dreams. In my warm haze I sense John sit up, and I get uncomfortable. With my eyes closed, I flip over to avoid looking at him.

"Want some lotion?"

"Uh, yeah, sure." I lean up on my elbows, drowsy from the sun, my mood relaxed and casual. John applies the lotion from my back to my legs as if it isn't a big deal. He has an all-natural, casual attitude, and I try to copy him to fit in. I hold my breath at his touch and think, *Well, Dawn, when in Rome . . .*

"Me too," he says, tossing over the bottle of lotion and quickly rolling over.

"Sure." I sit up and shrug. I see the brown of John's back and then his rear end. It is whiter than his back and has a few red pimples. My stomach tightens. I feel repulsed for a second that I'm looking at this old guy's butt. I try not to show any disgust and methodically rub lotion down the back portion of his body, still wanting to maintain my cool. When I finish, I am relieved that I haven't seen anything surprising.

After another nap in the sun, I am getting too hot. My skin can feel the beginning of a burn, and I want to find some shade. John turns his face toward mine. His eyes sparkle as blue as the Caribbean Sea. "They're doing body painting over there. Wanna go?" he whispers.

Cold sweat runs through me on the hot sand. "Sure." I'm nervous. I don't really want to get up. I don't want us to see each other in the nude. John stands right away and reaches his hand down to pull me up off the blanket. I fix my gaze on his face, and he keeps his on mine. His grip still firm in mine, he leads me over to a crowd of people covered with fluorescent body paints.

"Hello," John says in a syrupy, friendly voice.

"Step right up!" A woman with a wide straw hat and psychedelic swirls painted over her entire small nude frame smiles. "What can I do for you today?" she asks. She looks me straight in the eyes, raises an eyebrow, and grins. Her paintbrush poised in midair, she winks at John. "Flowers? Swirls? Peace signs? What will it be for the lovely couple?"

Fierce blushing burns my cheeks at her comment; I glance down for just a second, gather my courage, turn, and look back at John. From the sand, I slowly follow his long lean figure upward, taking in his full naked image at last. Inwardly I choke. I don't know what to think. Our eyes meet, and for an instant I think he looks scared. Quickly, my eyes dart away, and I blush even harder.

John nervously shifts his weight. "We'll take the flowers," he says decisively to the woman in the hat.

We stand side by side, next to two other brightly painted naked people, as the woman with the paintbrush adorns our breasts and belly buttons with large daisylike flowers. Any tension between us melts away at the silliness of having glow-in-the-dark petals painted on our bodies.

Giggling like children at the way the brushes tickle, we glance over to see Juan waving to us. His brown skin fiery red, he looks as if he has just woken up. "Hey! Let me get the camera!" he calls, dashing off like an excited tourist. When he returns, the artists working on John and me are just finishing, admiring their handiwork. "Okay, you guys," Juan says, panting for breath, "let's see a pose."

John and I beam proudly at the costumes of floral colors we are now sporting. I love the wild flowers, and the colorful green leaves cupping my small breasts match the hint of emerald in my eyes. John steps in, puts his arm around me, and nestles close as we smile for the camera.

"One more! One more," Juan shouts. "Come on. One more!" I haven't noticed that a small crowd has been gathering behind us.

In a whir of movement, John gallantly sweeps my tiny, budding child body up into his arms. My long golden brown hair flows behind me like a mermaid's as he stands, beaming from ear to ear for the camera. I giggle with delight, wrap my arms around his neck, and cuddle up to his chest.

"Good. Perfect." Juan snaps the picture.

Gently, John sets me down on the sand, turns immediately without saying a word, and walks into the water.

"Are we leaving?" Juan asks.

"I guess so. Why did he go into the water?"

"I bet *I* know," Juan smirks, raising his eyebrows.

"Hey, you're burnt." I change the subject, embarrassed. "Ha-ha. That's going to hurt." Laughing at his nakedness, I run back to our blankets.

John is out of the water and getting dressed.

Terry is happily packing as fast as she can. "We're leaving," Terry says.

"Oh, okay." I wonder if John has other plans. His mood is serious, and he speaks to no one, shaking out the blankets and packing the cooler. I get dressed, confused again. *He is so weird,* I grumble, following him back over the rocks to Zuma Beach.

"Well, he managed to get *your* clothes off, didn't he, Dawn?" Terry snaps as we approach the van. "I told you I didn't feel right about this."

I don't answer. I like John. In fact, I am getting very scared at how much I like him. His professional life is still very vague to me. I don't understand it and, anyway, I don't see him that way. *He's not that way around me. Besides, we're just friends,* I say to myself, pulling my mind back from the temptation of imagining anything more. There is Sharon too. That's another entirely weird thought.

"After you," John says, holding the van door open and helping me up. He is smiling, and his mood is light again. Naturally the first thing John does is plug in his favorite Jim Croce eight-track tape. Together we sing "Time in a Bottle" while Juan falls asleep in the back and Terry sits frowning next to him, keeping a cautious, silent watch on the two of us all the way home.

CHAPTER SIX
Early Morning Dawn

Nobody tells Dad the next day that we went to a nude beach. He probably would blow it off anyway. Still busy hanging out with Harriet, he tries to get rid of us whenever we show up. Occasionally, he comes over to see if Mike has any pot, but Mike is rarely home anymore. All we know is that he has some girlfriend a few blocks away. We figure he is selling pot pretty regularly about now and needs to hang out with a different crowd.

John continues to wake me for school every morning and stops in to hang out at Juan and Terry's cottage two or three times every evening. He sweetly brings us peace offerings of food and treats, easily melting any suspicions Terry might have about him. After all, John is a really nice guy.

Running into each other has become a daily habit. "Nothing's going to happen, Terry," I tell her. John loves to dash over several times during the day or evening, carrying a sizzling plate or frosty blender of one of his creations, getting the greatest enjoyment from sharing his meals with us. He's never without his corncob pipe, a member of his trademark paraphernalia, and he passes shotguns of smoke to everyone while we watch television together for hours and hysterically invent dishes to satisfy our sweet tooth munchies.

John and I gravitate toward each other naturally when we hang out. He is funny and kind to me. When he catches me faking a hit off a joint, he laughs. "Lightweight," he teases. "I like that." Then he swiftly reaches down and gives me an up close, killer shotgun. Stoned from the blast, John and I find things so funny that sometimes we hold each other in tear-streaked fits of laughter while Terry and Juan stare and shake their heads.

Gregarious and gaudy, John wears outrageous outfits without blinking an eye. Dinner, late-night talk shows, and the fairly new *Saturday Night Live* become our common ground. On an evening, well after dark, John races over carrying a steaming cookie sheet in his hand and wearing a full-length bright-yellow-and-black-striped caftan. "Try this!" he cries enthusiastically, handing each of us a gooey cookie.

Terry and I blush and hold back a laugh. "Sure." We take one of his treats. "What is he wearing?" we mouth to each other, rolling our eyes. "He looks like a giant bumblebee." Then we taste the creamy creation. "Umm, this is delicious! What is it?"

"Chocolate chip, peanut butter, brown sugar cookies with a dab of butter on top baked in the oven just enough to melt the butter," John says, smiling proudly without taking a breath. Bursting into laughter at the outrageousness of his dessert, we devour the cookies in handfuls.

It seems for a couple of months I have found a safe haven at my sister's cottage, a place that takes me away from the unwanted coldness of my father and Harriet, if only for a few hours a night. Politely, John leaves Terry's when I do and, like a gentleman, escorts me to my door at the end of the evening. I have found a safe haven with him also; at least I think I have.

John sees my father's lack of concern for my whereabouts and takes the initiative to ask me to join him on errands alone more often. With little or no excuse, we go on long drives and window-shop just to enjoy each other's company. Before heading home, we stop at John's favorite hamburger joint, Bob's Big Boy, on Colorado

Boulevard and with gusto we eat greasy cheeseburgers and fries dunked in Bob's very own blue cheese dressing—"the best," according to John.

John eagerly waits for me to come home from school each day. Giddy and happy to see me, he delegates a never-ending list of odd jobs so we can spend time together. On a rare day, when I came home late from school because I stayed to hang out with new friends, John acts terribly angry and hurt. Without warning, he pulls back from me, stops treating me warmly for a few days, and I feel bad. After that I am sure to be home on time, glad to see John smile and talk to me again.

* * *

"Gotta new job for you," John says invitingly one afternoon.

"Yeah, what?"

"You've got nice handwriting. Will you update my address book for me?"

"Sure!" Happy to be trusted with such an important project, I follow John to his cottage.

"Sharon? Dawn is here to work on my address book. Can we get a table set up for her and some pencils and things?" John says with authority as he barges through the door.

Sharon looks up from her handiwork and peers over her dark-rimmed glasses. Sitting on an overstuffed chair with her feet up on a matching floral footstool, she sews a button onto a nursing uniform.

"Okaaaay," she answers with a slight drawl, her expression stoic. Buttons jumps off her lap and follows her into the back room.

Oh, I wonder. *Is she mad?* I'm nervous and stand awkwardly waiting for her to come back with my table. John has left me to tinker with something in the kitchen. I shift my weight, extremely uncomfortable, and don't really know what to do with myself.

Sharon returns, squeaking in her nurse's shoes, with a handful of different-colored pens and pencils. Under her arm is a TV tray that she sets up next to John's ornate gold desk. I admire the desk again: grand with brass lion handles and a mirrored top to accent the slender golden wood legs. I take my cue from Sharon and sit down uncertainly. John returns from the kitchen and hands me a glass of iced tea. "Ready?" He acts as if everything is normal and, without blinking, passes me a large stack of messages. "Let's get started."

"Good night and . . . ha . . . good luck," Sharon calls out, gathering her needle and thread. She heads for the bedroom with John L, Pokie, and Buttons following close behind.

I look down at the stack of messages and recognize them as the ones from the answering service. About two-thirds are business related, and one-third are very flirtatious and personal. The thought that one of these messages might be from his girlfriend hits me in the gut again, and I feel my face flush and temper rise. The intensity surprises me. *Don't get too close,* I warn myself and repeat my silent promise in my head.

John pays attention to my reaction at the writing on his messages and smirks. "See these? These get tossed. I don't care about those numbers." He whisks them out of my hands and throws them in the trash.

Good, I think and take it as a compliment. I get the feeling John is trying to make a point for me. My focus stays on the address book, studiously copying old numbers into the new book and adding additional ones from another stack. As I keep working, I begin to notice mysterious codes near certain curiously written names, and I get a little nervous, uncomfortable at the secrecy. Some names have straightforward notes like "asshole" or "bitch" jotted next to them.

"I wouldn't even keep those if I didn't have to work with them." His voice is thick with contempt. "The sons of bitches. It's just a job, you know," John snarls and then stops and lets out a sharp, cynical laugh. He shuffles through another stack of papers. "Except for Candy Samples. She's a sweetheart. Older woman, but the nicest person you'd ever want to meet."

I make no comment. *Gosh. He really doesn't like them. Is he being forced to work for them or something?* I return my focus on the transferring of numbers and contemplate the idea of what John is saying: that world as a cold business separate from pleasure and home. *He must not have a girlfriend if he doesn't even like those people. Well, they must not be very nice then.* I brush it off, confused.

❧

With John's guidance Terry, Juan, and I become acquainted with many more of the sights of California. Everyone wants to take advantage of as much warm weather as possible, so camping trips soon became overnighters with the four of us. Farther north from Zuma Beach, John introduces us to another of his favorite hide-aways—Leo Carrillo State Park. Leo Carrillo has everything: beautiful beaches lined with prehistoric rocks jutting from the shoreline on the east and campsites secluded by giant sycamores backed by mountainous hiking trails on the west. Campsite number twenty-two is designated as our special spot. It has the most direct path to the beach and the largest trees to separate us from our neighbors. Lots of cool evenings under the starry sky, we warm ourselves by crackling bonfires built out of scavenged, dried wood. When the weather is bad, the van makes a perfect tent.

On a chilly night in early fall, Juan, Terry, John, and I pull into our campsite at Leo Carrillo. It is already dark outside when we arrive; the wind howls in deep bellows. We gather as many dry branches as we can, trying to start a fire, when the rain suddenly begins to come down hard.

In a matter of seconds, large drops of water fall from the sky, and we run to the van for shelter. In a good mood and laughing, we tumble over each other trying not to get wet, but we are soaked. I am shivering, my chattering teeth clicking loudly and out of control. John steps forward and wraps a blanket around me and, in his regular fatherly way, rubs my arms and shoulders to warm me up. Terry looks at Juan to do the same for her but is disappointed and finds her own blanket. "Awww. Here, Terry." John reaches over and warms her arms along with mine.

"Well, this trip is a disaster," Terry says, unhappy about the rain.

"What? No it isn't," John insists. His wet hair hangs in ringlets around his ever-smiling face. "We have food!" John grabs the French bread loaf, sausage, lettuce, and mustard and begins tearing off hunks of the crusty bread, passing them around. Crumbs fly everywhere! He is in a comical frenzy. We huddle in a circle in the center of the van, amused at John's performance. Sausage held high, he pulls out his Buck Knife and gives it a precision flick, then slices off thick hunks of meat and tosses them at each of us in a challenge to catch them. We generously load our sandwiches, piling them as high as towers, when John snatches up the lettuce and holds the entire head between his hands, tearing off pieces, flipping each of us a share. Lettuce falls down on us like the rain shower outside. Tears run down my face, my sides ache, and I can't stop laughing. I reach over and pick up pieces of lettuce and one that has fallen on John's lap, my hand lightly grazing his leg.

John freezes and pierces me with his eyes, jaw drops open in shock.

"What?" I ask, trying to follow his joke.

"What? What?" John lunges for the remaining head of lettuce and feverishly shreds the pale green leaves all over his lap.

"What are you doing?" I ask, still giggling. I'm puzzled at the joke.

"If I had known that was all it took to get you to touch me, I would have done this a long time ago." He beams ecstatically. Proudly covered in lettuce, John sports one of the biggest grins I've ever seen on him, hoping for me to pick up another soggy piece. Even Terry's cynical demeanor cracks, and everyone bursts into peals of laughter.

Oh God! Now I get it! Horribly embarrassed, I hide my face in my hands and bury my head in my lap. I want to disappear. I crawl into myself and refuse to move even after the snickers and giggles fade. After a while, John takes pity on me and changes the subject, finally coaxing me out of my fetal position.

"Come on, Dawn," John persuades, wiping the tears from his eyes. "I was just kidding around. Come on. Let's go for a walk."

"Hey! It's raining," Terry protests, her watchdog antennae kicking in again.

I can't look at anyone, especially Terry. *She will think I like him.* I am mortified that my private feelings are being made a spectacle. I am cornered and take a deep breath. *What the hell,* I think. "Arrrrrghh!" Quickly, I grab for the scattered, limp pieces of lettuce and, on impulse, fling them in John's direction. "You bastard!"

"Hey! Ouch! Sorry," John says. "I didn't mean to embarrass you."

No one is laughing. It's not as funny as John's game. "It's okay," I reply. I am glad that the shadow of the Coleman lantern hides my red cheeks.

"Okay. That's enough. Let's just go to sleep." Terry is abrupt. She is frustrated at the tense direction the conversation is heading. "John. You sleep over there." She points to the other side of Juan at the far end of the van. "Dawn. You sleep here . . . next to me. And don't even try it, John." Terry's finger points directly at him. "Juan! Turn off the lantern."

"Yes, ma'am!" John mocks a salute.

Scurrying about like bugs caught in the light, we dive into our sleeping bags. Juan turns down the light of the hissing lantern. I lie awake in the dark for a while replaying the lettuce scene and John's goofy expressions. He looked so funny. A giggle slips out.

"Ha." It's John from the other side of Juan.

My heartbeat thunders against my chest, and I'm sure everyone can hear it. *Is he thinking about the same thing I am?* I stay perfectly still, till my heart stops pounding. The summoning crickets send out their call long into the night, the last thing I hear when I finally fall asleep.

School is dull after only a couple of months. As much as I want to fit in, my world is now pulling me toward the cottages and mostly toward John. All the friends I thought I could make at school suddenly fall short of what I see in John; they seem boring compared to him. They aren't clever and witty like he is. They aren't worldly, considerate, kind, or nearly as fun. John, I find, is becoming more and more handsome and charming. I don't see him as a geek anymore, although I still see him as older. Nobody I know has ever shown me such kind attention. I feel lucky for the first time since I was a little girl and my father called me "princess." I didn't think I could ever feel so special again. God only knows how much I need that in my life.

I trudge through classes now, putting forth as little effort as possible to barely pass my tests. I feel invisible there anyway—just a brown-haired, blue-eyed, freckled speck in a sea of similar colors. Here at school, I'm not anything special, not like John treats me. Getting home is the focus of my day. Home—at least to Juan and Terry's place. Only then does the light shine down on me and I matter. To John, I matter.

On a typical school day at the end of October, I race to the cottage to see when everyone will be gathering that evening. Terry is home alone.

"Hey. Where is everybody?" I pant, wiping the sweat from my brow.

The low hum of static crackles from the television in the corner; lines cascade down the screen. Terry sits on her water bed in the living room. She is fidgety and nervous. Worry lines crease her freckled forehead.

I flop down next to her on the water bed. "What's the matter, Ter? What's up?"

"Nothing!" she snaps.

"Okay! Fine."

"Well, there *is* something I have been meaning to talk to you about."

"Yeah? What?"

"John," she says, averting my eyes.

"John?" My voice rises an octave. "What about him?"

"Well, uh, you know. I was wondering . . . how do you feel about him?"

Oh my God! I can't believe she is asking me this! my thoughts rage. *I can't tell Terry I am starting to have feelings for John. She doesn't even like him!* I get control of myself and decide to tread with care on this subject. *To make sure it is safe.*

"Feel about him? What do you mean, 'feel about him'?"

"You know. Do you like him?" she asks flatly.

"Terry! Like a boyfriend, like him?" I nearly shriek. I am stunned at her straightforwardness. "He's too old," I gasp and act as if it is unthinkable.

"He's not really, Dawn. He's only thirty-two."

Wait a minute. This doesn't sound like something Terry would say. I begin to doubt this conversation, getting the feeling someone has put her up to this. "Besides, Terry, he's married!"

"No, he's not, Dawn. They're not together."

"How do you know?"

"He told me."

"He did? What did he say?"

"He said they only live together. She lives her way, and he lives his. She cooks and does his laundry, but other than that they are mostly friends."

"Well, that's kinda weird. Are you sure?"

"Yeah, I'm sure. I asked him, and that's what he told me." She sounds positive. "So, I know you like him, Dawn. Don't you? Really, what do you think about him?"

I heard him say that about Sharon too. So I guess he wasn't lying. Wow! With the big question of Sharon answered, I suddenly realize I can allow myself to imagine a possible relationship with John. I get excited and I feel tingly thinking I can share my silly fantasies with my sister. I feel shy and lower my voice. "Well, he *is* cute!"

"I knew it. I knew it! What else? Would you go out with him?"

"He's really nice too," I add childishly. "I guess if he wasn't so old, I'd go out with him. I like being with him. He is really fun."

Terry's face pales suddenly; her cat-green eyes grow round as saucers. A rustle from the room behind me tells me we are not alone. Boisterous laughter rings out like children's on Christmas morning. In three loud steps, John comes charging out of the kitchen. The blood runs from my face, my skin prickles, and my throat tightens with embarrassment.

Swiftly John comes toward me, and for a moment I'm scared. He reaches down and holds my face in his hands, then plants a long, intense kiss on my lips. His eyes sparkle wildly as he loosens his grip, turns on his heel, and without another word, stomps out the door.

Stunned, I am frozen to my spot on the water bed. John's delighted laughter trails behind him across the courtyard all the way to his door.

"Terrrryyyy! Oh my God! I'm gonna kill you. I can't believe you did that to me. Arrrggggh! You set me up!" I yell and leap on top of her, wrestling and pretending to throw a few punches.

"He made me, Dawn. He made me," she shouts, fending off my lame blows.

"What do you mean, he 'made you'? How? What did he do to make you?"

"It was Terry food. He brought me Snickers and other food. Dawn, he likes you and you like him, and I'm tired of being in the middle of it."

"Middle of it?" I ask, quieting down. I want to know the truth about what she thinks.

"He likes you so much, Dawn, and you don't even see it. He's been crouched down in the kitchen like a high school kid, just to hear what you had to say about him."

"Wow! He really likes me?"

She imitates John's voice, "'Does she like me? Would she go out with me? Where is she?' He's jealous too."

"Jealous. Of what? I come here every day, right after school."

"Why do you think he's waiting for you every time you come home? He thinks there're all kinds of guys checking you out."

"I thought he might like me, but he can get any girl he wants, so I figured I was wrong. What about that porno stuff? I've seen the messages he gets."

"I know." Terry's voice hushes. "He says it's just work to him. It doesn't mean anything."

"Yeah, he said that to me too. But, Terry, don't you think he's kinda weird?"

"It don't matter. Do you like him, Dawn? You do, don't you?"

"Well . . . yeah . . . I do," I finally admit. "But do you think he really likes me, Ter? I mean, sometimes he acts so strange, and lots of times he just walks away for no reason."

"Dawn, don't you know why he does that?"

"No."

"He gets excited by ya, so he has to walk away. Why do you think he went into the water that day at the nude beach?"

"Oh my God! How do you know that?"

"He told me that too," she says without blinking.

I am silent. My head is spinning. *Wow! How long has John been talking to Terry about me? And about everything!* The thought makes me stressed. "But now what?" I ask, feeling my heart skip a beat.

"Just act normal and come over for dinner like always. He'll say something to you . . . I guess." She shrugs her shoulders. Terry's eyes meet mine, and her brow is furrowed again. She is biting her nails now—something she does when she gets nervous. I see the normally warm color in her eyes turn dark with worry. Silently, we agree to drop the subject.

⚜

Now that the "cat's out of the bag," John and I spend the rest of the week flirting heavily. He is extra charming and sweet, and I am more attentive and close. Things are much different since that day at Terry's. On every visit he makes to the house, he brings a gift for me now. A store-bought rose with baby's breath, a giant stuffed animal, or a blouse he thinks I might look good in. I am overwhelmed by his admiration for me, and the feeling of being adored makes me light-headed and happier than I have ever felt before. I truly have never known anyone like him. Purposefully he sits next to me, and this time I even let him hold my hand. As usual, he walks me to my door like an adoring gentleman and kisses my hand good night. I feel grand, like a queen on her throne, special. He brings extra treats for Terry too, but she sees through his ploy, sees how attracted we are to each other. She accepts them in silence, rolling her eyes.

By the weekend, John invites Terry and me to the movies. Juan can't go. He has to work on Saturday, so Terry doesn't want to go either.

"Please come, Terry," I beg. "I don't want to go alone."

Tired of being the continuous chaperone, Terry agrees only

reluctantly. As we cruise through Brand Boulevard in Glendale, nothing looks interesting. John doesn't give up and decides to continue searching. He hops the freeway and heads toward Hollywood.

"Let's see what's playing at Grauman's," he suggests.

Terry and I don't care, but Grauman's is showing something John doesn't like, so we turn around to drive back home to Glendale. At Western Avenue on Sunset, John unexpectedly makes an abrupt turn into a parking space in front of the Pussycat Theatre. *John C. Holmes XXX,* the marquee announces bigger than life. *Now Playing: Mitchell Brothers' Autobiography of a Flea.*

"Wait here," he instructs, shifting gear into park. Without making eye contact, he shoots out of the van.

"We're not going here, are we?" Terry panics.

"I, I don't think so. Maybe he has to do some business."

"Oh my God, Dawn! Look! He's signing autographs!" she shrieks and points in the direction of a small crowd. "He told me he was a movie star, and now he's signing autographs. Maybe he *is* a movie star!"

"Maybe he is." It is strange to watch John being treated like a star. Suddenly I become proud to know him.

John approaches the van. "Come on," he says, pulling the keys from the ignition. He walks around to open the door for us.

Terry and I nervously step out onto the dirty gray pavement. My palms sweat, and my heart pounds in my throat. I smooth down my hair and feel dowdy and inadequate in my tan-striped sweater and bell-bottoms. John takes control, holds one of my hands, and pulls me close to him. With his other arm, he guides Terry by the shoulder toward the ticket booth. The short, red-haired lady behind the thick ticket booth glass wildly blinks her over-the-top fake eyelashes. A clownlike lipstick grin is frozen on her face, and I can't stop staring at the streaks of red on her long yellow teeth.

"Do we go in here?" He points to the entrance to the right.

Mouth still open and mesmerized, she nods blankly. "Oh. Uh. Excuse me. Mr. Holmes. Do you think I can have an autograph please?" She steps out from behind the booth and races toward him, a small playbill thrust out in front of her.

"Oh. Yeah. Sure." Popping his gum, John gives a crooked smile and signs his name, slashing the black marker in all directions until his name resembles a giant scribble.

"Thank you. Thank you so much, Mr. Holmes," she gushes.

John lifts his mirrored aviator sunglasses, flashing a quick flirtatious smile, puts his arm around me, and leads the way in. My chest swells. He is important, and he just made me feel important to someone who admires him. I feel I have been lifted onto a pedestal. I smile at the woman. Terry smiles too.

The movie has already started. The theater is dark except for the glaring light from the screen, and we fumble to find an empty row of seats, asking a few patrons to excuse us. The three of us flop down and sink low into our seats. On the screen, Technicolor images of naked people pop out at me. I panic, flinging my hands up in front of my eyes. I sense John next to me get a little tense and nervous and then scoot down low into me. I wonder how Terry, on the other side of John, is reacting to the nude bodies up on the screen. *The Autobiography of a Flea* is an attempt at a Victorian era piece. Through my fingers, I can see large white wigs, hoop skirts, and canopied beds.

Then I hear something that nearly makes my heart stop; a voice that sounds familiar blares broken and awkward from the speakers above. It is John addressing the audience in a very bad phony English accent. Mortified, I stiffen and sink down even lower in my seat. I feel John's body freeze. *This is horrible. He is the worst actor I have ever heard.* I try not to breathe, to show my reaction, but unbelievably, a snicker escapes my lips. Immediately John's elbow jabs into my ribs. "Ouch!" I sink lower, almost to the floor. I try to make out Terry's image in the dark and spot the short, red-haired lady walking up and down the aisle, stealing blatant stares at us. Other people in the audience are sneaking random glances our way as well, but their attention quickly returns to the screen. Terry is staring straight ahead. A sudden feeling of bravery runs through me. I spread my fingers and look past them up onto the big screen ahead.

There is John, standing in a monk's robe, desperately trying to deliver a few overacted lines to a couple having sex on the canopied bed. A tidal wave of warmth engulfs my body, one like I've never experienced before as my senses take in the erotic movements on the screen. John knows I have peeked and squeezes my hand. *How can he know what I'm feeling?* I am self-conscious now, exposed.

Suddenly, the moment is lost as I think I see John's monk character on screen change into a flea and hop down the shirt of a French maiden's blouse. *Is John the flea?* I start to snicker, uncontrollably now, so hard I snort. John is aghast, but smiling, and it takes only a second before his loud laughter joins mine. The audience is annoyed, turning our direction to give us hard stares. We are uncontrollable.

"Let's get outta here," John manages to say, tears running down his cheeks. He grabs my arm and signals for Terry to leave. Nearly tripping over our feet, we race out into the lobby. The red-headed lady is hovering at the glass doors with a small group of moviegoers. John stifles his laughs and graciously signs his auto-graph for them, keeping Terry and me nervously at his side. The crowd glances over at us, making me uncomfortable.

"Thank you, John. Uh. We really enjoy your work."

"No problem, man. Thanks." He shakes a few hands and guides us out of the theater.

Terry shakes her head. "That was gross."

John and I roar even louder as we head for the van.

November comes that week. The weather gets noticeably colder, and the temperature between John and me gets increasingly warmer. The mood between us has grown deeper, more profound. *Soon,* my gut tells me. *Soon.* It is inevitable to me now: no turning back. I am terrified. We look at each other knowingly as we wait for time and space to open the door of opportunity for intimacy. It comes. On the following weekend, my world will forever be changed.

The week seems to drag on. It is hard to focus on anything except John. When Friday afternoon finally comes, John is in the backyard digging holes for a plumbing line, covered in dirt and sweat, when I arrive home from school. He is very serious, not his normal friendly self. "Hey. You wanna run to the store with me real quick?"

"Sure." I worry that something might be wrong; his face is stonelike.

We are quiet for most of the ride. I can't think of anything to say. Mostly around John I don't say a lot; he usually likes all the attention. Besides, he would think I was stupid; he is so worldly and smart. When we return and unload the van, John whispers in my ear, "Want to go to the beach?"

I swallow hard. *This is it.* Very clearly I answer, "Yes."

"Meet me here in an hour." His brow raises. We look at each other for a long while, his piercing gaze asking me if I am sure.

"Okay," I tell him, and then nod at his silent question.

We hold each other's stare for an eternity. John deliberately reaches his long-muscled arm out to me, firmly holds the back of my head and, bent low, brings his lips fully onto mine. We kiss. Passionate and tender, we seal the deal.

Through the courtyard we walk silently. The kiss still courses through me like a roller coaster, sometimes catching in my throat.

Without making a peep, I slip into Harriet's, gather my things, and wait at the van.

Our usual route to the beach now wears the heavy air of a clandestine rendezvous. John drives the van with methodical precision, following a path memorized from numerous visits past. The low pounding of my heartbeat sounds in my ears like a distant thunder, closing in with every pulse as we come closer to our destination. We do not speak.

Arriving at our spot in Leo Carrillo is as familiar as coming home. It feels right. Under the large sycamores, we gather wood without making a sound. John lights the sticks and branches and steps back. I stare into the fire as if it is my crystal ball, catching glimpses of my future through the flames. The fire speaks of passion.

Hypnotically, John reaches out and holds my hand. The reflections of dancing flames replace the blue that used to be his eyes, and his face shines with a soft, warm glow. He cocks his head for just a moment, turns, and leads me to the beach.

The tide is low, and the water is cool around my ankles as I play in the surf. Perched on a large boulder, John looks out over the horizon, deep in thought. The sun has set and the remains of light fade orange, yellow, and blue into the sky. A bright crescent moon hangs low above the inky water.

"It's getting cold," I finally tell him, timidly breaking his trance.

He finds my eyes and nods. Hand in hand, we amble toward the campsite. Abruptly John turns to face me and then sweetly, in a boyish tone, asks, "Would you make love to me tonight, Dawn?"

My heart stops; the ripples of the ocean stand still. The atmosphere is like the air before a lightning storm . . . wet, rich, charged. "Yes." I hear my voice quiver like a shy and frightened kitten's. *He really likes me now.* I hear a voice come from the back of my mind that comforts my insecurity.

Slowly he guides me into the van, lights a joint, and blows the smoke into my mouth. Shoving grocery bags and clothing aside, he unfolds a brightly colored Mexican blanket and lays me down against the scratchy weave. John takes charge, his nostrils flared like an animal's, wild from scent. He slowly peels off my clothes—jacket, shirt, pants. I recoil a bit, afraid of his intensity. He stares at me, surprised, and then gently kisses my arms, my neck, my breasts. I am mesmerized as I watch him gasp and caress every exposure of my skin, as if he is unveiling something precious. I begin to feel exalted, safe, and warm. His breath is heavy, and I can hear an almost catlike whine from the back of his throat. He bolts upright, rips at the snaps of his light blue cowboy shirt, and strips off his pants. Kneeling over me, he is fully erect. I panic at his size and quickly look around for a way to escape. John coaxes my hand to reach out and touch him. Frightened, I follow his lead, awkward, and silently worry if I'm doing okay. He slips down to kiss me between my legs as I lie there unmoving, frozen, not understanding what he wants me to feel. When he lifts his head, he doesn't look at me and rises up to cover me with the frightening hardness of his body. He is strong, and I can't move from under him. A whimper escapes from somewhere inside me.

"Trust me," he whispers hoarsely into my ear.

With a deep breath, I remain deathly still, pinned immobile underneath John's strength. I close my eyes and silently let the terrible searing pain of finality wash over me with the crash of the ocean tide.

CHAPTER SEVEN
The World According to John

For three days, the window shades keep the lights out in Harriet's living room. My head stays buried under the pillows to keep out even the glare of the shadows. Fiery images of my night with John burn in my mind, and the cold, silent ride home stings. *Everything hurts,* my body screams, *and I can't walk.* I tell Dad that I have bad cramps and can't go to school. Harriet gives me looks that say she knows better but, without any questions, she lets me keep the pullout couch open. I take painful steps to the bathroom every five minutes; I think I am going to die. Specks of blood and wrenching pain keep me doubled over and paralyzed. *Something's really wrong.* I panic that I have seriously damaged something inside, but how can I go to anyone for help? I can't . . . not after the beach.

Harriet answers when John knocks to wake me for school the next Monday. "She's sick," she tells him and sends him an icy glare. A pregnant silence and then his footsteps fading away are the only response I hear. I want to say something but can't find the words. I'm not well, and I'm way too scared.

Thankfully, Harriet is compassionate and takes me to the local clinic for antibiotics. Slowly my body heals. The bleeding stops, and the pain subsides enough that I venture over to Terry's again. *Oh God. How embarrassing.* I try to act nonchalant and ignore the nagging voice inside my head that shouts, *Everyone knows!*

"You okay?" Terry asks blandly. "Dad said you were sick."

"Yeah. Cramps." I cringe as I sit on the sofa. I had lost my virginity back in Carol City, at my girlfriend's house one night when her father was gone. My sixteen-year-old boyfriend had seemed huge to my five-foot frame, but he was nothing compared to John. That was awkward kids' stuff; this is undeniably real.

"John's been worried."

"Yeah. He has?"

"Yeah. He wants me to tell you he had to go to San Francisco for a couple days. He'll be home tonight."

"That's nice." I dully curl into a ball and shiver.

"Are you sure you're okay? Here. Here's a blanket." Terry hands me an afghan and turns on the TV. We watch television numbly late into the evening until we hear voices at the door. John and Juan walk in together. Juan is still wearing his cook's apron, and John wears his faded jeans and boots and his favorite hand-sewn patch jacket, a multicolored puzzle of patches collected from his different travels. He sewed each one on by hand and wears it only on special occasions. I know he has just gotten home from San Francisco.

"Thanks for the ride, man," Juan blurts, running straight for the bathroom.

"Yeah, man, sure." Seeing me on the couch, John says, "Hi. How ya doing?"

He props his briefcase up on the coffee table and sits down next to me, looking tired and unshaven. His arm stretches warmly out around my shoulder, and he hugs me close, kissing me on the cheek.

"Missed you," he whispers into my ear.

Don't grab me too hard, I think, my body tender. *God, I hope Terry can't tell anything.* My body still hurts, and I am uncomfortable with our secret. I don't really know how to act and, besides, I am annoyed that John has been away "working."

John sits up and leans over to open his briefcase. "Here." He tosses Terry handfuls of candy bars.

"Thanks!" she squeals, scrambling for the goods.

John reaches deeper into his case and hides something under his jacket.

"What's that?" I tease, pretending to grab at his chest.

He plays along and pulls away. Then, head down, he whips a small teddy bear out from behind his back.

"Oh! It's adorable. Thank you," I squeal and hug the soft plush toy. For a second, the memory of Aunt Ella and fireflies wraps around me like a soft, warm blanket.

John turns his body away and bends over secretively. "What size ring do you wear?"

I feel a rush of excitement. "I don't know. Why?"

"When is your birthday?"

"December 29. Why?"

"Let me see your hand." John reaches over to take my hand into his lap, admires my long slender fingers, and slips a sparkly light blue stone ring on my right ring finger. "Perfect." He holds my hand up in the light.

I am speechless. Tears well up, and it takes everything I have not to cry. "Th-th-thank you." I'm still not sure if the ring is for me. I am more than overwhelmed. No one has ever given me jewelry before.

John brings me close to his side. I can smell his scent again, that familiar green apple blended with maybe a hint of dogwood blossoms of my past, and I feel like I belong. I snuggle into his chest, and a tear falls from behind the veil of my long dark hair onto his colorful jacket.

"Blue zircon and white gold. Do you like it?"

I nod and sniffle softly. "How did you know my birthstone? And how did you know what size I wear?"

John chuckles.

He does really like me, I think and remember the ride home from the beach when he was so silent and cold. *This ring proves it.*

We cuddle for a long time, gingerly, lying on the couch draped by each other's arms and legs. It feels like a perfect fit. Cautiously, I sneak glances at Terry and Juan, checking their reaction to the closer intimacy between John and me. Blank looks that say *no big deal* and casual conversation help me feel comfortable lying so close to him.

"Ready?" John asks, yawning.

"Sure." I let him gently help me off the couch, my body still so very sore.

"Good night, you guys."

At my front door, we hesitate. It is late and the streets are quiet. "How about a date this Saturday? To the beach?" His voice is low and sensuous.

"Okay." I try to keep my voice in check; I don't want to sound too childlike; I want to be sensual. I reach up to let him kiss me deeply over every inch of my mouth.

John's breath is heavy; he steps back. "A date. A date. We have a date at eight," he whispers, mimicking the song of the rabbit in *Alice in Wonderland.* Then he kisses the ring he has placed on my hand, opens the door, and lets me in.

"Skulls. The human body is amazing," John notes as we scour the desert floor for bony specimens. John collects skulls—all kinds of skulls. We are somewhere out in the desert. John kicks the dirt around the silvery sagebrush. "Be careful of rattlesnakes."

Having grown up with my brother's boa constrictors, I don't mind snakes, but the poisonous parts make me nervous. "Here's one," I call, spying the white ring of an eye socket peeking out of the sand.

John runs over to see. Digging it out of the ground, he carefully holds the bleached bones up to the sun. "Jackrabbit. Nice one." He gives me a peck on the cheek.

I beam at the compliment and hold out a paper bag for him to carefully wrap it in.

"I think we have enough. Let's get outta here," he says, giving me a squeeze. "It's getting late."

We head back to Glendale, lighthearted. I'm happier than I ever remember feeling. I am John's girl, and he is my guy. We do everything together: mountains, desert, and John's favorite—the beach. At least, when he isn't working or I don't have school. He treats me like a lady, praises and adores me. We laugh and giggle like kids, get silly, and smoke pot. With everything we do, we get along. I am in love, and I'm sure John is in love with me too.

John always tells me I am beautiful. I have never known how much I need to be told those words; it feels so good. He plans trips, and I'm glad to come along. His presence, words, and actions fill every lonely, dejected void I harbor inside, and my presence seems to make him glow. John loves to surprise me with those secret moments behind closed doors when he can arrange just the right time to make love. I don't tell him that I'm scared when we're together like that, and I get good at hiding the pain.

"Let's go out of town this weekend," John says. "Somewhere special. Umm, let's see . . . maybe Palm Springs?"

"Really?"

"Just you and me, baby. Overnight. Nice hotel—Biltmore, maybe? I'll take you on the tram and to my favorite Mexican restaurant." He squeezes my hand and gives me a seductive up-and-down look.

"John, really? Uh, I mean yeah, I'd love to . . . But wait. What about my dad? Overnight without Terry and Juan. What do I tell him?"

"Can you tell him they're going? He won't check anyway. You

know how he is." John grips my hand convincingly tighter.

I nod in agreement, but I'm nervous. "Okay. I will."

I head to Terry's when we get home and take a hard dive for her couch to kick back for a while. Terry flips through the afternoon shows, cursing and twisting the rabbit ears. We are soon hypnotized into an old rerun of *I Love Lucy* when we hear a loud BAM, CRASH, THUD!

"What's that?" We race for the window. "It's coming from John and Sharon's." She lowers her voice to a whisper. "Shhh! Oh my God, they're fighting," she rasps.

"*Sharon! Sharon! Stop!*" John is shouting, but the shattering of glass continues.

A pregnant silence, then a different sort of smashing, like wood and pottery and metal, comes in hard, quick frenzies until we hear Sharon's voice scream, "*John! E-NOUGH!*"

The breaking noises stop, and you could hear a feather fall. Terry and I crouch behind the window shade, straining for a glimpse of the wreckage.

Slam! The screen door smacks hard, splintering its wooden frame. Sharon, in her white nurse's uniform, flings her purse over her shoulder and jangles a large ring of keys loudly in her hand. Marching down the courtyard, she storms into her Chevy Malibu and furiously speeds away.

The silence screams from their cottage. *She knows about us!* I panic. *And she's mad. Oh my God, is she going to the police? Is she going to kick us out?* I am beginning to get hysterical. I know my age is a huge problem, and I'm afraid John will get in trouble. Everyone who knows about John and me wouldn't say anything—and I figure most everyone knows. He doesn't really hide his affections. According to John, Sharon doesn't care who he is with because they live like brother and sister, but my being underage . . . that is a different story. *Sharon works for a pediatrician! She takes care of children! She might report him if she is mad.* My fears are spinning out of control, and I am visibly shaking.

Terry and I are still glued to the window, afraid of what John might do next. I hear nothing. All is quiet. For several minutes, both of us sit bug-eyed and motionless. Terry systematically bites her nails down to the quick of each finger until we again hear the sound of glass. But this time, it is the sweeping of it, the cleaning up. It is John. Solemnly he props the screen door open with a large plastic garbage can, quietly sweeps up the shattered glass, and gathers broken pieces of wood.

Cautiously, I walk out onto Terry's porch to see if I can catch his eye, but he won't look at anyone. I see his brother, David, standing outside smoking a cigarette and wearing a half smirk. *Is he gloating?* John keeps his head down, his face is red, and he is pouring sweat. He avoids looks from anyone who may have heard the argument. His long, hard sweeps are deliberate as he finishes the cleanup; then he disappears inside. He emerges with his briefcase and jean jacket in hand, storms to the van, and peels away to the gawks of more than half the tenants.

Oh God. What do I do? I throw myself onto Terry's water bed and fling a quilt over my head. I want to disappear.

"Dawn. Dawn!" Terry shouts.

"Whaaatt?" I whimper, willing tears away.

"I can't believe he left!"

"Yeah." I feel numb.

That evening John hasn't returned. He doesn't wake me for school the next day. The police don't come either, but I still believe we will surely be kicked out, and I know it will all be my fault. *Sharon's not going to put up with this.* But nothing happens.

John comes home the next evening, and Sharon soon afterward.

As mysteriously as the explosion appeared, it is gone. There is again a normalcy about their movements, almost as if nothing ever happened. No one asks and, taking their cue, everybody plays along.

⁂

"You up?" John asks softly as I answer the 7:00 a.m. knocking at my door.

"Hey. How've you been?"

"Hey. Yeah, I'm fine . . . and you?" He speaks gently, shyly.

"Fine," I lie. I want him to reach out and hold me, tell me everything is all right.

"So, uh, you still up for Palm Springs this weekend?"

"Yeah." I'm excited. I need him to know I missed him.

"Tell your dad we're going tonight and will be back Sunday. Tell him Terry and Juan too. You know. Like we talked about."

John opens the screen door. His thumb brushes across my lips. "Can't wait to be with you," he whispers in my ear. Then he kisses me warmly on the lips.

I want his kiss to linger.

⁂

"Gets hot here in the summertime. In the hundreds. But this is the time of year I like best." John speaks with familiarity. It is January of 1977, and the weather is perfect: in the seventies.

The Palm Springs Biltmore Hotel is a 1950s deco-style building with a grand front lobby. Huge crystal chandeliers, elaborate Spanish tiles, and massive live palms greet us at the front desk. I have never seen anything so rich and luxurious. I marvel at the way the room speaks to me. The air is warm and smells of secrets, lace, and confidence. John signs us in as Mr. and Mrs. Holmes. The clerk doesn't bother to check my ID even though I nervously fidget and obviously try to avoid his gaze.

"Lots of movie stars have stayed here. Still do," John whispers into my ear after thanking the clerk, and I fantasize that people are wondering if we are stars too.

He knows exactly where he is going. He's been here before. *How many times and who did he bring? Another girlfriend?* I wonder. We wind through stone pathways and giant palm trees and come to a private bungalow with a secluded porch and hammock. The inside is regal with a California king and a giant sunk-in tiled hot tub in the floor of our bath.

"Like it, baby?" He comes up behind me and hugs me close.

"I love it, John. I can't believe it. It's beautiful!"

"No, you're beautiful."

"John. Stop," I say timidly.

"No, you stop. Don't you know how beautiful you are?"

"No, I'm not. Quit it." I am blushing now.

John grabs my arms and flings me on the deep, soft mattress, holding me down. Playfully, I struggle to get free.

"Get over here. Yes, you are. Hold still. Hold still." He brings his body fully onto mine and pins me down. "Stop," he pleads sweetly. "Stop."

I relax at the gentle command he has of my body, lie trustingly under his weight, my eyes inches from the blue of his.

"Listen to me." He softly wipes strands of hair from my face. "Look at you. Look. Look at your face," he whispers admiringly, tenderly outlining my features with his fingers. "The shape, those cheekbones—and your eyes, the green, blue . . ." He shakes his head. ". . . and their perfect almond shape." His fingers lightly brush over my eyes, then stop. "You were my birthday present, you know? It was my birthday when I first met you." John holds my gaze for what seems an eternity before he lightly places his lips on mine. "I love you," he breathes, his mouth barely touching my skin. "You're the best thing . . ." His voice trails off.

"I love you too, John." My words come to life in my heart even as I speak them. Sparks light in John's eyes; my words ignite him. He is on fire. He lifts me up and showers me with dozens of kisses. He rips his shirt off, throws it to the floor, and tears my blouse open with his teeth. His lovemaking is frenzied passion. I follow his lead—he likes to tell me what to do—but I silently worry that I don't have the right moves. I'm getting better at blocking out the pain. I have never felt as loved as I do at this very moment.

We spend the weekend visiting John's favorite places, lying around the pool, ordering room service, and guessing the identities of the other hotel guests.

"I bet that one is his secretary and they are supposed to be out on a business trip." John starts the game playfully. "Oh, look, they're going to their room to fuck. I'll bet money! Wanna peek in their window and watch?"

"No way! Really? No, they're not, John. Quit it! They're looking." I'm embarrassed and blushing. But John is like a kid in a candy store. He loves this game; it excites him. He checks to see if the coast is clear, takes me by the hand, and leads the way to the back of the couple's bungalow.

"Shhhh!" John lifts his finger to his lips. We lie quietly for a few moments till he feels safe enough to steal a peek inside. He takes the first rubberneck look and lifts me up to spy on the unsuspecting couple too. A pile of clothes sits on the floor near the corner of the bed. I try to stretch my neck farther until John, unable to contain a laugh, can't hold me up any longer. We fall in the bushes laughing hysterically all the way back to our bungalow.

People stare at us constantly, and I finally realize that John is being recognized. I remember the group that followed us at Grauman's Chinese Theatre. He attracts people.

John loves the attention, but ever protective of me, whenever people look, he holds me closer, more possessively and intimately, as if to say, "She is mine." Holding my hand everywhere, John guides me to all his favorite haunts. We eat at an old family-owned Mexican place famous for its authentic food, ride the tram to the snowy top of the mountains that overlook Palm Springs to eat barbeque, and feed the squirrels as we look for the ocean through the large bluff-top binoculars. Then, back at our bungalow, we make love again until we fall asleep.

I don't want these days to end. Still Sunday comes, and it is time to go back to Glendale. Heaviness hangs on our final day, but on the ride home, a more comfortable feeling of permanence settles in between us. Our moves have become synchronized, and we sense each other's needs before words are ever spoken. John, taking the opportunity to kiss me every time we come to a stop, assures me that my father will not know about our weekend alone.

I hope he is right. I'm not looking forward to facing Dad with a lie on my lips.

John drops me off in the front of the cottages so I can walk in first with my sleeping bag and make it look like we have come from the beach. Instead, I make a mad dash for Terry's door to see if she has any news of Dad. No one comes to the door. "Shit." I kick the door and try not to panic.

Dad is sitting on the couch when I step in, his feet up on the coffee table. He's watching TV and smoking a Salem menthol.

"Hey," he calls out, looking up from his smoky corner. "Where you been?"

"The beach."

"The beach, huh? With who? John and, uh . . . ?"

"Yeah. Everybody went," I finish his sentence and quickly

duck into the kitchen, hoping that will be the end of the questions.

Dad follows me. "Listen," he says, lowering his voice. "I've been meaning to talk to you. You need to pack your things. We're leaving."

"What? Leaving?" I shoot back, reeling from the blow of his announcement. "I can't, but . . . but . . . what about school?" I begin to get hysterical.

"I'll sign you out. Shhhh. Calm down. Listen." He motions for me to bring down my voice.

Bracing myself, I hold my breath as Dad explains his latest *plan*.

"I got a place. In Riverside. Pen Ci is flying in to meet us. She's been waiting a long time. Harriet doesn't know, so keep it . . . to yourself." He stops, looks side to side. "I told her you want to go back to your mother's in Florida and, uh, I have to take ya. She, uh, well, you know, likes me too much and, uh, she just won't understand this thing about Pen Ci." He thinks for a moment and then speaks to me again as if I am his buddy. "God, I can't stand it anymore. It's like, like . . . *work* being with her . . . and pretending I love her," he practically spits as a visible chill runs down his spine. "Just get your things together, Dawn. Unless you got somewhere else to go."

"No. I, uh. No . . . I don't." I shake my head, scared of his backhanded threat to leave me.

Suddenly, it all makes sense. Dad is spending so much time alone with Harriet; Harriet tries to act like our mother; Dad is gone while Harriet is at work. She has fallen in love with him, and Dad's only intention has been to lead her on till he wants to leave. *Does John know what's going on between Dad and Harriet? Is that why he is so sure Dad won't say anything if we're together? Or maybe he thinks I'm in on it!* Like a dark morning gloom, the unanswered questions cloud my head.

"What about Terry?" I ask, little by little realizing the impact of Dad's decision.

"She's not coming."

"No! Why? Did you ask her?"

"She's with Juan now." He shrugs his shoulders. "She made her decision before we left Florida."

"Does she at least know we're leaving?"

"Yeah, I told her today," he mumbles. "So, uh, I'll go to school to tell them with you in the morning, 'kay?"

I nod numbly. He leaves me standing in the kitchen. Quick as I can, I race out the back door and take the few long steps to Terry's back porch.

Knock, knock, knock. No answer. *Knock, knock, knock.* Nothing.

So this is probably why no one answered at Terry's. I turn back to the house. *They're upset.* My mind whirls. It is difficult to breathe. *Does John know we're leaving?* I sit down at the table and put my head in my hands. *John? What about John and me? Will this be the end of . . .* I can't bear to think about it. Tears spill down my cheeks. *Do I have to choose between Dad and John?* I feel like I have no choice; I have to go. Dad is my legal guardian. *But,* I let out a deep sob, *I'm in love with John.*

Mom. She'll be worried. I haven't written her since before my birthday. I have to send her a letter. I rummage through the kitchen drawer for a pen and paper and find several drafts of the letter I sent Mom last month.

Dear Mom,

Sorry for not writing sooner. . . .

Thank you very much for the pictures. They are very nice. As soon as I got them I showed them to everyone in the courts (where I live). They all said I have a very pretty mother and foxy brother. Most of them think me and Wayne look like twins. I think so too. . . . I'm sorry I don't have any recent pictures of me except for the ones we took at the nude beach and I don't think you would like a picture of me naked. . . .

School ends Friday for the Christmas holidays and starts again January 3. Please forgive me for not sending anything except my love. But I have no money and no one wants me to do any work for them because they need the money for Christmas presants too.

Oh yeah! My bladder infection is gone. The doctor gave me anti-biotics for it. I've been taking them for almost two weeks now.

I will be sweet 16 in two weeks from Wednesday. Remember the birthday party last year. I had a good time. So did you I think? . . . I still thank you Mom it was one of the nicest things you did for me. I'll always remember it and you mostly. I miss you and Wayne so much. Especially now durring Christmas time. I only spent one other Christmas away from home 2 years ago. . . .

Well I better go now. . . . Sorry my writing is so sloppy. . . .

Merry Christmas early!
All my love,
   Dawn
      xxxxxxxxxx

It was all I could bring myself to say: tidbits of catching up, with no real mention that *maybe* something else is going on, *maybe* I was scared of being sick or the way things were playing out here in California. I know she can't do anything if I write her again, and I really don't want her to worry. I fold the letter and place it back into the drawer. Sad and exhausted, I pull down the sofa bed and cry myself to sleep.

John's morning wake-up call is a rap at the door. Today, I am already up and waiting for him. "Morning." He has a cheerful glint in his eye that says, *Remember our weekend?*

"Hey." I open the screen door, step out into the cold morning fog. John's face drops. "What's the matter?"

"We're leaving." I choke back a rush of tears.

"What? When? Now?"

"I'm not sure. I think tomorrow. Dad is checking me out of school today, and he told me to pack my things," I blurt out, a few tears breaking free. I lean against the stucco cottage wall, put my arm across my eyes, and let out a few sobs.

John steps in close to me and holds my hand. He is thoughtful, and I wish he would say something, fix this mess somehow. "Get me your address and phone number." He bites his lip a few moments more, staring into the gray, foggy sky. "Call me."

The cottage door flings open before we can say any more. John quickly jumps back off the porch and pretends he is just leaving.

"Let's go, Dawn," Dad purposely interrupts, his voice stern. He sends John a murderous stare.

John throws Dad a challenging look back. "You son of a bitch!" He turns in a huff, marches to his cottage, and slams the door.

Dad is shaken, and he fumbles with the lock and the screen

door. "Ready, Dawn? Come on. Quit standing around here, and let's get this over with." Dad storms to the car, shaking his keys against his leg hard and loudly; he is the one in charge.

"Why aren't you going, Terry?" I demand, banging on the door.

"He doesn't want me to go, Dawn. Didn't he tell you that?" She is about to cry.

"No. He said you were with Juan now."

"No. He did kinda ask me to go with him but, right after, said he understood I couldn't because I was with Juan. I feel like I have no choice, really." Her voice quavers, and she turns away. "Does he even love us, Dawn?" Terry looks back at me, her face streaked with tears.

"I don't know, Terry. I think so." I'm not really sure if he does.

"He withdrew me from school today, Ter. We are supposed to leave in the morning. What am I going to do about John? I don't even see his van. Where is he?" I hate the way my gut feels: hollow, like it's folding in on itself. I find the couch and rock myself.

"John knows—the whole courtyard knows—what Dad is doing to Harriet." Terry wipes the tears from her face.

"He does? He doesn't think I had anything to do with it, does he?"

"He's not so innocent! He did hint around a couple times, 'cause he didn't know if you knew about it. But he likes you, Dawn. It just made it easier for him to be with you."

"But you told him the truth, right?"

"I told him we didn't know what Dad was doing, and he believes me. At least I think he does." She gives it some thought. "And everybody knows about you and John too!"

"I know," I tell her with sober acceptance, but I am thinking, *Now what?*

I fall asleep on Terry's couch after hanging out with her the entire evening. I want to spend time with her before we leave in the morning, but mostly I am waiting for John to come home.

"Where do you think he is?" It is midnight, and I am getting anxious.

"I don't know. I thought he would be here by now. Maybe he *is* scared of Dad?"

We sit in silent worry, the both of us, as we have done so many times from our past in Carol City. Aside from our occasional getting up to look in the refrigerator, the cottage stays quiet. The only movement in the room is the spidery shadows cast by the television.

CRACK, RUSTLE, RUSTLE! The noise comes from outside a corner window.

"Shhh." Terry raises a suspicious finger to her lips and tiptoes to the window.

"What was that?" I whisper. "A raccoon?"

She keeps her finger to her mouth for a full few minutes while we both listen carefully for any more sounds. It is quiet. Silence.

"He's gone." Terry lowers her hand.

"Who?"

"John."

"John?" I jump to the window to see if he's there.

"Shhh. Yeah, John! But he's gone now. Don't you know he peeks in windows? He does it all the time. I coulda swore I saw him at your window a couple times before. Once I caught him face-to-face." Terry wrinkles her face in disgust.

"Yeah. I saw a shadow jump into the bushes a few times, and I figured it was John checking up on me." I remember the window-peeking in Palm Springs. *Why won't he come to the door?*

"Checking up maybe, and wanting to see you naked is more likely!"

I don't answer. I tear myself up inside trying to understand why he isn't here with me tonight, but is watching from the shadows instead. In my gut I know it's because of Dad. Nobody likes what he is about to do to Harriet, but nobody has the courage to stop him either. I jump at every noise I hear that night till a cold and dreary morning wakes me.

❦

Dad is saying his good-byes to Harriet when I finish hugging Terry. She is stone-faced and won't look at him. I can't stop crying and when I reach out to hug Harriet good-bye, all I can say is "Thank you." John's van is parked at the end of the courtyard in his usual space, and the door to his cottage is shut tight with the curtains drawn.

"I'll call John as soon as we get where we're going, Terry. I'm sure he'll give you a message," I assure her as well as myself. Things are complicated now. After a couple of days, Harriet will know that Dad has lied to her and, because I am with him, she will blame me too. All hell will break loose, and Harriet will see me as part of it. Everyone is bracing for the fallout. Terry doesn't have a phone, so the only number I can call is John's—and that will have to be when Sharon isn't home. I am sure Sharon will accuse me too. I've thought about calling the answering service, but John hasn't given me permission to call there.

The time comes to leave, and still John doesn't emerge. "Tell him I miss him, and I will let him know where I am as soon as I can," I tell Terry urgently. I grab my things and throw them in the car.

In front of the once-purple jacarandas, Terry stands on the damp sidewalk hugging her blue and beige sweater, eyes red and swollen. Then, expressionless, without a word, she turns and walks back to her cottage. It is the last time my sister and I will see each other as teenagers.

⚜

Riverside, California, is only an hour and a half away from Glendale. I make a note of it. The car ride is a sad blur. I notice nothing on the drive except the floorboards in the backseat. I feel carsick. Large gray and brown boulders jut out of dry desert hills to greet us, but I'm not excited. *The wind blows hard here in January.*

At the end of a cul-de-sac in a large apartment complex, Dad pulls up to a bottom-floor unit and taps on the door. A tiny, dark-skinned woman about four feet nine inches tall pokes her head around the corner and lets us in.

"Sawadee ka." The delicate lady clasps her hands together, brings them up to her eyes in a Thai greeting, and smiles.

"Pen Ci, kup, anee ben luk sow, sur Dawn, kup," Dad introduces me in Thai.

Pen Ci looks up at me and nods.

"Sa-wa-dee ka," I imitate the proper greeting the way Dad taught me earlier, my pronunciations bouncing awkwardly like a rubber ball.

She smiles, amused, and waves me in.

Pen Ci is a beautiful, fine-boned woman with jet-black hair and eyes. Her daggerlike fingernails are painted red, contrasting nicely against her brown skin. She wears a traditional bright-colored sarong, one of Dad's sweatshirts, and his oversized socks, which drag comically behind her tiny feet as she walks.

Right away she spreads a collapsible grass mat on the carpet. Then into the kitchen she scoops up bowls of different kinds of curries, soups, sauces, and rice. Dad changes into a more subtle, checkered male sarong, and we sit down to eat. I look around the sparse apartment, notice its dark green short shag carpet, a small television, and a roll of blankets against the wall.

After dinner, Dad and Pen Ci speak together in Thai, and he translates.

"She says to tell you she doesn't speak any English, but she thinks you are beautiful."

"Tell her thank you." I am flattered by the compliment. "And that she is too. I thought you said she wasn't here yet, Dad."

"I had to trust you. Shhh." Pen Ci speaks again.

"She asks how old you are, and she wants to tell you about Jack. He's two and a half." Dad finishes, and Pen Ci begins to cry.

"She misses Jack," Dad says.

My own tears fall down my face. "Yeah, I miss somebody too." Dad flashes me a stern look, then hangs his head, puts down his chopsticks, and exhales a long, hard sigh.

❧

Pen Ci and I spend the next couple of weeks communicating in sign language and crying a lot. *How long has Pen Ci been here?* I wonder.

"She keeps the green stone for me. She knows how to take good care of it. In her country, she is highly revered," Dad tells me confidentially. "She is a healer. People will line up outside of our house to have her lay her hands on them."

I am impressed, but then question silently why she hasn't taken away the pain in his face yet. I don't say anything. Instead, I can't stop thinking about John.

Dad already has a job with the phone company, so a black rotary phone sits on the green carpeted floor in the living room. *Man, when Dad makes plans, he really hauls ass.* I am amazed. Dad is strict about using the phone, though, and I know I will have to wait till he is gone to try to call John.

While Dad works, Pen Ci and I share household chores and melancholy.

I spend hours sitting at the front window, staring out at the parking lot, fantasizing that John will appear and take me away. I wonder how Terry is taking the flak of our departure and if she is waiting for my call. I have no money for a pay phone, and I can't figure out how to explain to Pen Ci why I need to place a long-distance call.

Pen Ci spends hours lying down in her room trying to stay warm under layers of Dad's clothes, rereading letters from Thailand, and listening to tapes with Jack's tiny voice talking to his mother here in the faraway United States.

"But why is she so sad all the time? Aren't you sending for Jack soon?" I ask Dad one evening.

"Yeah, we plan on it as soon as we get more settled. But she misses her country and, besides, it's way too cold for her here." Dad explains with compassion in his voice, and I can see he loves her and his new son.

The sun shines warmer than usual for a late winter's morning in Riverside. Pen Ci is in the kitchen motioning for me to help her pack some food and drinks into a picnic basket.

After we've packed she says, "Ma," with a *come with me* motion of her hand. "By teow."

I follow her out the door, carrying the folded grass mat and a plain green umbrella. She has spotted a huge rock perching high on the hill behind our apartment that is sunny and level enough for us to enjoy our small feast on. Laying out our spread on the warm rock and placing the umbrella nearby, we silently begin our meal. The sun feels good on my face, and Pen Ci's cooking is deliciously spicy and sweet. She makes a sign to me that she is happy I enjoy her food; it pleases her.

We finish quietly, staring out at the billowing clouds in the blue winter sky. A small lone bird flies close overhead and catches our eyes. Pen Ci looks at me; her small hands make the motion of a circle around her chest, telling me she knows I am brokenhearted. I break down. Tears of sadness pour down my face at the relief of finally having someone who understands. With broken English and crude sign language, I tell her of a true love I have left behind in Glendale and how deeply I miss him; that he doesn't know my whereabouts and how desperately I want to contact him. I tell her Dad doesn't like John and I'm scared to ask him if I can call. As I explain with my hands and my heart, she understands.

Decisively, she signals for me to pack things up. Then she leads the way back to the apartment and hands me the phone. Nodding curtly, she leaves me to my call. Fear engulfs me as I hold the receiver. *What if no one is there? What if Sharon answers? What does Harriet have to say about me leaving with my father?* I bite the bullet and dial.

"John?" I ask timidly after I hear his *hello.*

"Dawn?" There is a pause. "Is that you?"

"Yes. John, I'm in Riverside."

"Still with your dad?"

"Yes." I start to cry. "I miss you."

"I miss you too, baby," John says, his voice softening. "I've been waiting for you to call. Everyone here is pretty mad at your dad."

"I know. I can't help it," I sob, feeling a sting of guilt. "I don't want to be here, John."

"I know, baby. I wish you were here. Near me."

"How's Terry? Can you tell her that I called?"

"Terry and Juan moved out a couple of days ago. They went back to Florida. I thought you knew."

"Huh? No!" My voice catches in my throat, and sadness

overwhelms me.

"Baby? Dawn? You still there?"

"I didn't know, John," I forced the words through the telephone receiver. "I didn't know about any of it."

"I know; I know, baby. Let me think. Listen. You know my brother, David, right?

"Yeah."

"Call his number. I'll be there waiting at four tomorrow afternoon. Okay? I'll figure something out, baby."

"Okay, John. I will. Four tomorrow."

"I gotta go now. You know I love you, Dawn."

"I love you too, John."

"Tomorrow, 'kay? Bye, baby."

"Bye."

Pen Ci appears like a ghost and asks me in broken English if I am "good" and draws an imaginary circle around her heart again.

"Good," I answer, smiling. "Tomorrow?" I point to the phone. She nods.

John is waiting by David's phone for my four o'clock call. "Hey, baby." He sounds out of breath.

"John, I miss you."

"Me too. Listen. David and Karen are willing to meet you and talk to you about what happened with your dad. They just want to make sure you are cool, and if everything works out, they are willing to let you stay with them until we can get you your own place."

"Really?"

"Yeah, baby. I miss you . . . I can't wait to hold you, kiss you all over. When can you come?"

"I, I don't know, John. Anytime."

"Your dad—he doesn't like me. Can David or Karen come pick you up?"

"Okay. That's fine. I love you."

"I love you too."

We are in each other's arms making love that weekend in David and Karen's back room. John can barely keep his hands off of me, and he is very open with his affection, apparently not minding that they know about us.

There is nothing David and Karen want to know about my involvement with my father. They already believe John. David does take an authoritative moment with me, though. Still in his pajamas, he asks if I am willing to get a job and take being on my own seriously. I tell him I am. "Cool," he drawls slowly. He pulls a long drag of his cigarette, looks over his thick glasses at me, and asks, "Did John tell you about the garage apartment coming open?"

"No. What apartment?"

"You . . . John, you didn't tell her yet?" David grins slyly.

"Hey, not yet. We've been busy!" he says and proceeds to maul me playfully on the couch.

"I'll tell her then," David says, grinning. "The garage apartment is coming up for rent next month. If you want to, you can stay here until it's available. There's just one thing." He raises an eyebrow.

"What?"

"Sharon. You gotta clear it with Sharon. And as it stands, she thinks you knew about your dad using Harriet for money. And, well, you have to get a job and promise to pay rent."

John doesn't speak. I am scared now. My skin bristles. "Yeah, I'm serious about getting a job and"—I swallow hard—"I'll ask her if I can rent the place too."

"No, no, baby. I'll clear it with her if that's what you really want. Is it?" John comes to my rescue, hugging me tightly. He flings David a hard look.

Is John letting David test me? I let the thought go.

"Sharon is staunch about maintaining this place; you can't bullshit her," David warns. "You need to be responsible."

"I'm serious," I repeat and dig my face into John's warm shoulder.

Dad knows I went back to Glendale, even though I never said where I was going. "To a friend's house for the weekend" was the only explanation I offered. When I come back, he is in a foul mood.

"Is your pain bad?" I ask, concerned that his face may be feeling worse.

"Naw. Nothing. It's the same. It's just . . . I got served with papers. Harriet. She's moved back with her folks, and she's suing me for breach of promise! She knows I'm gonna pay her back. We're struggling here. Awww. This country. This is a load of shit! Only in this country!" He flings his newspaper across the room. Pen Ci says nothing. "We're outta here."

"What do you mean, 'we're outta here'? Where are you going?"

"Back to Florida. She's too cold here anyway"—he points to Pen Ci—"and when Jack comes, well, he can't take the cold weather either. Florida's weather is more like their home anyway. Sued for breach of promise . . . Can you believe this shit?" he mumbles angrily.

I think for a long moment. "Dad?" I muster up my courage.

"What, Dawn?"

"I don't want to go back to Florida."

"Yeah, I figured you wouldn't want to go. You want to be with John. I know."

Dull shock pounds in my ears, and I can't look at him. "Yeah. I love him."

"So what are you going to do, Dawn?"

"Get a job. Rent the back apartment. Be with him." I'm still not brave enough to look him in the eye.

Dad is silent for a while, then breathes one of his heavy sighs. "Okay. If that's what you want, Dawn. More power to you." His tone rings heavy with unspoken words: *Bad idea.*

❧

By week's end, Dad has quit his job and everything is ready to go. Standing outside next to the fully packed green Chrysler, I flash on moments of our trip to California: picking up Marty, the Grand Canyon . . . The slam of the trunk brings me out of my daydream. I hug Pen Ci and give her my best *wai.*

"Chok dee ka," she says, shivering from the cold air. Without further expression, she climbs into the passenger seat.

Dad stands next to the car with his hands in his pockets and stares at the ground. "Well, uh, I guess this is it." He kicks a small rock.

"Yeah, uh, I guess so." I don't want to get emotional. I know how much Dad doesn't like it when I cry.

"Well, uh." He thinks for a minute. "'Kay, here." He hands me a twenty-dollar bill from deep inside his pocket. "Oh, also, there are two days left on the rent, so I guess you can stay till then and, uh . . . well, let me know where you are, okay?" Dad scrambles to get our good-byes over with.

"Okay. I'll be in touch with Mom. Tell Terry to call me too. I love you, Dad." I wrap my arms around his shoulders and give him a kiss.

"I love you too, Dawn," he says and quickly climbs in the car to start the engine. "Good luck." Dad pokes his head out of the window and waves as dirt billows off the gravel behind the disappearing car.

"Good luck to you too," I call back weakly. In a trail of dust, I wave good-bye to my father as he heads back to Florida. In my hand I hold the twenty-dollar bill he has given me. *Two days' rent and twenty dollars . . . Thanks, Dad. Well, I'm really a Californian now.*

I feel a surge of independence lift my spirits. Little do I know that Carol City was only a boot camp compared to what California has in store for me.

CHAPTER EIGHT
A Rose of Sharon

Making it to David and Karen's is more of a hassle than I think it will be. John has to be in San Francisco for a shoot, and he leaves David in charge of helping me.

On the other end of the phone, David pulls an audible drag from a cigarette. "Got some problems. Can't get the car started."

"Oh. What do I do? I can only stay here a couple more days."

"Can you meet me halfway tomorrow?" His words slur, and I hear the cigarette sucking noise again.

"Yeah, I guess so." I am using up part of my twenty dollars for the pay phone and worrying about having enough.

On my last day in Riverside, I finish off the last of the rice from the plastic containers Pen Ci has left in the kitchen and gaze over the empty apartment. *How sad this place is.* Curling up in my sleeping bag on the cold living room carpet, I fall into a restless, uncomfortable sleep.

I am running for my life, being chased by something giant, invisible, yet terrifyingly real. It is coming closer . . . I keep running and running . . . trying to escape. Just as the darkness is about to pounce on me . . .

I open my eyes, thankful to be awake. *Whoa. I'm glad that was a dream.* I try to shake off the wrestling shadows of the night, but they linger miserably, their memories haunting until daylight.

In the morning I pack the rest of my belongings and, without looking back, walk out of the cul-de-sac to a busy part of town. Taking a deep breath to muster my courage, I stick out my thumb. Instantly, I get a ride.

An old man in his seventies driving a beat-up Chevy truck comes clanking to a stop. "Where you going?" He flashes his long, tobacco-stained teeth in a smile.

"LA," I pant. "Glendale."

The man looks to the sky for a second and says in a slow drawl, "Yep, well, I'm going in that direction. Hop in." The ride is long and bumpy. He pulls out a bottle of whiskey from his jacket pocket, takes a swig, and offers me some.

"I'm fine." I lean tensely against the door, balancing my bags between my knees.

"Is Long Beach close enough?" he asks after we have been driving awhile.

"Long Beach? If it's near LA. Sure." I figure that will be okay. I think I heard of the place when I was in Glendale. It shouldn't be too far for David to pick me up from there.

"I can take you to my sister's there if you want." He is drunk and offers several times to take me there.

"No, thanks. Right here is fine." I nervously point to a Denny's, pretending I'm not scared.

The old man takes his time changing lanes. He is getting agitated but finally pulls into the parking lot. I hop out and thank him again, walking quickly into the restaurant without waiting for a response. I dig for the last of my coins in the pocket of my corduroys, plunk them into a lone pay phone near the newspaper stands, and dial David's number once again.

"Hello."

"Uh, hi. John?"

"Dawn? Where are you?"

"Long Beach. At a Denny's off the 710 Freeway."

"Long Beach! Why are you there?"

"'Cause David told me to find a ride halfway. His car isn't working very well."

"What? That schmuck." John sounds pissed off. "Juss . . . just a minute." I hear the muffled sounds of voices; then John comes back on the line. "Baby?"

"Yeah?"

"Karen's going to pick you up. I gotta go to work, but I'll be home tonight and meet you here. Don't worry. I love you."

"I love y—"

He cuts me off, passing the phone to David's wife.

"He has epilepsy, you know," Karen says from behind the steering wheel of their 1969 orange Volkswagen Beetle. "He has to take phenobarbital every day so he doesn't have seizures. It wipes him out a lot. People think he's just lazy, but he's sick."

"I heard," I tell her sympathetically.

"Yeah." She is smacking gum and shifting gears like butter. Her straight, shoulder-length blonde hair is pinned back at the bangs with a modest barrette, and the late afternoon sun glares off of her thick bifocals. "So, you like John, huh?" she comes right out and asks.

Taken off guard, I am suddenly shy at how vulnerable her question makes me feel. "Yeah. He's nice."

She pulls her eyes off the road for a quick second, flashing me a smile. "You're lucky," she says, popping her gum.

"You think so?" I answer, but I don't really want to talk about it anymore.

She smirks, her head cocking to the side. "So is he."

Karen shows me where to put my things when we get to the cottage. David is passed out on a king-sized bed that sits directly in the middle of the living room. "His medicine has kicked in," Karen whispers.

Aside from the large bed, the room is adorned with a mishmash of just about everything. A patched orange beanbag chair props up against the front window, and odd pieces of furniture are placed in unusable parts of the room. Massive pothos plants hang from the ceiling in three out of four of the corners of the room. It looks like the dregs of a giant garage sale have found homes here. Nothing matches.

"Come on. I'll show you the kitchen." She motions for me to follow. The kitchen is in similar disarray. Bottles of prescriptions rest on the pale yellow and black tiles of the counter. A small table is pushed up against the curtains at the window with stacks of envelopes, bills, and paper strewn on top. Coffee stains on the tablecloth mark the visible parts of the table, and the sink is full of unwashed dishes.

"I'm just too busy to keep this place up." Karen sighs, frustrated by the look of the room.

"Mom." A small, dirty-faced blond boy appears from the shadows.

"In here. Shhh. David's sleeping. Dawn, this is my son, Jamie. Jamie, this is Dawn. She's going to be staying here with us for a little while."

Jamie looks up at me. "Hi."

"Hi."

"Honey, why don't you go wash up for supper?"

"Aww, Mom."

"Go." Karen snaps a dish towel at his backside and turns to do the dishes.

David is awake now and groggily enters the kitchen. "Hey, you made it." He loses his balance in the doorway and catches himself on the counter. He is wearing the same black-and-yellow-striped bumblebee outfit that Terry and I had thought was so funny on John. "And how's my sweet, sexy, beautiful mama doing?" He comes droning up behind Karen, rubbing his body against hers.

"I'm fine," she answers in baby talk, her bottom lip sticking out.

I have to turn my head. I know John and I were all over each other earlier and they probably feel comfortable being affectionate in front of me, but in my eyes this is sickeningly sweet and almost a show. *Well, I'm gonna have to put up with it. At least until I get my own place.*

John gets in around midnight. David and Karen are sitting up in the king-sized bed watching TV. "Hey," they greet him, smiling.

Half-asleep in the beanbag chair, I feel John crawl up next to me and nuzzle my neck. He smells of light, musky cologne, and his hands are strong and cold. Sitting up, he bends to pull his boots off, each hitting the floor with a *thud*. He opens his jean jacket, wrapping me up inside with him, warming me. He kisses my face, lips, and neck, then moans and pulls me to my feet. He throws David a film container. "Roll one up. We'll be back in a minute." He grins at David and leads me to the bathroom, where he swiftly pins me against the wall and passionately, possessively has his way with me.

I check the paper each morning for work. The trouble is the only places I am qualified for employment are burger joints, and at sixteen, I need a guardian's permission. "I am my own guardian now," I tell myself bravely. But I don't have any job skills.

David and Karen are patient but poor and very skimpy with any offerings of food or help. They assume that I will help out by taking care of Jamie when he's not in school, and I'm more than willing. John comes by every day and evening dropping off stashes of pot for them and leaving money to help with food. He often lies on the floor with me until early morning, when he quietly gets up, kisses me on the forehead, and goes home to his cottage. He is my savior. Gradually, I come to see that John has provided almost everything in David and Karen's house. From the mismatched furniture, to the food, carpet, shelving, pot, cigarettes, and, obviously, clothes, John is the one who supplies.

A couple weeks have passed, and I still have no luck finding work. John arrives early one afternoon, sits down next to me in the beanbag chair, and pulls out his corncob pipe. Taking a big toke, he passes it around the room.

"I gotta leave for about a week." He chokes back his hit.

"Where you going?" David tries to hold the smoke in as well.

"France."

"France!" My heart hits my stomach. "When?"

"Tomorrow. I just found out." He gives me a squeeze and kisses me on the cheek reassuringly.

David looks blank. "When is that apartment opening up in the back?"

"End of the month." John pinches my thigh.

"But I don't have a job yet." I worry I won't get the place, though John has already cleared it with Sharon.

"Hey, why don't you try signing on at one of the convalescent hospitals?" David offers, acting as if he has a brilliant idea. "They always need someone, and they will train. I'll bet if you tell them you're eighteen, they won't check. John can ask Sharon for some pointers. Can't you, John?"

John stays silent. He studies the pipe, his jaw clenched tight.

"Okay." I'm uncertain about what David is saying, and I'm not sure why John looks angry. I feel like I'm going to throw up. I excuse myself and get up to go to the bathroom for a moment of privacy. From behind the door, I hear the harsh words of an argument.

"You don't have to be so fucking rude, David. She's already scared." John's angry voice shoots out.

"What are you? Her father or her fuck?" David doesn't back off, his voice thick with sarcasm.

"Fuck you!"

Crash! Blam! The front door vibrates from the blow.

"What's happening?" I race back into the living room to see the screen door hanging from its hinges and David unfolding a pile of wadded money in the middle of the bed. He doesn't look up.

"Where is John?"

"He left." David continues coldly counting the money.

"Is he coming back?" I'm panicked. I don't want him to leave for France without saying good-bye.

"I don't know," he mumbles, not really paying attention to me. "God damn it!" he says, looking up at the broken door.

I don't like David.

༄

I sit on the front steps of David and Karen's cottage, leaning against the railing and staring blankly at the few pebbles at my feet.

"Ahhh! Ahhh! Ahhhhhhhh!" The wailing noises come from inside the house. Karen is having another orgasm; that's what John tells me it's called. It sounds unnatural, and it sounds throughout the entire courtyard. *You can probably hear it down the street.* The king-sized bed beckons them from the middle of the living room floor to come have wild sex. It is always a show, and if I don't walk outside in time, they have no problem starting in front of me.

"Whooooooh! Whooooh! Ahhhhhhнннн!"

Ugh, I think, *they're not done.* I lay my head in my lap and put my hands over my ears. My hair hangs limp and stringy around my face, and I am starving.

John's trip has been extended another two weeks, and there is no food in the house. I am still wearing one of the nurse's uniforms that John brought me before he left for France. One of Sharon's old ones, I guess. He stuck his head in David's door for a quick second the evening before his flight and called me outside to say good-bye. Pulling me around to the side of the cottage, he picked me up and hugged me tightly, kissing my entire face.

"I'll try and call you while I'm gone," he said softly. "I love you." He stroked my hair and cradled me.

"I love you too, John."

"Here. These are from Sharon." He handed me a bag of nurse's uniforms. "She said to tell you that if you need any help to let her know."

"Wow. Really?" I'm amazed and wary of her gift.

"I'll be back soon, baby. I'll miss you. Be good, okay? For me?" His words feed my aching heart. I don't want him to go. I'll be scared without him here, and I'll be sad like I was in Riverside.

"I will, John. I promise. Call me! Please!"

The next morning, I apply at the nearest place looking for a nurse's aide. Royal Oaks Convalescent Hospital on Verdugo Road is only two miles away. The place is a dump, a sad place where people go to die, so shorthanded that they hire me on the spot. When the application asks my age, I lie and write *18.* No one questions me. *I have a job!* my heart sings. *Now I can have my own place. John will be so proud of me.*

Still I have to wait for my first payday, and suffering another two weeks with David and Karen feels unbearable. They are mostly into themselves. I am invisible to them, and when I am noticed, I feel like I'm in the way. John calls, as he promised, and that is some relief. But David and Karen don't have him there to supply them with their normal *treats*, so they are grumpy and the kitchen cupboards are literally bare. It is obvious to me that they are doing John a favor by letting me stay there but can't wait for me to move out. Hanging out on the front steps keeps me sane.

"Can't stand that howling either, huh?" A wry voice shoots out from across the courtyard.

I look up. Sitting in the shadows, Sharon is smoking a cigarette on her porch steps. Spotting her I laugh, realizing she can also hear Karen's wailing.

"Are you hungry?"

"Who? Me?" Now I am embarrassed. *Can she tell?*

"Yes, you. Have you eaten lately?"

"This morning. Toast or something." I can't remember.

"Wait here." She gets up and goes into her house. A few minutes later, she returns carrying a steaming plate of meat loaf and potatoes.

"Here you go. Eat it while it's hot, and hurry before they see you." Her cigarette dangles from her lips as she hands me the mouthwatering meal.

"Thanks." I feel awkward and have a hard time looking at her.

"You wouldn't think an Italian could make meat loaf, but it's the best I ever tasted if I do say so myself." She is smug and proud of it.

"Mmmm. It's delicious." I shovel large spoonfuls of mashed potatoes into my mouth. "I found out I have malnutrition. The results of my physical came in today. They gave me some vitamins at work. Ha. No wonder I can't stay awake," I blurt out for no reason other than that I know she's a nurse. I inhale my meal.

"I could have told you that. Look at you . . . you're just skin and bones," she says matter-of-factly. "How's your new job?"

"Fine. I'll have the rent for you next Friday, if that's okay." I want her to know I am still being responsible even though things look bad at the moment. "Thanks for the uniforms."

"You're welcome."

We sit for a while on the steps of the opposite cottages, Sharon finishing one cigarette after another and I scraping the last bits of food from my plate. In the quiet, I listen for any signs of animosity. Any hint of anger or jealousy. It isn't there. I don't think so, anyway. Instead, I sense a paralyzing, acute cautiousness.

Breaking the spell, I walk over and hand her the empty plate. "Thanks. That was good."

"No problem." She butts out her smoke and disappears unceremoniously behind her screen door.

Moving day arrives, and I am ecstatic. I carry my few things in quickly and stand in the narrow hallway that is now my new living room. Karen packs a bag of canned goods to start me off, but she won't come down to see my new apartment. It is a simple bachelor pad: a ten-by-ten bedroom with crude burlap walls, an L-shaped hall on the far side for the kitchen, a small bathroom, and a living room. The apartment door is nestled between two garages. A bed, table, and sofa come with the place, and nothing is finer in my eyes. With a huge smile on my face, I pay Sharon, thanking her for renting it to me. John will be home soon too. Oh, how I miss him. These days at his brother's without him have been hard on me. But now, things are looking up.

Lying on my new bed, I stretch out luxuriously like a cat with a full tummy. I hear a knock at the door, my first guest. It is Sharon.

"Oh, hi!" I'm surprised to see her. She looks nervous standing outside the screen door, wringing her hands.

"Have you eaten?"

"No. I was going to heat up some beans that Karen gave me, but I'm too tired to get up."

"I thought so. I'll be right back."

In a few minutes, she returns with a casserole dish in her hands. "Here. This ought to fill you up for a couple meals." She hands me the hot dish. "See ya later." Again she turns and leaves abruptly.

"Oh, thanks . . ." My voice trails off before I can ask what kind of casserole it is. *That was a little strange.* It seemed as though she wanted to talk to me at first and then changed her mind.

As I open the lid to the savory smell, I am touched at Sharon's kindness and insight to my needs even if she doesn't want to get too close. I say, "Thank you," to her disappearing shadow loudly enough for her to hear me. On my newly acquired sofa, I devour the creamy meat-and-potato mixture till my stomach aches.

The days pass until it is time for John to come home. I can think of nothing else. My gut churns as I wait for time to move forward, dreading that another call might come to tell me he will be gone even longer. That call never comes.

He barges in—John does—flinging the door open wide in a grand entrance. Grinning from ear to ear, he takes long strides to greet me on the couch.

I'm still pretending to flip through a magazine that I quickly grabbed when I secretly saw him drive up. "Oh. Hi!" I try to fake surprise, but my heart pounds like a hard, steady bass guitar as he approaches.

Sweeping me off of my feet, he carries me into the bedroom and tosses me onto the bed. He positions his body above mine, spreads wild, passionate, longing kisses over my face, neck, breasts . . . makes a few swift, deft moves, and, in a flash, has me undressed . . . my panties torn on the floor. He makes love to me . . . fast and furious.

Tousled and spent, he caresses me till he catches his breath, letting our bodies slowly return to normal. He takes my hand and runs it through his hair, takes the other and places it between his legs. "You can touch me, you know."

Stiffly I comply. I feel embarrassed and juvenile. *I hope he doesn't think I'm not good at lovemaking.*

John remembers something all of a sudden, jumps up, grabs his pants up off the floor, and starts digging in the pockets. He elaborately searches, pretending to have lost something, then rummages through his other clothes until he finds several folded pieces of paper.

"Here, babe." He tosses the papers onto the bed. "These are for you. But wait . . . You can't open them now. You have to wait until I'm gone."

I notice how his hair has grown quite long and curly these three weeks away. A halo of dirty blond waves circles his head as he stands above me. "Okay."

Fumbling through his clothes one more time, John grabs something small and turns his back toward me.

I get excited. *He usually does this when he has a ring.*

He takes my hand. "Let me see your ring." He twists the small diamond-chip ring off my finger.

"Hey! What are you doing?"

"There." He turns toward me and proudly smiles.

I gasp. "Oh, it's beautiful!" On my hand is a new, thick platinum band lined with three large diamonds.

John puts the old ring on my other hand. "I wanted you to have a nice one, baby. I missed you so much."

"I missed you too, John." We rock in each other's arms till my body is stiff. I don't want to move 'cause I know this is what he likes right now, and I wait until I fall into a sweet, exhausted sleep. When I wake, he is gone.

On the bedside table is the stack of folded papers he gave me earlier, topped with a small metal replica of the Eiffel Tower. Carefully, I open them . . . one by one. It is poetry. Beautiful poetry, and the first one is titled "Early Morning Dawn." It is about the night we first made love and how I fill his heart. *Wow. He's a good poet.* I nearly start to cry. There are other poems too, about the days we spent together, verses about his innermost thoughts and how much he missed me while in France. Lying next to the poems is a hand-carved, heart-shaped wooden box with a note underneath that says, *I love you,* his elaborately scrawled signature, and *John C. Holmes* printed below. A giant heart circles the message. I gather the poetry gingerly and bring it back to my bed to carefully read again while admiring my new ring. *Wow. This is special,* I think happily. *This is real now—the real thing.* The wheel of time has turned. John is no longer courting me; I am his.

Tap, tap, tap. Tap, tap, tap.

Sleepily, I inch the front door open enough to see it is Sharon.

"Are you going to work today?"

"Yeah. What time is it?" The bright sky hurts my eyes, and I blink. Across the parking lot, the sun peeks over the trash bins by the Jehovah's Witness building.

"Ten after seven. I'm headed to the grocery store, and I remembered I didn't see you leave at your normal time this morning. Thought I'd come by to see if everything was all right."

"Oh my God! No, I overslept!"

"Okay. All right. Calm down. You just get dressed and I'll get my keys." She heads for her house.

Sharon is ready in a flash; she has the car warmed up and waiting. I scramble into a crumpled uniform from my laundry basket, pull my long hair back into a ponytail, and grab my sweater and bag. The door slams shut, and I race for the poised Malibu.

"Thanks." I'm panting as I struggle with my sweater.

"No sweat. I'll have you there in a sec."

"Thank you so much. How did you know I wasn't up?"

"I'm always up early. Five. Five thirty—sometimes earlier. When your light wasn't on, I wondered if you had slept in. Then, when you didn't leave at a quarter of, as usual, I waited a few minutes and then decided to come by. I figured your alarm hadn't gone off."

"I guess not." I shake my head. "Thanks."

"Really, it's no problem. I know it's a long walk from here to Royal Oaks, and I need to do my grocery shopping anyway. Don't worry about it."

I gaze out of my window and focus on adjusting my workday, my mind a million miles away. *Damn. I forgot my name tag.* Suddenly, I remember my new ring and start to hold it up but stop myself. *Will that disrespect her?* Instead I sneak an admiring look at the sparkling diamonds in the morning sunlight. A warm glow envelops me as I remember the homecoming the night before, and my whole being smiles. Sharon glances over. Quickly I conceal my hand in my lap and direct my attention to the passing landmarks outside. "Two miles," I mumble, thinking out loud.

"What?"

I have forgotten for a second where I am. "Two miles. It's exactly two miles from work to home. Karen gave me a ride to work one day and clocked it." I'm still not sure what Sharon thinks about me. She acts like a very nice lady, easygoing and all, but I don't want to give her any reason to ask me questions. John always said Sharon lives her way, in her world, and he in his. He is adamant about how to treat her. *No matter what,* we are to *always* respect Sharon and never insult her. And she never asks any questions.

John delivers all kinds of furniture for my apartment, odds and ends that he has stored away. Some antique pieces need refinishing, so he sets up the shop in his garage and strips and revarnishes them, teaching me the fine art of sanding and applying linseed oil along the way. Back and forth from his place to mine he brings bundles of towels, sheets, and comforters—items Sharon is handing down from her carefully stocked shelves. Boxes of food come next, with mixes of silverware, plates, and bowls. I am speechless. The way the boxes never end, it is like a good Christmas morning. John sneaks a kiss and a squeeze every chance he gets, even throwing me onto the bed a couple times. But when he thinks Sharon might be turning the corner, he heads right back to the garage to seek out something new to bring over. "We can't let her see us too close," he tells me when I try to stop him from leaving. "It would be rude."

John L and Buttons run happily back and forth alongside John and Sharon, stopping occasionally to sniff the edge of my couch and inspect every piece of laundry on the floor. Finally, it is evening and time to call it quits.

"How about a pizza?" Sharon offers as she enters the lacquer-smelling garage, jingling her big ring of keys. She's wearing a pink and gray paisley print muumuu.

"Sure." John's voice is muffled behind the carpenter's mask. He is sanding a drawer at his workbench, teaching me the right way to work the wood grain. The muscles in his arm bulge with each stroke of the sandpaper as he holds the drawer down with his body weight.

"Cheese, okay? I got a coupon." With cigarette in hand, she happily waves the Shakey's Pizza Parlor coupon like a flag.

"Great!" I watch her step away, dark blue fuzzy slippers on her tiny feet, carrying her broad-strapped, multipocketed handbag firmly under her arm. I think she looks much older than John, especially with her long, gray and black hair.

She's kind of like a grandma—very old-fashioned and wise.

"Dawn," Sharon calls from her car. "Can you get the dogs, please?"

"Okay." I run over to pick up a wandering Buttons and to herd John L toward the garage. I know it's a big deal for her to trust anyone with her *babies,* and oddly I am glad to be of help.

John is gaping at me in disbelief. It seems Sharon approves of me. Why, I don't know, but it makes me happy. *John cares a lot for Sharon, and she likes me.* John shakes the daze off and returns to his sanding. For a second, I wonder if that's a smile underneath the mask.

⚜

"Come on. You ready?" John's voice is hushed as he peeks into my bedroom. In his arms he carries a wicker laundry basket filled with old towels and a flashlight.

"Coming." I tie the laces of my shoe, jump off the bed, throw my multicolored knit poncho over my turtleneck, and follow him outside. "Where're we going?" I whisper. I'm used to John showing up at all hours wanting me to go on trips with him into Hollywood to pick up his messages or downtown Glendale to run an errand, but tonight I'm tired. It's been a hard day with the patients at work.

"Shhh. Barstow. You can sleep in the van. You'll see."

Heading off into the night, we drive for hours. John has layered several blankets and pillows on the floor in the back, and the soft humming engine lulls me to sleep. The radio is playing an old Cat Stevens tune as I'm bounced awake in the back of the van.

We must be on some kind of a dirt road. I grab the seat ahead of me and make my way up to the front with John.

"What's this place? It looks creepy—out in the middle of nowhere and all."

"You have to help me pick out a present for someone," he says, smiling as he pulls the van into park.

"A present? For who?"

John looks at me as if I should have guessed. "Sharon. It's her birthday tomorrow."

"It is? I didn't know. What are we picking out?"

"You'll see." We walk up the driveway to the door of a lonely ranch-style house at the outskirts of Barstow. John knocks.

The desert night is chilly in early June, and I shiver as we wait for someone to answer. Looking up, I admire how vastly the bright stars blanket the dark midnight blue sky. *Where is the moon?* I wonder.

"Coming!" a voice calls from inside. A rotund, bald-headed man appears. "Yeah?"

"Hi. I'm John. We're here for the Boston bull puppies." John uses his deep, businesslike voice.

"Hi. Right. You called. Right this way." We follow him to a small, dark utility room, where he flips on the light switch. "Here they are. Take your pick."

A dozen black-and-white, squished-nosed faces poke their heads up out of shreds of newspaper, whining. "I think they're hungry." John bends down to pet the circling crowd. "Which one do you like?" he asks me, laughing as they vie for his attention.

I bend to take a closer look. "I don't know. Let me see." I study the furry, bug-eyed group. "Oh, look at that one!" I squeal. "Look at his eyes and head. They're huge!" Off in the corner is the tiniest puppy of the bunch struggling to get out of a fold in an old, torn blanket. The head is so much larger than the body, it's comical. The puppy is always falling over on its face. I stretch out my hand and gently pick it up. "A girl. Look at those eyes!"

John tenderly takes her and holds her up to the light. He winks and clicks his gums from the side of his face, bringing her down for a closer look. Squirming desperately, the tiny dog obviously wants to sniff his face. Determined, she lands a paw on either side of his nose, clamps down, and licks. "Ha!" John laughs out loud, amused at her sweetness. "Sold!" Tenderly he puts her inside his jacket and pays the breeder in cash.

On the drive home I hold her protectively in my lap, keeping her warmly nestled in my poncho. "She's gonna love her, John," I say softly to them both. John reaches over and holds my hand. Everything feels right again.

When we arrive home, John is excited. He puts the sleeping bundle into the laundry basket, gives me a quick kiss at my door, and heads for his cottage. I stay put in the shadows of the garages and watch him place the basket at the front door, ring the bell, and run into the bushes. He waves in my direction for me to hide as well.

"Yes?" Sharon's voice inquires from behind the screen. There is a moment of hesitation. "Oooooooh! Where did you come from? Awww, you poor little thing. Did someone leave you out here in the cold all by yourself? Let's bring you in and get you warmed up." She reaches down and, without looking around, brings the basket in.

John and I smile, entirely pleased with ourselves. He jumps back over to me and hugs me close, giving me a long, loving kiss. "Good night, baby," he says sweetly, brushing his hand across my cheek.

"Good night." Loneliness falls upon me as I watch his silhouette take long strides toward the house . . . Sharon . . . and her new gift. I am sad. I want to be a part of the birthday present surprise, more than just a spectator.

Work is exhausting and the two-mile walk up the hill and back makes it even more so. John gives me rides when he is home, and Sharon offers occasionally when he isn't. John is gone about two to three evenings a week. I know it is for his movie work, and it makes me sick inside. I hate that he goes to be with other women, but I don't say anything. I'm painfully aware that I'm younger and less experienced than the women on the film marquees, and I get scared that I can't compare with them.

But John can tell it makes me sad. "It's just a job, baby. It doesn't mean anything. I love you. I'll be home early."

His work schedule does, however, gradually coincide with mine. He tells me it's so we can spend more time together, and I believe him. On days when I pull a double shift, he comes to Royal Oaks to pick me up. "It's too late at night to walk home," he insists and shows up often wearing kneepads and smelling of varnish from working in the garage.

Days off are ours, and we do everything fun. John loves time at the beach, hiking the mountains of Malibu, working on refinishing projects, or collecting donations and selling bumper stickers for Greenpeace (*save the whales* and *save the seals*). But as usual, John always goes home for dinner. John arranges special surprise trips with me and Sharon to Disneyland and Knott's Berry Farm. He and I love the roller coasters and stand in line to ride the big ones over and over as Sharon shops for boysenberry jam.

Slowly my apartment takes shape. Sharon's gifts of curtains, clocks, color-coordinated towels, and patterned dishes are left at my door at intervals, surprising and delighting me. "Everyone has to have matching decorations too," she laughs while taking me on a trip to Kmart to choose a kitchen motif. I'm a giddy kid and can't stop laughing when I pick a yellow and brown mushroom theme for fun.

Sharon has taken a real interest in me, and I'm not always sure John likes it. I get the feeling that he is jealous sometimes, but of what, I don't know.

I also don't know if Sharon's interest is completely her idea. "I don't like you being alone when I'm gone," John tells me. "Go see Sharon if you're scared."

But it is Sharon who starts inviting me over for dinner, instead of bringing meals to my door. Unsure at first, I feel strange at being her houseguest, and sit timidly on the couch. John L, Buttons, and the newest member of the family, Pokie—Sharon's birthday present, Pocahontas' Pixie Pride—maul me with sniffs and snorts.

"Don't worry about them. They just want to see if you have anything good to eat." Sharon loves to cook and treats me like family. She sets up TV trays for each of us with her usual delicious home-cooked meals. The days roll by, and life feels good in comparison to the uncertainty of my past. I am glad, although at times I feel old for my years.

On a breezy autumn day, I walk home from work exhausted. It is the end of a long, five-day workweek, and my legs and back ache from lifting patients. My body hurts with each step, and all I can think about is falling onto my couch and sleeping. *Almost there.* I turn onto Acacia and drag myself through the courtyard. John's van is parked in his spot by the tree. *He's home early today.* I was not expecting him that evening. But my body needs to lie down, and I plug along down to the garages. John pops out from behind his van. "Here she is," he shouts loud enough for the neighbors to hear.

"What's going on?"

"Ta-da!" Sharon sings. Around the corner of the van she wheels a brand-new bright red ten-speed bicycle.

I blink, scared for a moment. Then, dumbfounded, I look

back and forth at the bike, then John, then Sharon.

"Surprise! It's for you, silly. Here! Take it!" Sharon rolls her eyes, exasperated, realizing I don't get it.

"It is? Really? Oh, thank you." I look at John for assurance. Smiling at me, he gives a slight nod of approval that says it's okay. "Thank you."

"Baby. Baby." John strokes my hair from my brow. "Wake up."

"John. What are you doing? What time is it?"

"Watching you sleep," he whispers. "You're so beautiful when you sleep."

"Ummmmm." I roll over and snuggle his waist.

"Hey. Wake up. You want to go to Vegas?"

"Humm? Vegas? What time did you get home last night? I waited up as long as I could. Sorry I fell asleep."

"It's okay, baby. I just got home. Had to work late. Listen, I got a Harley outside. Let's go to Vegas for the weekend. You're off work, right?"

"Yeah. Harley! Motorcycle? You're kidding."

He leads me out to the parking lot to show me a 1976 Hardtail. "It's a beauty, isn't it? Get your things together. Let's go. I'll let Sharon know we're going." John rushes off singing loudly with excitement.

The screen door bangs as Sharon comes out a few minutes later to look at John's newly acquired machine. "You gotta be kidding. You're gonna ride *that* . . . through the desert . . . in this heat? Well, it's your funeral!" The three of us are lighthearted for a moment; then Sharon shakes her head and walks away.

John and I smile at each other. "Woo-hoo!" we yip. "Let's go to Vegas!"

From her front porch, Sharon watches us mount the shiny chrome machine. She looks serious. "You better take some water with you," she yells.

"We did," I call back, waving good-bye.

David and Karen stand near the driveway watching us leave as well. "Meet us at the Aladdin," John calls out over the popping engine. David nods and Karen smiles and gives us a thumbs-up.

The road is long and hot. Our smiles wear off about an hour after we leave; our muscles ache, and the heat is atrocious beating down on our black-helmeted heads. It isn't long before I get weak and feel my fingers lose their grip from John's leather sides. He feels my legs buckle and my body go limp. Placing his hand firmly on my leg, he squeezes and pulls off at the nearest stop, a desert coffeehouse with a shaded space to park, and helps me off the bike. Groping desperately at the straps of my helmet, I need air. My fingers numb, I can't find the clasp and I begin to collapse. Instantly John scoops me in his arms, gently resting my body on his knee. Swiftly, he unleashes my helmet and douses the top of my head with water.

"It's okay, baby. I got you. Just breathe; just breathe." He caresses the water through my hair and dumps the rest over his head.

The sky is spinning, and the heat is suffocating. "John," I pant, "I'm gonna get sick. I need to turn . . ."

"Here, here you go, baby." He helps me roll over and places my head between my knees. "It's okay. It's okay."

Against an old oak, I lose what little I have in my stomach.

John wets a bandana and wipes down my brow. "Better?" he asks after a few minutes.

"Yeah. I'm better. John?" I've been wondering if we should turn back. "What am I gonna do in Vegas? I'm only sixteen. I'll get busted if I'm in the casino."

"Ha! You don't have to worry about that. You're with me, babe. Now come on. If you're feeling better, let's get out of here."

We drive on through the arid summer heat. The blazing lights of Las Vegas greet our tired bones, rejuvenating us. On the Vegas strip, we approach the wondrous, blinking Arabian lamp and Taj Mahal–style castle, the Aladdin hotel. Passersby smile and wave at us, the Harley-riding couple bellowing down the strip, and I sit a little taller and prouder in my seat.

"You okay?" John dismounts in the parking lot.

Delicately, I step off and grin. "No . . . I can't feel my ass."

"Ha. Me either." Stiffly we walk hand in hand toward the hotel entrance. "Looks like we've been rode hard and put away wet," he says, making fun of our bowlegged cowboy shuffle.

❧

"Hold still. I can't get it straight." He playfully puts the last of the blue eye shadow on my lids.

"I'm trying. John, you sure this is gonna work? I'm nervous. I don't want to get caught." I squirm at the application of makeup. I never wear the stuff—John likes it better that way—and I feel stupid in the hideous mask of colors.

"Just stick close to me, baby. Nobody's gonna say anything." He takes one last look at his work. "Ha-ha! You look great! Mmm, mmm, mmm!" Kissing the top of my head, he hands me a pair of wooden platform shoes and a low-cut paisley popcorn blouse that he has borrowed from Karen. "Here. Put these on."

David and Karen have driven John's Chevy van to the Aladdin and met up with us soon after we arrived. The plan is to spend the night gambling and see the sights, then load the Harley in the back of the van and drive home the next day. Since John wants to

189

keep me by his side, he will have to get me into the casinos where he likes to gamble. John is good at gambling. Poker is his game, but he'd play anything. David likes to tell the story of how John was discovered in the bathroom of a poker parlor in Gardena. His point for telling it is lost on me. I don't care about that stuff.

Walking down the luxurious red carpet to the lobby of the hotel, I clutch John's arm for balance. The platform shoes are large and awkward on my feet, and I've caught my balance on the wall twice already; I don't want to fall.

John guides me through the casino and to the poker tables, beaming with pride at the stares of the crowd. He finds an open table, pulls up a couple chairs, and sits down next to me.

"Deal me in, boys," John commands lightheartedly.

"And your partner?" the dealer asks, lifting a brow.

"No. Uh, this little lady here—she's my good luck charm," John tells the group half grinning; he pulls my chair in close to his and slides his arm around me in a showy manner. Large men in black cowboy hats, a man who looks like he has come off a yacht, and old fat men leer at me. I sit very still. Determined not to engage anyone's eye contact, I stare at the table. The players nod in sly understanding, and the dealer distributes the cards.

"We won. We won." John rubs it in every chance he gets on the drive home.

"Shut up." David tries to sound like he is kidding, but he's mad. David and Karen have lost the money they came with, and Karen is pouting in the back of the van. Lost as well is the money John doled out every time David came by the poker table to see how we were doing.

"With my good luck charm, I couldn't lose, huh, baby?" John

winks at me and smiles.

Modestly I look his way and blush. *John is lucky, very lucky,* I think, remembering his dramatic winning bets on the roulette wheel.

"I play aught—double aught on this one," he told me, "and always, always, I play lucky number thirteen." Thirteen won big for him. Every game he played, he won. We go home with what John came with and over a thousand dollars extra. John pulls the roll of cash from his pocket and peels off a few hundreds from the top. "Here, baby. Hang on to these."

David stares for a minute and then sticks his hand out.

"What?" John snaps, annoyed at the gesture.

"Hey. Don't I rank?" He sounds insulted.

John clenches his teeth and drives faster. His good mood quickly fades, and the air remains tense the rest of the long way home. When John gets mad he holds a grudge, and who knows how long it will take him to get over it? Could be days. He resents that his mom pressures him to take care of his younger, epileptic brother. David is in his late twenties, old enough to take care of himself, but he still expects John to share almost everything, and that infuriates John.

Pulling into our parking space, John yanks the van into park, reaches into his pocket, and throws a couple one hundred-dollar bills at David. "Here," he says angrily, then stomps away, leaving the motorcycle in the van.

I unload my things and head to my apartment. "Damn it, David. Now he's mad!"

"Fuck you." David slams the van door.

⁂

"They found the body of a young girl strangled to death in La Cresenta," Sharon tells me, her brow deeply furrowed over her thick-rimmed glasses. "Can you come over?" It is Halloween in 1977, and I am sixteen years old. La Cresenta, just north of Glendale, is the town where Sharon works.

Sharon has come by to invite me for dinner and to see if I am okay. We aren't sure if John will be home tonight, but she doesn't want to be alone and I definitely don't want to be in a solitary garage apartment by myself either. Daylight savings time has ended, and the clocks are turned back, bringing dark evenings along with the dark news of the murder.

We pick at our dinner, our nerves on edge, startled by any loud unfamiliar noises. Locking and double locking doors and windows, we venture outside together with flashlights and large, weaponlike key chains to let the dogs go pee. Without much conversation, we watch the evening movies, then listen again to the horrific headlines on the news. "The body of a sixteen-year-old girl . . . She is described as being about five feet, small, with long, reddish-brown hair." We gape at each other, our jaws frozen wide open. *That sounds like me.* My stomach is turning. I feel as if a speeding truck has rushed past me, barely missing me, and I fall back onto the couch. It is late, and I need to go home but can't manage to budge. Sharon doesn't call it a night as usual. Instead, we decide it is safer being together. Soon, I can stay awake no longer and wearily fall asleep, my head draped uncomfortably over the armrest of the brown floral sofa.

When I next open my eyes, John is carefully setting down his briefcase at the table. Tiptoeing in his socks, he comes over to me on the couch.

"Where's Sharon?" I ask, remembering I am not home.

"Shhh. She's in bed. Go back to sleep, baby." Kissing me on the cheek, he pulls the sofa blanket over me and turns out the light. "Good night," he says, quietly walking toward his bedroom and leaving the door open.

"Good night," I call back. Instantly I miss his embrace. The house is large and full of shadows in the dark, yet strangely I feel secure in these new surroundings. I stretch out on the couch, and comforted that I'm not alone, I fall into a restful sleep.

❧

"Dawn! Your mom's on the phone," David hollers through the court-yard into my apartment. It startles me; I spook easily these days.

"Coming," I yell back, taking a minute to calm down and grab my keys. Mom calls on Sundays whenever she can, and the only number she has since Dad left is David and Karen's. It doesn't cost them anything, so they don't mind.

"Hi, Mom. How are you?"

"Yah. Goot. How are you?"

"I'm fine. No, they haven't found the strangler yet. Yeah, I'm still working, and I'm helping with work at the cottages when they need something. Oh, John and Sharon let me do filing for the owner and collect tenants' rents now in exchange for a lower rent." Mom is asking all the right questions trying to make sure I am all right. "Yes, the emancipation papers are finalized. Yeah, things are good. Yes, he is still my boyfriend. She doesn't care. They just live together." I answer her casually, especially questions about John and Sharon, until her list of inquiries dies down and it is my turn to find out about everyone. "How's Terry? Wayne? Good. Oregon? When are you moving there? Well, let me know, okay? Thank you for the bath mats and towels. Yeah, they match my bathroom. I love you and miss you, Mom. Talk to you next week. Good-bye."

Our conversations are only surface. My mother does her best to be a part of my life even from so far away but her world, I know, is hard. I can't bring myself to talk about my love for John. Mom is always suspicious at best, and I'm not sure what Terry has told her. John is right: It is best not to tell her much. And Sharon? Well, Sharon's a whole other story in itself. Sharon is turning out to be a friend. A good friend. How am I supposed to explain that? I can't even explain it to myself.

CHAPTER NINE
It Takes Three to Tango

The rain falls steadily in the winter of 1978. Hillsides crumble and old graveyards wash down onto neighborhood streets. Rumors of contracting typhoid run rampant, and people stop drinking the water.

"The Hillside Strangler struck again," Sharon reports to me on a gray morning in February. "It's another girl who lived on Garfield. She was on her way to work at Glendale Community College. Somebody took her in broad daylight!"

"Oh my God!" That particular address on Garfield Avenue is only two blocks away from us on Acacia, and Glendale Community College is just past Royal Oaks on the same road. "I go that way to work every day!" I am scared. After the first killing last Halloween, seven more bodies have been discovered on the local hillsides, five of them during Thanksgiving week alone.

All of Glendale is up in arms, frightened at every turn. Nobody walks alone. John is tense and furious. Every time the dogs bark, he is outside with his .357 in hand, walking the courtyard and ready to take aim at a moment's notice.

The sense of fear triggers my Carol City survival demeanor like an old, familiar coat. "Touch me and you die," my body language says to anyone I pass on the street, but inside I am a frightened seventeen-year-old who really knows no one in this place. I imagine that if anything happens to me, no one will know. No one except John and Sharon.

We spent that strained Thanksgiving together. Sharon baked a turkey, teaching me the proper way to sew the stuffing in and describing how John liked his gravy with the giblets. "Hillbilly upbringing," she said snobbishly, flipping her head. She was referring to his Ohio roots.

"I heard that," John called from the other room, teasing.

David and Karen were invited, although Sharon confided in me that she hoped they wouldn't come. "Maybe one of them will be sick, as usual." She turned her head in disgust.

John stayed quiet but had a smirk on his face.

"The only reason you even ask them over is because your mother makes you feel guilty if you don't watch out for *poor* David," she told John, trying to embarrass him into standing up for his true feelings and retracting the invitation.

Having been through this same argument with Sharon before, John didn't answer. He stomped off to his back office and dug out some clay for sculpting, ignoring Sharon's ploy.

Later, like clockwork, David called. Karen was sick, and they couldn't make it. "I'm *so* sorry," Sharon lied in her best nurse's voice, then winked at me with relief.

The Hillside Strangler didn't know it, but the widespread fear he had caused naturally brought us closer than we normally would have been. Besides, I think we liked each other's company.

❧

Christmas was the three of us again. Sharon loved to decorate, and all things Christmas came out in droves. She invited me to help with the festivities, and we mulled cider and put ornaments on the tree. John came home in the evenings after being gone for short afternoons and helped with putting up décor. We had fun hiding a few gifts for each other and loved finding just the right one for each of us.

The holiday spirit was broken suddenly when another young body was found nearby about a week before Christmas. The light-heartedness disappeared and, sobered up, we again focused on staying safe.

Four days after Christmas was my seventeenth birthday. John brought over a dozen beautiful sterling silver roses, a gold necklace, and a .22 automatic handgun.

"You remember how to use this, right?" he asked me as he filled the small clip.

"I remember."

"Keep it with you at all times," he stressed harshly. Satisfied that I took him and the gun seriously, he softened and kissed me warmly. "Happy birthday, baby. Now come on. Sharon and I want to take you to dinner."

At Clancy's, my favorite restaurant on Brand Boulevard, Sharon had a small stash of gifts wrapped and waiting for me. I tore into them wholeheartedly, feeling comfortable now with the exchange of presents between us. There were whimsical porcelain figures of my favorite style of fairies, feathers, and penguins. We stuffed ourselves with egg-dipped abalone, and a flaming cupcake topped it all off. Back home, we said good night and headed our separate ways.

At home I sat alone on my sofa, frightened, holding the .22 and reflecting on the small celebration. I didn't want to be by myself on my birthday, but I had nowhere else to go. Nowhere felt safe anymore. Twenty minutes later, a light tapping at my door scared me out of my thoughts. Heart pounding and gun in hand, I tentatively pulled back the curtain of the door's window.

"Hey, watch where you point that thing!" John joked, quickly slipping inside.

"John! I'm so glad it's you."

"I know, baby. I know. I miss you too. Happy birthday." He picked me up and carried me into the bedroom, making love to me until we fell asleep in each other's arms. In the morning, he was gone. I was seventeen now. Only one more year till I would be eighteen. Then maybe we wouldn't have to hide anymore.

⋅⋅⋅

February, the news of the killing of a local girl causes a new level of paranoia. The air is thick with foreboding; people stare suspiciously at each other in the neighborhood. Soon after hearing the news of the death of the girl who lived on Garfield, I ride my bike past her street on my usual route to work. Something pulls me in. A morbid curiosity draws me to take a closer look at the place she last called home. The children playing on the street eye me cautiously as I pedal slowly by the house. In just two seconds, I have seen enough. The strong sinister aura of this place is overwhelming; I pedal double time and race to work.

Directly after I get back home, I knock on Sharon's door and barge in as soon as she turns the key. "I passed the murdered girl's apartment on Garfield today." I pant, breathless.

"You what? Are you crazy? The cops think there's two of them and they are dragging girls out of their cars in the middle of the day! And don't forget about the Trash Bag Murderer they caught last summer. There could be copycat killers around. You're too smart for that, Dawn. Be careful!"

"I know, but for some reason I wanted to see what her place looked like. It was real creepy, Sharon. There was a cop car outside. They may have been searching her apartment."

"Those dirty rotten bastards!" Sharon's voice rises. I know she's thinking about the brutal murderers. "Let them try to take me! I'll pop their eyes out of their heads before they know what hit them!"

"Yeah, me too!" I puff myself up. Then I think about it for a minute. "I'm scared back in my apartment, Sharon," I confide. "I dread going home to my place with the Hillside Stranglers out there. I've got two windows facing the alley and another butted up against a courtyard off of Chevy Chase. I hear noises all night!"

"Well, you can get a pit bull." I can't really tell if she is joking.

Hey . . . I think for a second. "No. I don't really like pit bulls, and my place is too small for one anyway."

"Well, it doesn't *have* to be a pit bull," she says, a bit of sarcasm in her voice apparently defending the breed. "You can always get one of those little yappy things you *love* so much like the one at the house on the corner."

"Ewww! Chihuahuas? I hate those dogs. They aren't even dogs. They're pests, making all that noise. It's so annoying. Ahhh, *any* dog is better than that!" I say dramatically.

Sharon laughs hysterically at my reaction, and it is contagious. Soon we are both giggling and making bad jokes about the tiny dogs. Our moods lift. "Let's play some rummy." She heads for the kitchen drawer. "But let's eat first."

"Sounds good to me." I jump up and open the refrigerator door. "What shall we whip up tonight?" I make myself at home.

❧

John brings the newspaper over on Saturday morning. The weather forecast is still dreary and rainy. I don't mind today, though; I finally have a weekend off after working split shifts for the past three weeks, and that means John and I will be able to spend time together.

"Here. Circle the garage sales you want to check out today." He hands me the *Los Angeles Times*. "And be ready in ten minutes." He leaves without waiting for an answer.

Oh, okay, I think. *That's a little strange, but garage sales are fine with me.*

A few minutes later, I walk over to meet him at the van. He and Sharon are waiting; the engine is running, exhaust billowing.

"Hi. Oh, good, you're coming too?" I try to hide my surprise and climb into the van.

"Seems like a good enough day to do garage sales," she says cheerfully.

John drives farther than he has to any other garage sale before. *This is a little out of the ordinary,* I think. *Maybe they have somewhere else to go first.* Deep in the Valley, we pull up to a Spanish-style house in a quiet residential neighborhood.

"Come on," John says to Sharon, and they climb out as if they know someone here.

"And you . . . wait here a minute," he instructs in his best fatherly voice. He and Sharon walk to the door and knock as I sit staving off an uneasy feeling.

This is too weird. What are they up to?

Disappearing inside, they leave the front door ajar, and a moment later John steps outside and waves me in.

As I approach, the door swings open. "Come in. Right here. Take a look." A gray-haired woman standing near the entrance points her cane.

In the middle of the floor, a child's safety railing forms a circle lined with soft blankets, water bowls, and the teeniest of elf-eared faces. Four tiny puppies hop up and down on their twiggy back legs, beckoning for someone to pick them up.

I stand in the middle of the room confused. "What are they?"

I ask, not recognizing the ratlike creatures.

"Don't you recognize a Chihuahua when you see one?" Sharon teases. She and John have their eyes glued on me. I feel as if I am on display.

"*Those* are Chihuahuas? They're so cute!" I bend to pet their wrinkled foreheads. "Are you getting one of these?"

"Pick one." John beams.

"Huh?" I reply blankly.

"Well, pick one!"

Speechless and thrilled, I stoop down to take a better look. A lone pale brown and pink face stretches up above the others. It has more wrinkles than body, a tiny pulled-back mouth, and desperation in its eyes that grips my attention like an iron clasp. "This one," I immediately decide, attracted to the struggling puppy.

"Lucky choice. That's the only boy in the bunch."

"Sold!" John eagerly reaches into his pocket for the cash, reminding me of the night we picked out Pokie for Sharon.

❦

The tiny creature nestles under my poncho shakily, sticking his wrinkled head out of the V shape of my collar as if to see where we are going. The sky grows darker and heavier as the day progresses, escalating into a full-blown thunderstorm by the time we get home. In John and Sharon's kitchen we set up a basket with towels and John's old T-shirts.

"So. Have you decided what you're gonna name him?" Sharon asks. "Make it a good one. He's your protector now."

A loud clap of thunder rolls through the darkened sky, shaking the china in the cabinet.

"Thor!" I shout. "I'm gonna name him Thor. God of Thunder."

"Good one!" Sharon agrees enthusiastically. John cuts the

ends out of one of his old socks to make a sweater for my little guy and beams proudly at both of us.

My mind soon quiets. A dog. He's really mine.

Thor's Aquarian Prince is his AKC registered name. He is the sweetest little chocolate-brown cutie pie with a pink nose and white patches on his toes and chest. Immediately, Chihuahuas are the best breed of dog in the world to me, causing bouts of heated banter among Sharon, John, and me. Thor is never yappy and never annoying. My shadow, he goes everywhere with me, except to work. He is my own little life to nurture and care for, returning only playful, loving companionship. John takes a fast shine to him too, playing tug-of-war and warming him tenderly when he shivers . . . and Thor both adores and fears John.

Little Thor brings me so much joy. His puppy kisses and playful snuggles are warm and soft, and he loves John L, Buttons, and Pokie. John, Sharon, and I get a great kick out of watching the older dogs train little Thor in alpha etiquette.

Sharon, in her constant housecoats, relishes digging out her doggie meat loaf recipes laced with gobs of vitamins or boiled beef kidneys, livers, or hearts. I try to cook all of it at my apartment, and I do really well, but the kidneys smell horrible and I can't stomach their greasy steam. I don't tell Sharon, though. I'm afraid she'll think I'm a wimp, and I want her to be proud of me.

Sharon, I can tell, loves to teach me things that she has mastered. "I bet you can't guess why John doesn't mess with me. My IQ is 160!"

"Is that high?" My ignorance shows. I figure she wants me to know she is smarter than John.

"Let's put it this way. My high school career counselor wanted me to go into nuclear physics."

"Wow. What did you say?"

"I told him no way. I like helping people too much. I'm going into nursing. And that was that."

I want my IQ to be 160 too. I'm ashamed of myself because I dropped out of high school. Still, we begin to spend most of our time together as a threesome now. Whatever Sharon shows me I learn with earnest: how to cook John's favorite meals, the way he likes his clothes folded, and how to set up his chair at the television with cigarettes and wooden matches set next to an ice-cold glass of milk when he gets home.

John gets used to me taking care of his personal things under Sharon's supervision. His days and evenings are mostly spent at home, being the man of the house, guarding the courtyard, and maintaining the cottages. When he is at work, he is only gone for a few hours in the afternoon, returning around five o'clock as if he has a normal job. I am expected for dinner in the evenings, having helped Sharon to plan them around John's tastes and to grocery shop for them on weekend mornings. After dinner we watch a movie, settle into a good game of Scrabble or penny rummy, listen to Beethoven or Ravel, and teasingly accuse the winner of cheating as he or she rakes in the coins.

John has a temper, I notice, and sometimes gets too angry when he loses a game. In a childish fit, he'll flip the entire game table over, scattering the pieces and pennies to the corners of the room.

"John! Quit it!" Sharon scolds him.

"What, Sharon?" he hollers back.

Sharon doesn't answer but calmly stubs out her cigarette.

Knowing the night is ruined, I help Sharon pick up the pieces—the game tiles, cards, or pennies. After the mess is cleaned up, Sharon wordlessly storms off to bed. John L and Buttons dutifully follow.

Embarrassed and uncomfortable by his outburst, I sit very still in a corner of the couch. Pokie and Thor shiver, frightened, on my lap as if there's a thunderstorm. Arms crossed, John glares at the television, sulking, and I try not to look at him until a short while later when he calms down.

But these moments are rare compared to the good times, and I easily dismiss John's behavior as an occasional bad mood. We all have one sometimes, right?

John and Sharon love old movies and test each other's memory of who won which Academy Award for what picture in what year. Sharon wins a lot, and sometimes it worries me that John will get mad about losing the game. He also likes to keep us on our toes and feign anger, stomp out of the room, and laugh from behind the walls.

I declare *Wizards, Fantasia,* and *Harold and Maude* my all-time favorite movies in the world.

"You add *Rooster Cogburn* and *The Good, the Bad and the Ugly* and we agree," John tells me. Then, stepping into his John Wayne character, he pulls two invisible six-shooters from his hips, shuffles his feet, and drawls his favorite cowboy saying from the side of his mouth: "Live fast, die young, and leave a good-looking corpse!"

If it isn't games or movies, we each work on individual projects at the house. Sharon demonstrates the basics of embroidery to me, and I love to sit on the couch for hours practicing with the colorful thread. On his favorite patch jacket, John lets me embroider a butterfly and a bluebird on each of the sleeves. Relaxed in her recliner, Sharon clips recipes from ladies' magazines while John sculpts skillfully with clay in front of the television. He fashions beautiful busts of old, wrinkled, weathered fishermen so lifelike I swear they wink at me.

Poor Pokie is forced to sit still on the couch for hours while he sculpts the wrinkles and delicate details of her brow and cheeks. Thor wants to play with her, but John pulls her back and commands her to stay. But the end result is stunning: a magnificent likeness of a Boston bull terrier's head and neck. We encase the bust in glass to showcase it proudly on the mantel.

Hitting the best restaurants in Glendale and the latest releases at the theaters gets to be a game: *Star Wars* at Grauman's, *Alien* at the Cinerama Dome, and *Close Encounters of the Third Kind* at the Alex on Brand.

Our weekends include trips to Saugus Swap Meets, where John and I seek out old jewelry for parts to create our own designs. Often, we get lucky and score old pieces with undetected authentic diamonds for a steal. We smelt down some of the gold we collect at a local jewelry maker's in Glendale on Brand to make a beautiful belt buckle with an image of a mother whale and her nursing baby swimming beneath her. John chooses it as a symbol of our support for Greenpeace and our respect for nature.

Our pride and joy is the completion of a huge gold dragonfly ring that stretches from knuckle to knuckle on John's ring finger. Encrusted with twenty-two diamonds of all shapes and sizes, ones we collected from various sales, the ring is beautiful, extraordinary, and quite a sight. Since we've met, John has never worn a wedding ring, but he loves wearing his dragonfly in its place. *It matches his personality,* I think, and for moments when he's flamboyant and wants to make an impression, it works. No matter what, John always makes an impression.

❧

As strange as it appears, I look up to Sharon. I'm growing up inside, maturing. I can sense an awareness blossoming in me. My desire for more knowledge increases and, like a thirsty sponge, I absorb whatever bits and pieces Sharon hands down. She savors answering my never-ending questions and in great detail describes intricate nursing techniques. Medicine is Sharon's forte. Bones, blood, muscle, skin—there is nothing she doesn't know about the body or, to me, about anything really. I become a certified nursing assistant through a program at Royal Oaks because I want to be like her, and Sharon's tutoring helps me pass with straight A's.

"David and Karen don't understand why we are friends," I tell her. "You're a mentor to me. Don't they understand?"

"They're jealous. David doesn't have a backbone; he's worthless. He used to be in my good graces. Not anymore. Not after John and I supported him through high school and he returned the favor by bringing pot into my house. He's a juvenile delinquent who refuses to grow up." Her resentment for David is set in stone.

Wow, I think. *When Sharon doesn't like you, she really doesn't like you.* I'm scared of her too. I don't want to be, and I try not to think about it too much. I already know that if she did get mad at me, I would be very hurt, and I can't stand the thought. *I'm glad she likes me.*

Every Thursday evening, Sharon is on call for her employer, Dr. Nuttycomb. I love to listen attentively to the calm reasoning and detailed remedies she gives worried mothers over the phone. Seeing my keen interest, she actively includes me in patient relations, prompting me to give blood or talk to sick patients from her office for support. It is meaningful for me to be there for someone so terribly ill.

One patient in particular is special. Gena is an eight-year-old suffering from something Sharon calls prehepatic portal hypertension. "In layman's terms," Sharon explains, "her veins in her liver, stomach, and esophagus are so enlarged that any bump or irritation causes severe life-threatening bleeding." When John's not around Sharon encourages me to reach out to Gena, and I talk to her occasionally on the phone about Girl Scouts, the *Dukes of Hazard*, or making crafts. Sweet and smart, she is easy to like and we become fast friends. Once a week I give a pint of blood specifically for Gena and with words and homemade gifts, she says thank you more than an eight-year-old should.

On a particularly gloomy day, when the dark low clouds of Los Angeles mingle with fog, Sharon is home early. I sense something is terribly wrong; her mood is blue.

"What's the matter?"

"Gena's critical. Her lungs collapsed, and they're losing her fast." We rush to the hospital to discover the worst. There is no hope; she is slipping away. Sharon and I take our turns with her in her room, holding her hand to say good-bye.

"Gena?" I whisper calmly. "Do you know who this is?"

She squeezes my hand.

"Yeah. This is Dawn." I wipe away a tear. "You're doing a great job, sweetheart. Everything is okay. We all love you."

She squeezes my hand again really hard for a moment and then lets go. Her mom and dad have made a decision. It is time. Sharon pulls me aside to explain to me, step by step, what is about to happen. We are called in one final time to stand on either side of her small, tired body as the nurse delicately unplugs the life support and we watch little Gena pass away.

"She had the best parents and a beautiful life ahead of her. Why her?" I cry with Sharon privately.

"I know; I know. Life isn't fair." She takes her glasses off and wipes her eyes.

"But, but she wanted to be a Girl Scout, Sharon! Why couldn't she be a Girl Scout?" I don't understand why Gena has been chosen to die. She had what I always craved: a loving family, willing to do anything to give her a bright future. She wasn't from a broken home, like me; she was wanted and she wanted to live.

Sharon and I accept one of Gena's stuffed animals from the small mountain of gifts brought by well-wishers and weep in each other's arms.

❧

The funeral is set three days later at Eternal Valley Memorial Park in the small desert town of Newhall. The chapel is full of friends and family. On the altar at the front of the church, among sprays of tea roses and baby's breath, is the smallest, most delicate white coffin; it is almost doll-like.

When it is time to proceed for the viewing, my steps drag.

Gena's mother approaches us from behind, looking bewildered and worn. "Sharon, Sharon, I'm so glad you came." She leans on Sharon's shoulder for a moment, then collapses into tears. Sharon holds the grieving mother compassionately for a long time, gently guiding her out of the chapel to the waiting procession.

"I didn't know there was a children's section in cemeteries," I observe through my tears, piercing the heavy silence on the drive home.

"There is," she sighs. "It's a nice one too. It sits up high and green against the hillside—seems to look over the whole valley."

"Yeah. We can see her when we go to the swap meet now. We can wave and say hello."

"Yeah. She'll be right there, won't she?"

I focus on Sharon's face, her salt-and-pepper hair severely pulled back from her small, chiseled features. Her eyes are slightly red, but there is no expression on her face. I understand why John says no matter what, we respect Sharon. She is a lady worthy of that, and I feel glad that we have bonded. Then I think about John and me. *Does she really know about us? How can she not know? Everyone else does. But she doesn't act like it, and why doesn't she care?* Only an occasional mood swing ever gives me the slightest hint that she knows a thing.

Sharon and I are sullen for over a week after Gena's passing. John is sensitive to our feelings; he, too, is down in the dumps. We don't feel like playing games or being creative; instead, Sharon passes out Valium and goes to bed early, leaving John and me to watch television by ourselves.

John and I sit stiffly on the couch, his arm around me until I fall asleep with Thor and Pokie cuddled close. I'm not feeling very romantic these days, and John continues to understand. Instead, he wakes me and leads me to the spare bedroom, tucking me in with a kiss on the lips. Turning out the lights, he whispers, "Good night," and shuffles off to his bed.

In the mornings I run to my apartment to dress in my uniform, then hop on my bike and head for work. Pedaling home after a particularly exhausting day, I ride into the courtyard to find Sharon smoking a cigarette on her steps and letting the dogs out to do their business.

"Hi." I catch my breath. Thor has been at her house, and the dogs run up to greet me, jumping on my leg.

"Hi." Her cigarette dangles as usual. "How's work?"

I light one up too and sit down next to her. Taking a good, long drag, I launch into describing the antics of some of the funnier geriatric patients I have cared for that day.

John opens the door behind us. "Coffee?"

"Sure," I reply.

"You know I don't drink coffee, John," Sharon says icily.

Uh-oh. Something's going on.

The screen door bangs repeatedly against its wooden frame. John disappears and returns a few seconds later, balancing cups of lukewarm coffee.

"Thanks." I scoot over a bit so he can sit between us.

Sharon dismisses John like a child and keeps her attention on me. "So how is your new stroke patient?"

John is bored and instantly fidgets. He wants my attention; I can tell. *It's been a while since we've been together.* Little annoying tugs pull at the back of my neck. His hand is at my waist, his fingers pinching long strands of hair. I ignore them and swat the air behind me, but John snickers and keeps pulling. I try to swipe his hand away a few times more, but he persists. It hurts, and I've had enough. "Stop it, John!" As if he doesn't hear me, he continues pulling, now a little harder. "John! Quit it!" I snap at him. I've never done that before.

Sharon's head whips around. "John!" she sounds exasperated. "Do *you* mind?"

I smile a *thank you* at Sharon and roll my eyes. She has taken my side. John's neck veins bulge; his face flushes as if he's been dabbed pink with paint; his eyes harden. He does not approve, and the challenge is on. Again he childishly pulls at my hair, this time even harder—a yank.

"Ouch, John. That hurts!" I grit my teeth and try hard to ignore his laughing. My coffee at my feet, I reach down and slip my thumb into the now-cool liquid. *Do it, Dawn. It's perfect,* I think. *Well . . . if he does it one more time I'll . . .*

John pulls down hard again.

Whooosh! The coffee flies midair and lands on the bull's-eye of his taunting face.

Stunned and motionless for several seconds, John sits there. His huge blue eyes grow dark, bulge out of his head.

I can't believe what I have done. Sharon belts out a mocking laugh. John looks humiliated, stung.

Then Sharon sees his eyes. *"Run!"*

Adrenaline surges. I jump to my feet and fly through the courtyard, John trailing inches behind. *I hope this is a game.* I panic. As I turn the corner in the front yard, his long legs catch up to me. A sudden searing force at my head stops me midair, pulls me hard to the ground. John is clutching a huge chunk of my hair. "Ouch!" I cry, shocked and in pain. He circles me like an animal surrounding his prey. Gasping for air, he points his finger and pants, "Don't you ever, EVER, throw anything in my face again!"

I stare at him, chin quivering, ready to cry. "But you . . . I didn't mean to. You started it." My mind races, my feelings ripped from my heart.

He says nothing more, furiously storms to his house, and slams the door.

My feelings punched and bruised, I get up, brush myself off, and walk, humbled, back over to Sharon on the steps. "I guess I need my dog," I tell her, keeping my head down. I try not to cry.

"I guess so." Sharon tiptoes inside and retrieves a shaking Thor.

"Good night." I'm trembling, and I don't want her to see me. I don't want to get in trouble for that too. Sad and dejected, I walk to my lonely apartment. I feel kicked in the heart. *What does this mean? Are we broken up? Does this mean I can't come over anymore?* I don't know. I'm scared. This is our first fight.

The van's engine revs hard out in the parking lot; burning rubber chokes the sky. John peels out, screeching through smoke, leaving me alone for the next three days to agonize over what has happened.

⁂

Every time I hear a car, I jump up to see if it is John. The first night he's gone, he stays out late. *He's really mad,* I worry. Sharon doesn't go to work, and she doesn't invite me over either. *Did they fight too?*

I knock on the door after the second day.

"I have the stomach flu. Diarrhea, cramps . . . you know. Not fun. I'm in bed, not going to work." Sharon keeps behind the door in her grandma nightie, a well-worn soft flannel.

Internally I am tortured. I hate the loneliness, the rejection of the cold shoulder treatment. I try to tell myself everything will be all right, he is only making a point, and this will soon blow over— but I'm having a hard time believing myself. From the garages I think I hear David's and Karen's voices as they talk to someone. *It's John. He's hanging out with them again.* But he still doesn't come over. By the third day, I stop looking out of my window when I hear an engine, even if I know it's John. *I'm not gonna care anymore,* I lie to myself, but I know I want him to come to me.

At the end of the third day, it is late and I'm hanging on to thin hope that John will show up at my door.

Then there is a knock. It's Karen. "Hey! How ya doing?"

"Fine. What's up?" I'm suspicious. Karen rarely comes over.

"Haven't seen you in a while. Just came by to invite you for a cup of coffee." She tilts her head, makes a silly grin.

I give her a slanted look. *She's stoned,* I think, *and up to something.* "Sure." I am curious and lonely.

I grab a robe. At the door to their cottage I can hear David talking to another man. It's John. Relaxed in the bright orange beanbag chair, he has the corncob pipe smoking in his hand.

"Hey. Look who's here." David's eyes are red and glassy.

"Hey." I stand awkwardly at the door.

"Come on in," he says with a twang. "Sit down."

I walk across the room, past John, to the clearest spot on the bed and sit down. I avoid his eyes and he avoids mine, but I can feel him steal peeks in my direction. John passes the pipe to David, who takes a deep, long drag. Then, reaching over to Karen, he bends to give her a powerful shotgun. Karen rolls her eyes and, with a huge grin on her face, falls back near me on the bed. David, pleased with himself, turns toward me next, signaling my turn. He reaches down to give me the next blast from the pipe. From the corner of my eye, I see John tense up and shift his weight. He doesn't like it, and David makes me feel uncomfortable too. Quickly I pull away, holding back a choke, then blow out a hazy stream of residue, surprising myself at how much I've taken. I close my eyes and prepare to feel the high.

Like lightning, John jumps up, relieves David of the pipe, re-fills it, and shoots Karen a stream of smoke that engulfs her face. Coughing wildly, she falls back on the bed, banging her chest with her fist, unable to speak. She motions with her hands and says,

"No more. You're killing me."

John turns to me with an *I'll show you who can give a shot-gun* look, clamps the back of my head, and blows a giant cloud of smoke over my entire face. Rocking back on his heels, he grins. My chest hurts, the burning grows too strong, and I join Karen's coughing frenzy because of the harshness of the weed. Grateful that the wall is behind me, I feel the echoing buzz rush in. My body is limp, and my eyes are mere slits.

John smiles and reaches in close for a sensual kiss. "I missed you, baby."

His voice is soft in my ears. My mind hums as I breathe in smells of fresh pot and cigarettes.

"I missed you too," I murmur. The pot dries the words to my mouth like paper. He falls on top of me, his body just as disconnected as mine, and we begin to laugh. My body and senses move in slow motion. John and I roll awkwardly on the bed, bumping and banging into each other in an attempt to cuddle. Finally we give up.

"Got any chocolate chip cookies?" John asks with a goofy smirk. Without waiting for an answer, he heads for the kitchen.

❧

John and I make up. After we've come down from our high a bit, he politely excuses us and guides me back to my apartment. Taking my hand, he pulls me into the bedroom. His arms are strong and tender. I fumble a lot because I'm still too high, but John doesn't let on that he notices. We make love in a blur, and he falls asleep in my arms as if nothing ever happened. *We haven't done this in a while. It feels so good to be next to him again.* I squeeze him tightly, letting my bare foot run down his long, muscular leg. *We fit together just right. Just right,* I muse. Content in the warm familiar smell that is John, I drift off.

For the rest of the year our lives pass in the courtyard with a sense of normalcy, albeit a strange one. No more bodies are found in the neighborhood, and our intensely worn fear shifts to a subconscious hyperawareness. Occasionally we hear about a potential copycat killer, but that is considered typical for Southern California, I learn.

Sharon and I have our jobs, and John has his. Rarely is John gone at night anymore, but when he is, Sharon and I make sure we are together for the evening. Many times, exhausted from work, I can't keep my eyes open and I fall asleep on their couch. Sharon leaves me to rest, turns out the lights, and goes to bed.

Eventually, John broaches the subject of me moving in permanently. My apartment is in dire need of repairs and close to unrentable. The ravages of time and tenants have taken their toll on the old brown burlap walls, and I'm not there very much anymore. The decision is made without much concern or need for thought, and my clothes and a few of my favorite things are casually brought over one lazy weekend and set up in the spare bedroom.

Aside from worrying about disrespecting Sharon, not once do I question the strangeness of my relationship with her and John. When John and I want to hang out together, we head to David and Karen's (John can be counted on to hand down *extras* when he is in their lives), and when he wants to be intimate, well, that can happen anywhere. John and I still make weekend trips to the beach, mountains, and Palm Springs. Sharon usually declines our invitation but does go to the Saugus Swap Meet and flies to Vegas with us once, vowing afterward never to be in an airplane again.

"Flying is not for people. It's for birds," she snaps. She is terrified of flying and takes some kind of pill to get through the flight.

When in Vegas, we hit it big, the three of us. John plays poker machines and scores a royal flush in hearts. Drunk with laughter he peels off hundreds for us to play our own machines, and when that is gone he peels off more without flinching. Sharon and I mill around watching the gamblers and find a "hot" slot machine of our own, banking almost eight hundred dollars each. She puts the coins in, and I pull the lever. "We'll split whatever we win," she tells me. "If they ask you for ID, tell them you're just watching." I'm glad she is covering for me. Winning my own money is intoxicating, and I am on cloud nine.

John checks us in at a small desert motel, where we share a room and splash in the pool. Sharon watches mostly, but with a lot of teasing, we do talk her into dipping her feet into the cool aqua water. I'm surprised when I see there is only one king-sized bed for the three of us to sleep on. John acts like it's nothing. "It's all they have," he says, avoiding our eyes. Lying in the middle, he acts nonchalant and proper but reaches over to hold my hand after the lights are turned out. I sense Sharon tense up; she is not asleep.

It is like living three different lives: the one with John and me; the one with Sharon and me; and the one with John, Sharon, and me. But I do question every day whether or not Sharon knows about us. Some days, I have no doubt that she is well aware of our relationship and simply has no desire to discuss it. But on other days, I am completely baffled and afraid to think about it. Even so, the three of us all seem content with what we have and unwilling to rock the boat.

⁂

The holidays come again, and this time David, Karen, and Jamie are able to stop by for a few minutes on Thanksgiving Day. Karen is cooking this year, and they can't stay long. "Just in case she burns the turkey," Sharon whispers to me in the kitchen, "I want to make sure they don't have to come back for anything." She sends them home with as much food as they can carry away. They like Sharon.

With a little more money in my pocket this year, I enjoy plotting with Sharon to buy gifts for John and vice versa. Among his other passions, John loves collecting cobalt blue glass, scrimshaw, and knives, while Sharon enjoys shells and dragons and mice. Proudly, I hit upon some beauties to add to their collections as gifts. After searching for hours in secondhand stores, I uncover a small antique cobalt vase delicately adorned with hand-painted white roses, and I bargain at the swap meet for a belt buckle that pulls out as a double-edged knife. *These will be perfect for John.* And I save for months to buy Sharon her favorite things, the best find an exotic seashell sold by a crusty old man who ships them all the way from Africa.

John brings home a huge Douglas fir for us to decorate and, like a child, is caught occasionally shaking the packages and peeling back the paper. "Come on. I bet you can't guess what you got," he entices, and I join him. We know Sharon will scold us, but we do it anyway.

Christmas Eve comes, and I run around energized and happy, waiting to give them the treasures I have found.

John deliberately takes a long time getting ready, futzing in the garage and stopping in at other cottages around the courtyard to wish tenants a "Merry Christmas." For some, he delivers fruitcake, chocolates, and bags of pot.

"Come on, John," I yell out the window impatiently. "The presents are waiting."

"Just a minute. Just a minute." He chuckles.

"Well, hurry up or we'll hide your presents till next year," I tease.

John comes in at his own leisure anyway—he never likes being told what to do—and when he finally walks inside, he torturously takes his time settling down in front of his pile of presents. On cue, we tear into the multicolored wrappings, squealing and delighting between packages, and in a short time the frenzy is over. A few of my favorite fairy figures are among my stack of gifts, as well as anything Chihuahua, feathered, and my newest love, penguins. They are gifts chosen as carefully as the ones I have purchased for John and Sharon. I am happy.

"Wait a minute. We're not done." Sharon gives John a nod.

"Nope. Sure aren't." He grins and steps into the kitchen.

"What are you two up to?"

John sets a large, brown paper bag in front of me. "Open it," he says smugly, leaning back in his chair. Striking a wooden match underneath his table, he brings the sparking flame up to light his cigarette, draws in a breath, and blows out the match.

"Wait a minute. What is this?"

"Just open it!" Sharon's voice is mischievous.

Very light, the bag is folded over several times and stapled all along the seam. Carefully, I unfasten it. Inside is a large ball of toilet paper. "Toilet paper!" I laugh and scrunch my nose. I begin to unwind it. I unravel . . . and unravel . . . and unravel until finally, after at least a roll and a half of paper, a large gold metal object plunks into my open hand.

I gasp. "Oh my God! It's a gold fairy!" I yell. She is spectacular. A large, golden art nouveau replica of the popular winged, long-haired, nude fairy so heavy the herringbone chain has to be linked from wing to wing. John places her around my neck and stands back admiringly.

"Do you like it?" he asks, throwing Sharon a nod and me a look that says she approved of this gift.

"I love it. Thank you," I cry out loud, rolling my fingers over the sleek, slippery metal. "Thanks!"

Full and satisfied with a great Christmas, we clean up and get ready for bed. "Do me one more favor," John says as I pick up the last of the ribbon.

"What?"

"Go over to your room and get me Thor's leash, would ya?" John points to the spare bedroom in the house.

"Sure," I tell him, thinking it odd that he needs it this late. On my night table rests Thor's leash and a type of scroll with a large red bow attached. Gingerly I unroll the paper. It is a hand-drawn charcoal sketch of me in profile looking down lovingly at Thor in my lap. At the bottom are John's flamboyant signature and name printed below. I smile warmly. *Now, this is special.* My heart warms like the sweet taste of chocolate melts in my mouth. *I am loved!* I stash the drawing in my closet. This holiday is much better than last year's when we were all still so uncertain of each other. It is the best Christmas I have had in a long time, and I go to sleep that night wrapped under a warm blanket of childhood memories of a New Jersey summer evening . . . and fireflies.

From here on we do predictable family things, and when my eighteenth birthday comes along I know John and Sharon will take me out to dinner and have gifts waiting for me: presents carefully wrapped in birthday paper, not Christmas paper! *This is like my family now,* I think, *disjointed at best, but mine.*

Memories creep into my head. I think about Mom, Wayne, Terry, Dad, Pen Ci, and baby Jack. I wonder what their holidays are like. *Do they think about me as well?* I convince myself they do, even though I haven't heard from them . . . this year.

CHAPTER TEN
The Evolution of a Fall—Cocaine

Whistling down the courtyard, John breaks into song. *"If you could read my mind, love, what a tale my thoughts could tell. Just like an old-time movie, 'bout a ghost from a wishing well."* I look over and love him. He is singing our favorite Gordon Lightfoot tune, and when he sees me watching, he sings even louder.

After the New Year we put the finishing touches on the spare bedroom, turning it into my own personal haven. John carries in the few heavy things left in my old apartment, singing brazenly like a little kid.

Wow. He's really happy I'm living here, I think, feeling the warm welcome.

With Sharon's help, the walls of my new room are decorated generously with my favorite pieces—items gifted to me by both of them in the last two years. I make a mental note of how the wheel of time has turned once again in John's and my relationship: Now I am living under his roof.

I help around the house, doing my share of the chores. Since I am eighteen now, Sharon suggests I take classes for my GED at the local adult school. "You're smart enough, Dawn," she lectures me. "It'll be a breeze."

I do. In April of 1979, I anxiously open the results of my exam.

Despite my doubts, and to my amazement, there is the diploma.

"Didn't I tell you you could do it?" Sharon applauds maternally.

"Wow. Yeah, you did," I tell her, feeling good about myself.

My self-esteem rises when Sharon offers me more and more of the bookkeeping duties for the cottages and invites me to attend medical seminars with her for her two-year license renewal. We study together like coeds and both ace the finals. It seems that being eighteen is opening some doors for me and I feel stronger, full of hope.

Since my move into the house, John and I goof around all the time, much to Sharon's chagrin. He loves to flirt and tease me, often playing silly games of chase or covering my eyes and telling me to stop looking at him. "Those eyes! Stop!"

Sometimes, too, he can be on the edge of annoying. Enough so that he provokes me to threaten him, "Quit it, John, or I'm gonna smack ya!"

It amuses John to get my goat, so he eggs me on. "Promise?" But a tiny flame of caution burns deep beneath my consciousness, and never do I go too far again, as I had the day I threw the coffee at him.

Sharon is like a parent trying to control her children. Admonishing us for our bad behavior, she covers her amusement with seriousness. She excuses herself when our playfulness gets too rambunctious and refuses to lower her dignity by joining in the banter. "I'm not a touchy, feely type of gal," she throws back at us. "Grow up." Or "Touch me and I'll deck you."

I'm confused by Sharon sometimes. I know she and John are like brother and sister and she has little patience for most of the fun John likes to have, but there is a day that my understanding of them is tested. It is a piece of paper in Sharon's long, sharp handwriting, left haphazardly on the counter by the television. "What does the mad rapist want for dinner tonight?"

What? Rapist? What does she mean? There is no one around

when I find the note. I hold it in my hand, emotionally stuck. I read it again and again. It's like a brick wall I can't climb over. *This can't be anything,* I tell myself. *I wouldn't be here if they were together. This has to mean something else.* I am worried, though. My thoughts spiral in bizarre twists.

John appears, walking in his white-and-red-striped tube socks and robe from his back office, and sees me. Gently he takes the paper from my hand, folds it in two, and kisses me. "Get me a glass of milk, will ya, baby?"

"Sure." From the corner of my eye I see him crumple the page and toss it casually across the counter. *Oh, it's nothing important. Good.* I fold this new nagging seed of uneasiness back into the recesses of my heart and get John his milk.

* * *

There are no restrictions or rules in the house besides common courtesy, and there are no mysteries to me here, except for one— "Big Tom." I don't understand Big Tom. He has something to do with John's arrest years ago in my birthplace, Point Pleasant, New Jersey. I have strict orders whenever he calls to "ask no questions and immediately hand the phone over to John." If he isn't there, I am instructed to get Sharon; she will know what to do. He seems to call every few weeks, cautious when I first answer, but friendlier after a while. As time goes by, he even adds a "How ya doing, Dawn?" when I pick up the phone, acting as if he knows me, familiar with my voice. But even with the friendliness, I abide by the rules and pass the calls along without question.

It is an overwhelmingly hot day in July, and I can't believe he has taken me to this place. Farmer John's Slaughter House in downtown LA has a happy farm scene painted on the stucco wall surrounding it, and the stench of blood, urine, and fear hangs like an ominous cloud above. He tries to coax me inside, but I refuse. "It's one thing looking for them in the desert and shops, but *fresh heads!* Ugh, John! Just hurry up!" I snap, annoyed at this not-so-brilliant idea to add to his skull collection.

"Come on. Let's get these in the house." John hurries, sweat pouring from his brow.

"I am *not* touching those," I warn, holding back a gag. "John, this is disgusting!"

He lugs them through the front door, and I follow with his briefcase and keys. Dropping the bags on the kitchen floor, he grabs the giant cooking pots from under the stained wood butcher block he found at a yard sale and fills them with water. I stand watching him, my hand over my mouth, a few steps back for distance from the gruesome unveiling. *Plop*—the pig is the first to go in. Mortified, I step back farther. Next comes the cow. I can take no more and walk away, leaving John to position the heads in the boiling pots of water.

"I'll just check the mail." I excuse myself, relieved to get away from the kitchen. A pattering of little furry feet follows me to the front door. The dogs, panicked by the smell of blood, are sticking close to someone safe.

On the porch under the mailbox sits a plain brown box. I bring it in. "John!"

"Whaaaat?" he yells back, coming around the corner wiping his hands on a dish towel.

"You got a package." I set it on the table and back off, not wanting to get near his hands.

Looking down at the label, John tears into the package. "Woooo-hoooo!" he cries. "She's here!"

"Who's here? What is it?" Curiosity has gotten the best of me.

"Louise!" he says, holding up a shining, creamy white human skull. "Ahhh! She's perfect!" He turns her, admiring every angle.

I gasp. "Where did you get that?"

"Well, ha." He tosses his head back and decides against a lie. "I told them I was a UCLA premed student studying anatomy, and they sent her to me."

The student part is bull, I tell myself. I think about his story for a moment, blink, and laugh too. I believe him, guessing it can make sense. "Good one," I admit, extremely impressed. I reach over and kiss John's beaming face. "This must be the day for skulls."

"Hey! Wake up, you lazy bum!" John calls through David and Karen's window as we walk up to knock on their door.

"Whaaa da ya waaaant?" David slurs.

"Look at this baby." John holds up the ivory orb.

"Cool," David says, blandly turning her in his hands. "What are you gonna do with that?"

"Her name is Louise," I jump in, "and we're gonna mount her with the rest of the skulls, David. What do you think?" I'm bothered at his lack of enthusiasm for John's prize.

"Yeah, I gathered that. But, well . . ."

John shoots back, "No, man, I'm gonna use her for when Dawn's sleeping and I need to get off. Look at her, man. She's a beaut!"

"Yeah. Yeah. Okay, I see. I'm just not into that kind of thing, man. Sorry! But, ah . . . you know what kind of thing I'd *rather* be into . . ." David pauses for a minute, raising his eyebrows. "You know what I mean?"

"And what *do* you mean, David?" John challenges, knowing exactly what he means. "You can't even take half the shit I'm around on the set every day, man! John Holmes can get any kinda dope he wants."

"What! Bullshit! I can take anything you bring into this house and more, suckah!" he insists, calling the dare with a half grin on his face. Karen steps out of the kitchen holding a cup of coffee and smiling at where she knows the conversation is heading.

"You're *on,* asshole! Tomorrow night. Nine o'clock. Be here!" John points his finger at David's face. He grabs Louise, then my hand, and we head home.

The next day John is gone into the evening and calls me from work. With disco music blaring in the background, he tells me to meet him at David's by nine o'clock. "Make sure that asshole knows I'm coming," he says jokingly. "And tell them I got a surprise for all of you."

"Ooooh, a surprise. What is it?"

"You'll see, baby. You'll see. 'Cause we're gonna have some fun tonight!" he says, sensually cupping his hand over his mouth on the receiver. "I love you."

"I love you too, John."

"He's here," Karen calls, hearing John's van pull up.

"I told you," I mumble, stretching my legs in the beanbag chair.

"It's about time," David gripes.

It is almost midnight, and we are tired, dozing where we sit. Echoing up the courtyard, we hear the soft thumping of John's boots against the cement walk and the whistling of the tune from Rudyard Kipling's "Gunga Din." The door opens and John enters singing the end of the song into the air. "Though I've belted you and flayed you, by the livin Gawd that made you, you're a better man than I am, Gunga Din!" He pauses and, as always, waits for applause. Finding none, he grins anyway and shuts the door. He is in a great mood.

"It's about time," David whines.

John ignores him and steps over the mess on the floor to be next to me. "Hey, wake up, baby. I got a surprise for you."

"Mmmmmm. Hi, John. I'm awake. What is it?" I sit upright, my skin squeaking against the vinyl beanbag chair. His hair is tousled, and he is wearing his blue jeans and a skintight, scrub green T-shirt. The large dragonfly ring on his left hand stands out in contrast and in size. He reaches for a kiss, and I notice his breath is stale from too many cigarettes. David and Karen gather around voraciously.

Nestling down on the edge of the bed, John opens his briefcase, pulls out a mirror from its top compartment, and sets it next to him. Next comes the surprise. From the watch pocket of his jeans he removes a small glass vial with a black screw-on lid. Inside are the shiny white crystals—cocaine. He doles out four fat lines with a single-edged razor and swiftly snorts up the first line with a short, white gold straw. *Snnnnnnnnnufff.* The *tap, tap* of the straw cracks on the glass. He runs his finger along the remaining residue of his line from the mirror and rubs it on his gums. "Tiffany's," he chokes out. As his face reddens, he throws his arm across his eyes and plops back on the bed, cringing from the sting of the powder in his head.

It takes me a minute to understand that *Tiffany's* refers to the white gold straw.

John hands David the mirror next. "Ahhh! Shit! God damn, that's good!" he exclaims after he inhales his line and falls back on the bed with John. Karen has her own method, and I watch her carefully, knowing it will be my turn next. John knows I snorted coke with my father a couple times back in Carol City; he got mad about it when he found out. He is very strict when it comes to me getting loaded. He is the one who passes out the pot or shares a shot of aged Scotch. Sharon gives me a Valium occasionally when John's not home, but he doesn't like that either. He only approves if he hands it to me when he does one too. This time John is watching me, and I don't want to make a mistake. When Karen takes her turn, she lies back and holds her face, as if painfully gripping for the rush. John hands me the mirror. Shakily, I accept and bend to snort my line. Large clumps of my hair fall around my face, blocking my view. Awkwardly, I swing the long locks back and try to sniff the line a second time, but my hair slides in the way once again.

"Here. Let me show you," John says firmly. "You hold one side of your nose in with your thumb while you use the straw to snort with the other." John sets the mirror on the bed and holds my hair.

Snnnuuuuuffffff! I shake visibly and cry out in pain. Instantly I roll into a fetal position, covering my head. My eyes water uncontrollably. The pain takes forever to subside, and my face goes numb.

"That's pure shit!" John sniffs.

David and Karen are in a deep embrace on the bed. Karen begins to moan.

John, feeling his high, nestles next to me on the beanbag and leans in for a deep kiss. "Let's get out of here," he says, pulling me up and out of the chair. On the mirror he taps out a small pile of coke from the glass container and closes his briefcase. We tiptoe out of the house, David and Karen oblivious to our departure.

Quietly, John unlocks the darkened door of my old apartment and we sneak into the bedroom giggling like kids. John lays out two more lines for us on the side table, pulls my hair back gently from my face, and afterward falls with me on the bed holding me tightly till the burning pain of my sinuses clears and the euphoric rush of the coke takes over our bodies.

Just before sunrise, the two of us, red-eyed and bedraggled, slowly creak open the front door of our house. Sharon is still sleeping. Pokie and Thor lethargically greet us. John kisses me on the cheek as I scoop Thor into my arms and we head for our separate rooms to sleep the day away.

John and I wake late that afternoon and stumble out into the living room wearing our pajamas. Sharon is folding her laundry. "Well, look what the cat dragged in," she scoffs, loading up her basket. "You both missed your cartoons." I shuffle to the bathroom, look in the mirror, and groan. I feel sick.

We spend the rest of the day hanging out on the couch, unable to do much of anything. We try to play off our cocaine hangover as if we just want a day to be lazy.

Sharon becomes bored with us easily. "If the two of you insist on being brain-dead, then I'm going to bed!"

Neither of us has the strength to argue.

John lies on the couch next to me until *Saturday Night Live*, when the phone rings. We look at each other to see which one of us will move first, until I give in and get up to answer it.

"It's David," I tell him, holding out the phone.

John stiffly gets up. "Yeah? How ya feelin, asshole." He laughs, then laughs harder at David's reply. John's expression quickly changes, and his body tenses. "Fuck . . . you!" he snaps coldly and slams down the phone.

"What's the matter? What'd he say?" I'm shocked. John is furious.

He falls down next to me, jerky and tense, flings his arm around my shoulders roughly, thinks hard for a minute, then snaps, "You don't want any more of that shit, do you?"

"No. Baby. I don't . . . really." I look deep into his eyes and hug him reassuringly, guessing that David has just asked for more.

John studies my gaze intensely. Then, satisfied, he faces the TV clenching his jaw. "I've seen people sell their lives for that shit. People who had everything—everything—sold it all. Lost their houses, their cars, their jewelry, their wives. Now they're sleeping anywhere they can . . . and can't even bum a cigarette." His lip curls with disgust.

Standing, John reaches up to the shelf above his chair and pulls down a bottle and two shot glasses. "Old Parr. Thirty-year-old Scotch." He stares somberly into the amber liquid, then pours us each a drink. "The older, the better. Skoal!" He slugs down the shot, and I do the same. Then we call it an early night.

As if he hasn't remembered his own words, John arranges for us all to meet at David and Karen's once again the following weekend. They are very happy, and it doesn't take a lot to make a gram of coke sound like a fun time to me either. *Was it the dare from his brother, or has John been doing some coke all along?* I wonder as he spreads another round of crystalline lines. *Naw. He's just a fast learner,* I calculate. *Besides, he hates the stuff. He told me so.* I blow off any doubts about John's sincerity. He wouldn't lie to me. Whatever it is, to me, this is the beginning. Before my eyes, the warm colors of my contentment are rapidly turning to a cold, cold gray.

⌘

Within a few months, our weekend cocaine high turns into twice and three times a week. John begins to need to work again on overnight shoots and comes home looking haggard and grumpy. On those weary days, the minute he steps in the door, David and Karen call or come over to discuss something *important*. A ruse only; their true motive is to score more coke. They like to party, and John is their connection. Tired, and complaining that David won't leave him alone, John drags himself to their cottage to hand down a line or two from his little glass vial with the black lid. But by now, John *always* makes sure he has enough for a wake up for himself when he sleeps into the afternoon.

The days when John is in a good mood anymore are the days he comes home with a nice amount of coke, ready to party. The tiny container is full most of the time, accompanied now by a couple of folded paper bindles, each containing a gram of coke. John calls me at the house. "Be at David's in an hour." Sharon knows it is John on the other end of the line, and by my voice she can tell we are making arrangements to be at her brother-in-law's that evening. Sadly, of late, our conversations have run dry. We never tell Sharon about the pot. Never have. She is straitlaced, and getting high is another thing we don't talk about. I know how she blames David for bringing it into John's life in the first place. We definitely can't say anything about the coke. Sharon and I watch television in silence until it is time for me to make some excuse to meet John a few doors down.

After a while, I resent going to David and Karen's cottage. Always vying for his attention when a bag of coke is present, they aren't giving him time with me or with anything else he enjoys—or so I think. I blame them for constantly wanting more coke. David knows John is unwilling to let him down, and he knows just the right buttons to push. To me, it seems David manipulates John, and I agree with Sharon: I don't think John can see it.

Things are getting creepy too. Sometimes, when the coke runs dry, mood swings and paranoia kick in and John will order us to take turns peeking out of the windows at the slightest noise. David and John get antsy, and Karen and I find it harder and harder to make it to work after a night without sleep. It doesn't seem like much time has passed at all, but it is flying. And our worlds . . . our worlds are changing . . . dramatically.

❦

It is late October 1979 and the tail end of Indian summer when John and David hatch their plan. After a usual call telling me to meet him at his brother's, John shows up at David's door, looking over his shoulders, a large grocery bag and briefcase in hand. "Hey. Here. Take this," he says, handing Karen the briefcase. Gently, he places the brown paper bag on the kitchen table.

"What cha got there, bro?" David's words roll smoothly.

John doesn't answer but races past him over to the windows to pull the curtain shades closed. Deciding it is safe, he opens the bag. "Check this out." A large, pale green, black, and chrome gram scale appears from its brown wrapping. He sets it on the table and kneels down to meticulously balance the arm. Out of his briefcase he removes a small wooden box. Inside is a metal incremental weight set. John pulls out the weight marked *one gram* and sets the scale.

"God damn." David pulls a drag off of his cigarette.

Grabbing for my own cigarette, I watch John proudly display the precision of his latest acquisition, announcing breathlessly his intention of a new business venture. He taps out lines for each of us, then passes around the mirror and the now-worn and dull Tiffany straw.

"Here." He hands me a ruler and an eight-by-eleven sheet of heavy bond paper. "Cut out a bunch of squares that look like this." He draws out several even lines, then lets me do the rest. "And here. You get to fold," he says, handing Karen a sample bindle to duplicate. His words race together, his breathing shallow and fast; then he pulls out the big stash. From his jacket pocket he carefully retrieves a plastic sandwich bag about one-eighth full of powdery cocaine.

"Son of a b—," David whistles, and John throws back his head and smiles admiringly. Quick as a flash, he is rummaging through the cabinets looking for bowls and pans. Again, from the brown Samsonite, he fumbles for a small metal strainer, the kind Sharon strains gravy with, and a half a brick of another white powder wrapped in paper.

"What's that?" I ask.

"Menita."

"What's menita?" I ask naively.

John chuckles slightly and winks at me. "Anyone want to tell her what menita is?"

"Baby laxative," David answers, helping John dig for the right tools from the kitchen, his arms loaded with pans.

"Baby laxative! Why do you have that?"

"This is pure shit, baby," he says, holding up the coke. "You can't sell people this. They'll never come down!"

"Oh."

I don't want to look stupid, but I still don't quite get it until Karen mumbles under her breath, "You mix it with the coke. You get more that way."

I nod.

We all dutifully get busy taking on our specific jobs. John hands out lines of coke, and we are like bees intent on gathering pollen for the queen. I cut squares until the scissors leave an indentation and slight blister on my hand, and then John promotes me to bindles. He teaches me how to fold the perfect one, the edges and corners tight, with flaps secure.

John and David use the strainer to mix the menita and coke together. Then they weigh one-gram piles and set the powdery gold aside for Karen and eventually me to scoop up and fold securely in bindles. During the night, the lines of cocaine flow. My face and throat stay numb, and my nose runs constantly while I focus intensely on my job. We are like robots, thinking only of doing another line when we begin to feel run down. This is a business now, a way for David and John to earn a little extra cash. Karen helps her man, and I help mine.

The pale pink of the breaking day shines through the side of the kitchen window shade. I realize I have to work this morning and have no time for any sleep. *Ugh!* I think, feeling the ache of my joints from sitting in the same position all night. Stiff and woozy, I leave the table. "John? I have to get ready for work." I lean in to hold him. Snuggling up, he relaxes in my arms and for a moment we drift off right where we stand.

"Run down and get dressed, baby, and I'll give you something to get your day going," he says, wrapping things up and sending me on my way.

I walk down the misty courtyard to the house, pulling my sweater around me in the cool morning chill. Sharon is in the kitchen getting the dogs their breakfast and doesn't come out to see who's at the door. I am glad. I don't want her to see me high. Quickly, I dress, play with Thor for a few minutes, and step lightly toward the door.

"I need to talk to you when you get home from work today, Dawn," Sharon calls out from the kitchen, stopping me in my tracks.

"Okay," I call back. My heart begins to race.

There is a pause. "Is John letting his brother talk him into being stupid again?" Sharon's voice echoes wryly.

"Yeah. I'll see ya later," I answer quickly, not quite sure if she really knows what is going on. I wait politely for an answer.

"Have a nice day," she replies.

⁂

It is a miserably long day of lifting, feeding, and bathing patients. Time drags to 3:30, the end of my shift. My body aches, and I'm so worn out I can't keep my eyes open during my breaks. I return from work, dreading what Sharon might have to say to me. I take a deep breath and open the front door. Jumping off of John's bed, the dogs run out to greet me. *Good, he's still sleeping,* I think.

Sharon steps out of the kitchen holding a dish towel. "Hi. You're home."

"Yeah." I collapse on the couch. "I'm exhausted!"

"I can see that. Listen. I've been meaning to talk to you about something. John and I have discussed it and . . . well, how would you like to be in charge of maintaining the books and organizing repairs, gardening, cleaning and such for this place? It'll be full-time . . . with pay," she offers enticingly.

"You mean I can quit my job?"

"Yup. Your hours will be up to you so you can also look into enrolling in some of those classes at the adult school you've been talking about."

"Really? I'd love that!"

"Good. I'll let Dr. Nuttycomb know you've agreed." She folds the dish towel into a square, pivots, and walks out of the room.

Giving notice at Royal Oaks is a relief. The place has given new meaning to the term "overworked and underpaid." Many patients die here after years of suffering. I am glad when they go. To finally prepare their bodies for the morgue and see them in peace is an odd relief. It's a difficult state of mind to come to, but after working there for over two years, I am burned out.

Feeling good about changing jobs, I can't foresee the power cocaine will have over my future. Although I am already uneasy with its powdery bitter presence, it gives me a powerful rush and sweeps me away at times.

I take on my new responsibilities at the cottages with gusto. Setting up a little table in the corner of John's office with my own typewriter and file cabinet, I settle into organizing the property's files. The arrangement gives me and John more time to spend together. We do—together with cocaine.

Instead of meeting at David and Karen's throughout the week now, John brings the glass vial home to the house while Sharon works. I feel guilty about doing this, but I never question anything John does in his own home. He is always in command of his domain; John is a Leo, and this is definitely the lion's den. It is also a place where David and Karen won't enter unless specifically invited. They rarely are; Sharon makes sure of that. John drops off large bags of coke for them to weigh and wrap, keeping them supplied, but the party isn't being held there anymore, for the moment anyway. No matter what kind of influence David has about scoring drugs now, John is the one in control. Cocaine is his new instrument of mastery. And he likes his newfound power.

John dishes out *wake up* lines, *let's get a job done* lines, and *pick me up* lines. In the evenings, so we can still have an appetite for dinner with Sharon, he lights up his corncob pipe and passes around the mellowing weed. Then, just to be sure we can sleep, down comes the thirty-year-old Scotch from the shelf above the television to wash back half a Valium each.

Steadily the coke becomes the center of our world, and when John has to go to work it is rarely on a set—he is only out to score the drugs. Camping, day trips, or dinners out cease to exist anymore. He can't be away from a private spot to do a line. He is ever careful of how much of the coke I take in, but his own personal stash is growing in leaps and bounds and his personal doses are getting larger. I sit and watch without question as he snorts extra amounts over and above what we share together, and the shots of Scotch and doses of Valium he needs to come down with have increased dramatically.

Still, I try to manage the cottages well, maintaining the books and scheduling repairs. Even though I am keeping everything up-to-date, it is hard to cover up John's unusual behavior, which the tenants notice and mention. John's standoffishness and secretive paranoia, along with their sometimes incoherent encounters with him, make them all nervous, afraid to trust him to watch their property anymore.

"Is John all right?" an elderly tenant named Marian asks me one day after John rudely rushes past her mumbling obscenities. "He almost knocked me down."

"Oh, he's fine." I cover for him with the first excuse that pops into mind. "He probably didn't see you."

Still they take the complaints to Sharon.

The phone rings. It is an evening with Sharon watching TV, lying on the couch, as I wait for John to come home. As on any other evening Sharon, knowing it is John, lets me answer.

"Hey, baby." He sounds out of breath. "Meet me at David's tonight. It's important."

"Okay. What time?"

"Go now . . . and tell David I got the ether. I love you." He hangs up.

Sharon peers over in my direction, curious about the confused look on my face. "Something wrong?"

"I don't think so. He wants me to give David a message. Right now!" I add with emphasis.

"Wonderful," she says sarcastically, turning away as if to say she wants nothing to do with the subject.

Karen opens the door after the first knock. "Hi. Come on in." She looks behind me as if she's searching for someone. "Where's John?"

"He's coming. He said it was important to meet and tell David he's got the ether."

"Alllllllright!" David sits up against the wall.

"Ether. What's that for?" I hate that I have to ask.

"You'll see," he says, smiling with a shit-eating grin.

John's van pulls into the driveway only a few minutes later. He looks more paranoid than ever, pulling shades and peeking out the windows like a scared rabbit. *He smells different.* I register a whiff of medicinal perspiration coming off of his clothes.

Convinced the coast is clear, he settles down in the middle of the room delicately opening his briefcase. Gingerly he removes two glass bottles of liquid, a petri dish, single-edged razors, and a large bag of cocaine.

"Ladies and gentleman, I am about to show you how to do things *right!*" His eyes dart frantically at each of us, his grin robotic. Finally I get a good look at him; I see the red in his eyes and the sallow, sunken look of his face. "But first we'll try this." He whips off his jacket and dips into his briefcase, retrieving a glass water pipe. It has a round base for the water with a stem for smoking out of and a bowl with screens to place the drugs on. He opens one of the bottles and pours water into the pipe, replacing the stopper. Then, from the familiar glass vial with the ebony lid, he taps a pile of small white crystals onto the screen. John sets the pipe on the glass coffee table, rubbing his sweaty palms on his jeans in anticipation. Rummaging farther, he withdraws a pint bottle of Bacardi 151 Rum, a cotton ball, and paper clip. The wire clip is unwound on one end, bent like a metal tooth, and curled on the other. He hooks a piece of the cotton around the tooth into a ball and opens the Bacardi, pouring some of the liquid into the lid. Lifting his head to nod at us, his audience, he directs us to ready ourselves to join in at his signal. Dunking the cotton into the liquor, he squeezes off the excess and lights the tip. Wavy, blue, the flame silently purrs. Holding the pipe at his mouth and slightly tilting his head, he positions the flame underneath the bowl until the white of the crystals melts into the screens. John quickly dives in to pull the cloudy smoke through the water from the bowl and into his lungs. Holding in as much as he can, he lets go and holds the pipe up to David's lips, keeping the flame beneath the bowl until it fades out.

John's face is bright red and bursting. Unable to hold in his breath any longer, John wraps his hand around the back of my head and brings my lips onto his, exhaling the smoke from his lungs into mine. I see his face smile, as if to say, *See? I told you this was good.*

Then the tingling and ringing in my head begin. I close my eyes. Sensing my mouth, throat, and chest go numb, I feel dizzy and fold over to my knees. John's delighted laughter echoes in my ears as I can hold the drugs in no longer and release a paler cloud of smoke. Head still spinning, I lie down on John's lap.

Running his fingers through my hair, he takes me in hard and steady, then goes about the task of preparing the pipe for me to take a turn passing the exhale to him.

My mind has shifted to turbo mode. I sit up attentively, checking everyone else's reaction. David and Karen are looking for a cigarette, and so am I. Lighting up almost simultaneously, we all look to John to lead the way. "Freebase," he tells us, releasing a twitch in his neck. "Pure cocaine! No cut, no crap. None of that quinine shit that kills you. Doesn't burn your lungs because you roll the smoke through water and the flame is pure. No lighter fluid to cough up." John rambles on, "*And* it's three times as expensive as a gram of powder." John's education is thorough, and our interest devoted. "Now it's tricky to cook this shit up. You gotta use ether, and it's been known to explode in your face if it's not done right."

He and the freebase coursing through our veins have our undivided interest. John is determined that we learn the process completely. Then he issues directions for how to prepare coke and ether for cooking in boiling water, releasing the pressure every few minutes until the cut is separated, then spreading it on the petri dishes to cool in the freezer. With the razors, in a process similar to the weight-and-scale method, we scrape the dried pure crystals off of the curved glass and arrange the oil-based powder in piles to package.

We are busy bees, and the freebase runs freely. With this stuff, the initial high is the best and it lasts only a few minutes. The more I take in, the more introverted and agitated I become when the first euphoric rush soon wears off. The same thing happens to everybody, especially John. We take the freebase hits so frequently that we have very little left to package as the sun rises on another sleepless night.

John sends me into the kitchen to check on the last dish cooling in the freezer. *"Ahhhh!* Shit! No way!" A round of curses come from the living room.

"What is it?" I run out to see what happened.

"Son of a bitch." John is standing with his hands on his hips, looking down at his briefcase, very angry.

"What?"

Silence, then, *"Shit!"* He kicks the briefcase across the bed into a side table and against the wall.

"John! Stop!" David yells.

John stomps into the bathroom, leaving us to stare at the mess he created.

"What happened?" I ask for the third time.

"It melted," David says, shrugging his shoulders. "We put it in tin foil, and it had a bad reaction to the metal and melted. Who knew?"

"Oh."

Karen, David, and I begin carefully picking up the broken pieces of an ashtray and placing John's strewn things in a pile on the bed.

Twenty minutes pass by the time John comes out of the bathroom with his hair wet and face looking washed. He walks into the kitchen, opens the freezer, removes the petri dish, and dumps the contents in the dishwater. Without hesitation and with dogged determination, he gathers his things from the pile, dismantling the glass pipe and paraphernalia from his briefcase. I watch in quiet appreciation his moment of clarity. No one else says a word either. Then, taking the pieces of the pipe in one hand and my hand in the other, he leads me outside to the street.

Feeling the moisture of the early morning fog on my face, I feel better than I did in David's claustrophobic box of a cottage.

Mist glows in the streetlights as I hold his hand tightly and follow. It has been a long time since I have connected so intimately and warmly to John; the coke has been changing that between us. At least, I believe it's the coke. We have each lost the child inside who promises to never leave, so often laughs, and loves.

John bends down on one knee with his head poised in thought for a moment. Then, stretching out to hold my cheek, he looks into my eyes. "I promise you, baby. I . . . I *promise* tonight was the last time you will *ever* see this glass *dick* in my mouth! Ever!"

I simply nod, awed at his apparent desire to make those words true.

"I love you, baby, and . . . and I'll . . . I'll lose you if this shit stays in our lives . . . and I don't ever, ever want to lose you. You're my baby." A tear glistens in his eye as he strokes my face.

"I love you too, John," I breathe. "Are you okay? Can you do it?" I feel sorry for him. His attraction to the coke is very strong.

Things will get better again, my heart wishes through the waning effects of the drugs. *We'll get the warmth back now.* Memories of the chemistry between us rush back, and I realize how much I've missed him. We have become like mannequins, only remnants of "John and Dawn."

He stands up. The sky is beginning to brighten into daylight. Then, with all his weight, John steps back and throws the pipe down with a crash. "*Fuck you!*" he shouts defiantly at the shattered glass. "*Fuck you!*"

We hug one another desperately, John kissing me all over, as if to seal the promise and make it stick.

⊱✦⊰

It is near Christmas and we are expecting a visit from John's mother and niece from Ohio. David and Karen are excited. David, the baby of the family, is going to see his mother, and he has good news about his life. He has enrolled in a locksmith certification program and is scheduled to graduate next spring. John, on the other hand, is somber about the news of her visit.

John's mother, Mary, is a strict Baptist woman who has seen a lot of heartache in her life. Religion has given her solace in her suffering over bad husbands. I picture her, a habitual rocking chair occupant, the Good Book in her lap, praying feverishly over her family's sins. A Bible thumper—that's what Sharon calls her. John and David agree. They have a nickname for her—"Mother Moses"—and they're serious.

Things are going to be uncomfortable for us while they are here; neither John nor Sharon is partial to religion. "If there's a God, he's a sadist," Sharon has said, passionate in her anger toward God, and John agrees wholeheartedly. It is the first time I have ever heard that word, *sadist,* and I believe them, especially after Gena's death and the others I've witnessed at Royal Oaks.

Mary favors David and puts a lot of pressure on John to take care of him. John doesn't talk about it with me much. Mostly he hides out in his office moping and, I know, getting high on coke. It is arranged that their mother will stay with David. Julie, their sister Anne's girl, will stay with John and Sharon—in my room! I am depressed.

I wake up on the day of John's family's arrival with John L's, Pokie's, and Thor's faces inches from my mine. "What is it, you guys? What's the matter?" They wag their tails excitedly as I roll out of bed.

Sharon is up flipping through the channels, smoking a cigarette.

"Did you know that these guys were all staring at me in my sleep?" I ask her, rubbing the grogginess from my eyes and yawning.

"Uh-huh. They do that all the time. Didn't you notice?"

"No. How come?"

"You mean you don't know? You grind your teeth in your sleep. And it's *loud!*"

"I do?"

"All the time." She says it like it's old news.

"I must be restless about something."

"It wouldn't have anything to do with certain visitors, now, would it?" She clears her throat.

"Yeah, that must be it. I don't want to spend Christmas in that old, dusty, empty apartment, Sharon. I want to be here, where I live."

"I know. Well, you can fall asleep on the couch all you want and definitely on Christmas Eve, if that will make you feel any better. You're still going to eat here anyway. It's never good when we get a visit from Ohio. It upsets John every time, but we'll get through it . . . as long as we don't let them do any of the cooking." She rolls her eyes in mock horror.

"What about presents? Aren't they going to think it's kinda weird that the three of us go all out with presents?"

"We'll open ours when they are visiting David and Karen. That way they won't have any questions to ask."

John picks them up from the airport that afternoon, and the first place they head is David's.

Sharon and I have been in the kitchen cooking all day. Wafting smells of macaroni and cheese, meat loaf, antipasto, and everything we can think of to stock the refrigerator keep the dogs tap dancing at our feet and, according to Sharon, give John's family no reason to pull out a pot or a pan. No matter what, there is to be no back-woods, hillbilly cooking in her kitchen!

At dinnertime the visitors finally make their way to the house. John's mother and niece walk in, scanning the assortment of skulls, sculptures, dragons, and odd antique wall décor. The dogs bellow their alert at the strangers, their nails scratching the wooden entryway. Julie puts her hands up in front of her legs, swatting and squealing in a goofy fright.

"Hieeeee," Sharon's doctor's office voice shrills off-key. Mary walks up to hug her, and Sharon pales and freezes, stiff as a board.

"Mary, this is Dawn. She's, well, a part of the family."

John's head looms behind his mother's. With Julie's suitcase in hand, he closes the door, and we lock eyes.

Mary takes a step back at the rush of information. She has small, pinpoint brown eyes, graying brown hair severely pulled into a ponytail, and some kind of drooping palsy that makes one side of her face look like it's melting. She burns a single lopsided look my way, without a flinch dismisses me and, stone-faced, turns to introduce Julie, a mousy, brown-haired, brown-eyed, bottom-heavy teenager. Julie is eighteen, my age.

I fall back on the couch and shrug my shoulders at John. From across the room, I can see his jaw tightly clench as the tension mounts.

⚜

Everyone in the house is on edge, and I am happy to get away. *Did David tell his mom about me? Probably. He would do something like that to get John in trouble with his strict Baptist mom.* I sleep the first night at my old apartment, and thankfully John checks on me before bed. Although I don't like being alone, it is better than enduring the silent treatment I get from his mother and niece.

"I'd rather stay here, with you," John tells me, trying to get under the covers with me and not go back home.

"Come on. She's come all the way from Ohio to see you. You can spend some time with her, John," I coax insincerely.

"She's here to see David," he blurts. "I'm not her favorite, you know. She thinks I'm a freak."

"A freak? No, she doesn't, John. She's your mother."

"I've always been one. She never knew what to do with me when I skipped school. She wanted me to play sports, but the kids called me a freak. Fuck them. Fuck them all. Those low-life backwoods idiots are in that small town doing their sisters, and

243

I'm here. I can have any woman I want at the snap of my fingers."
He raises his hand and gestures a snap at the wall, then looks over
and holds me. "But I got you, baby." He rocks me in his arms.
"I'm sorry you're over here. Come first thing in the morning for
breakfast. Okay? I love you." He reaches down, pets Thor's pink
upturned belly, and kisses me good night.

I understand his pain. Being an outcast as a kid, I can relate.
Walking him to the door, I watch through the window as he climbs
the steps to his house. Then, as his front door shuts, I see the light
to my room at the house go out.

The next morning, John is missing from breakfast. I can't blame
him; the meal is a miserable experience. The air reeks with so
much bitter hatred that even the smell of food can't entice the dogs
into the kitchen. Mary insists on making eggs in lard, and as much
as I know it bothers Sharon, she begrudgingly concedes. Mary
doesn't make any for me.

I find John instead, in his back office. He is high on coke
and won't look at me. "Damn it, John. You're not supposed to be
getting high anymore. You promised! Not with your mom here.
And besides . . . it's Christmas." I am furious. I need his support.

"Not the pipe, baby. Just a few lines . . . till they're gone." He
rambles the excuses, fidgeting from side to side. "Now you go on
and visit." To assure me that everything is fine, he bends to give
me one of his big bear hugs that he knows I love so much and sends
me to keep his family entertained. I hear a muffle and a tap at the
other side of the door. Julie is listening from the next room.

Mary hardly speaks to me the entire time I am there, deliberately looking the other way when she needs to walk past me. Like
a bungling informant, Julie scuttles and bumps behind entryways

and doors a few feet behind me, watching everything I do. *Jeez. Is she trying to catch me and John together or something? What for?* To my relief, they prefer to spend most of their time at David and Karen's cottage. I don't understand right away that it is because Mary is disgusted by me, but I start to get the message because of some sharp quip David makes that his mom prefers him over John on this visit. I try to be polite and offer her a chair or a drink, but I am constantly ignored.

"What is it with her, Sharon? Why is she so mad at me?" I ask after Mary has iced past me one more time.

"Nothing. She just doesn't understand our relationship. She feels you should have no place in this family, that you make yourself at home and it is disrupting our house."

"What? How do you know this?"

"She said she needed to talk to me last night, and she dumped that on me."

"Oh my God! She doesn't even know me!" I cry, shocked. "What did you say?"

"Basically, I told her to mind her own business. No, I was polite. I said, 'Thank you for your concern, but Dawn is in this family by choice and no matter if that makes sense to you or not, it is our decision.'"

"Our . . . what do you mean?"

"Well, she pulled John into the conversation."

"She did? What did he say?"

"The same thing. It wasn't her business and would she kindly butt out, in not so many words. She didn't take it very well."

I am stunned. Both John and Sharon stood up for me. Now I can't wait for Mary and Julie to leave. *She doesn't even know how her son feels.* I stop trying to make polite conversation and decide to keep to myself. Sharon says they aren't worth it, and now I believe her.

John keeps to himself also, walks puffed up and tall past his mom, avoiding her eyes. I suspect he is doing lots more coke and getting angrier.

Mary's anger also grows . . . and grows. She doesn't like the tables turned on her in *her* son's house. She doesn't like it one bit. But how can she make John and Sharon see what she knows is an obvious abomination? Bible in one hand and finger pointing toward the heavens with the other, she storms into the house to confront me as we watch television one evening.

"You! You, you *devil!*" She pokes her finger wildly in my direction. "You don't belong in this house."

John gets up from his chair and stands between us. Sharon sits like stone.

"Mother. Mother! Enough!" John's voice commands.

"Get out! Go!" she yells, her face covered in angry red blotches.

"Mary!" Sharon snaps.

"You mark my words, John. She will bring this house down. Can't you see it?" Mary teeters; her arm presses up to her brow. Dizzy, she falls back into a nearby armchair, out of breath, a clammy sheen of sweat glazing her forehead.

I gape at her, unbelieving. *Does she know how nasty and mean she is being? Why does she want to hurt me? That's not Christian.*

"Dawn . . ." John starts to apologize.

"No. It's all right." I feel my throat constrict with that familiar feeling of hot tears on the verge of eruption. "I have to feed Thor anyway," I lie. I can't reach the door fast enough. On the cold concrete steps outside, in the harsh December sunlight, my internal volcano explodes and I break down. *So this is what it's like to be the devil. Huh. It doesn't feel very powerful . . . or scary,* I think, feeling the sting of Mary's cruel judgment run down my cheeks like an unexpected slap across the face, the kind I got as a child by my own mother. *Great. Now I'm unwanted, here, in the place I call home.*

New Jersey—
Me at 6 months
sitting on the
lap of Great
Aunt Ella

With my Grandma
Dora at age 6
months in New
Jersey. She passed
away waiting for
Dad to come back
from Asia.

My mom, great-grandma, and Great Aunt Ella in the back of the house in New Jersey. You can see the branches of my favorite climbing tree.

Opposite page bottom: With my father, brother, and sister at Asbury Park, NJ. This was one of the last times I spent with my father before he left for Vietnam.

Me, my brother, and my sister took a portrait our first year in Carol City, FL. I was 8 years old, and just about to start the 3rd grade.

My mom and dad in 1977. Dad went back and saw mom in Florida after he left me on my own at 16 in California.

Above: Summer 1977 on a day back from Zuma Beach with John and his sister-in-law, Karen. This light blue Chevy had the plates W-ADD on the back. John's infamous brown Samsonite is packed with his "goodies".

Left: David and Karen's living room surrounded by temptation.

Christmas, 1979. Visit from John's mom & niece. John is strung-out on coke while putting on his good "show" face.

John being escorted out of the courtroom, and later acquitted of murder.

Early 1981. After I ran from John, before the Wonderland murders. I'm at mom's with my brother in Oregon.

I wrote this two weeks
before turning 16.

① Dec 13, 1976

Dear Mom,
        Sorry for not writing sooner
but as you heard I broke my finger.
Well I just got the cast off
yesterday. I had to wear it for 3
weeks.
        THank you very much for the
pictures. They are very nice.
 As soon as I got them I showed
them to everyone in the courts (where
I live). They all said I said I have a
very pretty mother and a foxy brother.
Most of them think me and Wayne look
like twins. I think so to (except the eyes)
I'm sorry I don't have any recent
pictures of me except for the ones we
took at the nude beach, and I don't
think you would like a picture of me
naked. We will probably take some
pictures during the christmas holidays
and after they are developed I'll send
you some.
        I got a letter from Caprice She
said you were buying a non-sergical face
lift when she got my adress from you.
How did you manage to see her? I thought
you would never go to Carol City again?
        School ends Friday for the Christmas
Holidays and starts again January 3.
Please forgive me for not sending anything except my love. But I have no money
and no one wants me to do any work for them

because they need the money for christmas presants too.

Oh yeah!! my bladder infection is gone. The doctor gave me some anti-biotics for it I've been taking them for almost two weeks now.

I will be sweet 16 in two weeks from Wednesday. Remember the birthday party I had last year. I had alot of fun and so did you I think? Man there was about 500 people there. It was great!!! I still thank you mom it was one of the nicest things you did for me. I'll always remember it and you mostly.

I miss you and wayne so much especially now durring Christmas time. I only spent one other christmas away from home before 2 years ago when you sent me to Kentucky.

Well I'd better go now my finger is starting to get sore.

Sorry my writing is so sloppy but this is the first thing I've written since I got my cast off.

Merry Christmas early!

ALL MY LOVE,

LOVE YOU, mom

Dawn

Love you, wayne or Bill.

xxxxxxxxxxxxxxxxxxxxxxx

Dawn Schiller with actors Kate Bosworth and Val Kilmer.

Dawn, Jade, and Max (who played Thor) on the set of Wonderland.

To our Dawn. ✗ We love you

On the set of Wonderland with Kate Bosworth (left), Kate's acting coach, Warner Laughlin (center), and Dawn Schiller.

CHAPTER ELEVEN
When the Bough Breaks—*Snap*

J ohn stumbles home late and kicks off his boots. I have been
    waiting up to talk but have fallen asleep. The familiar *thud*
wakes me from my dozing on the couch; I open one eye and watch
him. He heads straight for the refrigerator and guzzles milk from
the cold metal pitcher, saying nothing. I hear the toilet flush and
the soft sound of socks on linoleum brush past; a blanket falls over
my chest, and he shuffles to bed. I pull myself up and glare into
the dark doorway of his room. *I wish he would have wanted to wake
me. I miss him.*

After his mother and niece leave to go home to Ohio, I move
back into my room at John and Sharon's. Soon after, I enroll in a
typing class to sharpen my office skills. John acts supportive at first
but becomes jealous of my time in school and the countless hours
of homework. "It takes time away from us," he complains. Not
that he spends much time with me lately anyway.

In short order, John continues to break his own promise. I
suspect that he's doing lines of coke again; it isn't hard to figure
out since he leaves remnants of his use, mirrors laced with the fine
dust of coke on the bathroom tile and empty vials rolling at the
bottom of his briefcase. Although he is doing his best to maintain
an appearance of normality, he can't hide the dramatic Jekyll and

Hyde changes taking over his personality. He stays out late, not telling anyone where he's going. There is only one possible explanation: He's out to get high.

In only a few weeks, John's behavior grows darker and darker. When he is home he heads directly for the bathroom, holing up for hours, sitting naked on the toilet, briefcase splayed at his feet erupting paraphernalia, cigarettes, and scribbled bits of paper. Water rushing to fill the tub is a good sign. It means John is ready to come down and his mood will be safe again, goofy and sweet.

The bathtub is also where John gets honest. Scrubbing the dirt and sweat from his body and his soul, he talks about the dogs, asks about the neighbors, and curses porn as he scours his skin red. "Those fucking assholes. They'll ride you hard and put you away wet. Have no morals. They'd sell their mother if they thought it could get them a buck and laid." He laughs at his own irony.

I sit next to the tub and listen to him purge and belittle his profession, glad that when he finally feels clean he will be ready for bed. John and Sharon have stopped communicating altogether. He is avoiding her, and she has nothing to say to someone who "lives" in the bathroom.

"Dawn!" John shouts crossly from the bathroom on an afternoon when Sharon is at work.

"What? What's the matter?" I run from the back office. John's anger flares at the drop of a hat these days, and I don't want to give him any reason to explode.

"Get in here," he orders.

I slip into the bathroom, squeezing past him on the commode, and take a seat on the small step in front of him. His briefcase is open, and on the edge of the bathtub rests a delicately balanced mirror with four lines drawn.

"Here." His voice is gruff as he shoves the mirror and a rolled-up twenty-dollar bill for me to snort the lines in a hurry. I haven't seen the Tiffany's white gold straw for a couple months now.

Snnnuuff, snuff. I inhale quickly, feeling the instant burn bring tears to my eyes.

John hastily snorts and shakes his head wildly. He keeps his face down, staring into the trashed-out briefcase as if deep in thought. "So, uh, where you been?" he asks, running his fingers through his curls, purposely trying to keep his voice calm.

"What do you mean?" I answer casually, my throat and tongue numb as I feel the effects of the drug.

"You know what I mean!" John's tone is venomous, his eyes large, his chin jutting at an accusing angle.

I'm confused. "No, John, really. What are you talking about? You know everywhere I go. Here. The cottages. School. Here mostly," I stammer.

"David told me." He acts as if he knows something.

"Told you? Told you *what?* David doesn't know anything about me. I hardly see him anymore. He goes to that locksmith school all the time."

John's head stays glued to the ground as I defend myself. He picks up a piece of white lint from the corner of the floor and throws it down. Sounding hurt, he asks in a quieter tone, "You sure you're not checking out some young stud from over there in your class?"

"No! John! No! I would never do that to you. I love you. You're everything to me, baby." I walk over to him. "Awww, baby . . ." I cautiously reach over to stroke his shoulder.

He grabs my hand and pulls my arms around him, his head still down. Rocking in my embrace, he mumbles, "Just checking."

I am touched that he is vulnerable at the thought of me leaving him. *Aww. He still wants me.* A glimpse of his fading tender side sputters, a flame on candle wax, reminding me for a moment of the good John.

The doorbell rings.

"That's David. Go and answer the door for me, will ya, babe?" He gives me a quick kiss and shoos me out the door. As I shut the door behind me, I catch a glimpse of him reaching for the mirror again, and the tender moment is gone, replaced with the vision of a robot of a man.

David stays in the bathroom for over an hour before he steps out, wiping his reddened nose, and smiles. "So, you ready to get to work?" he says smugly as he heads to leave.

"I already work, David," I reply defensively. David likes to boss me around as he thinks John does. But I don't love David.

John falls out of the bathroom hopping from foot to foot, pulling on his heavy Frye boots. I can see why he avoids me; his eyes are bloodred, his face drawn and pale. His head whips from side to side as he pats down his pockets checking to make sure he has everything. "A business," John says loosely, looking around the room and still patting his pockets. "Oh. Ha." He laughs awkwardly, finding his smokes in his jacket pocket—a pocket he's already checked several times.

"Business, yeah. How would you like to help us open a lock-smith shop?" David holds the door open, smiling, his lips liver purple and thin.

"Yeah, uh, we'll talk about it later." John pulls a long drag off of the True Blue. "Finish up what you gotta do around here and, uh, come down to David and Karen's." He is gesturing wildly with his hands. "Oh, uh, I love you." He hops over to kiss me, then leaves.

How much coke has he done today? He's acting way messed up.

David has scoped out a small corner shop for his locksmith business next to a liquor store on Pacific Avenue in Glendale. He will be graduating shortly and has everything ready for John to finance the location and buy the equipment. "I'll have it all back to you within a year. Including tuition," he promises. John approves, and David is in hog heaven.

"I agree on one condition," John tells Karen and me. "Dawn works with him."

"What?" I snap.

"Hey, you're my girl and, besides, I need you to look out for my interest." He scratches his head nervously and smiles.

David throws him a hateful look from across the room and thinks for a moment. "I can teach her to cut keys, I guess." He shrugs his shoulders and exhales an endless stream of tobacco smoke.

I'm stunned. After John's earlier comment in the bathroom about David telling some lie about me, David is the last person I want to be around. He needs to stay in John's good graces; that is obvious. The way he depends on John for everything makes me nervous. I can see why Sharon calls him a user. David also knows John loves me. As Sharon has warned from the beginning, John is a jealous guy. He wants to know every little thing I do, so anything David can offer up on me, even lies, will gain him favor in John's eyes. And favor, to David, means more drugs. Now I understand another reason Sharon doesn't like him. "Two-faced," she calls it.

"John?" I ask on the walk back to the house. "You know the three of us don't get along. What are you doing?"

"I need you, baby. To make sure he isn't fucking off and using me. He's a fucking cokehead. You gotta let me know how much shit he does and where he gets it from." He is serious; he wants me to play the middleman. "I think the motherfucker's lying to me."

"Well, I know he's lying if he has anything to say about me!" I don't mention anything about how much coke John himself uses. *Good. He knows what David is like,* I assure myself. *He won't believe him anymore.* John swings a comforting arm around me, staggers slightly, and walks me up the steps.

Keyways Locksmith Service Ltd. opens its doors for business in the spring of 1980. It takes only one month for John and David to notice it isn't doing any business.

"You gotta give it some time, John," David insists, sniffing back a long white line John has handed him on a mirror from the bathroom of the shop. "We need to get established."

"How much time, David? We can't afford this shit without any money coming in." John holds up the mirror and plastic straw in his hand. Clear, viscous snot runs from his nose, but he sucks it up hard and does another line anyway.

The only thing that has been established is John's routine of coming into the shop and using the bathroom to get high. No announcement, no hello, he sneaks in without a peep. Like a specter materializing, he spooks me. *How long has he been in there?*

John's paranoia is growing. He wants to know what is going on when he isn't around and tries to listen through the walls while hiding in the bathroom and getting high. I catch myself paranoid too, jumping at every noise or movement to lean my ear toward the bathroom, fully expecting to hear John tapping and snorting in the back.

David and Karen know he has drugs when he shows up, and they want some. So do I.

John takes turns calling us each into his porcelain shrine to sit at his feet like begging, starving puppies to do a line. Each of us is giddy when he calls us one by one.

When it is my turn, John carefully, intentionally takes his time. "Where did you go today?" His voice is stern, not showing any hint of softness. Again, he acts as if he has inside information.

Tap, tap, tap. The white nuggets crumble under the sharp razor's edge.

I twist my hands nervously around each of my fingers, stomach tightening, eyes glued to the crystals on the mirror. "Nowhere," I answer truthfully. I hate that he dangles the drugs like a carrot in front of my face. It makes me want them more, and I know where his questions are leading. "Here. That's all, baby."

Tap, tap, tap. He keeps on.

I get anxious. He's pressuring me to falsely come clean. I know what to do. To prove I am faithful, I recite my exact steps from waking this morning to sitting now on the floor at his feet. *He has to believe me if I tell him everything.*

"Yeah, right." He is not satisfied.

I don't know what else to tell him, but I beg him to believe me.

John pulls back his cheek with his thumb to clear his sinuses, dives in, and snorts the large, fatter line. "Here." He shoves the mirror at me with the thin, small line and dismisses me.

I hate how John is acting. I hate how I am acting. He is cold and angry and growing more and more distrustful of me. He is scaring me; my fear is covered by the high of cocaine. *Why?* I ask myself. *I know I'm faithful. I do everything to be trustworthy. He knows that. He's gotta know that!* I rack my brain trying to figure out why John is so irrational and suspicious of me. *It has to be David,* I think angrily.

⚜

"We're adding on," John yells, surprising me by barging into the front of the shop one afternoon.

"What?" I'm shocked to see his upbeat entrance. "Hi. Hey, you're happy for some reason." I run over to hug him.

"You betcha! We're gonna have two businesses. A second-hand store in the front, perfect with a locksmith shop in the back. You and me, baby! We're gonna be in business and in charge of the front. Can you do it?"

David's trailing behind him and heads straight for his desk in the back. They are both high as a kite.

"Yeah, I can do it. I'd love it. We can resell all our finds from garage sales." I am hesitant about the idea but like it much better than being under the constant scrutiny of David and Karen. I resent working under David's thumb cutting keys, and I distrust him every time he watches what I'm doing. *He's lying about me to get drugs from John,* my gut tells me. *I just know it.*

⚜

John, Sharon, and I sit down for what is now a rare evening dinner together. It is another of John's weak attempts to hold on to his rapidly declining personality. He hasn't slept for at least three days, and his eyes are bloodshot, his skin pale, his mind spacey.

"What should we call the new business, John?" I ask, trying to get him to participate in a mealtime conversation.

He shrugs, barely interested, and makes a feeble nod toward Sharon. "You two think of a name." It looks like his high is wearing off.

Sharon loves the idea: a brain challenge. She stops for a minute to mull it over. "Mmmmm, let me see. Aha! The Just Looking Emporium!" I can tell her enthusiasm is an attempt to bring John out of his sullen mood.

"Yeah! I get it," I join in. "You mean name it so people won't be pressured to buy, but once they come in and see something so cool, so unique, they'll have to buy it."

"Exactly!" Sharon is pleased with herself.

We begin the renovation with dedication. At least I do. John's enthusiasm is fueled by the speedy effect of the drugs. When he shares with me, together we are a frenzied team. Sharon stops by after work to drop off boxes and supplies while John and I design and build brick and wood shelves for the front windows, hanging plants to dangle and absorb the full sun. Days turn into nights as we race to get the Just Looking Emporium open for business. John sparingly issues lines of coke to help me keep up with him, but I know he is sneaking more when he disappears into the back. We paint and hammer into the wee hours of the morning, stopping when the rising sun streaks through the windows and burns our tired eyes.

Gathering inventory is easy for us. Our collection of yard sale booty has been growing for years. It's simple enough to stock the shelves with knickknacks and still-worthy pieces of dismantled treasures salvaged from the depths of John's garage. Outside, on the redbrick north wall of the shop, John and I paint a massive arched rainbow and *Just Looking Emporium* in bold colors underneath. Beneath the rainbow and tucked in the back corner is a conservative black and yellow *Keyways Locksmith Service* logo, which seems out of place against our giant psychedelic hippie sign.

❧

Proudly I stand admiring the shine on the glass display case John and I have arduously placed in front of my large oak desk. *Where is he?* I worry. *He promised to be here for the opening.*

"Just have to pick up a few more things for the store," he told me on the phone earlier, but now he is nowhere to be found. He's like a noisy ghost who has suddenly evaporated, leaving a gaping hole of nothing where it once haunted. In my heart, I know he is out scoring drugs. Still, I try to believe he is telling me the truth. I want to believe in him.

The business opens uneventfully. A few stragglers wander in to browse through the store. Perhaps there is a sale or two, but my mind is only on John. I'm hurt that he hasn't shown up on this special day, the opening of our business.

He doesn't return until late the next day, slipping in through the bathroom. I figure it out when David constantly disappears from his workbench for over an hour and Karen paces into the back, pretending to get supplies. My stomach begins to tighten. I want to see him too. I walk to the back to interrupt the creepy hovering of bees to the cocaine pollen.

"John?" I tap on the door and hear a muffled, hurried fumbling, then silence. "John." I tap even harder.

"Yeah?" His reply is short, suppressed.

"What are you doing?" My mouth presses into the wooden door.

It flings open. "Come in, quick!" David is hunched in the corner, staring at the floor and smoking a cigarette. John, on the toilet, bends over his briefcase. He palms the freebase pipe.

"What is that?" I point to the pipe. I know he broke his promise for good this time, and I have been expecting it.

With an awkward laugh, he motions for me to be quiet. Then

he draws a long, bubbling toke from the glass pipe, pulls me down, and blows the rancid smoke into my mouth. I hold it in as I have been taught. Falling into place as another cocaine bee, I hang on to my breath until I'm dizzy and then fall to my knees to exhale. My ears instantly ring, and in that split second it seems as if freebase has never left my memory; it is an insidious tumor in my temporal lobe. I look up at John. He grins at me, a clownlike nubby-toothed grin. *He looks like the Grinch who stole Christmas,* I say to myself.

"Now go back out and close up the shop," John orders. Obediently, I do what I'm told.

❧

Freebase is back in our lives; there is no questioning it. I never ask John why he broke his promise about the pipe; I only accept that this is now the way it is. Once his secret use isn't secret anymore, John makes a last-ditch effort to show that he is in control of his drug habit and not the other way around. The effort is lame, and John is again gone for days on the pretense of purchasing more inventory for the shop. Predictably, when he eventually comes home, he is empty-handed. The back room is bathroom central again, and David and Karen use every excuse to be granted entry by the *king*.

A few months have withered away, and business for the Just Looking Emporium is bad. We have no customers, and we have nothing of value to sell anyway. John doesn't seem to care, and when I complain to him about the lack of inventory, he casually rips apart a cabinet or shelf and displays the fractured pieces for sale. I'm embarrassed to assist a customer in the purchase of obvious junk. But John ignores my pleas to shape the place up and, instead, hides out in his cramped porcelain cocaine haven.

Indian summer September, late in the evening, I hear a bang. *What's that?* I am working late dusting the shelves and cleaning the glass on the display cases. I wonder if it is the ghost of John. I grab my protective baseball bat, the one I keep hidden by my desk, and walk slowly into the back room. "John? Is that you?" There is silence. I think about calling 911, then decide to check out the window to see if his van is here. It is. *It wasn't there a minute ago.* But something is wrong. The bang I heard was angry, and the silence is tense and mean. "John?" I walk slowly toward the bathroom door.

Wham! The door flies open. John rushes like a gale force wind in my direction.

"So! You gonna tell me who ya been fucking?" He is shouting an attack song like a martial arts expert, storming toward me, his eyes bugged out, maniacal, his arms and body stretched out on the offense.

Walking backward into the shop I stammer, "N-n-n-nobody, John! Quit it!" I clench the smooth, wooden bat in my hands.

He charges me menacingly, veins bulging, a furious scowl distorting his face.

Fear washes over me. "Quit it, John!" I shout again. "Nobody! Stop it!" I peek down at the bat in my hands dragging the ground. John looks at it too and strains to compose himself. He takes a step to the side, settles down for a moment.

He snatches a paper towel and some Windex and begins to roughly clean the already clean glass of the cabinet.

I circle to the other side, distancing myself.

Fuming, John purposely calms his tone. "So who were you with today?"

"Today? Nobody, John. Really. Who told you that?" I watch his every move.

"Didn't you go to lunch today?"

"Ye-yeah!"

"Who did you meet there?"

"Meet? I didn't meet anyone. I went to the Mexican place down the street in the Galleria, but I ate by myself!"

"You mean you didn't meet the busboy for a quickie after you ate your taco?"

Fear turns to terror when I realize he is serious. I get really confused. Anything I say will be wrong; he will find a way to make me guilty. "Busboy? What busboy?"

Bam! John's hand flies out across the glass and lands hard across my face.

I hit the ground with a *thud* that sends the air from my lungs. I immediately feel the searing pain of the blow rip through my jaw. It cracks with a loud *snap* and aches like it is broken. Stunned and in shock, I have no vision except for sparks of light against a black background.

In an instant, John is on top of me, hands grasping the collar of my shirt and shaking me. "Who is it?" he demands. "I'll kill the motherfucker!"

A quick rush of adrenaline and a flash of Carol City have me bucking and flailing for my life. *"Aaaaahhhhhhhhh!"* I let out a banshee scream at the top of my lungs, throwing wild punches and grabbing at his clothes.

John tries to hold down my arms, and I fight even harder, sliding across the room. The back of my head hits the wall as he pins me against it. "Fuck you, bitch. I know you're fucking around on me. Now tell me. Who? Who?"

"Fuck you! Fuck you! Fuck you!" I wrench a knee up to kick him in the groin. His face pales with surprise and pain as he loosens his hold on me. Scrambling out from under his weight, I crawl over to the baseball bat and hold it up against him. My cheek is numb except for the sharp pain deep inside my mouth, and I feel

something warm trickle from the corner of my lip.

John jumps up and stares, surprised. He looks at his finger, disbelieving, and shakes off a droplet of blood. Beet red and panting for breath, he lunges at me, grabbing for the bat. Falling to the floor, we fight to gain control of it. John's strength overpowering, he rips it out of my hands.

I curl into a fetal position, close my eyes, cover my head, and expect to feel my skull crush in like a grapefruit.

Crash! John brings the bat down into the glass display case and smashes down over and over. *Crash, bam, crash!* The shattered pieces fly everywhere as he demolishes the once-shiny case into a pile of rubble. I curl into a tighter ball and try to avoid the debris until, finally, the breaking noise stops.

John, exhausted, bleeding, and breathing hard, slides to the ground and lays down the bat. I hear a breathless whimpering sound, like a wounded desert coyote, and then an unfamiliar sound.

Carefully, I take my hands away from my face and peek over at him.

His head in his hands, he is sobbing, pitiful, and poor. "Baby? Baby, I'm sorry." He chokes back tears and wipes the sweat from his eyes. Still weeping, he reaches out his bloody hand. "Come here, baby. Please?"

Emotion gushes out of me like a tsunami. "John! John! Why, baby, why? Why did you do that? Why did you hit me? Oh my God, I can't believe you hit me!" I sob uncontrollably. I touch the side of my face and the blood from the corner of my mouth. My heart aches as I weep. "I *love* you, John . . ."

John inches his way over to me and wraps me up in his lap. "Are you all right, baby? I'm sorry; I'm sorry; I'm sorry. Let me see." He gently traces my face to assess the damage.

I close my eyes. The physical pain of my cheek is nothing compared to the searing pain in my heart. The man I love has hurt me. He hurt the very person he loves and cherishes and adores.

My thoughts numb. Nothing makes sense anymore. I don't understand how love can hit you and make you bleed. "Why, John, why?" I cry into his lap.

"Oh, baby, forgive me . . . please. I'm sorry. It was just . . . you're here every day and I never get to see you. David tells me stuff, and I miss you."

"I never cheat on you, John. Why did you hit me? I never cheat on you!" I insist. "David doesn't know anything. He lies to you."

"I believe you, baby. I believe you. Please forgive me. I never meant to hit you, baby."

We cry into each other's arms for hours, rocking back and forth and cradling our wounds. Kissing my head and my cheeks, John promises over and over that he'll never let it happen again.

The morning sunlight stings my eyes. Raised red welts already show on my arms. John helps me up and guides me through glittering shards and splintered wood to the back door and the van. We head home to leave the mess for David and Karen to clean.

My mind cannot wrap itself around John's violence. *This didn't happen. This didn't happen.* My mind chants the mantra to reverse the hour before. With all my being, I need to believe this will never happen again.

What I don't realize is that before John exploded, he was seriously out of dope.

⁂

I don't open our part of the shop for a week afterward. I can't bear facing the scene of such heartbreak—or seeing David and Karen. In my eyes, it is their fault that John hit me. *If it weren't for David feeding John all those lies for dope, this would never have happened*, I seethe.

John doesn't push going to the shop either. Every spare moment he checks and double-checks on me to see that I am all right and not planning to leave. For three days I lie low at the house, hanging out and watching TV.

Sharon goes to bed early, oblivious to the newfound strain between us and John's nervousness and tender doting on me.

On the fourth day after the terrible destruction of the Just Looking Emporium, John is spunky and silly, telling jokes and playing with the dogs. "Come on. Get dressed, baby," he says warmly. "Come with me on a quick errand."

"Where?" I ask, making sure he isn't taking me to the shop.

"Just an errand. Now hurry up!"

In the van, John holds my hand and serenades me with Gordon Lightfoot tunes again, trying to lighten my mood.

I haven't seen him like this in a long time. I start to feel relaxed, sensing a lifting of the endless dark edge of the melancholy cloud that has hovered over us since that day at the shop. As the tension melts, the painful memory of violence begins to wash away. I want to forget it ever happened and feel myself starting to believe that this normally warm, loving, attentive man has come back to me, even if it has taken such a horrible fight.

It isn't to last long.

Waiting outside of the fancy white house on the cul-de-sac, a gray-haired man in his bathrobe is calling his dog in the yard to the left of me. A small fuzzy-headed poodle bolts out of the bushes, happy to be done with his business. The sun is bright as I look up from under the street sign: *Dona Lola Drive.*

Stretching, Thor wiggles out from under the covers, licks my face, and snuggles into my neck.

"Hey. Good morning, sweetie. Whew! Your breath! Thor, stop it!"

He has to pee and nips at my nose. *John. Where is he?* I sit up against the blue vinyl seat back and block the sun from my eyes. The early light glistens off the remaining dew on the outside corners of the car window; the condensation on the inside has dried. *I have to pee too.* I wiggle urgently. Thor gets antsy. "Shhhh. I can't, Thor. You gotta hold it too," I whisper and squeeze him tight to my chest, slinking down again and trying to fall back to sleep.

Almost an hour later, John slides into the driver's seat and nudges me over. "Stay down," he hisses. Half-asleep, I don't move.

"Almost, almost," he chants, driving around the circle and out toward Laurel Canyon Boulevard. "Okay, now!" He helps me peel off the blankets and pulls me up. Thor jumps into his lap and leans on his chest, happy to see him. "Ha-ha!" John lets out a laugh. "Yes, yes. I know, Thor!"

"I gotta pee too! What took you so long?"

"Oh, man. The dude wouldn't let me leave!" John sounds exasperated. "He likes me so much he insists I stay. And this ain't the kind of guy you say no to! Sorry, baby. Did you get some sleep?" He is smacking gum like a full-speed locomotive.

"Yeah, we slept," I pout. "Thor and I gotta pee, John." I'm really not in the mood to hear some story when I can easily figure out that he hung out to get high.

We stop at DuPar's Coffee Shop at the bottom of Laurel Canyon on Ventura Boulevard. John lets Thor out on the grass while I head out to make a beeline to the bathroom inside.

"Here. Bring me a cup of coffee?" He calls me back, digging for change from his pocket.

When I pay for the coffee, John is at the end of the counter talking on the phone with his hand cupped around the receiver. He hangs up as soon as I approach him.

Back in the car, he says, "One more stop and we'll be home."

He reaches over to give me a reassuring kiss that smells of stale cigarettes and plaque-lined teeth.

"One more stop? John!" I grab his pack of cigarettes off the dash. A huff of disappointment escapes my lips.

His face shimmers with an oily sheen, and his wrinkles are deep with dirt from being awake and unbathed all night. "I know, baby. I know. Just one more, please." He kisses my forehead as he steers the car onto the road with his coffee-free hand. "I promise it will be quick this time."

"I hope so." I give in, not happy about having to wait outside again, and I kick my feet angrily up against the dash.

"I promise." He smiles his jesterlike ear-to-ear grin. "Gum?" he offers, switching the subject as smoothly as he changes lanes.

***

The car winds back up the twisted road of Laurel Canyon Boulevard, passing Dona Pegita, the road to the cul-de-sac I waited on the night before. Turning up on Lookout Mountain Avenue at the other side of the hill, we follow the signs to Wonderland Avenue. Twisting up the narrow, curvy road, we stop on the hill in front of multilevel terraced homes sandwiched next to each other on all sides.

"Wait here and stay really quiet," he whispers harshly enough that spittle flies onto the steering wheel. He pulls to a stop, does a quick double take up and down the streets, and hops out of the car.

John's voice jolts fear into me. I grab Thor and slump onto the pile of blankets at my waist. "Hurry!" I rasp after him.

***

John comes back in about an hour: fast, as he promised, this time.

I stay down again until we are well on our way home. When I finally sit up, I stretch my aching bones. "Well, that wasn't fun!" I tell him sarcastically.

"I know, baby," he says, reaching over to hold my hand. "But I couldn't get away. I got some goodies for us, though!" He winks.

"Cool. That's cool." I don't really feel like partaking in any goodies. I want to be in my bed, but I know what will happen instead when we get to the house. John will hole up in the bathroom, twitching and barking orders until the drugs are gone. *I'm just going along with John's plans right now,* I tell myself, because my plan of having a comfortable business in Glendale is pretty much extinct and I know I have nobody else.

John reminds me of this nearly every day. "Your family doesn't care about you, just like mine doesn't care about me. Your father left you, and Sharon will be pissed if she finds out about the drugs." Throughout the passing months and years, John has often reminded me of how my horrible family dumped me in California. Only lately, he's been saying it more often.

❧

As expected, the Just Looking Emporium closes its doors forever by the end of September of 1980. I can't stand to look at it anymore, and I think John can't either. David keeps his part of the business open while John removes our inventory and sells it all for coke. Back at the cottages, stucco peels and mold buckles the exterior of every unit in the complex. John and I sneak into my old apartment to get high. The obscure door between garages is boarded up and the inside is dank and dark, a perfect mimic of John's mood. The burlap walls are stained and shredded, smelling like wet cardboard. Still, it's better than doing drugs at the house with Sharon there, and John isn't interested in sharing with David and Karen anymore. "David has to keep working to pay me back," he justifies.

John's pace is frantic and worried. His calloused hand and eagle eye make sure I'm always by his side. My jaw still aches from *that night,* and John makes me jumpy and nervous. But with just the right amount of freebase in my lungs, I stay in foolish hopes that this craziness will soon end. It doesn't. My bookkeeping duties are barely manageable with the amount of drugs John brings home, and the tight, paranoid leash he has wrapped around my whereabouts is suffocating and cruel. If I need to collect the rent for the month and simply knock on tenants' doors, he interrogates me ruthlessly for hours on end, holding the cocaine in my face as leverage for me to *tell him the truth.*

John's interrogations are regular now; morning to night and over again.

"Stop it, John," I implore in tears, scared to death that he'll get violent again. "I'm not lying."

Sometimes he believes me, or pretends to believe me, and dismisses me military style. I know he's still angry; I turn away and swallow hard, apprehensive. *Something bad is going to happen. I just know it.*

It does. He takes it out on other things now; the small pieces of my heart that over the years he has allowed into my life—other than him. My beloved garden: destroyed in a flash. I find my entire lovely, tended garden—ready-to-be-harvested squash, tomatoes, and cucumbers—piled and rotting in the middle of the courtyard on a day I let Thor out to pee. Startled and bewildered tenants step gingerly over the pulverized mounds of vegetables. My heart bleeds, pierced straight to the core at the cruelty of John's destruction of my small, nurtured space.

Sharon sees me crumpled on the porch holding my gut and crying. She steps back into the shadow of the house, emotionless, as if she has accidentally walked into a private conversation.

John is becoming steadily abusive on every level now and steadily more insane.

⁕

"Where's your ring?" I ask him after answering his frantic rapping at the garage apartment door.

He was wearing the large dragonfly when he left, and I have a bad feeling now that it's no longer on his hand. *I know men who have lost everything. They'd sell their mothers to get high.* His warning lectures from months ago echo eerily in my head. *Lose everything they own. Lose everything they own.*

He doesn't answer but only brushes past me to set up his pipe in the bedroom.

"John, are you all right?" I follow him nervously. "What's the matter?" He looks shaky and in a foul mood. Snapping his pipe together, he makes himself a big hit of freebase, grabs his stomach, and holds it in.

The stream of residue billows around my head as he exhales at my face. *Uh-oh.* My heart thumps like a drum in my chest; my palms sweat and twitch. *He's mad again.* I straighten up the room, desperate to become invisible.

"Where did you go today?" He flares his nostrils and glares accusingly.

"Nowhe—"

Wham! In one forward lunge, he flings his pipe into his brief-case and throws me on the bed. As I struggle to get free, John sits on top of my chest, pressing my arms down above my head. I am paralyzed. *"Now!"* he hisses dangerously, deliberately slowing his breath from our scuffle. *"WHERE—HAVE—YOU—BEEN?"*

"Stop! John!"

He yanks my arms down and pins them with his knees, taking

one of his free hands and covering my mouth. "I'll rip your eyes out, you lying bitch!" he sneers, plunging his thumbs into the corner sockets of my skull.

"Noooooo!" I try to yell, but his forearms muffle my voice. Like a bobblehead doll bouncing wildly on a bumpy road, I frantically turn my head from side to side.

The sweat from the battle and the heat of the claustrophobic apartment cause John's thumbs to slip roughly off my eyes, his nails slicing the edges of my lids.

"Ahhhh!" I scream at the pain.

John's bloodshot eyes widen in disbelief at my ability to escape his grip; then, in another fit of rage, he draws his arm back and punches me in the mouth.

The room is black with flashes of light like electric sparks. Blood splatters crimson on the pale sheets at my head.

John pushes himself off of me, smears the blood from his hand on the pillow by my face, and walks away.

I spit out a warm metallic mouthful of blood and roll to my side, holding my face. I feel the hole in my lip and the tooth that juts through, and I scream pitifully from the pain. I want to die. *How can this be?* I can't comprehend. *What's going on?* The horribleness of *this* overwhelms me.

On the way out the door, John holds up a stack of papers that look familiar through the burn of my cloudy vision. "Here. Now you can give these to your new boyfriend!" he spews venomously. One by one, he tears them to shreds, tossing mutilated pieces of the deepest, most private years of my life in the air before leaving me to my wounds.

"Noooo!" My breath catches in my throat when I recognize the scattered papers. *Oh God, no. My poetry!* I stagger over to the fragile paper fragments now littered on the gray and mildewed carpet. Precious words from all levels of my soul—words that brought me comfort, joy, release, and love—now scattered like a discarded jigsaw puzzle. "I wrote this one for my father," I cry out loud, a new stab of pain stinging me with the loss of treasured memories, all I have left of him. "And this one. This, this one. I wrote this for *him*." Unbelievably, more tears find their way down my bloodstained cheeks as I realize John mistakenly assumed these were written for someone else. *He really doesn't think I love him . . . How can that be?* Eyes stinging and mouth throbbing, I clutch the precious tattered bits of me in my arms and rock in place for hours, blocking out the violence, willing the devastating destruction gone.

To and fro, to and fro, the constant, simple rhythm carves a space in time.

A safe place.

John sticks his head in the doorway later that evening. I jump out of my skin. "Come eat," he says, abruptly turning to walk back to the house.

Sharon, I think. *She probably wants to have dinner. I gotta think of something to say about my face! I can't tell her what happened. But what can I say? Oh God, maybe she'll figure it out! Maybe she'll be able to stop him. He's out of his mind. He'll hurt me again; I know it. Maybe she'll help me. Maybe?* My mind races wildly, seeking a way out of John's torturous grip. I head to the sink to splash cold water on my face. My lips and eyes are swollen red, the right eye almost shut. I roll my tongue over my bottom lip, numb now, and poke it easily through the hole made by my tooth. *Oh shit! She'll definitely see this.* I hold out small hope that I can still make this not real. *I'm gonna need some bandages,* I acknowledge, feeling a jab in my heart. I clean up the blood and sweat as best I can, take a deep breath, and harness my sinking sadness. Hiding my face with an old cleaning towel, I follow John's order and make my way across the courtyard.

The big front door squeaks, and the doorknob clicks my way in loudly. *Please don't let her hear me.* I rush swiftly across the varnished floor to my room. I don't want to be here. The shame of Sharon seeing me beaten and bruised pains me as much as being punched by John did, but I'm scared John will get violent again if I don't obey him.

In the back of my mind, though, I pray Sharon will see how badly I have been beaten and help somehow. John is afraid of Sharon. "I'm Italian, John," she has said. "I can kill you in your sleep. Remember the penicillin you're allergic to? How about some spaghetti?" Sharon has always let him know she's the boss if he pushes too far.

John is in the bathroom. I can hear the water running, and the *tink, tink, tink* of porcelain on glass from the kitchen means Sharon is washing the dishes. *He won't do anything with her around,* I reason. Thoughts about my poetry slam into my spirit again, and my eyes are ready to cry. But I'm spent; the weeping well is dry. In my room, I fidget with my stuffed penguin and shift the few knickknacks on my nightstand. There is my jewelry box, pink and heart-shaped with a delicate ballerina that spins to "Somewhere Over the Rainbow."

Something doesn't feel right. I open the box, cautious, hoping my gut is wrong. *Oh no! Not my rings! And my fairy—my beautiful gold fairy's gone!* I stifle a wail. *Drugs! He's been selling our stuff for drugs. Just like the guy who lost everything. Just exactly the same.* I can't believe it. *How can this get worse?* Numbly, I walk into the kitchen. "Shh, Shh, Sharon." My voice cracks, barely a peep. "Do you have anything for a cut eye—eyes? An, an, and my lip?" I stutter, raising my head into the light, averting her gaze.

"Oh. Okay?" She sighs and studies my face. "All right. Let me see what I've got."

"I, I, I had an accident." My lie falls flat, like the hollow *ping* of rain on a cheap tin roof, but I desperately want Sharon to *know* what John's doing to me—killing me—without having to tell her. *She will know. She has to know,* I pray.

"Oh," she responds simply again. Removing her glasses, she squints at my face. She says not a word, but squeaks over to the bathroom door in her white, polished nurse's shoes. "John. I need to get in there," she calls into the doorjamb. There's a rustling, and a minute later the door flings open and she steps inside, closing the door behind her.

She doesn't know, I tell myself with disbelief. *Did John tell her something?*

She returns with eyewash, antibiotic ointments, and bandages. "Come over here and sit down." She guides me to the couch and silently commences tending to my wounds, wrapping a patch on my right eye and placing a butterfly bandage on my lip where my tooth has punctured through. Her tone sharp and crystal clear, she recites the proper instructions for the continued medical care of my face.

"Thanks," I mumble, forcing back a sob. I sit for a stinging moment in a last, hopeful silence, willing her to ask me for the truth. *Please, please. Just ask me how this really happened. Please see. See what he is doing.*

Sharon gathers the bandages and tubes, lines them neatly on the counter. She snubs out her cigarette and wordlessly walks to her room, leaving me to sit on the couch, staring blankly into a dark and dusty corner of an overly decorated bookshelf, numb with despair.

Hours later I lie in my room, the lights turned out, pretending I'm asleep. I'm too scared to really drift off. I know John is listening for any noise that may come from my direction. He and Sharon watch television together, parts of a *Benny Hill* episode I know Sharon doesn't care for, in the living room. A thick, suffocating silence hovers like a deadly fog on a winding highway; not one word is spoken. The tapping of the dogs' toenails on the polished wood floors tells me of Sharon's movements. She is up and heading to her bedroom, leaving John by himself. *No!* I think futilely. *Don't leave me alone with him!* I can see her shadow cast against the entryway walls from her bedroom light, on for only a minute, and then out with a final *click,* leaving my desperate, silent pleas unheard.

Just as I have dreaded, John comes into my room after plenty of time, when he thinks Sharon is sound asleep. A silent tornado ready to wreak havoc, he hisses, "You can't hide behind Sharon." He walks past the foot of my bed into his back office. "I'll find out sooner or later." He slams file cabinet drawers and rifles through books up on high shelves. I hear the familiar tapping of a razor on glass and a quick, harsh snort of cocaine.

If I'm loud enough, Sharon will hear and he won't do anything. I get brave. "I'm not cheating on you, John!" I yell out. I hope he will get nervous enough to leave me alone if he thinks Sharon will wake up and catch him. I want Sharon to catch him. *Maybe she can stop him.*

It backfires. John's temper flares. He jumps quickly from behind his office wall, pretending he'll walk past me to the living room, but then he spins around and springs on top of my chest in an instant replay of the action earlier that day. This time I'm expecting him and thrash ferociously before he can pin down my arms. I struggle free and run. John charges after me. I think for a quick instant about calling out for Sharon, but head for the bathroom instead, locking the door behind me.

Adrenaline slams my heart against my chest; my breath is ragged and wild. I can take no more.

Bang, bang, bang. "Open this door, Dawn. *Now!*" he demands, his voice, demonic, burns through the crack of the door.

I can see the wood molding buckle from his crushing weight. Desperately, I search the room. *Escape! I've got to escape. I gotta get out of here.* For a second I imagine squeezing through the tiny window above the sink and know there isn't enough time. *He's almost in. He'll catch me for sure. What do I do? What do I do? There's no way out!* My mind frantically examines every corner, every crevice I can possibly disappear through. *Where? Where? Where? There's no way out! There's no way out!* Pure, doomed terror engulfs me as if I'm falling through quicksand.

Then I look down . . . and I see a way. The long white cabinet drawer . . . the medicine drawer where Sharon keeps the medical supplies for the house . . . the multicolored bottles of pills smile at me like a friend who has shown up to help. *Darvons*, I remember with clarity. *That's where Sharon keeps her Darvon.* I leap for its shiny brass handles, yank it open, and plow through the meticulously lined prescription bottles and tins one by one until I find the pills that will grant me refuge, give me peace, blessed oblivion.

John's banging gets louder, but I can ignore him now. I have a way out.

"*Dawn!*"

I'll take them all, I convince myself. *I'll get out of here right now. This is enough to never come back. I have to get away from him. I have to get out of here!*

I hear tapping at the lock. John has a set of David's lock picks. A surge of fear races through me, and like a cornered animal willing to jump to its death, I hurriedly fling off the lid and down the entire bottle, scooping handfuls of water from the sink faucet.

There. I slide to the floor. *It's over. He won't be able to get to me; he won't be able to get me now!* I curl in a ball and weep.

The door bursts open. "What did you do?" John yells harshly with acid under his breath. He picks up the empty bottle, smashes it into the sink. Bits of broken glass rocket out across the room. "What the fuck did you do?"

I don't move. *Let him do what he wants now,* I think. *It'll be over soon.*

He yanks me up by my arm and scans my eyes. *"Shit!"* he curses, then panics and runs to the refrigerator.

Almost instantly I feel lightness in the air, a floating, and then my head begins to spin in a centrifugal force like on the Gravitron ride at the carnival as I sense the downers spreading through my bloodstream. Grabbing hold of walls and doorways, I stagger back to my bedroom, uninterested in John's banging in the kitchen, and collapse back on the bed. The room and ceiling whirl wildly around me; my body is the only thing in the room not moving.

John's distorted features appear near my face. He is kneeling next to me on the bed. "Here. Drink this!" he demands in a low, short hiss, pushing a glass filled with half a dozen or so raw eggs in my face.

I shove the glass away, my hand feeble and lame, almost spilling the slimy liquid.

"Drink it!" he orders again, his face swollen red with anger. Then, in a second that I don't understand, Thor's little face is sandwiched between John's large calloused hands. "If you don't drink this right now, I'll squeeze his fucking head till his brains pop out!" The brown of my tiny Chihuahua's eyes bulge out of his skull; he is terror filled in John's viselike grip.

"Stop!" I cry.

Thor lets out a paralyzed yelp, his face crushed brutally tight. John keeps squeezing.

"Okay!" I wish the pills will take me faster, but they don't.

"No. Don't hurt him, John. Stop!" I let out a sob. "Okay!"

John drops Thor like a worthless river rock and thrusts the glass to my lips. He tilts my head back and pours the slippery fluid down my throat.

Falling back on the bed, I look up at the ceiling and smile. I already see stars, like the heavens have come. John is pacing back and forth from his office to my room. *Those eggs aren't going to work,* my body tells me. The pills are beginning to take a stronger hold. The room swirls . . . stars spin . . . sounds fade away . . .

"Are you dying yet?" a male voice rings like a bell tone through space . . .

Since birth, a voice answers from deep inside my core.

"Are you near?" The male voice is impatient.

I don't know . . . I'm afraid to look.

As if sucked through a vacuum of time and space, I become aware of a shape—my body—spiraling, consumed by a black hole abyss. Then, without effort, body and mind are one again and spontaneously the vomiting begins, purging my entire body, from the roots of my hair to the veins in my toes.

The next morning I feel rough, like I've been run over by a semi. I awake not knowing where I am. It takes me several minutes to pierce through the blurriness of my vision and see Sharon standing at the foot of my bed, dressed in her uniform for work. She asks curtly, "You up?"

I raise my throbbing head. *Whaaaa—?* Quickly, I lie back down. The pounding is immeasurable, splitting my temples. I gather my bearings as best I can. Slowly I remember the night before. *Oh no. John.* I wince. *I'm still here.* Despair consumes me. *The vomiting—all over the floors, the walls . . . Thor! Where's*

Thor? I lift myself up on my elbows with difficulty. *My skin. What are these bumps all over me?* I am covered in red, swollen welts that look like bee stings and itch like mosquito bites.

Sharon brings in a pail of soapy water, a mop, and rags. "I'll do that, Sharon," I rasp. "I'll get that." She throws me a dirty look and walks out. *She had to have heard everything. She must know the Darvon is missing.* As I worry, I laboriously set about cleaning up the smelly mess. Then I numbly walk into the living room to face her. "Sharon, I'm sorry. Ssssorrry for the mess."

"Here. Put this on your skin." She hands me a tube of ointment. "It'll help you with the swelling and itch." She stares at the television as if she is using it to hypnotize herself away from this moment; the flashes of light and conversational tone of the narrator take her to a safe place for a moment. Her eyes still mesmerized with the glow of the TV, she robotically recites the physiological reasons for the welts on my body. "Your circulatory system was in the process of shutting down when you took the pills. You puked before the major vessels were affected, but the capillaries near your skin collapsed—they're the first to go—and that's what's causing your reaction."

"Oh." I blink. *Is that all she's thinking?* I wonder, amazed. I scan the house for John and notice with relief his leg sticking out of the blankets of his king-sized bed. A few minutes more, her eyes still fixed on the TV, Sharon picks up a white envelope from the counter and presents it to me. Then, walking into her bedroom she turns and, for the first time, shuts her door.

It is a letter. My hands are shaking, and my skin is crawling with itching bumps. Nervously I open it and cry. The long, sharp points and curves of her handwriting are like daggers in my open wounds. Through the blur of my tears, I read.

Dear Dawn,

How could you do such a thing? I am a woman who respects life; nurtures and cares for it. My career in nursing is a reflection of how deeply I feel about human life. I have always believed that I taught you that and that you understood and believed the same. To treat life with such poor regard—to do this to yourself—is to me, an insult to my kindness in letting you live here in my home. I am extremely disappointed in you, that you would have such little respect for me and especially for yourself! We will talk more when I get home from work. There has to be some changes from the behavior I have witnessed last evening or you can no longer have a home here. I hope you can see my point and can find the strength to look into yourself for this utter failure of character. This must never happen again.

Sharon Ann Holmes

Oh my God! I weep. She doesn't know. *What am I going to do? Now she's mad at me, and she doesn't know the truth!* The feeling of being a caged animal returns; it is a sharp, gut-wrenching aware-ness. My skin, my chest, my buttocks, my back, and legs burn and sting, walls close in on me, and my brain shuts down. *This isn't happening,* I chant, willing time to reverse. *Everything is really over now. No! This can't be happening!* But it *is* happening, and I know deep down my time in what I used to call home is over.

CHAPTER TWELVE
The Worst Day

The underground parking lot of the Holiday Inn on Hollywood Boulevard is dark and piss-stained. John wants to lie low before we check into the place; he is scanning the lot for easy hits. Lately, he's helping himself to anything worth trading that isn't locked or bolted down, using me as a cover.

It's over—our time as a family with Sharon. The dinners, the holidays are just a blur and a topic John doesn't want me to talk about. It is John and I now, living in seedy motels and in the Chevy Malibu when there isn't enough money for a room. The van is gone. It has been traded for an old postal truck that never runs and has been abandoned back in Glendale. Here, in the backseat of the car, our belongings are shoved into black, plastic garbage bags. On the floor is a bowl for Thor's water. At least I have Thor. The few precious pieces of knickknacks left in our possession I wrap in T-shirts and a brown paper bag, which I set carefully next to me in the front passenger seat. I am scared of John now, all the time, but he is all I have and the memories in the bag are, to me, a small portion of the dwindling proof that our love really existed.

He won't let me out of his sight now, not after I tried to kill myself that day. He takes me on all his runs and has me wait for him in the motel room or the car outside the drug deal houses. Rarely do I know where I am. I've never gotten my driver's license—John never allowed me—and the freeways scare and confuse me. I know a few homes are in the Hollywood Hills; I recognize the large wooden Hollywood sign that hovers over us from the side streets. It's eerily prophetic when Bob Seger's "Hollywood Nights" plays on the radio as I lie on the front seat of the car, waiting; or when the depressing lyrics of the Eagles' "Hotel California" wash over me as I wait in front of their manager's house while John delivers and deals inside. The houses on Dona Lola and Wonderland become the most familiar, the ones we most frequently drop by.

A couple months ago we stopped sleeping at the house in Glendale with Sharon. That part is okay by me, I guess. I am too ashamed to face Sharon any longer, and John has stolen more from the house than he can get away with.

"Does Sharon ever ask about me anymore?" I ask John one day after he has returned from Sharon's with freshly laundered clothes.

"Nope! Why would she?" His tone is flippant; his scowl implies, *How can you ask such a stupid question?*

"Of course not," I remind myself, agreeing immediately. The pangs of shame and guilt ravage what hope I have left for our relationship. *This is all my fault,* I admonish myself silently. *Just as John says, this is all my fault.*

⚜

It is Thanksgiving week, and the Holiday Inn is a grade better than what we are used to lately. John has made a little extra on a run he's just finished for a man named Eddie Nash. John simply calls him Nash, and he gives me strict instructions: "He's the baddest motherfucker there is. People who try to fuck him over die. That's why you're a secret. He can't find out about you or Sharon or the family. It's not safe. Do you know how many bodies are buried in the desert that no one will ever find?" John is passionate, dead serious. He reiterates his orders to never cross this guy, until he's satisfied that I understand.

Nash is the owner of the house I wait in front of on Dona Lola Drive, and I can never let him or any of his bodyguards see me—or else . . . "you might turn up missing like the rest."

A strange kind of dealer–runner underworld friendship has started up between John and Nash. "This guy is all about the drugs, baby. *And* he calls me brother," John confides with a smirk as if to say, *Boy do I have him fooled.* In a short time, the friendlier John and Nash become, the waiting gets longer and longer—but his payoffs are also higher.

John's foul moods and cruelty soon become greater and greater as well.

❧

John has me wait in the car in the Holiday Inn parking lot before we bring our things to the room, giving him time to slink through the parked cars to check for an unlocked door. Jumping up from between a couple of cars a few rows down, John walks casually down the middle of the lot wearing the appearance of an innocent guest. "Come on," he snaps from the side of his mouth, motioning for me to hurry out and walk with him.

Clumsily I pull a large garbage bag from the backseat while holding on to Thor and my precious brown paper sack filled with breakables. "John, help me," I ask, getting nervous about dragging our clothes and things in such a disorganized way. "There are security guards."

"What? What is all that shit?" He sounds annoyed and whips quickly over to see what I'm carrying. "What is this?" he snaps again and yanks the brown bag from my hands.

"It's, uh, uh, stuff," I answer, frightened at his demeanor. Protective of the sentimental items in the bag, I hold my hand out to get it back. "They're presents. Presents I gave to you . . . and you and Sharon gave me. You know. Back at the house," I explain, trying to take back the bag. I hope he will soften up at the memory, that he'll appreciate my caring enough to cart them with me . . . affectionately, as awkward as it is. Yet the opposite is true.

"Presents! What kind of presents?" He rummages through the bag and smiles when he wraps his hand around the one gift that means the most to me—the cobalt blue vase.

Smash! "Those kind of presents are over!" he barks.

"No!" I cry, feeling a knife rip through my heart. I fall to my knees to try and pick up the shattered pieces of blue, willing the hand-painted white rose back together.

"Pick up that garbage," he scorns, "before security sees us." He walks away and tries to cover the commotion with a nonchalant stance.

Tears burn my eyes and face. The grimy ground of the parking lot is slick with dark brown grease. On my hands and knees, I pick up every tiny cobalt shard and hurry over to where John's standing. Not wanting him to get any angrier with me, I wipe the wet from my face. I try to act cool and swiftly stuff down the huge knot of raw pain in my throat and quiet the well of echoes from the back of my head that beg for the bad feelings to go away.

Growing impatient, John flings one of our large garbage bags over his shoulder, puts his arm around me, and walks past the surveillance cameras trying to act as though we are a couple in love.

Two men in tan sports jackets pass us casually as we walk through the garage door into the lower level hallway.

"Huh, those look like cops," I whisper into the crook of John's arm. He pulls me roughly closer to his side and guides me to the elevator.

Once on the second floor, we dash across the hall to room 252, where John immediately jams the desk chair under the doorknob, slides the chain into its lock, and presses his eye against the peephole. "Close the drapes," he hisses, then runs to do it himself instead, peeking out for ten minutes or so, head bobbing like a chicken's.

Satisfied we made it without being noticed, he undresses and sits on the bed, leaning against the headboard. The hair on the back of Thor's neck stands up like a porcupine's quills, and he disappears under the bed.

Snap, snap. John opens the brass clasp of his briefcase, pulls out the freebase pipe, and lights the bowl.

Oh no! I think. *He doesn't have any base, and he is scraping his screens.* I am quick to assess the drug situation. I have to. The more he has, the less likely he will be cruel. My insides cramp up and become paralyzed with panic. *No wonder his mood was ugly downstairs. Maybe he has some Valium and can get to sleep soon,* I tell myself in an effort to stay calm. *He's real tired too.*

After coming back from a run, John is always tired, having been up for days. When I wait for him in the car I sleep mostly, hidden under blankets with Thor. But on days John knows he will be a while, to make sure I won't leave him and run to my mother's, he drops small amounts of freebase with a pipe on the floorboard. For me, the drug is an escape that blocks out the pain of my reality, if just for a short while. After it's gone, I have the warmth of little Thor and sleep—sweet sleep that takes me away to a place of warmth and safety—until John climbs into the driver's seat and orders me to stay down.

Back in the motel room, he gruffs, "Draw me a bath."

When I return, he is searching for something in his briefcase once again. "Did you take my other glass pipe?"

"No, John, I didn't take anything."

Crash! His pipe goes flying across the room, and I start to cry in fear.

"No, John . . ."

"Fuck you, bitch. All you want are the drugs!"

"John, stop." I try to calm him, but he is on a roll, frenzied, throwing everything from his briefcase on the floor and up against the walls. He picks me up, throws me across the room. I slam into the motel room door and land on the broken glass.

"Owwww!" Blood gushes from the bottom of my foot. A large piece of the pipe is sticking out of the tender part of my arch.

Bang, bang, bang! "Security! Open the door!" Voices barrel through the walls.

I hobble over to the bed to tend to my foot.

Bang, bang, bang!

John's eyes bug out, and he jumps up nearly out of his skin, pulls on his pants, and throws me a towel from the bathroom. "Here. Wrap that up," he whispers, picking up the scattered glass.

"Yeah. Just a minute. Hey, who is it?" He slides the chain off the door and opens it just a crack. It is the two men in tan jackets we saw in the parking lot.

They push the door open farther, flashing badges and barring it from closing. "We'd like to ask you to come with us, sir. Neighbors are complaining that there's a loud argument in here." They scan the room, looking at the broken, silvery shards covering the floor, and make note of the bloody towel pressed against my foot. John turns his back to them and throws me a threatening look.

"I, I cut myself on some glass. It was an accident," I lie, afraid that if I don't John will really hurt me, as his look suggests.

"Shut up!" John snarls at me under his breath, then turns back to smile cunningly at the two men. "We, uh, had an accident, officers," he says with a smile. "She'll be fine—"

"Can you come with us, sir?" they interrupt.

John looks scared for a minute and then nods. Searching for his shirt, he holds a hand out to me. "Can she come with us?" he asks, acting loving and concerned toward me.

"As a matter of fact, we would like her to come with us too, sir."

John bends to wrap one of his socks around my foot, and we follow the two security guards to their office at the end of the hall.

Oh my God! We're going to be busted!

John squeezes my hand hard as we are led inside.

The guards shut the door securely behind us. I can tell they want to keep the noise level down. "We have reason to believe there's drug activity going on here. You were witnessed downstairs in the parking garage acting very suspicious . . . looking into patrons' cars."

"Drugs? Uh, what? There are no drugs . . . we got no drugs," John rambles.

"Then you don't mind if we search you, do you, sir?"

"N, n, no. G, go ahead." He steps back nervously, spreading his arms wide. "You don't really gotta do this. I can assure you, I don't have an, an, anything illegal on me," he tries to convince them.

Both men approach John on either side. "Then we can search you and we won't find anything, sir. Right?"

"Y, y, yeah!" John agrees.

"Spread your legs, sir, and place your hands in the air."

John does as he is told, and I begin to cry. *They're gonna find something. I can feel it . . . and then what am I gonna do? I can't even drive.* My mind races illogically.

"And what do you call this, sir?"

Keeping his hands up, John looks down at his pockets. "That? Well, uh, that is a pipe . . . for, uh, you know . . ." His voice trails off as he peers down at the small piece of paraphernalia in security's possession. He knows he is caught.

"We're gonna have to call LAPD, sir," the taller man informs him. "Is there anything else we're gonna find on you?"

"N, n, no. Nothing." His face is pale as they pull out his corncob pot pipe from his other pocket.

I cry louder. Knowing John is definitely under arrest, I hobble over to hug him and interrupt the search. I'm afraid they might find more. But they have enough evidence and aren't fazed by my intrusion. John lowers his arms carefully and pretends to give me a big, despairing hug. "Baby, baby. I'm sorry, baby." He kisses my forehead and lowers his mouth to my ear. "Get my phone book when you get back to the room and call Eddie from a pay phone. Tell him his brother is in jail. He'll know what to do." His breath is hot and hoarse.

"O, o, okay." I nod in his embrace and continue to cry.

"Make sure you talk to him *only*. No one else! Got that?" He grips my arm to the bone.

I nod again, sniffing back my tears.

"Uh, excuse me." John is laying on the charm. "Do you gentlemen mind if she goes back to the room till checkout time tomorrow? She needs to take care of her foot and, uh, well, I don't really want her to see me like this."

The two men give me the once-over and discuss it for a moment. "All right, Miss . . . ? Do you have any ID?"

"Dawn Schiller. No. No, I don't have anything."

"You know your boyfriend here wasn't exactly honest. Say your good-byes, Miss Schiller. He can call you from the station."

The taller of the two officers picks up a phone to call for back-up and warns me to keep the noise down or they'll return to the room and ask me to leave.

John pulls me in closer for what is supposed to look like a final hug and kiss, and presses his lips into my ear again. "Wait a couple hours after their shift changes. Then use the pay phone outside. Remember: tell Eddie it's his brother!"

John's briefcase is open on the bed as I scramble to find the address book in the top folds. "Here it is," I say out loud to the beat of my racing heart. Lying in the bottom of the case are a joint and his pewter flask. Immediately I drain the flask, downing the bitter shot of liquid to calm my nerves. Wiping my nose on my sleeve, I pick up the leftover pieces of glass from the carpet and crawl under the covers, checking the time on the clock.

I hear a slight whimper and remember little Thor. He is scratching at the side of the bed and his eyes are watering, telling me he wants up to snuggle. *He feels safe with John gone.* I reach my arm down and let his quivering warmth hop into my hand.

I am still shaking; the gash on my foot is throbbing; I need something more. Lighting the joint, I take two very large drags and snub it out. *John will get mad,* I panic. *He will know I took some.* The mellowing effects of the pot take hold. The staticlike sting of my nerve endings numbs, fear subsides, and I am safe in the moment, a capsule in time. I pull the covers up under my chin and fix my eyes again on the clock. The large digital numbers of the alarm clock flip past, and I spend the next two hours in the dark, waiting . . .

⁕

"He, he, hello," I stammer in response to the deep male voice on the other end of the line.

"Who is this?" The hard tone sounds like stone, demanding.

"I need to speak to Eddie." There is silence. I swallow a lump in my throat that threatens to take my voice. "I have a message from his brother."

Still, silence and some shuffling in the background. In a short while, there's another voice. "Hello," an accented male voice answers.

"Eddie?"

I can hear his breath pull in . . . hesitate. "Yes."

"I have a message from your brother." I wait a moment, then

continue. "He's in jail. Your brother is in jail, and he told me to call you," I gush, wanting to get this call over with. I am scared out of my mind. I feel violated, like I'm being mentally stripped, my private parts examined without my permission.

Thick silence permeates the line. "Yeah . . . who is this?" The thick accent turns slightly kind, coaxing.

I think for a moment about what to say next. The fear of the man I'm talking to sinks in further, and I picture myself being driven to the desert and executed.

Click. I hang up.

My heart's pumping. *Questions. No questions. The less he knows about me the better.* John's many terrifying reasons to fear Eddie Nash continue to swirl through my consciousness . . . kidnapped, tortured, murdered . . . I can't seem to stop it. I race back to the room, smoke the rest of the joint, and lie motionless under the blackness of the polyester bedspread and a starless night.

❧

John arrives back at the room early the next morning. He's in a hurry to pack up and leave. "Fuck this place," he snaps with contempt, opening his briefcase for a cigarette. I notice him rummaging around for the joint, but he says nothing about it.

"I, I called Eddie like you asked," I tell him.

"I know, babe. Thank you." He leans over to peck me on the cheek.

Good. Eddie must have bailed him out, I tell myself, hoping everything's okay now and his good mood will last.

Heading over the Laurel Canyon pass, John has only one destination in mind—Dona Lola Drive. He parks near the entrance of the cul-de-sac and lowers his voice. "Stay down and don't let anyone see you." He checks the contents of his briefcase and covers me up with a blanket he pulls from the backseat. "This might be a while." He grabs his briefcase and steals a kiss. As if he's forcing a genie into a bottle, he nervously contains his breathing. "I love you."

"I love you too, John," I mumble to his disappearing shape. He makes a quick dash across the street, head turning from side to side, fast, exaggerated, as he scans the neighborhood scene.

"Well, Thor," I say to the chocolate brown face, "I'm glad I have you." And we both settle down in a huddled, awkward ball as familiar as the couch in our old living room, to pass the time in slumber.

❧

"Come on. Come on. Scoot over." John pushes, and I awake with a start. It seems that only a few hours have passed.

"Huh? What? Okay . . . I gotta pee, John, and so does Thor."

"Shhh. Stay down till we're down the road."

Turning toward the valley on Laurel Canyon, then right on Ventura, we travel about half a mile till John spies the Valley Chalet motel and pulls in. *Oh . . . we're gonna get another room first. This is good.* We usually do a run after leaving Eddie's, but I'm happy to think I can take a bath and wash some of the grunge off my stiff, aching body. Sadly, I have misread the situation. The time in jail has made John's already worn and haggard face even more leathered. But there is something else, something terribly more demoralizing. It's as if a mask covers his face—one of those rubbery, wretched faces people wear on Halloween.

John checks us in and, as usual, inspects the busy street outside. Opening the door of the small room, he waves me in. Grabbing one of the garbage bags and stuffing Thor under my shirt, I scramble in through the open door. The motel is a particularly seedy place with old green shag carpeting, rust stains in the sink and bathtub, and see-through spots on the sheets from years of wear. Everything is bolted down, including the cheap, velveteen

Spanish matador pictures on the walls covered in peeling paint.

As always, John immediately places the desk chair under the doorknob of the front door. He strips off his clothes and hops on the bed, snapping open his briefcase. The freebase pipe is lying on its side at the bottom, already assembled. He opens a small film container and taps a few crumbs onto the screen in the bowl. He motions for me to light the end of the Bacardi-laced cotton ball, and I dutifully comply. John pulls in a long, slow draw, holds it in till his face bursts flame red, and plugs up the stem with his thumb. His shoulders slump as he leans back against the headboard.

Sitting on the edge of the cheap cardboard bed, I pull at the invisible nylon threads on the bedspread, anxious for him to share his exhale of the mind-numbing solution. John knows I'm craving the drug. I want to disappear too. I can see the tension in him deflate, like air seeping from a giant blow-up doll. His body relaxes. I reach out and gently touch his leg, a puppy begging for a table scrap.

Finally, after what seems like forever, he leans forward and offers me his lips. They taste of burnt screen and plastic, a taste which means these are the last scrapings of his briefcase; he is out. *Why? We just got back from Eddie's.* I try not to think and force myself to search for any bits of altered state to blur my thinking. I suck in another gulp of air, holding my breath for as long as I can manage. It will let me think I am high, have a "buzz" if I can hear ringing in my ears. When I release my lungs, as I suspect, there is no cloud of residue. I'm depressed and don't want to look up. *He's gonna get mad any minute now.* John sits staring at his pipe lying relaxed in his hand, wearing his nakedness like a comfortable suit of clothes. Then he raises his head to look me up and down.

"Get dressed," he orders sternly.

"What? I am dressed, John."

"No. Something nice."

"W, why, John?" I ask, nervous about being part of one of his plans. *Is he going to dress me so he can rape me? What kind of perverse sex game is he going to play this time? God, please, I don't want him to tie me up again, like he's been doing lately when he shows me how he can hog-tie an animal. It hurts too much. I'm not high enough for that. Please.*

"You know . . ." John's voice is eerie, like a mortician's: flat, hard, and cold.

It is late afternoon, I note from the way the light falls orangey yellow through the shabby, faded curtains. My gut sends a wave of cold sweat through my body as understanding falls, my shroud of ignorance lifts, and John's intention pushes its way into my consciousness. This place . . . his request . . . is a reality I have always feared but hoped would never come. Quickly I force the ugly realization out of my mind, and with a terrified hard gulp I will John's motives away. I sit motionless, silent, wanting time to stand still.

For a few pregnant moments, John tinkers aimlessly with some loose jangling pieces in his briefcase. "What are you waiting for?"

Slowly, I struggle to get up. I don't want him to get angry—I don't want to get hit—so I obey and open the plastic bag of clothes. *Maybe if I do what he asks he will change his mind.* Aimlessly, I pull out jeans and T-shirts and heap them on the floor. "This is all I got, John."

"That one. That flower top I got you. And those jeans. Put those on." He flips his thumb menacingly on the pipe as he points to the pile.

The air gets thick and heavy, and the size of the room shrinks and suffocates me. His thumb keeps an angry beat on the glass. *Tink, tink, tink . . .*

I steal a glance at his face to check his mood. The blue of his eyes is a bright contrast against the red background, and his nostrils flare like a crazed bull's. I remember when his face looked like that in the past; it used to mean passion, sweet and strong. Now it is a clear sign of danger, of his impending rage.

Quickly looking away, I do as I am told. With my head held low, I keep a fearful watch from the corner of my eye, hidden by the long dark strands of my hair. With the trash bag emptied, its contents dumped unceremoniously on the floor, I cautiously stand up and sit next to John on the bed.

"Let me see your face," he tells me, tapping the pipe harder.

Lifting my head obediently, I quiet a sob.

"Quit it!" He curls his lip, shoots a daggerlike glare at me. "You got any makeup in there?" He motions with his head.

"John, no, I . . ."

"Shut up and go look!"

Startled, I jump . . . then walk over to the bag, afraid he will throw a punch in my direction, and rummage blindly around. I can hear more tapping on the base pipe, the *chink* of the lighter, and a sucking noise of the bubbles rolling through the burned-out stem.

"Come here," he chokes, still holding in the hit.

I walk over and robotically kneel on the floor next to him. He blows a faint, plastic-tasting mouthful of air hard into my lungs, and I hold it till I get dizzy again from lack of oxygen. I pretend to feel more of a high than is really there and slump down, stalling for time.

But John is not fooled. "Go wash your face and come here." He indicates the spot next to him on the bed.

Again, I do as I'm told and, with my face damp from the metallic-smelling water, I lie next to him on the bed and tentatively reach over to hold him. John puts the pipe away and scoots down close to me, wrapping me tightly in his arms. Softly he begins to caress my back and legs, buries his face into my neck, till my body guardedly relaxes. He makes love to me, more gentle and loving than he has in a long time. He lifts my arms, my legs, scanning every inch of them, snapping a mental picture like an Instamatic camera. His kisses sweep over me from the base of my belly, up between my tiny breasts, into my neck. I melt into them, still scared yet desperately wanting the kindness, the sense of compassion, to be real . . . enough to erase the degrading moments earlier.

It's over quickly, and John is back digging in the bottom of his briefcase for a few dirty pieces of freebase that might be floating loose in the corners with the lint and sand.

With his lovemaking having stopped as coldly as it began, I lie under the sheets and stare at the ceiling, my mind trying to fall asleep. The noise coming from John's direction, every *bang* and *crash,* sends a jolt of fear through my body. I don't like how urgently he's searching for crumbs, and the familiar tension churns loudly in my stomach.

"It's getting dark. Get cleaned up and put your clothes back on," he says, his back turned toward me. "You're going out!"

"No, John . . . Why? I can't go . . ."

He snaps back and lunges at me. Taking me by the throat, he growls, "You thought it was good enough for me when I had to sleep with those bitches. Now it's your turn."

"John, I, I, I can't. I don't want to sleep with anyone else. Really. I only want to be with you. I swear!" Tears come gushing out as I tell him the one thread of truth I have left in me, and I beg him not to do this. "No, John, please. No. I don't want it. Please. Please!" I don't know what to do. I plead to calm his unfounded fear that I am secretly lusting after others. I am convinced he's just jealous and if he'll believe I only love him, this torturous mistrust will end. "John, please!" My tears stream down onto his hand as I try to kiss his arm and loosen his grip on my neck. "Please. I don't want anyone else. No strangers, no threesomes. Only you, John, please. Only you!"

The hatred clears from his eyes for a moment, and his gaze connects with my pleas. I think I recognize a flash on a memory of our love. Then I see rage again.

"Do you know what it takes to keep a roof over our heads and dope in the pipe? Besides, we owe him. *Eddie Nash* had to bail me out of jail! That did *not* make him happy. Now we owe him *big- time!*" John's nostrils flare again, stretching his lip in a sneer as he glares accusingly at me.

"Then quit the dope, John. Please. This is all because of the dope. I hate it. I hate it. Stop it! Please!"

John lets go and takes a few long strides to the window, standing at the corner behind the curtains and looking out at the street. Again, I pray and say nothing more, hoping that if I stay quiet he will have a change of heart. It has gotten dark. He stands for a long time, naked, leaning against a side wall, peering out of the drapes—and finally, without saying a word, he picks up his clothes and gets dressed.

Rummaging in the pockets of his pants, he pulls out some condoms and flings them on the table. "Twenty bucks for a blow job and forty for all the way." His face is expressionless. "And I'll be in the bathroom watching. So don't let the motherfucker go to the bathroom."

I cringe at his words and go numb. *I want to die. I want to die.* That language slices through me like a razor-sharp Japanese suicide sword. I feel like nothing; less than trash. He hasn't changed his mind at all, and my pleas go unheeded. I am exhausted and know that no matter how much I beg him, it won't work. "What do I do, John? I don't know what to do."

"What do you mean you don't know?" He comes out from the curtains, yanks me up off the bed. "You walk up and down the street till someone stops. Let him talk first, then ask him if he's a cop. He has to tell you. Tell him to meet you here. Don't go with any of them." His voice is deliberate, every syllable sharp as broken glass. His fingernails dig deep into my shoulders, tearing quarter moon cuts in my skin. "Now get dressed!" he orders, releasing me hard and throwing my chosen clothes at me on the bed. He raises his hand, sending me a look that says he's had it. "Go!"

I cringe and cower. "Don't, John. Please." My skin stings with

293

a rush of adrenaline. I'm scared that if I say anything else he'll attack me. Slowly, zombielike, I put on my clothes. In the bathroom I stall for time, letting the water wash the tears and dirt from my face. I can't breathe; my blocked sinuses press against my cheeks. My eyes are red and swollen from crying, with dark sunken bruises underneath, and my tangled hair is hard to comb through. Time is heavy, standing still; I'm in a bubble of space. I travel through it in slow motion as if I'm walking through a thick layer of slime. I have no sense of the shell that is now my body. All understanding of who I am is leaving me; I am completely unfeeling, detached from my movements, a fractured casing of who I once was. I dress carefully in the clothes John picked out, smoothing down my flowery shirt over my jeans again and again. Robotically, I walk past John, who takes a hard look at me and again peeps through the curtains, sucking at the barren pipe.

"Don't get into anyone's car!" he shouts without looking back.

I walk to the door, place my hand on the knob, and quietly turn. The knob sticks a little, and for an instant I believe I won't have to go any farther.

"Go!"

My hand jumps; the door clicks open. I step silently into the humid air and the buzzing sound of heavy traffic, and become another street child of the Los Angeles night.

❧

Knock, knock, knock. The tapping at the door is furious. I jump up to look out the window. John isn't supposed to be back from Eddie's yet, and I get nervous that someone might have followed me from the street. It is the black girl, Frosty, from the long-term bungalow at the other end of the motel. It has been a few weeks since John and I first checked in, and John has talked to her several times as we've come in or gone out. She waves at me every time she sees me leave the room to take my turn on the filthy streets. She knows John watches for me.

The evening's street activity comes alive on its own, I find out. It is like the twilight zone, or a channel on television with programs I've never seen before. The actors and actresses all know their lines. I don't feel like I'm doing anything different, just walking down the street, but I'm approached almost immediately. The one blessing, I think, is that it is over quickly. Paralyzing fear and horrific internal pain are over quickly, if I can set my mind on checking out for those moments. Then I can block it out . . . and then I can look at myself in the mirror.

After the night is over, John draws a steaming hot bath, removes my clothes, and ritually scrubs me clean. He counts and pockets the money, apologizing profusely that our lives have sunk so low. "Does that still hurt, baby?" He wipes the washcloth carefully over my cuts and bruises. "I'm so sorry. It'll be better soon, baby, I promise. Just gotta get clean. Everything is better after you get all the dirt off." John makes sure I am extra clean. It has to be this way before he can lie down with me, touch me. Sporadically, out of jealousy, he attempts to throw me a question or two about whether I enjoyed myself with those other men, and recoils instantly from my piercing death stare. In that moment, I could kill him. I know it, and I don't care. I also know I will die doing it. But I relish the thought of tearing his body limb from limb, John screaming in pain and in fear of me this time. My thoughts scare me. I numb my brain again, slip away from reality. I let him dry me off and carry me to bed, where he will make love to my body under the sheets as I watch from a distant corner of the room.

"Can you help me?" Frosty asks, looking frantically from side to side. Small boned and large breasted, she is bouncing on the balls of her feet. Her hair is unkempt and matted, and a thin layer of nervous sweat beads on her upper lip and brow.

I unlock the chain on the door and let her in. "Sure. What's the matter?"

"I, I just need your help holding my arm. I can't find a vein. Can you just come over and help me? For a minute—just a minute—p, p, please?" she begs. Her brown face looks like dry ashy wood and is wrenched in agony.

"Uh, yeah, sure. I'm not supposed to leave the room, but okay. Let me get the key." Her eyes, deep wells of black ink, are deeply creased in pain, pitiful. I can't say no.

I follow her quick pace, practically running to keep up with her. *I hope John doesn't find out I'm helping her.* She barrels through her door, pulls the chain across to lock it, and leads me to the built-in vanity, where her needle waits loaded and ready. Frosty is fixated, sweating profusely now. She grabs a belt lying handy on the chair and pushes her arm through the readied leather circle. Yanking back hard, she bites down on the loose strap with her teeth, contorting her face into a misshapen smile. She slaps the innermost part of her arm and picks up the needle.

I watch in horror, stammer uncomfortably, "Wha, wha, what do you need me to do?"

"Hold my arm. There." She points with her chin through the strap in her teeth.

I race to do as I'm told and squeeze her arm tightly, cutting off the circulation so her veins bulge between my two hands. Frosty grunts and groans, digging into her skin with a bending needle, as

I keep my grip secure. I want to throw up. *Please, please, please. Let her find the right spot,* I think, hoping she'll hurry. I am painfully sympathetic with my neighbor. I have seen her on the street at night, in that other evening world, usually smiling and throwing me a subtle wave. Tonight is different. She is so agonizingly desperate. Sweat and fear reek acrid and foul from every pore of her skin.

"Shit!" She drops her arm and releases the belt. "This isn't gonna work. Damn it!" Grabbing the needle, she places it in her teeth and pulls off her shirt and bra. The belt dangling in her hand again, she does what I cannot believe and wraps it securely around one of her large breasts.

I struggle to keep a sudden rush of vomit down.

"Here. Hold this." In a panic, she nods toward her chest, belt in her mouth, fingers slipping off her sweaty skin.

"Oh my God! Okay. Here." I scramble to help, finding it hard to keep a firm hold on her slippery breast. We wrestle with the large mound of flesh to keep it motionless enough to catch a vein that won't collapse. *She's done this before,* I notice.

Blood runs profusely from the edge of the areola where Frosty continuously pokes her way to a working vessel. Then, in blessed release, she hits it. Her eyes roll to the back of her head, and she lets go of the belt. Splatters of crimson droplets spill a sinister-looking trail from the linoleum to the carpet until she finally puts her hand over the wound and collapses on the bed. "Mmmmmm," she groans. "My medicine. Can't go to work without my medicine." Her words float through the air, dreamy and buttery smooth.

My face is flush with sweat and tears. I stand there awkward, not knowing what to do with myself. Frosty has forgotten I am here; she is drifting further away with the heroin. I clumsily grab a pile of cotton balls from the vanity and, sniffing back my tears, wipe up the drops of blood from the floor. How horrible and sad, and so close to home. *Is this where John and I are headed?*

"You, you okay now?" I ask, standing at the foot of the bed and paying close attention to her breathing.

"Yeah, baby. You can go home now. Thank you, baby." She waves her one free arm loosely in the air. "Hope you don't get in trouble for helping me, sweetie. I'll talk to him if you want me to."

"No. Thanks. It'll be okay . . . I'm gonna go now. You sure you're all right?"

"Yeah, baby. I'm good. Frosty's got her medicine now. She's good," she says to the shadows on the wall, and I leave.

John comes back late, around midnight, in a rotten mood. I can guess from the look of him that it is going to be a bad night—a night when no matter what I say or do, nothing is going to be right. The familiar apprehension over the brutal side of his presence washes over me, and I brace myself for the inevitable.

Visually taking in the room as usual, he settles his hands into his briefcase. "Where have you been?"

Fear seizes me. *How did he know I went anywhere?* I search the room for what clues might have given me away. I'll be in trouble if I lie. "The black chick's place over there," I tell him, pointing out the window and trying to stay calm. "She needed me to hold her arm 'cause she couldn't get the needle in by herself."

John's head perks up. "And did you help her?" His voice carries an eerie tone.

"Yeah. I guess. She couldn't get it in her arm, so I helped her get it in her tit. It was really bad. Gross. She was shaking so hard."

"And did you do some too?" He is tense, purposely staying calm.

"What?" I'm taken off guard. I suspected he'd be mad that I went out without his permission, but I didn't think he would ask me that. "N, no," I answer honestly. "She needed help and begged me, John."

"Who was over there?" The strain in his voice cracks, his temper hidden with more and more difficulty. I inch my way toward the door, afraid the violence is about to blow.

"Just her . . . and me," I mumble, hoping the path to the door will stay clear for an escape.

John notices my moves. In an instant, he bolts for the door and intercepts my feeble jump for freedom, pinning me up against the wall. "Where do you think you're going, huh? Back over to *Frosty's?* She introduce you to her pimp? Fucking tell me, bitch. You got a pimp now?" His nose pushes into mine as he screams louder and louder, his face red, his mouth spraying me with spittle.

Crazy, crazy, crazy! I gotta get out of here. He's out of his mind. Run. I gotta run! "John. Stop. No!" I yell at the top of my lungs. I want to be loud . . . loud enough that maybe someone outside will hear. Maybe Frosty will hear me and come and explain the truth to John.

Unexpectedly, he lets me go. He puffs himself up like a rooster, confident that he has proven he's in charge. Then he turns his back and reaches for the brown briefcase that has fallen from the bed.

Oh, good. I breathe. *He didn't chain it.* My eye is still on the door. *He's gonna snap again; I know it.* John is bending, busy picking up the pieces of the spilled pipe parts, and I see it: my chance to run. I bolt for the door.

I make five or six long strides ahead of John out the door before he realizes I have actually broken free, but just as quickly he is up and running full force after me. I quickly scan the parking lot to see if there's anyone or anywhere I can run to for safety. There isn't. John is catching up to me, and I panic. *The 7-Eleven!* I race across traffic on Ventura Boulevard toward the green and red building on Tujunga and rush inside the double glass doors. Pushing frantically past a man and a woman at the entrance, I run to the back of the counter and jump behind the clerk at the cash register.

"Please, please, please," I beg. "He's gonna kill me. Help me, please. Help me!" I clutch his shirt at the waist and pull him in front of me. "He's out there. He's after me. Please help me."

The clerk panics, nervously trying to turn to face me while I scoot around him, keeping him in front of me for safety. He sees my red, tearstained face and the fingernail welts on my arms and then scans down to see that I am wearing only a large nightshirt and black sandals. He nods, satisfied that I am really in danger, and spreads his arms out to block anyone who might come close to us.

"There he is!" the couple I crashed into yell out. "He's standing by that car looking in!" The guy points to John's figure slinking in the dark.

"Look! He's hiding. He's going behind the building!" The couple and the clerk have jumped in to the rescue.

"Call the police!" the woman shouts.

"No, don't call the police!" I cry. Suddenly I'm afraid . . . of the police. *They'll arrest me. I'll have to tell them about John and walking the streets, the drugs, and . . . oh God, no . . . . Eddie Nash.* A flood of tears pours out of me. "Just take me to Glendale. Please! I have somewhere to go, but I only need a ride. Glendale. Can I get a ride to Glendale, please?"

The clerk raises his arms in the air helplessly. "I, I can't leave the store," he explains honestly. "I'd help you, but I can't leave."

"Oh God! He's gonna kill me. I can't go out there. Please!" John is still lurking, poking his head in and out of the shadows of the side of the store, waiting to jump me. I know it; I can feel his ominous presence nearby. But this time I have some protection: The clerk and the young couple know it too.

"Where in Glendale do you need to go?" the young man asks me, making a decision to help. His girlfriend locks eyes with him and nods. They are in their early twenties, sweet and clean-cut. They are also leery of me . . . and deep inside, I don't blame them.

"We saw him running after you and then run to the side of the building. Where can we take you?" the woman adds.

"Glendale: 1012 East Acacia," I recite my old address. "Thank you."

The three of them—the clerk, man, and lady—form a barrier around me and walk me to the backseat of the couple's Volkswagen Beetle parked out front. John is nowhere to be seen now, but I can still sense the danger, that invisible angry threat that wears his face and lurks right around the corner. Nervously, the young man starts the car and takes off. Something scurries behind a dirty gray pickup truck.

"There he is!" the lady yells.

The car backs out onto Ventura Boulevard and peels away.

I wipe my face—tears, mucus, and fear—on the bottom of my dirty, stained nightshirt, and I pray that Sharon will be home.

Tap, tap, tap. My frozen knuckles knock painfully on the cottage door. *Tap, tap, tap.* Shivering, I keep a continuous plea on the painted white wood. *Tap, tap, tap. Tap, tap, tap.* My knocking flows steadily with the rhythm of my cold, shaking bones. I haven't seen Sharon for months—it seems longer—and I am horribly ashamed to face her again, especially like this.

The sweet couple with the Volkswagen has just let me off in front of the courtyard. I assure them I will be all right. "My friend Sharon is like a mom to me. She is always home," I tell them. They look worried, but agree.

The street is empty; a soft buzzing noise hovers over the trees from the distant freeways. *It must be after midnight.* I feel the damp chill of the December fog soak through my skin and down to my bones. I pull my nightshirt to the front of my body, tightly clenching in as much body heat as I can with my arms, and crouch low on the dimly lit porch of my former home. Here I am, nineteen. Things aren't supposed to be like this. John and I aren't supposed to be like this, and Sharon, who is like family to me, is always supposed to be here. I will be twenty in exactly a week, and I'm not sure if I'll make it. *Dear God . . . let her answer the door,* I pray over and over in sync with my chattering teeth.

I can hear the dogs prancing on the other side of the door. They know it's me and don't bark, only snort and sneeze and scratch in friendly anticipation. *Thor.* I wince. *Thor's with John. God, I hope he doesn't hurt him.*

I have to stop knocking. My hand is too cold. So cold it seems if I knock one more time the bones in my hand will shatter. A light flickers on at the neighbor's cottage. Quickly, I duck. *Oh shit! What am I doing? John's right. Sharon doesn't want me here. She'll just call the police. Then what will I do?* The light goes out. *Oh my God! It's so c, c, cold.* My teeth begin to chatter harder, uncontrollably, as I stay on the porch curled in a ball, my knees tucked tight under my nightshirt and my chin. *M, m, maybe I can find a warm spot to sleep here.*

The cold air is too much—too thick and damp and chill. There is no place warm to escape the frozen first night of winter. My body is in pain. I thought extreme cold was painless, but it's not and I'm finally forced to lift myself off the freezing concrete porch. I tap on the door one last time, using as much strength as I can muster. This time the dogs bark. I hear a rustling come from the bedroom. I knock hard and fierce, then listen.

The response is silence.

She doesn't want me here, and I don't blame her, I tell myself. John's words of disgrace tear through my wounded self-esteem. *God. What do I do? I have nowhere else to go. I can't go back to John.* I hunker down again. Now my legs won't stop shaking back and forth, mechanical like a fifty-cent horse ride outside of the supermarket. They won't hold still no matter how hard I try.

God. I can't stop shaking. I have to move, have to get warm. I have no choice. I have to go back to John.

Dejected and desperate to get out of the cold, I quietly step off of the porch and walk down Acacia to Glendale Avenue to stick my thumb out and hitch a ride back to John.

"Where you going?" the Hispanic man asks with a broad grin from behind the wheel of his early 1970s model cream-colored Chrysler.

"I, I think Ventura Boulevard." My teeth still won't stop chattering. "Near Laurel Canyon. My boyfriend and I have a room there, and I need to get back to him. He's waiting for me and will be real worried."

"Yeah, come on. Get in." He gestures for me to hurry to keep the cold out. "I know where it is. Come on."

I jump onto the front seat, keeping my arms across my chest. The driver has dark hair and an olive complexion and is dressed in black slacks and a white dress shirt. He makes a clicking sound with his cheek, as if he's annoyed. With a sideways glance he looks me up and down, but he says nothing about my attire. "What's your name?"

I smell the alcohol billow from his breath and notice a slight slur. "Dawn," I tell him. "And yours?"

"Dawn. *Si.*" He pauses. "Jose. Ieee just came from a Christmas party and had a fight with my boss. So Iee, uh, leffft." His slurring is becoming more pronounced.

"Oh, really? Where do you work?" I ask, hugging myself tighter and remembering the date, December 22, near Christmas.

He shoots an angry stare my way, letting me know he doesn't like my question, and takes another long moment to answer. "Nordstrom. At the Galleria."

He doesn't like me; I can sense it. "Oh," I answer uncomfortably and decide not to ask any more. Slowly, I inspect the inside of the car. It has a dark interior. I can't quite tell the color—maybe a deep bloodred. I notice it has power windows and long push-down door locks. They are up. Scanning down, I notice the control panel. *Automatic locks,* I note. *He can control all the locks.* Cautiously, I lean up against the car door and ever so slowly place my two fingers under the smooth, knobby lock, making it look like an attempt to keep warm. This guy is acting strange, and I want to make sure he can't lock me in. We drive in silence for a long, long time. John has neither allowed me to get my license nor given me directions anywhere, so I don't know whether we're going the right way. Even though my gut screams, *This is wrong,* I have to trust this stranger for the moment.

We enter a freeway. "You know Ventura Boulevard, right?" I ask again. I'm getting more worried that I don't recognize the freeway we just got on.

"Iee know. Iee know. Chut up!" he snaps.

I gulp. *Did he tell me to shut up?* Paralyzing silence permeates the air, and my heart catches in my throat. *Oh my God! This guy is angry! He's not going to take me to John!* I push myself away from him against the side of the passenger door, using my body to cover my hand on the lock. Farther and farther we drive. My insides are screaming, *He's going the wrong way!* Houses seem to be fewer and farther between, and all I can think about is the Hillside Strangler, the Trash Bag Murderer, and the girl on the news who got her arms chopped off while hitchhiking.

In a drunken haze, the driver sees my fear and sneakily lowers his hand to fumble at the control panel, flipping the switch that will lock all the doors. I feel the tug of the lock between my fingers, while the audible *click* of the others snapping down echoes like a gunshot in my ears. *I'll jump!* I think, keeping a weird sense of calm at the idea. *But where?* He looks over at me and smiles.

He thinks he has me trapped.

"W, where are you taking me?"

"Chut up, bitch!" he snarls. He methodically frees one hand from the steering wheel and like a vise grip bolt grabs my throat. *"Chut up or I kill you!"* He squeezes tighter.

Beating his hand from my neck with my free hand, I keep far away from him, never releasing my grip on the lock with my other. "Okay. Okay," I choke. "Stop! Stop!"

"You *chut up,* bitch. Okay . . . *Okay?"*

"Okay! Please stop!" I beg. *I need to get him to trust me,* a voice from inside my head speaks plainly and clearly.

He lets go. With a wicked smirk on his face, he puts his hand back on the steering wheel and keeps driving. Lights pass sporadically now, and I can see the silhouette of the mountains in the background.

"Please, please—," I plead. "I'll do anything you want. Ju, just stop. Here—right here. I promise I won't tell anyone. I'll do whatever you want!" I try to reason with him, soften him, hoping he will stop near enough to people that when I jump I'll see someone someplace near enough to run to.

He pays no attention, as if he can't hear me, driving steadily onward as if he has someplace in mind. The air in the car grows heavier . . . ominous . . . dark, as if the deadly presence of evil has crept into every crevice of the car—and then I know! I know this man wants to kill me. Not just hurt me, like John, but kill me. He knows exactly what he's doing.

Now the tears come, violent flooding tears, and I beg him for my life. "Oh my God! Don't do this! Please!" He turns his head to look me dead in the eye. *He knows I know.* In his eyes there is death. There is rape and violence and pain. In his eyes there is anger—boiling, seething hatred—and it twists his face into a mask like one my little brother wore one Halloween that scared me so bad . . . the mask of a killer.

"Chut up!" he says one final time harshly.

I can almost feel my neck snap. I obey. Counting every street-light we pass, I try to calculate when to jump. *I gotta do it now, before he takes me any farther. But he's going too fast. I gotta get him to slow down somehow!* The houses and buildings are disappearing. On either side of the freeway there are only mountains, twinkling with a sporadic sprinkling of lights as we speed along. On the left I recognize the distant isolated glow of the Eternal Valley Memorial Park. *Gena. That's where Gena is buried! The upper desert. Oh no! He's taking me to the upper desert!*

The speed of the car is too fast; there are no more buildings now. The only streetlights left are near the periodic off-ramps. Traffic is sparse, and things look bad. *I have to get him to pull over . . . and then I'll jump!* Up ahead is an on-ramp with another lone streetlight. But as we approach, I see something different: a second light. *A small building maybe? Maybe someone is there. I have to try now. This is my last chance.*

"Please, mister. Please. Just pull over, and I'll do anything you want. Anything!"

He turns to look at the side of the road, nods, seemingly satis-fied, and slows to pull over. The car comes to a stop.

Bracing myself, I lean my full body weight into the door and pull the handle. *Whoosh!* The door opens.

Instantly, his head whips around and just as quickly he stomps on the gas. The car lunges forward. The door flies open.

My head snaps back and forth with an invisible slamming force. As if in a vise grip my hands are glued onto the door handle, holding on for dear life. I dangle there, hovering stretched out over racing asphalt and gravel, long enough to catch my breath. Then, in a split-second decision, I let go. Over and over I roll, blinded by my momentum on the pitch-black pavement that burns hot into my skin and crunches rock into bone. Like a cat that's fallen from several stories above, I land on my feet, wind whipping my hair in my face. I run full speed toward the just-passed on-ramp. For a moment I can't believe I am really able to run—and not just run, but race like I'm going for the finish line in the 300-yard dash in seventh grade. Peering down I see I have lost one of my black sandals and both my knees are bleeding. I turn to look behind me. The white blob of the car is parked on the side of the road, and *he* is running after me!

A huge rush of adrenaline surges through my body and, with superhuman strength, I double my pace. Eighteen-wheelers fly past, honking a long, eerie, banshee scream; a car or two whiz by. My arms are frenzied flags, but no one stops. I turn to look behind me once again, and gasp. *The car's still there, but he's gone! He couldn't have made it back to his car in that little time! Oh God, no! He's in the bushes!*

My pace quickens; air rushes hot in and out of my lungs, pushing me forward. I make it to the freeway on-ramp and my only hope—that second light. *No! Please no. It's a utility box. No!* My heart falls. Then I hear him. Twigs and branches snap just a few feet away. *He's right behind me!* I gasp and keep running down the ramp for something . . . anything.

Suddenly lights—bright, blinding lights—flash like a searchlight. Two of them. *Can those be headlights? Yes! A car!* I jump—I don't care—in front of the oncoming vehicle, waving my arms like a lunatic in distress. A small, light blue Ford Fairlane slows to a moving stop. I dash to the passenger side and bang wildly on the window.

An elderly woman, shaking and nervous, rolls her passenger side window down a few short inches.

"Please. Please," I plead breathlessly. "There's a man behind me in the bushes! He's trying to kill me! Please take me to the police. Please! He's right behind me in the bushes!"

The woman visibly trembles. Looking back and forth from me to her husband, she has no idea what to do.

Crack, snap, rustle, rustle. The noises from the brush are right behind me.

"Open the door! Hurry! Open the door! He's behind her!" the elderly man in the driver's seat shouts urgently. "He's right behind her! Hurry!"

The lady fumbles for the lock, her gnarled fingers pulling deftly at the handle. The door swings open, and I scramble into the backseat, a rush of wind pushing me in with the slamming of the car door.

"Thank you! Oh, thank you!" I weep with relief, my body convulsing with the flow of adrenaline that still courses through my veins.

"There he is!" the gray-haired man shouts, stepping on the gas and barreling onto the freeway. "Let's get out of here!"

"We saw a guy chasing her on the side of the freeway, so we turned around to see if we could help," the old man reports to the police.

I sit trembling, in shock, clutching a scratchy wool blanket an officer has handed me. My elbows, knees, and back are bleeding from my fall out of the car. The bottom of my shoeless foot is bruised and swollen, and skin is missing from the top of my big toe. I have already told the police everything that happened: everything except the part about John beating me and sending me out on the street. "We just had an argument. He pushed me a little, and I, I wanted to go to my friend's house."

"You're a lucky girl." The officer at the desk taps his pen on the stack of papers in front of him. "Truckers saw you but couldn't stop, so they called it in. We had someone on the way, but it only takes a few seconds for something really bad to happen. Like I said, you're a lucky girl. Now, where can we take you? Your family's not in California, right?"

"No. No family here."

"To your boyfriend's then? Maybe he's calmed down by now."

"Okay. Yeah. T, t, to my boyfriend's room, please. I guess that's okay," I stammer. I am exhausted and again have nowhere else to go. *John,* I call out in my head. *John. I just want you to hold me like you used to. Hold me in your arms and keep me safe. Please don't be mad anymore. Please, John. My God, I was almost killed.*

I watch the desert sun rise outside a gray cement window behind the officer's desk and realize how I nearly missed seeing this morning. This very light could have found me lying dead in the thick dry brush on the side of the freeway.

Nothing can be worse than this. I'm sure of it.

The police car pulls up next to the Chevy Malibu in front of the warped and water-stained orange door to our room. One of the officers knocks while I wait in the backseat. I hear Thor barking and get excited. Moments later, John sleepily opens the door, shirtless, scratching the shaggy curls on his head. The officer speaks to him briefly, then gives his partner a nod.

"Thanks, officers," John calls brightly, waving with his other arm tucked around me protectively. Their car pulls off, and John guides me inside.

I sit on the bed, wanting to lie down and sleep. Thor sweetly dances for my attention, hopping about like a Mexican jumping bean. "Hey, little guy." I bend to pick him up and kiss his little cheek. "My goodness, Thor! You sure have started to turn white." I think about what I will see if I look in the mirror. John is in the bathroom taking a pee. The toilet flushes, and I look up to greet him with a faint smile. He says nothing.

"John, I . . ."

"Shut up!"

I freeze. *No! No!* my mind screams. *This isn't what he's supposed to say. No! God! Not again.* I have no strength. No energy left to fight. No heart to battle what I know, but can't believe, is coming once again: John's violent hand. Before his body strikes mine, I close my eyes and curl into a ball, covering my head. Over and over, his fists hit my back, sides, and neck.

For the first time ever, I hear Thor growl at John and I catch a glimpse of the small champion charging at his flailing hands. I barely raise my head in time to see Thor's tiny body hit the wall, give a breathless yelp, and slide lifeless to the floor. Slipping off the bed I try to crawl where Thor lies in a puddle where he fell; then I feel the swift kicks of John's boot ram into my ribs.

Like a child about to rest in her mother's arms, I curl into a fetal position again while John yells like a crazy man, a stranger. "You were asking for it, weren't you? You wanted him to rape you. You little whore."

The battering continues over and over into my right rib cage till I hear a *snap* and then . . . then I block all pain from my mind, leaving nothing but the thudding sound of his boot reverberating against my side. I don't know how long it lasts or when it stops. I only remember relief when I hear the door slam behind him, the car start up and drive off.

Squeezing my eyes shut, I want to disappear; I want the world to go away. The cruelty, the violence—I don't understand any of it. I am hurt. I know it, but I'm not going to look at my body. *Never get up; never move again,* I tell myself, forcing down the pain.

I wish myself into hopeless oblivion, pressing deeper into a fetal ball, never wanting to see the world again. A strange shivering warmth touches my cheek; lightly, delicately, timidly at first. Then with more persistence, the warmth pushes again until the shivering furry face presses so hard and intense that I have no choice but to roll my face toward it. A thick veil of sweat- and blood-drenched hair is stuck to my cheek, covering my eyes. I try to lift my head to see and let out a moan. The warmth presses harder, more desperate into me, and I open my eyes. Blurred, and through strands of sodden hair, I see him. "Thor!" I feel my heart take a beat again, and tears spill onto the old, filthy carpet. It is Thor. He is alive and in pain, crawling on his belly over to see if I am all right. He licks my tears and wags his tail, snuggling under my long, matted hair, reminding me, like an angel, that I am loved and not alone. We both lie close, burrowed unmoving into each other, until we eventually fall asleep.

CHAPTER THIRTEEN
My Name Is . . . *Dawn*

La, la.
La, la.
Pretty bird.
Oh, you poor thing.
The thorny cage
prick your wing?
La, la.
Pretty bird.
Poor thing.
Flapping about,
On one crippled wing.
La, la.
Don't feel so pretty.
Sorry thing.
Smell the sweets
But can't reach your swing.
La, la.
Pity bird
Withering . . .
Surprised no one hears?
You thought you could sing?
La, la.
So sad. Pretty bird . . .
Dead thing.

My poetry comes dark, full of self-loathing. How could it be anything else? Once I was a queen in his arms, beautiful and prized; now I'm alone and broken like an old discarded doll. My mind, my only sanctuary, is no longer safe.

I stay very still, afraid to sit straight because of the stabbing pain in my ribs. My head slumps over onto my chest as I stare numbly from my paper on the bed to a long, red welt on the inside of my leg. I feel sad, tired, and old—ancient, in fact. *I get it now,* I tell myself. *I finally get it. If I don't resist, he won't hit me anymore.* Thor, my little hero, stays glued to my side. *Little man, little man,* I speak to him silently with my eyes, *how is it you can keep me caring . . . about anything? You're so sweet.* I stroke his wrinkled, worried brow and flash briefly on the rainy day when John and Sharon let me bring him home for the first time. Nestled in my arms under the warmth of my Mexican poncho, his tiny, shivering, hairless body ached to be loved with every ounce of his being, and we bonded instantly. "Yes, we are still kindred spirits, aren't we, boy?" He closes his eyes.

When John comes back late in the evening, I am in bed and the room is dark. Keeping the lights off, he undresses in a few swift moves, crawls under the covers, and quickly turns his back to me. Thor and I lie motionless. *God, please don't let him touch me.* I cringe as he rolls onto his side. Thankfully, he doesn't, and instead acts as if *his* feelings are hurt, covering us in a blanket of silence.

In the morning John continues to mope, banging around the shabby rented room with loud noises and jerks. A stained chair falls against the splintered desk and over onto the floor. Slowly, he becomes aware he has no audience and registers my mental absence . . . the severity of my injuries. Through his creased and bloodshot eyes, John sees I'm not moving and my trips to the bathroom are labored; I'm bent over in pain.

My own eyes, though swollen, tell me he is out of dope again. Half-assed, he tests me to see if I am faking, casually asking me to hand him an ashtray or a match. Ignoring him, I tell him flatly, "My ribs are broken, John."

He locks eyes with mine and, for one desperate moment, looks frightened and lost. We both know from the gleaned medical knowledge we picked up from Sharon that there is nothing you can do for broken ribs except to keep them immobile enough to heal. *I might be stuck here,* I tell myself as I turn my back on him, *but he doesn't have to be important to me anymore.*

In the days that follow, John realizes how badly he has beaten me and is apologetic, loving, even doting again. *He's really scared.* I can sense it and am curious at his vulnerability. As with every other time when an episode of abuse ends and he finally comes down from his high, remorse consumes him. But this time the reality of how close he came . . . to killing me . . . strikes a twisted sense of panic in him.

He brings Thor and me food, gives me Valium to help me sleep through the pain, and carries me to the bathroom when I need it. He is nervous and jumpy. He tries to crack awkward jokes, hoping I will respond with something—a smile or a nod, some gesture that will relieve his terrible mounting guilt. *He looks like a gangly monkey,* I note, still not connecting him to anyone familiar.

John kneels down beside me on the bed, reaches for my arm, and begins massaging. "Baby?" he chokes and moves in to hold me. "I love you." His head presses hard against my chest, and he melts down into my lap with a groan when he realizes I'm not responding as I always have when he's said those words to me. He knows those are the words that move me. It is the love I live for that he manipulates. I freeze and then robotically touch a curl of his dirty blond hair that lies needy; he is more like an unkempt stray dog in my lap than a man I love. An audible sigh escapes him as he wraps his body around me, thinking my resistance has softened, careful not to disturb my ribs. I allow him to draw me a bath and brush the tangles from my hair, hiding the clumps that he has pulled out, as if I can't see. Putting on his best performance, John moves in to make love to me. I let him guide me through the motions, my arms and legs lifeless, limp like straw. He pours desperate kisses over my naked skin, across my breasts, down my sunken belly. His eyes are closed, and his mouth is pursed tight as he displays for me his erotic movie face. I stare at him as if he's a stranger. His pounding slaps the headboard above me, sounding oddly like distant hammering, until he is sweaty and spent, holding me as if we have made passionate love.

※

Thor, who once loved and trusted John with all his little might, now moves warily from him, jumping in fear at every move he makes. John makes an effort to try and be gentler and more playful until, nervously, Thor complies. His tiny legs dance halfheartedly, like a run-down windup toy's. John knows he has broken more than bones this time. He seems aware that he has fractured the most innocent of hearts and with feeble, stumbling attempts, tries to pick up the shattered pieces.

I can tell from John's movements that he will be going out again soon and he is trying to make it okay by being overly nice and fussing over me. My stomach tightens when I see the signs that the insanity is about to begin all over again. I keep ignoring him, though. I don't believe any of his lies anymore, and they are all lies. I am actually glad to have what I guess will be at least a couple days alone.

"I'll be back as soon as I can, baby," he says, sweating and looking like he can't stand to be in his own skin. He bends down to kiss me good-bye. I recoil at his gesture of intimacy. *Don't kiss me on the mouth.* I turn my cheek toward him instead. He backs up, sadness flashing in his eyes for a moment; then without hesitation he shrugs it off, grabs his briefcase, and walks out the door.

As the car chokes then sputters off, my stomach unwinds. I'm relieved that he is finally gone. Then panic seizes me. *Did I let my guard down too far?* The thought that he might be outside shoots me off the bed like a bolt of lightning, and I run for the window.

Snap! The loud sound like a breaking tree branch reverberates inside me.

"Ohh! My ribs!" I cry out into the darkened room, doubling over in pain from the rebreaking of my bones. Falling against the window, I clutch awkwardly at the sill and push off toward the bed, not daring to breathe. I drop onto the slippery polyester spread, pop a Valium, and try not to think about the burning fire in my side, the searing pain in my heart—or the fact that tonight is Christmas Eve.

✤

John comes back the next morning, just before checkout time, high as a kite. "Come on, baby. We gotta get out of here!" He is frantic and reeks of sour sweat.

Mmmmm. Shit, I think, rolling over onto my good side to try to shake the Valium off. Reluctant to leave my dream state for the reality of being with John, I lie perfectly still, until the clamor of the midday traffic forces its bleak way into the room. I keep my eyes squeezed shut anyway.

Then the memory that it is Christmas comes over me, and for a brief moment a dream appears . . . a tiny hope. Maybe, just maybe, we will go home and see Sharon today and have some kind of celebration. A welcome image appears behind my resistant eyelids. It is our old house—John's, Sharon's, and mine. The door is open . . . beckoning. Our once-treasured red stockings glisten with the gold of our names: *John, Sharon,* and *Dawn.* They hang over the stone fireplace behind a slightly crooked Scotch pine decorated to the brim with the bright and silly ornaments we've collected over the years . . .

Light burns its way in, disrupting the warmth of my fantasy and forcing me to open my eyes. John's face is sweaty. He is biting his lip and, with one look at him, I feel my dreams wash away. *It doesn't look like he got much from Eddie*, I notice, disheartened.

I roll out of bed, stiff and sore, trying to be careful not to shift my ribs again. Eddie has been strict with John ever since he bailed him out of jail. Their relationship has changed on another level as well. John doesn't act confident, like the favorite child, anymore. *Does Eddie still trust John?* I wonder. *He looks dope sick every time he comes back from a run at Eddie's—ever since that night.*

When Eddie Nash gets mad, John gets very scared. "We owe him," John keeps repeating, but the money isn't the only pressure he gets from the house on Dona Lola Drive. Eddie wants to know who that *other* voice on the phone was—the one who referred to him as John's brother.

John grabs up our things from around the room and begins throwing them into plastic bags. "Take a shower before we go. It may be a while before we get another room."

Here we go again, I think with a sinking heart. I don't want to know anything else, and I do as I am told. Gingerly I move to make my way to the bathroom, mildly surprised that my body is feeling better. I watch hypnotically the steaming water cascade over the diminished bruise marks on my side, running my hand slowly down the length of my ribs. My fingers fumble around a large circle of calcium that is forming over the break, keeping me sorely aware that my injuries are real.

John has my clothes set out on the bed. Jeans, tennis shoes, and an oversized gray University of Oregon sweatshirt. "Put this on," he says as if he's talking to an assistant. Again, I do as I am told. Happy to be wearing warm clothes, I sit on the edge of the bed and, with difficulty, comb my long, wet hair.

John packs the rest of our things in the car and comes in to sit next to me on the bed. He opens his briefcase and uneasily lights the pipe, baking the sides of the stem to melt down the brownish residue that clings to the glass. He manages a large cloud of smoke and uncharacteristically puts the pipe to my lips. "Here. Suck." He offers me the first pull of freebase.

I draw the billowing smoke into my lungs, feeling the stab of my right side catch my breath and stop me halfway. I choke back air, squeeze my eyes shut, and fall on the bed to search for that blissful numbing oblivion when John, anxious for some of the high, reaches down to suck my breath into his.

"Is that good, baby?" he asks after a while.

I don't answer; only barely nod.

Without a sound, John closes his briefcase, helps me up, and escorts me to the waiting car. Latching on to what bit of high I can, I try to stay numb but can't resist stealing a final peek over at Frosty's door and whispering a silent good-bye. *Good luck.*

❧

On the side of the road off of Dona Pegita, a street near Dona Lola Drive, John finds a vacant spot under a thick patch of eucalyptus trees. He parks the Malibu, sets up his brown Samsonite briefcase between us, and lights the pipe, once again melting down the darkened resin from the glass and the screens. The glass reddens with the heat and looks ready to explode as he attempts to drain every drop of the drug from a bone-empty pipe, this time blowing only gases of burnt screen ash into my mouth.

So this is Christmas, I say to myself flatly as I watch John manipulate the pipe. *What did I expect?* My body begins to hurt again. I am moving around more than I should and the drugs, what little there are, have worn off. I desperately want to be numb again, and watching John's frantic scrapings of the pipe only makes it worse. I turn away from him, lay my head back against the sticky vinyl car seat, and stare at the grimy headliner.

"He wants to see you," John finally says to me, not looking up, and spits a piece of tobacco from his mouth.

My heart pumps loudly at his words. "Wh, wh, who?"

"Nash," he says, using Eddie's last name. He spits again.

I say nothing.

"We got no choice. He wants to meet you."

"Me? Why, John?" My voice is panicked.

"He wants to know who called him that night I was arrested."

I look at John in disbelief, remembering that night, the claustrophobic narrowness of the phone booth and the way my body shook when I spoke with the heavily accented drug lord. *He'll kill you and dump your body in the desert. Don't fuck up. He'll kill you. If he asks you your name, don't tell him. Don't tell him anything. He'll kill you.* John's warnings are still very clear in my head.

"Who did you tell him I was, John?"

"At first I didn't tell him anything, baby, but he got pissed off. Then the fucker stopped paying me for deliveries." His fist hits the steering wheel. "He's starting to not trust me; doesn't think I'm loyal if I don't tell him." He angrily looks down at the exhausted base pipe. "Now he's real mad, baby, and I, I tried not to say anything, but he wants to meet you."

"No! John! Who did you tell him I was?" I ask again, mortified that he is planning to take me to meet Nash—Eddie Nash.

"Baby, baby." John turns to hold my hand. "Baby," he murmurs.

I am crying now. Streams of tears run down my face.

John brushes them away, holds my chin, and looks me dead in the eye. "You're my niece, from Oregon. You're eighteen . . ."

"I'm nineteen, John," I correct, interrupting his cold tutorial.

"Tell him you're eighteen and your birthday is in a few days. He'll be generous."

Oh my God, he's serious. I sob.

"Tell him you're a nursing student from Portland. Tell him . . ."

Blocking out the noise of his words, I let his voice trail off. I watch as his mouth fervently continues to move, but no sound registers. His face squints and frowns in animation, yet I hear nothing. It feels safe here within my tears. He grabs my arms and shakes me. "Are you listening? He'll kill you! If you don't get this right, he'll kill you. He'll cut your head off! And, and your body will be dumped in the desert with the rest of them . . . and believe me, no one will ever find you!"

"*I'M LISTENING, JOHN!*" I shout, halting his familiar torrent of fear. "What—is—my—*NAME?*"

"Gabrielle. Your name is Gabrielle." There's a long silence. John's face twists as if he is going to cry, until I acknowledge him with a curt nod and lower my head. "Thank you. Thank you, baby," he gushes, kissing my face all over. "It's just work, baby, right? It doesn't mean anything. Just a job, okay?" He pulls me in close, then gets dead serious. "He's no one to fuck with, baby. He'll offer you drugs. You can't let him know you know how to smoke base. Tell him you only tried it once before, and ask him to show you how to hold the pipe. He'll like that." John nods, seeming to agree with his own plan, and runs his fingers nervously through his greasy curls. "Now listen carefully. Are you listening?"

"Yeah . . . I'm listening."

"There will be a bodyguard at the door, a big black dude. He's one mean fuck. Don't talk to him. He'll show you into the living room and ask you if you want anything. Say no!"

I nod and absently roll my tongue over the peeling skin on my cracked lips.

"The bodyguard will leave you there, in the living room, probably for a long time. If you see anything—anything at all . . . coke, money, jewelry—*don't touch it!* Don't touch anything! Do you hear me? *ANYTHING!*"

"I, I understand, John."

He jerks me toward him; eyes glare like cold blue steel. "*I mean it!* There are two-way mirrors all over the house, even the bathrooms. If you touch anything—I mean *anything*—you are a dead girl with her arms cut off!"

I am scared. *What if I mess up? Oh God, what if he can tell I've done drugs before?* Fear turns my blood icy. *Eddie Nash kills people, and John's selling me out!*

"And if he asks if you have a boyfriend, tell him, yeah, you have one back at school, but he doesn't mean anything to you—mostly a friend."

All I can hear is the thrumming of my heartbeat in my ears. I want to block out his voice; I wish he would just shut up.

"Stick to talking about nursing, Dawn. You know, the way you learned from Sharon . . . and play dumb with everything else." John finally connects with the fear in my eyes. "Don't worry, baby. Just do everything like I said, and it will be okay. Eddie will see that he can trust us again and then . . . then everything will be all right, baby. We won't have to do this anymore. He'll let me do the big runs again. Okay, baby, okay?"

Us? I think sarcastically and wonder how else I fit into his scheme.

John turns the ignition and grabs the charred pipe for one last, desperate pull of dope. He lets the flame go long against the translucent glass, till the heat is unbearable and he can hold down on the striker no longer, his finger black with soot. He curls his lip, throws his head back, and lets out a stream of hot, colorless butane. I can tell there's nothing left to smoke, but I have no shame. I want to disappear and can't stop the urge to taste the pipe, hoping desperately that John will offer me a turn. Instead, he slams the briefcase shut and puts the car in gear.

We backtrack our way down the road toward the Dona Lola cul-de-sac. This time John deliberately parks in front of the white stucco ranch-style house. The Christmas lights hanging from the gutters of Eddie's massive roof flicker on, and I remember again what day it is. *Am I supposed to be a Christmas present?* I wonder dryly. I robotically look down at myself and notice the clothes he laid out for me to wear. *University of Oregon—how long has he been planning this?*

John gives me a nervous once-over, making sure I look my part, and then scans the other houses on the street for an all clear. "Come on. He's waiting." He opens his door, keeping his distance to shake off any kind of familiarity that could make it look like we are a couple.

I straighten up and follow the haunting echo of John's boots against the concrete footpath, over the valley, and into the twilight, up to the colossal brass knocker of Eddie Nash's front door.

❧

As John described, a large black man opens the door and lets us in. He's wearing a thick gold necklace and matching bracelet.

"Uh, Eddie here?" John twitches.

"John. Yeah. Wait here," the man at the door commands firmly and points at a space inside the door. We stand in the front entranceway as he disappears far into a back room. The lights in the house are dim, as if the occupants might be ready for bed, except for a glaring light that comes from our left. In front of us sprawls a formal dining room adorned with an elaborately carved table and chairs upholstered with plush velvet seats that stand in majestic formation. An enormous coat of arms hangs from the wall and casts an ominous shadow across the well-polished table. I sneak a glance over at John and see he looks worried and is pacing his breath to not look as if he is jonesing. I take my cue and do the same.

The hulking man returns. "Okay, folks. Eddie will be a little while. She can wait for him in the living room." He gestures toward the darker side of the house and gives a half-cocked smile. "John, you can go." He places his body between us, edging John back toward the door. "Come back in the morning." He waves him out. John's brow creases as he darts a worried look my way, then turns to leave without a word and without a glance back.

"This way, hon," the man says, changing his expression to a friendly smile. "Can I get you anything to drink?" He leads me to the right into a huge, sunken living room, where a man and woman stand together speaking melodically in some Middle Eastern language. Their conversation halts as we approach. They are both dark-featured, but the younger woman is taller, striking, as she casts a hardened gaze with her large almond eyes.

The gentleman, dressed in what looks like a maroon bathrobe, cracks a smile. "You must be John's niece," he says politely and cocks his head.

I grin and nod nervously.

There is an uncomfortable silence as they continue to scrutinize me. "This is my daughter. We are just saying good night." He reaches over to place something small into her palm and kiss her fondly on each cheek, mumbling again the strange notes of their language. In her black, flowing shift, she walks past me as if she's gliding on ice, with a demeanor just as cold.

"Can I get you anything to drink?" the black man interrupts, taking the lead again and guiding me into the sunken living room, allowing the gentleman to disappear behind the bodyguard's massive build. He walks me through the grand room and gestures for me to have a seat on an expansive, deep red velvet sofa. Before me, the ornate brass and glass coffee table immediately grabs my attention. A solid gold Rolex, a fully loaded money clip, and remnants of cocaine in full view send my heart pounding.

"Umm, no. I'm fine. Thank you," I say, barely able to speak and trying hard not to stare at the table. I pry my eyes away and am stunned by my gaunt reflection coming from across the room in an elaborate gold-framed mirror that covers almost the entire wall. *That's the two-way mirror John told me about.* I sit up tall and pull a loose strand of stringy hair behind my ear. The room appears enormous now, as if every picture and piece of furniture has its eyes on me. I break into an anxious sweat and force every muscle in my body to maintain a perfectly nonchalant appearance.

As if he didn't hear me, the bodyguard comes back with a glass of water and sets it down. "It'll just be a while. You don't mind waiting, do you?" he asks, giving a hard sideways glance at me and the table.

"N, no. Thank you," I say politely, and he leaves. I take a drink and sit back, wringing my hands to keep them occupied, and I conspicuously look everywhere . . . except at the table.

A nearby clock ticks torturously slow. What seem like hours pass. My bones ache from the tense stiffness of my posture, and my gut churns from hunger and the need for drugs. As the twilight turns to blue, then the deepest shades of black, I am finally called in to see Eddie Nash. Escorted to a back bedroom in silence, I am announced and stand frozen at the door. The same small, dark, curly-haired man I met in the living room sits on the side of the bed, his maroon bathrobe lying open, his bikini underwear exposed. He smiles seductively when he sees that I notice his appearance, and he raises his face. "Come. Come on." His accent is thick, and he waves me in. I walk toward him, eyes engaged with his round, bulgy, bloodshot ones. His stare pierces through me, and I jolt at the flash of callousness I see. "You need anything, uh? Your name again?"

"D—Gabrielle." I've waited so long I've almost slipped up and forgotten the name John has chosen for me.

Eddie catches on and shoots me a mean look. "Sit," he tells me and pats the bed next to him. He reaches over to lift a large water pipe from his bedside table and places a fat rock of yellowish freebase on the screen. "Sit down; sit down," he insists and points to the floor this time. "So, uh, you're a college student? Eighteen, eh?"

"I'm eighteen. I'll be nineteen in a few days," I tell him as I kneel down on the floor at his feet.

Eddie looks me over intensely, watching my eyes as he moves the pipe from one hand to the next. An ominous air charges the room. He turns his attention to the side table and picks up a small propane torch. "Do you, uh, like this stuff?"

It's a test, my mind screams. *Act cool!* But I am helpless. With every ounce of strength in me, I try to feign innocence; yet my body is fixating, my mouth watering, all for a taste of the drugs paraded before me. I know Eddie sees me. "Well, I don't know . . . uh . . . is that that cocaine stuff you can smoke? I think I've tried it. Once. I think."

Eddie raises his eyebrows at my rambling and gives me a leering nod. Then he lights the torch and begins to melt the rock down, rolling it from side to side till it is completely dissolved. Quickly he dives in to pull on the pipe and suck the thick brown smoke off the bubbling water. He holds the smoke in his lungs and looks over at me. Instinctively I rise up to be ready to take his exhale. He pulls away, surprised, and releases a cloud around my face. "You know how to do this?"

I realize I have messed up again and shake my head. *God, I'm doing terrible.*

"Come here." He holds the pipe to my mouth and heats the stem. I lean toward him, purposefully trying to make my movements look awkward. This time the ache in my rib cage makes it easy for me to appear new at handling the pipe. Eddie notices and falls into his high, relaxed.

I draw in the dense smoke and almost choke. Eddie smiles at my weakness. Then I make a final mistake. When inhaling the smoky cocaine, I suck in my breath and hold in the hit the way John taught me, the way a pro would. Eddie's head snaps up, and he glares hard in my direction.

Oh no! I blew it. He knows this isn't my first time. He knows I'm lying! Panic seizes me as I quickly release the hit and steal a peek at him. Face stone cold, a man in total control, he watches my reaction. The room begins to whir, and my head starts spinning. My stomach lurches into my throat, and I think I'm going to be sick. *He's watching everything you do!* John's words swirl in my head. But I can't help it. I have to lie down. I feel like I'm going to pass out. I let my guard down and fall back on the bed. *What's happening? What is this stuff?* the voice in the back of my head yells out. *Oh God. Is this heroin?* Everything hums, and I can't focus beyond two feet away. Covering my face, I can hear a steady laugh—Eddie's—float past my body into the background. I brace myself to see him, but the door slams shut and the laughing stops instead. Sitting up through the fog of numbness, I try to understand what is going on. *Did he say something?* I wonder. I try to bring my eyes into focus and look around the room. The drugs and pipe are still on the nightstand, and the closet next to it is ajar.

John told me about the safe being in the floor of his closet. *Oh shit! I'm being tested again. Don't look at anything, Dawn. Don't look at anything!* I tell myself frantically. *If he's not here, he's mad. Oh God. I don't want to end up in the desert! Please!* I hold on to the side of the bed, keeping my balance and gazing downward. *Just don't look at anything,* I chant in my head, over and over and over . . . for hours . . .

The groan of the bedroom door tells me someone is finally here. I look up from my drugged paralysis, my vision cloudy and blurred. I hear steady mumbling and see a shadow approach me, then loom overhead. A hand reaches down to pull me up and guide me onto the bed, laying me slowly on my back. My clothes are pulled off, and instantly I am self-conscious; bruises cover my body. An image, the outline of a dark-haired man, stands before me. He casts off the maroon blur of his robe, and his face comes closer to mine. This time it is real; he is here, next to me. I cringe as I feel his breath on my neck, then my cheek, and register the lack of compassion in his eyes. He knows I am helpless, and he takes obvious pleasure in me and even in my fear. But I can close my eyes . . . I can still disappear . . . and I gratefully vanish.

It is barely morning when John raps on the door to pick me up. The bodyguard returns and gets me from Eddie's room, where I have been waiting alone. Acting nervous and jumpy, as usual, John leads me out onto the front pathway. My head is in a fog.

"Can I see him, man?" John begs, referring to Eddie.

"No, John," his booming voice fires back firmly. "He said call him later. You got everything he wants to give you." The figure stands defensively, as if to say, *That's it.*

We walk silently to the waiting Malibu. My eyes squint from the rising sun. John's jaw is clenched, pulsating. *Is he mad?* I wonder vaguely as I count every step closer to the safety of the car and farther away from Eddie Nash. Briefly relieved once we turn onto Laurel Canyon, I face reality in only a moment. I am shaking and hollow inside. The daylight hurts every part of me, and I don't want to think. *Please, God, keep everything out.* Drained, I slump down in my seat.

"What happened?" John snaps as we continue driving.

"Whaaat?" I ask, dazed, then realize he must want me to recap the night. I begin. "First the bodyguard . . ."

"No! I mean what *happened?"* John's veins bulge at his temples, and his nostrils flare.

I look at him in disbelief. *He is mad! Oh my God!* "What do you mean, John? I'm telling y—"

SMACK! The back of his hand hits me hard across my mouth.

"No!" I scream. *"No!"* Desperately, I scramble for the door. *I'll jump . . . like I did before. I'll jump!* my mind instructs me. *Not again. This can't happen again!*

John sees me fumble for the handle and reaches over to roughly grab my hair at the scruff of my neck. "You're not going anywhere! He only paid me half! *Half* of what he promised! Now, tell me *what* the *fuck* happened! What did *you* do?" He whips my head back and forth.

I am trapped. John is stronger than me, and he knows I will try to run. I can't speak. Fear paralyzes me. I feel my lip swell from his backhanded blow and the steel-force tug of his hand at my neck, and I start crying. Then, as if I'm standing outside of myself, I only register the distant monotone howl of my voice.

"Noooooooooo . . ." The cries shriek through my being, blocking everything else out.

❧

When consciousness returns to me, I am under the covers in the bed of another dark, run-down motel room. I know what John did, but strangely I see it as only a memory of what happened, as if I weren't there, as if I left my body. I take a mental inventory of myself *and* my ribs. John is sitting in the corner of the room at the table, naked and sucking frantically at the freebase pipe. It seems the more he does, the less high he gets. But that's not the way he sees it.

"This isn't even the good shit!" He cringes, sweat pouring down the side of his face. "What the fuck?"

I bury my head farther under the covers. *What day is this? How long have we been here?* I try to get oriented. John keeps mumbling curses at the pipe as I tap into the memories of his brutal interrogation of my night at Eddie's. This time he was careful not to touch my ribs. *God, why not?* I think. *Why doesn't he just end it for me?*

John didn't get paid what he thought he was going to get, and Eddie is letting him know he isn't stupid . . . at my expense. Getting busted that night at the Holiday Inn opened up a can of worms that John hoped would never be opened—me! Now John is vulnerable. I know everything personal about him—his family, Sharon, where they live. Everything. I know exactly what he has been keeping secret, and that scares him. John sees firsthand that Eddie is powerful—enough to get what he wants if he thinks something is being hidden from him. In this game, John holds only bluff hands and he has already played them all with Eddie. All except for me. I am the ace up his sleeve: the last one who will stay loyal, he hopes, and by force if necessary.

But all I want to do is die.

"Get up," he orders, snapping his briefcase shut. "Eddie wants to see you again."

"Oh God. I *am* going to die, aren't I?" My heart skips a beat, and I lie motionless.

"Get up," he commands again, whipping the covers off of me. "And this time do *exactly* like I told you. It'll be fucking New Year's in a few days, and I don't want to have to search for a body in the desert!"

The desert? He means me, dead in the desert. New Year's . . . in a few days, I think numbly, and I quietly obey. *Then it has to be around December 29, my birthday. How old am I? Oh yeah, twenty. Going to Eddie's again. I think it's my birthday.* The ideas don't connect to anything familiar in my mind. As alien as my name anymore. My name?

Suddenly, black envelops me. The chugging noise of John's engine keeps the darkness constant, and the smell of exhaust fills the tiny space. *Air! I've got to have air!* I press my nose close to the left wheel well, where the only light in this suffocating place comes up through a small hole. I can see the speckled gray of the pavement and the tire spinning below, yet all I can think of is breathing—staying alive in the trunk of this car.

CHAPTER FOURTEEN
The Queen of Spades

New Year's Day has come . . . and gone. After the second time at Eddie's, John questions me again. As before, I mechanically give him step-by-step replays of everything that happened and, devoid of any emotion, suffer through his abuse. I feel sick to my stomach mostly and stay comfortable in the shroud of sadness I have befriended.

"Eddie likes to smoke speedballs," John tells me. Heroin and cocaine combined. I know I am feeling the effects of something different: heroin. My mind, remembering Frosty, screams a warning. *This is next! I know it! This is where we are headed!* My senses recoil.

We hole up in another motel until a particular morning about a week past New Year's when John checks us out and loads our things into the car again. The January air is crisp, and daylight glares bright against the metal from the cars on the street. *So this is 1981,* I think, looking to the sky for signs that this New Year might bring a change for the better. I can barely walk, my body hurts so badly, and I am thin as a rail. Food. I know I need food, but it is almost as if I have forgotten what it tastes like or how to forage for any. Approaching the now-run-down Chevy, I stop in my tracks.

"John? Wait. I don't want to go." I stand frozen in the parking lot. "I want to go away. I want to leave. Please!"

"Where do you think you can go? I told you Sharon doesn't want you around anymore. Oh! I get it. You think you can go to your mother's. What makes you think she wants anything to do with you either?"

John has said all these things before. Many times, repeatedly. I don't care anymore. I just want it all to end, one way or another. One more step toward the car will only prolong my agony. Something has to give.

"I want to try and call her. I just want to see if she'll send me a bus ticket. Maybe she will. Let me go. Please. I can't go with you! I can't, John. I can't go with you anymore!" I sob pitifully, hoping to be released.

John looks offended and then scans the parking lot for anyone who might overhear us. "You what?" He forces a half smile as if to say he knows I purposely began this fight while outside so I'd have witnesses. "Shhhh! Come here, baby. It's okay." He keeps his voice intentionally calm and, still wearing a plastered smile, walks to the back of the car to throw a bag in the trunk.

His smile and sympathetic tone soften his hard edges and, with the light of day, give me a false sense of security . . . just as John knows they will. Somehow, I feel he is going to listen and I let my guard down. Trusting, I follow him.

Whooosh! In a terrifying second, John's hand is over my mouth. As if he's handling a rag doll, he lifts my body up and shoves me into the trunk.

"Waaaiiitt . . . John! No!" I let out a terrified, muffled scream.

"Shut up! Shut up! Just be quiet. It'll be okay. Be quiet!" he insists in a low, husky tone, trying to talk my panicking voice down.

I nod feverishly, wanting only for him to let go of my mouth, and when he does, the lid of the trunk slams shut. The engine turns over, a loud rumbling growl; then it shifts into gear as I brace myself for the bumps and turns of the drive. My head finally rests near a small hole of light and air. "Jooooohnnn!" I yell, trying to get his attention, but he doesn't answer. The sound of the engine in my ears and the smell of fumes stop me from yelling anymore and wasting my breath. Bumps and turns level out into a smooth high speed, and I know we are on the freeway. I focus on staying calm . . . and air.

⤬

When we finally come to a stop, I hear John open his door and get out. Footsteps round the Malibu toward me. "John!" I call out. The sound of my voice reverberates in the enclosed space. "John!"

WHAM! A crushing fist smashes down hard on the lid of the trunk. "Quiet!" he hisses into the keyhole. "I'll let you out if you swear you'll stay quiet!"

"Yes! Please," I quickly reply. "I promise. Just let me out!"

Moments go by, and I wonder if he is still there. Then the key turns sharply and quickly in the lock, and a blessed rush of cool air gushes over me. John's hand reaches in to grab me and pull me to my feet. "Now relax. Take it easy and be quiet. This is a security building."

My arms fling wildly to move my hair out of my face. "John . . . I . . ."

He bends down to give me a hug, then stands back. "I'm sorry, baby. Are you okay? You can't leave me . . . please. I need you."

"Where are we?" I demand, looking at the massive apartment complex in front of me. Terraced up against a hill, the white, faux stucco building winds toward the street, each unit with features the same as the next.

Swiftly he takes my hand and, passing ivy and dwarf palms, he motions for me to stay quiet, leading me to a hallway, then a door. He knocks.

"Hey," the woman answers in a sexy voice. "Come on in."

John steps forward and gives the woman a kiss on the cheek.

333

"Hi, uh, Michelle. This is Dawn." He enters as if he knows the place and walks straight into the bathroom.

Michelle—a tall, cigarette-thin woman who looks to be about thirty-something, stands in the doorway draped against the metal frame. Her features are long; her cheeks and bloodshot brown eyes sunken. Stringy, dark brown hair hangs limp over the shoulder straps of her full-length magenta negligee. She looks me up and down. Pursing her thin lips, she says not a word to me and turns to follow John.

Timid and shy, I walk through the tiny studio apartment. *Is she gonna give us a place to stay?* I wonder. John has his briefcase open and the base pipe out. In the bottom, floating loose, are a few of his Swedish erotica playing cards. The queen of spades faces me. A dark-haired, naked woman, provocatively posed, catches my attention. *It's her . . . this lady. She's the queen of spades.* I know John is in the deck of cards, and now I know they must have worked together in the past.

Michelle's dishing out the white crystalline rocks onto the screens. Choking back the smoke, he passes down part of his exhale to Michelle and the rest to me. I let it out quickly; my lungs still feel the need for air after being in the trunk.

John notices me and lights the pipe again. He takes his time holding in the hit, pondering the bitter smoke as if it possesses wisdom, then blows the rest into Michelle's mouth. "Dawn needs a place to stay, uh, for a while." The bubbles purr as they run through the water in the pipe again. "She's willing to work too."

I look over at John and say nothing. *I don't want to live here, in this strange lady's place. I want to go to my mother's. I want to leave.* The dialogue in my mind is angry and stern; full of power that I wish I had.

Frowning, Michelle glances toward my crouching figure on the bathroom floor. "Oh yeah? Shit, John. Do you see how small this place is?"

"She'll work for it," he interrupts. "Now come on. Here—have some more of this." He holds the pipe to her lips.

It takes a few minutes for the smoke to clear. John dismantles the pipe, places it back in his briefcase, and stretches, straightening his pant legs. "Well, what do you think?"

"Yeah. All right. I'll work something out. But that dog can't stay here." She reaches into the bra of her gown to hand him a wad of money.

"I owe you one," he whispers into her ear, his voice syrupy sweet and loud enough that I can hear. "I'll be back as soon as I can." John pockets the money, snaps his briefcase shut, and tucks Thor under his jacket. He plants another kiss on Michelle's cheek and makes a straight shot out the door, not a word to me or even a glance my way.

"So," Michelle sneers. "You better get cleaned up. I got some-one coming over in half an hour, and you can take him for me."

"What?"

"What do you mean, 'What?'" she snaps, whipping her body around like a tiger ready to attack.

Slowly . . . I grasp her meaning. *Oh shit. That's why she's dressed that way. That's why John took Thor with him. Oh my God, no. This is why he put me in the trunk of the car! I can't do this anymore.* Degradation chokes me. Ready to throw up, I grab my stomach.

"Oh, don't look so pathetic!" she snarls. "Why else do you think he brought you here? What's the matter? Scared? Here. Go take a bath and wash your face. Christ, I can't stand crybabies." She storms out of the bathroom and chains the lock on the front door.

Oh God! I don't want to be here. I don't want to be here. Where am I? I don't even know where I am. Who is this woman? Why is she so mean? I can't understand how someone I just met can spout such hatred. *Is she like Eddie?* I am scared of her right away, and she knows it.

"*Hurry up* . . . and *don't* touch anything!" she yells from the other room. Again, I have nowhere to go. I am trapped. A cold chill runs down my spine and quickly, fearfully, I do what I am told.

Almost a week has gone by in this dungeon of a place. I am nothing more than a prisoner. Michelle watches my every move every minute of the day and night. Right away I find out what kind of a businesswoman she is—one who works out of her home and who now expects me to work for her. This small studio apartment has little more than a bed in the center and small tables on either side. A tiny kitchenette is sectioned off in the far corner of the room with a counter and a few bar stools. At the far end of the room is a sliding glass door that leads to an undersized patio surrounded with stucco planters that are filled with curtaining shrubs and trees for privacy.

Michelle tells me what to do, when to do it, and how to do it. She gives orders sharp and coldhearted, like an Army sergeant, and has no patience for back talk. *Don't mess with me or else* is the message she sends. Stick-thin and hard, drug-driven and mean, she reminds me of John but in a female's body.

There is a list. A list of "visitors," a "date book," that names each person scheduled to arrive that day. A special coded knock signals when a customer is here. Michelle simply checks her book and gives the order to either hide in the closet until she is done or to answer it and "welcome" the visitor. I do as I'm told, scared out of my mind that I might be hurt if I don't, remembering I'm completely lost somewhere in LA and don't know how to get away.

John returns intermittently and rushes into the bathroom with Michelle to get high. He doesn't look at me sitting there on the bed, skinny and pale, in a shabby beige negligee Michelle threw at me to put on when I work.

"John?" I try getting his attention at the bathroom door.

"Hey, baby. How's it going?" he answers sweetly, stepping out of the bathroom jumpy and wired.

I can hear Michelle flicking a lighter and the bubbling of the freebase pipe behind him.

"John? Where's Thor? I want to leave. Go to my mother's. I, I, I just want to go. Please give me my dog!"

"Okay. If that's what you want. He's with me, in the car. He's okay. He's safe. They don't allow pets in this building, baby." His emotions and words are erratic.

"I just want to leave, John. Please!"

"*Fine!*" he yells, packing up his briefcase and storming out, leaving me behind.

John makes a few drug drop-offs to Michelle, and I figure she is giving him the money from the men who come to the door.

Michelle is mean, but when she is out of drugs she gets meaner. "Whatever you do, don't eat anything when I'm not looking," she orders while I make a peanut butter and jelly sandwich that she has allowed. "I can't afford to feed you too! That's up to John."

"No? Okay." I feel badgered, guilty, and obligated for taking anything. I eat what she gives me because I am starving, but there is no taste; it's like forcing down cardboard.

I don't know my days anymore; the drapes are always drawn, keeping any light out of the tiny living space. It is confusing, but I don't think about it. I don't think about much. There is no more poetry in me. I'm a zombie . . . the walking, lying, breathing, living dead. I know weeks have gone by.

Michelle sometimes has to leave me in her apartment alone. "I'm going to see the manager," she tells me. "I'll be right back. Don't answer the door for anyone while I'm gone. I'll fucking know if you do, Dawn. And don't fucking touch anything!"

I listen to the locks of the dead bolt click behind her and feel caught in an inescapable trap.

Time is nothing to me now, but I know it's there. John is skipping days before he shows up with any drugs, and Michelle is getting pissed. She doesn't like how John comes in loaded out of his mind with only scrapings to show for the money she's given him. She throws fits and flings shoes against the wall. It isn't long before she hatches a plan.

"Where the fuck are my things? Where is my money?"

"What things? I, I don't know about your money."

"Bullshit! I know it's you!"

I can't convince her I'm not stealing from her, and I don't think I could if I tried. *Is she starting a fight with me so she can complain to John and get rid of me?* Silently I wish it will happen, praying for this door to open so I can get away. *At least here, John doesn't hit me. Not in front of Michelle, anyway.*

⚜

"I have to go out for a few minutes to see the manager and go to the store. Lock the door, and don't let anyone in. You know the rules." By the light through the bottom of the curtains, I know it is morning.

"Okay." I'm amazed that she lets me know she will be gone so long.

"John likes me," she says, a stab of jealousy in her eyes, and bolts the door shut.

I sit on the edge of the bed and wait a few minutes. I know this is my chance to do what I have been waiting for: to call my mother. I jump up to listen at the door, my ear pressed hot against metal. The coast is clear. Kneeling in front of the red rotary phone at the side table, I dial with a shaky hand. *This will be on her bill, and she will be real mad,* the frightened voice in the back of my head screams. "Yes. I'd like to make a collect call," I whisper into the receiver. My heart pounds out of beat for a moment. I hear a rustling noise outside the door and almost hang up.

"Hello."

"Hello. Mom? It's m-m-me. Dawn. I don't know where I am. Wait. Listen . . . John has been hitting me." I let out an audible sob. "He has me trapped at this woman's house. No. Listen please. I don't have a lot of time. She'll be back in a minute, and I'm not supposed to use the phone. I know you don't want me, but I, I want to come to Oregon. Please. Yes."

"Vaht! He is! Ver are you, Dawn? I vill help you. Ver do you want da ticket?"

"Really? Mom, thank you. But . . . I don't know where I am. Can you call the Glendale Greyhound station? I'll try to get there somehow. Please, Mom."

"Ya, Dawn. I luff you. Did he hurt you? I had a feeling something was wrong."

"Thank you, Mom. Thank you. I love you too. I gotta go. She's coming back. I can hear her. Glendale bus station, please. Love you. Bye." My pulse is beating hard in my throat as I hang up the phone. *Mom is glad to hear from me. Oh God, thank you. She isn't mad. She doesn't know what's happened to me. I can't tell her. Not now anyway. I have to get out of here first. I have to get to Glendale, on the bus—but how?* My mind races, like an engine that hasn't run in ages and is raring to go.

I hear Michelle tap at the door and I jump up to answer it, checking the musty room for any sign that I used the phone. *Does she think I am so completely afraid of her that I wouldn't try to make a call?* I think, feeling a bit triumphant.

Michelle bursts in, fumbling with her grocery bags.

I panic as she walks into the room scanning every nook and cranny with an eye that shoots daggers. *Does she know?*

Creasing her face into a satisfied frown, she looks at me. "Get some sleep," she barks. "We're going out tonight."

John shows up to wake us in the evening, haggard in dirty, faded jeans and jacket. His curls are limp and dirty, like his stained clothes. He and Michelle immediately head for the bathroom, their favorite spot. John steps out a few moments later to brush a cool, robotic kiss on my cheek. He is jumpy, energetic, as if he has just done a hit.

"How is Thor?" I ask, feeling my heart break.

"Fine, baby, fine. He's back at the house." He leans in for a better kiss. "I'm gonna get you out of here soon," he whispers in my ear. He glides over to the faux fireplace mantel on the wall, picks up a carved stone figurine of a woman in a Roman toga, slips it into his pocket, and hurries back to the bathroom.

Oh shit! He's the one who's been stealing from Michelle, and she thinks it is me!

Michelle steps back into the room, showered, dark blue eye shadow over her hollow eyes. "You ready?"

"Yeah. I guess." I'm glad to be getting out. It's been so long, and I miss my little Thor. I want to find out where I am, take note of the surrounding landmarks, and find something familiar that will get me to Glendale. But there is a freeway entrance near the apartment complex, and John jumps onto it almost immediately. *Denny's. There's a Denny's near the on-ramp.*

"This is the Marina," John tells me as we approach a long, white metal gate and security hut. "They watch everybody that comes in and everybody that goes out!" The Marina is a massive water parking lot for boats. Long wooden masts and white rolled sails line the sharp edge of the rocky shore with weblike finger docks that stretch in uniform rows—places to park the yachts.

Michelle politely calls her friend, a big businessman, on the house phone at the security gate and smiles at the guard as we're granted access. The underground parking structure of a giant, square luxury apartment complex sits next to the water. John finds an open spot, and we head to the top units. Different sized sailboats sit anchored in a row on the docks just below us in the glass elevator, the horizon black with a sprinkling of stars. Michelle leads the way to a grand corner unit guarded by massive double doors, and knocks.

"Come in. Come in," a slender, silver-haired man greets us. In his late fifties, he has bright blue eyes and a tanned and polished pockmarked complexion. He guides us into the main room, and I'm taken by its magnificence. The entire west side of the warehouse-sized room is lined with floor-to-ceiling windows, a deep, black sectional sofa, and a baby grand piano that seems to hang over the twinkling lights on the sea. The marble floors, covered with plush animal furs, seem twice their size because of the many giant mirrors on the opposite far walls.

Michelle introduces me as Gabrielle and John, proudly, as himself. He vigorously shakes the hand of the deeply tanned man. Michelle beams at having "Johnny Wadd" as her escort. Fidgeting nervously, John smiles with as much glamour as he can muster and immediately begs to excuse himself, slipping out of the apartment. The silver-haired gentleman doesn't hide his irritation and uneasiness. "Asshole," he calls after John, loud enough for John to hear. He spins on his heel, marching across the sprawling room, and slams a back room door.

"Wait here," Michelle demands, pointing to the couch. "I can tell he only wants to see me."

I'm relieved and keep my comments to myself. I wonder if this place is a drug traffic house, like Eddie's, with two-way mirrors. To keep safe, I fold my hands neatly in my lap and fix my eyes down at my crossed thumbs so I won't be tempted to make a mistake. The quiet elegance of the room is hypnotic though, not like the tension at Eddie's, and I doze for a while right where I sit, like a frozen mannequin.

Michelle startles me awake. Her hand bumps my shoulder as she brushes her hair and tucks her purse under her arm. There is no one with her; the silver-haired man never reappears.

"Let's go," Michelle mutters in a hurried voice, and I jump up to follow.

John is waiting outside, hanging out near the Chevy Malibu, trying to act nonchalant. He's leaning up against the trunk, his head turning back and forth wildly as if he has no control of his body and can't help but scan the entire area. "Get in," he commands, voice low and rushed.

The backseat is packed with garbage bags spilling over with laundry, soda cans, and trash. I climb in. John and Michelle are in the front. The air is tense as John deliberately obeys the slow speed laws and gently crosses every speed bump. *He's stolen something,* I sense. *I just know it.* John is a thief at every opportunity; he can't help it anymore. I saw how he checked out the cars when we arrived, and when he almost ran out of the apartment to hang downstairs I was suspicious right away. And now he's paranoid, grabbing for a cigarette, wiping his palms on his jeans. *Damn, John. What did you do?*

John rolls up to the security gate, and the guard flags him down. "Just leaving, sir," John says, forcing a casual smile as if he's an old friend and there's nothing to worry about.

"Can I ask you to pull over to the side for a moment, sir?" The guard motions with his flashlight to the side of the road. They arrive out of nowhere: a swarm of flashing red and blue lights barreling in on us. In an instant, the police have circled the car, blocking every escape route. Uniformed officers charge in, opening our doors. "Can you step out of the vehicle please?"

"Can you tell us your name, sir?" they ask John, guiding him out of the car by his arm.

"John."

"John. Do you have a last name, sir?"

"John Holmes."

"Mr. Holmes, is there anything in your vehicle you want to tell us about?"

"Uh, no."

"Then you don't mind if we look in your trunk, sir?" The guards are on their hands and knees, rifling through the garbage and clothes. Two other officers guide both Michelle and me to the other side of the road, far away from John. "Do you two ladies have any ID?"

"No," I answer. Michelle pulls out her wallet from her purse.

"May I ask you ladies what business you have here tonight?"

"We're visiting a friend," Michelle replies.

John, pale and nervous, leads two officers over to the trunk of the car. He fumbles with the keys for a moment, stalling. An officer helps him pop the trunk, and his shoulders sink. Flashlights beam into the dark opening. "And what is this, Mr. Holmes?"

John says nothing. From my distance on the other side of the car, I can see a thin sheen of sweat on his face and detect a faint scent of adrenaline reek from his body.

"Is this your computer, Mr. Holmes?"

John still says nothing. In an instant, the guards are handcuffing us and reading us our rights.

Oh God! He's stolen a computer! While we were upstairs, he stole a computer! We're being arrested! I can't believe this.

Three separate police cars drive off with Michelle, John, and I handcuffed in the backseats. Sharon's Chevy Malibu is impounded.

Early in the morning on January 14, 1981, the Huntington Beach

Police Department, a dank cinder block of a building surrounded with barbed wire topped fencing, is crowded and busy. Michelle and I sit handcuffed on the bench in front of the booking counter on the female side of the jail.

"Dawn Schiller." The woman police officer calls my name. The wall with the lined height measurements is cold, and instantly I shiver. "Hold still, please." She poses me to face a camera for my mug shot and fingerprints and then leads me to a holding cell. Several women crowd the tiny eight-by-eight cell, and each of them scurries to see if the new person is big enough to make her move. "You're gonna have to find a space," says the husky officer.

Two bunks, a top and a bottom, are overflowing with bleary-eyed women, some leaning against a gray concrete wall and the rest sitting wherever there is leftover space on the floor. Near the door of the cell, a metal toilet, yellow and plugged up with paper, is the only space left to sit. I prop myself up against the cell wall and try not to look at anyone or think about the smell. *This is an all-time low,* I tell myself, and I want to break down. *I have a bus ticket waiting for me, and I'm stuck here. I don't want to go to jail because of John.* The hard stares from the others keep me from crying. I want to, though. I want to wail like a baby. Keys jingle again at the lock; the officers have come with Michelle.

"Move over," she hisses. She is boiling.

"Oh God, Michelle. What are we going to do?"

"We? What do you think? John's going to call Eddie to bail us out of here."

"Oh, good."

"Good? He's not bailing *you* out!"

"What? Why?" I am mortified.

"He knows how you've been stealing from me. He's not going to bail you out so you can come back and rip me off some more!" Her eyes are fiery mad.

John's grabbing the hand-carved figurine from the mantel plays before my mind's eye. "It wasn't me," I promise her desperately.

"Don't fucking lie," she snaps, then turns her back to me. "John told me it was you!"

Oh no. It was John. He's the one who made her suspicious of me. She's going to make them leave me here. I replay his movements in my head. I can't bear it. "John did it! John's the one who has been stealing from you. I saw him take a figurine from your shelf. I swear to you I haven't been taking anything. I promise. I promise." I am terrified to be left in jail. *I can't be left here. What will I do?*

"Don't fucking bullshit me." She lunges back like a cobra.

"I'm not. I'm not. I saw him take it. Please! It wasn't me!"

She curls into a ball on the floor. "You better not be bullshitting me!" She closes her eyes and drops off to sleep.

I lie awake on the hard concrete floor until daybreak, cold to the bone, wondering if I will be left behind in jail. Breakfast is served early, and a few of the drunken women who are there to sleep off their buzz are released. Every time an officer appears at the barred metal door, I hold my breath, hoping my name will be called and I will be released. Midmorning an officer calls for Michelle. My heart sinks.

"See you later, bitch!" she snaps as she steps over me.

Her words cut me like a Samurai sword, swift and sharp down to my core, and I shrink back dejected. But it is short-lived. Immediately behind them, another officer is at the door calling my name. "Oh. That's me." I leap to my feet, relieved, and follow Michelle and her escort. I wave good-bye to a couple of the girls who, in the night, were kind and showed me how to use the toilet.

The booking desk is bustling; inmates in handcuffs and shackles shuffle by, escorted by detectives in suits. We sign for our few things and are released out into the harsh morning light.

John is waiting out front, pacing and chewing anxiously on a plastic cigarette filter. Michelle ignores the bogus grin he displays as we step through the jail's metal doors, and she storms briskly ahead to the waiting Malibu. Without a flinch, John saunters up to hug me.

"How did you get us out?" I ask.

John's plastic smile stays plastered for the surveillance cameras and he shoots me a look. "Nash. How do you think?" he breathes from the corner of his mouth, still chewing on the filter.

In the car, we are quiet heading back to Michelle's. The relief of getting out of jail is wearing off, and my next concern—how to not get beaten again—is crowding in on me. Michelle will challenge John about my jailhouse confession. *This is not going to be good.* I wince. *I'm going to run. As soon as I can, I'm going to run,* I promise myself. *Please. Please. Let my bus ticket still be there. The next chance I get, I'm going to run.*

Back at the studio apartment, Michelle and John head directly into the bathroom. This time I don't hear the bubbling of the freebase pipe but their muffled arguing instead. *She's confronting him about stealing. He's gonna be mad.* The feeling of walking on eggshells is taking over again. My stomach shrinks into a nervous, acidy knot, and I swallow back a taste of bile as I scan the room.

Suddenly, a chilly breeze blows across my arm. The drapes by the sliding glass door ebb and flow with a January wind and faintly billow at my feet. For the first time, that glass door stands out as never before—a way out.

The arguing gets louder. Something bangs against the wall. In an angry rush, Michelle storms out and grabs her coat. "I've got an appointment. I'll be back in half an hour. Nobody had better take anything from this house, or else!" She slams the door behind her, and she's gone.

"Dawn!" John calls from the bathroom. I can hear the gushing of the running water fill the tub. His voice sounds mellow . . . tired, not angry.

This is good. I figure jail wore him out. "Yeah?" I brave an appearance and come to the doorway.

John is stripping, shedding the grungy jeans and T-shirt from days of being high and sleeping in jail. He steps into the steamy, hot bathwater. "Get me a cup of coffee, would ya, babe?"

"Sure." My voice is purposely soft. I don't want to give him any reason to flip out.

I catch a glimpse of my reflection in the mirror. My hair hangs limp and dull. My eyes are sunken with circles beneath them so dark that the blue-green that used to be their color is now a cold, steel gray. John's oversized T-shirt and jeans drape loosely on my bony frame, and my chest, where my B-cup breasts once were, is completely flat. I don't know the person staring at me in the mirror; she is like a ghost, a hollow shell of who I used to know as Dawn . . . a complete stranger.

I pull myself away. I don't want to look at myself anymore, and I don't want to draw John's attention. I head into the kitchen to make him his coffee.

A draft of cold air rushes through the room, and the drapes of the sliding glass door billow toward me again like long arms reaching out. I shiver. *The door.* The low hum of traffic plays like an eclectic distant radio station, and I can smell dusty humidity in the air. *It's open wide.* I have never noticed the door open before.

"Are you coming with my coffee?" John shouts impatiently from the bath.

"Yeah!" I answer quickly, unable to take my eyes off the wispy arms of the drapes. I time how long it will take to get through the screen door and for John to realize I'm gone. *Do it. Do it now!* In a split-second decision, I run, making a mad dash for the sliding glass door and freedom.

Sprinting in the cold air through the maze of the apartment complex, I stumble on a major street and spy the Denny's near the freeway on-ramp ahead. I turn to look behind me to see if John is following, and run with all the strength I can muster to make it to the restaurant's pay phone. I am panting, can't catch my breath. The receiver keeps slipping out of my nervous, sweaty hand. I dial zero. "Hello. Operator? Operator?" I try to make a collect call, but I keep getting disconnected. *Damn it. I need a quarter to get through.* I'm desperate. *Maybe someone will loan me one.* I still don't see John. I try to tap into my internal radar on him and picture him searching the apartment for me.

I hold my head down, in case he might be lurking around, and I go inside. The waitresses pinch their faces at me—I'm sure I look homeless to them—and ignore me. I begin to cry.

An old man, in his late seventies, with crinkly eyes and wiry gray eyebrows, studies me from the counter. "Are you all right?" he asks, limping fragilely over with his cane.

"No." I cry harder. "I need a quarter to call my mother. I need to see if she has a bus ticket waiting for me. I ran away from my boyfriend. He is beating me, and he'll be coming after me. I'm trying to get to my mother's," I blurt out like a balloon losing its air.

The elderly man sits down in the seat across from me. His face is covered in deep wrinkles, but it is soft, oval, and kind. "I'm Sam. Here. Here's a quarter. Now go call your mother, and come back and have a nice bowl of chili with me."

"I'm Dawn. Thank you. Thank you so much."

I hurry back, paranoid that John will catch me.

The old man is still there with a steaming hot bowl of chili waiting for me at the table. "Well? Did she send you a ticket?" His voice is raspy, like an ancient heavy smoker's.

"Yeah, she did. She has one waiting for me at the Greyhound station in Glendale. Do you know how to get to Glendale from here?"

"Well, I, uh, know, but I don't really have any way to get there. This is San Fernando and, uh, you see, I live in the senior home around the corner. I don't drive anymore. Don't know anyone that does." He sees the worried look on my face. "But let's think about it for a minute, and you eat your chili, sweetie. It'll warm you up."

Whispering a thank-you, I devour my food.

"Maybe you can call the ticket agent and see if you can transfer it to this area. Glendale is pretty far. Or we can look up the bus schedule. But they don't run on Sundays, and it's getting late. Do you have anywhere to sleep?"

"No, I don't. My boyfriend is crazy. I know he will start looking for me as soon as he finds out I'm missing. He'll kill me. I know he will. He's always told me that if I leave him, he will hunt me down and kill me!"

"No, no, no. Now stop it. Calm down. He's not gonna kill anybody. You can sleep on my floor in my dormitory. I'll have to sneak you in. They don't allow overnight visitors, and I share the room with another old fart. Hell, he won't mind, and it's just until you can catch a bus in the morning, right? Come on. Finish your food, and let's go."

"Really? Thanks." I gobble down the rest of the beans and grab a handful of plastic-wrapped crackers to shove in my pocket. I follow him out the door and around the block, trusting that somehow I've gotten lucky and run into a person who cares and will help. What other choice do I have? "Dear God, let this be someone who really cares," I whisper under my breath.

"Shhh. We gotta be real quiet." We sneak in through the kitchen entrance, a two-story, tan concrete block of a building, and tiptoe up a flight of stairs to a semi-hospital-style room. The floors are shiny and polished, and the smell of disinfectant burns the insides of my nostrils. "Here's Ted." He waves his arm across the room at a hospital bed. Ted groans in acknowledgement. "Here you go." Sam hands me his extra pillow and blankets and points to a clear space on the floor.

"Thanks," I whisper, ready to lie down in my makeshift bed.

"Uh, there's one favor I'd like to ask you if you don't mind."

I freeze. "Uh, yeah?" The thought of Sam wanting sex for the favor of taking me in makes my skin crawl. *Oh shit. No.*

"I, uh, really hope this isn't too personal but, uh, I would really appreciate it if I could just, uh, touch your butt."

"What? My butt?"

"Uh, yeah. I, uh, just got this thing for butts, and I thought maybe you wouldn't mind."

"Well, uh, I guess so," I answer, quietly praying that's all he'll want. *I hope he won't turn mean.* Very lightly and cautiously, he places his hand on my rear end and then quickly pulls it off as if it's fire, too hot. He giggles to himself and mutters a thank you, crawling under his covers, a grin plastered across his face.

"Wait till I tell old Bill here what he missed. He's not going to believe it. Ha! Good night." There is a pause. "By the way, what's your name again?"

"My name?" I hesitate. "My name . . . is Dawn." I feel a small sense of pride stir deep down inside me, in a place that has been hollow for so long.

"Dawn, huh? Good night, Dawn."

I'm relieved. It sounds like he will just go to sleep. *Tomorrow I will be free. I will be out of this terrible place.* "Good night." I crawl under my blankets, happy for this polished antiseptic floor, into a grateful sleep.

※

Morning arrives, and I am the talk of the senior home. Sam sneaks me down to the main lobby, telling the front clerk I am his guest who's just arrived and needs to call the bus station. The clerk nods and hands me the phone book.

"Greyhound, Glendale." The voice on the other end of the phone is young and chipper.

"Yes. Hello. My name is Dawn Schiller. Is there a ticket there for me? Did my mother call and leave one?"

"Uh, let's see . . . from an Edda Schiller in Oregon?"

"Yes. Yes. That's her! Is it there?" I hold my breath disbelieving that this is real, scared that he will tell me he made a mistake and there is nothing there.

"Uh, yeah, uh, it's here, but, uh, someone just called looking for you. Some guy. He said he was your boyfriend."

"Oh God! What did you tell him? You didn't say anything, did you? He's not going there, is he?" In my chest, the pounding sounds like thunder.

"Well, uh, yeah. I told him. He said he's on his way."

"Oh no! No! Don't tell him anything! I ran away from him. He's gonna kill me if he catches up to me. Please. Don't tell him I called."

"Well. He said you had a fight; he wants to make up with you. He made me promise to not let you get on the bus."

"No! He's lying! He just wants you to believe he's a nice guy, but he's lying. I ran away from him because he hurts me. Please, don't tell him you talked to me!"

The crackling, silent line tells me he is really listening, believing me. "Well, yeah. Okay. The guy did sound pretty crazy, and your mom has been calling too. What do I tell him when he gets here?"

"My mom called? Tell him I already left. Tell him I never showed up. I don't know—tell him anything!"

"Yeah! Okay. When are you going to be here?"

"I don't know. I'm in San Fernando, and I have to find a bus that will go to Glendale. I don't have any money, so I have to figure something out. I don't know yet."

"Well, uh . . ." There is that silence again. "Well, maybe I can come and get you after I get off. Your mom asked me if I would help you. She told me you were running from your boyfriend. She's got five dollars here for you too, for food. I get off in a couple hours. What's your address?"

The world around me seems to get lighter. Lighter than the colorless shroud that's darkened everything in the past years. *Thank you, Mom.* A touch of hope is filtering in like the sun through a dirt-caked screen. I give him the address of the retirement home and hang up. Sam arranges for me to sit in the dining room with the other residents while they eat breakfast. The kitchen won't serve me an extra plate. The residents will get in trouble, but that doesn't stop them: Somehow my story gets around to them, and it isn't long before extra pieces of toast and bacon wrapped in napkins and tin foil are smuggled to me under the tables.

The hours pass quickly. I dwell on the thought that I am actually going to get away. *This is gonna work this time*, my senses forecast. An old, white delivery van pulls up in front of the home, and a young man in his late twenties sporting a ponytail gets out and asks me my name.

"Dawn?"

"Yeah. That's me." I wave good-bye and yell a thanks to Sam and his elderly gang of bandits.

"He was just at the station. Your boyfriend."

"Who? John? What did you do?" I'm sweating now. I'm not out of here yet. Maybe I won't get away.

"I told him you just left a few minutes ago on another bus."

"What did he say?"

"He asked which way it was going. Ha! I told him the opposite way, through Las Vegas."

"Thanks, man. Was he mad?"

"No. Well, I couldn't tell. He acted very concerned."

"He's crazy." We pull into the Glendale Greyhound bus station, and my bus is already boarding. "Thank you so much. Thank you. You saved my life. I can't tell you how much you saved my life."

"Yeah. It's cool. Your mom is real worried. Here's the five dollars she sent for you and, uh, here." He hands me an old long-sleeved, button-down shirt. "It's cold in Oregon. Take care, and good luck."

"Thank you. Thanks a lot."

I board the long, silver bus and head for a window seat in the back. In my baggy jeans pocket is a piece of contraband toast, broken a little, the crumbs rubbed off. I lean against the cool glass, relaxed for the first time in so long, and bite down on the dry bread. *Wow. This is the first time I have ever been away from John in years.* It is a strange, queer feeling. Never having imagined that we would ever be apart, I make a mental note of my entire body. *So this is how it feels. How it feels to be without him.* So far, I am feeling okay—better than I have felt in a while. Still, I can't deny the pain that lies deep beneath the numbness in my chest: the pain of the million bleeding pieces of my shattered heart.

CHAPTER FIFTEEN
One Last Wonderland, Baby!

ights flash in colored blasts around me. There is a whirlwind. I am in the eye of a tornado; the force from the surrounding current is spinning and sucking me down. A long, frayed rope hangs in the middle of the twirling black tunnel, and with bleeding hands I clutch it. It takes all my strength to not be pulled into the treacherous gale.

"He's bad news." The clear, sharp voice of sanity speaks clearly through the raging blast of the storm around me.

"But he's all I know." My defensive voice is frail, but audible through the noise.

"He hurt you."

"But I've known him since I was fifteen. He taught me everything."

My fear grows louder. Suddenly, my arm slips from the life-saving rope, yanked into the whirling tornado.

"My arm! I'm being sucked in!" I fight to wrench it free.

In a desperate internal struggle, I force my eyes open, hurrying to escape the deadly abyss. Slowly, soaked in sweat, my body breaks free of the paralyzing nightmare.

Mom is here—on her knees, next to me with my wrist in her hand, crying. *"Mein Gott!"* she whispers. "Look! You're so skinny."

"Hi, Mom." I can barely muster a half smile.

"Vaht's happened to you, Dawn? You're so thin! I tought effrything vas good. Vas it drugs?" She wipes the tears from her cheeks as she stands to hover over my emaciated frame.

I avoid her eyes, stare out of the big picture window behind her onto the winter-barren Blue Mountains on the eastern horizon, and nod.

I can't talk about it. Not to my mother. Anger is still buried deep, and it hurts too much to look into myself right now. Quick, short images of my life, a horror film, play in my head like shredded frames of a movie reel. John's evil sneer as he ties me up and beats me mercilessly with a belt; my body crudely sold to strangers; being dragged by my hair on my hands and knees. *Stop!* I can't do this. I can't.

I stand up. "It was bad, Mom." Not allowing emotion to raise my protective walls of silence, I walk into the kitchen. "Got anything to eat?"

Berrrrring! Berrrrring!

Thinking it's my brother or sister calling about my arrival, I grab the phone that hangs off the cabinet above the stove. "Hello?"

"Baby! Wait! Listen!"

It takes only a second for the anger to reach my throat. *"FUCK YOU!"* I scream at the top of my lungs.

Blam! I hang up.

"How long has he been calling?" I snap, waves of rage causing my body to tremble.

"Vell, you slept a long time. He's been calling all morning. I . . ."

"NOTHING! Tell him *nothing* about me. And tell him to go *fuck himself* if he calls again. I never want to hear his voice. *Ever!"* I am shaking hard now, and I want to throw up.

"Dawn!" Mom's eyes are full of shock and surprise at the intensity of my words. She can see her daughter has been hurt, but I am like a stranger to her, and she's helpless.

"You don't understand, Mom! I can't tell you how much . . . he

. . . Never mind!" I lose my appetite. Memories stab sharp, tortured pain from my gut to my throat, and I need to lie down. I curl into a fetal position, the most heart-wrenching of sobs bellowing from the very bottom of my soul. Sorrowfully, like a Holocaust survivor, I weep.

The month of January fades into February, and the phone continues to ring . . . two, three times a day. I stop picking it up for anyone, just in case it is John on the other line, and let it ring and ring. Morning, noon, and twice at night the phone rings. Only my family answers. In the beginning they hang up too, but soon enough John gets them to stay on the line and coaxes them into talking. "No. I'm sorry, but I don't tink dat she vahnts to talk." My mother stays polite while I signal for her to hang up.

There is snow on the ground, ice—and the sky is solidly gray. Eastern Oregon is barren in the winter. Brown, creepy, lifeless sticks for plants and trees. Wind chill in the teens. It suits my mood and the way I feel about life. Mom's in a new place, a light blue two-story house nearly a hundred years old. She is recently remarried and seems happy to finally have a place of her own. They are struggling though and don't have much, so after a month of isolating myself I finally feel well enough to apply for a job and help out. *I'm a CNA,* I tell myself with pride, remembering a good part of my past. *I can find a job.*

I secure a position at Evergreen Convalescent Hospital—not a difficult thing to do; they so desperately need the help for the elderly—and begin a three-to-eleven shift. I am blending in with people who don't know about John or my past, and the anonymity helps me to reconnect with the part of me that's been waiting to bloom. I am earning my own money now and helping Mom and her new husband, Phil, with the bills. But when I'm not at work, burning memories creep up, and overwhelming indignation at the degradation I've recently been through consumes me. The anger, the buried rage, smolders and bubbles, threatening to rise to the surface like lava overflowing from a volcano and destroying the village below.

My steam vents are my job, a crochet hook and ball of yarn, and my grandma's old wooden rocking chair. And when I can't sleep or bear to feel, I have alcohol to burn the memories into hated blackened ashes. Scheduled days off from the convalescent home scare me—too much time to think. I find some comfort falling back into childhood memories of the big house in Toms River, sitting in Grandma's smooth rocker. The vision of how her arms rested across her chest embraces me as I rock and gaze out of the big picture window in Mom's living room. I listen to the phone ring and ring and ring, muttering curses under my breath. Back and forth, back and forth I rock, remembering her consistency and faith, imagining her anger at the betrayal of my father. Full of rage, I crochet steadily. Yarn twists around my finger tightly, cutting off blood and denting the skin near my knuckle. The lack of circulation leaves my fingers blue and cold, but I don't pay attention to it and certainly I can't release my grip even if I try.

I associate only with my family. I am embarrassed at the way John falsely made me feel distrustful of them. He lied to me about everyone, telling me they didn't care. Slowly, I am able to share with them bits and pieces of what happened, and my brother fumes and wants to strangle John for hurting me, his sister. He met John a few years back when he ran away from Mom to visit me in Glendale. John disliked him right away. Someone else who loved me was not allowed in the picture of John's perfect world, so he fed me lies that caused me to distrust my brother and to send him away. It was painful to see how hurt he was then that I would believe John over him, and I am sickened to see how wrong I have been.

The few details I share with Terry have her dumbstruck. "How can he have turned that way? He wasn't like that when I was there!

He loved you so much, Dawn, and he was so nice to me!" It is a shock to her, and she thinks it's clear that the drugs are to blame.

I see the drugs as the culprit too. True or not, it is the only way I can accept that any of the violent abuse has ever happened. *It had to be the drugs.*

Winter's end brings days of sunshine and snow, spring, the robins that build nests in my mother's maple tree out front. I watch them play and forage for food while I still rock and pull the yarn ever tighter around my crochet hook. The phone rings constantly, and Mom continues to tell John, "She said no."

"He says he understands and to tell you that he loves you." Mom passes messages along, giving in a bit with John's pleadings and weeks of relentless calls.

Exhausted from the endless ringing, everyone really just wants him to stop. Yet Terry is over often and has no problem answering the phone when it rings. She lets John talk to her. Curious, she wants to know what happened. Finding an open ear, John jumps in . . . he's done that before with her. He knows Terry and speaks to her of times when he brought her food and helped us out. "He says he doesn't want anything from you, Dawn. He only wants to talk to you." Terry holds the phone out for me, telling me she thinks he's sincere.

For a moment, I feel the power of an upper hand as he exposes his vulnerable side. I have only one thing I need to know . . . "Where's Thor?" I yell my first words to him, breaking my icy silence.

"He's fine. He's okay. Do you want to talk to him?" Terry repeats his words to me.

"No!"

She continues to speak for a few minutes, then hangs up. "He wants me to watch out for you. Make sure you're okay."

Blankly and unflinching, I stare at her. *Can he be for real?* I think. *Now he wants to make sure I am okay? Yeah, right!*

"Is he high?" I ask her.

"I don't think so. He sounded normal. I don't know everything that happened, Dawn, but he said he's real sorry. He said it was the drugs. He said he and Thor miss you."

I see her face, furrowed brow, believing eyes, and understand how easily she is swept up in his sweet words. She is remembering the John from years ago, from the beginning. She doesn't know how violent the drugs have made him. I can't bear to tell her.

"He said he's gonna send me money to buy some film so I can take pictures of you. He wants a picture."

"God, Terry! What did you say? He *has* pictures. He has Thor too. He's sick and on drugs, and I don't believe him."

"All right, Dawn. I guess so. But he didn't sound high to me." Terry and I leave it at that. The charming John, the *Terry food* Snickers bar John, has the power over her emotions—a lot because I haven't told my family many details, but mostly because his seduction is controlling . . . and for me, dangerous.

***

A few days later a large package addressed to me waits on the kitchen table when I get home from work. I pick it up and flop on the couch. It's from John. His large, exaggerated scrawl on the wrapping is unmistakable. I open it with apprehension. Inside rests photos in a mound almost two inches high of our times past. They are of happy times when we smiled and cuddled, camping trips, romantic moments at the beach and mountains, the tintype of us as a couple from Knott's Berry Farm, and lots of photos of Thor. On top of the pile of colorful photos is a small, stuffed, brown Chihuahua with a note attached that reads:

Dear Mommy

I miss you very much and wish you were here.

Daddy is taking good care of me.

I Love you.
Thor

I Love you baby!
John

I melt. The armor protecting my emotions for the last few months is cracking. Picking up the photos carefully, one by one, I relish the tender, happy moments they represent. My mind floats on the clouds of happier times. Times I remember as the best I've known in my life. Pictures that pull me back into the vortex of John. After all, there are no photos of the bad times, and God knows how badly I want to forget them, pretend they never happened. I miss Thor terribly. My little, brave guy who loves me so much he'd stand up to John, a figure he loved too. *I hope he's okay.*

The phone rings. Perfect timing. I know it is John. It's his routine late-night call he makes after I get off of work—the call I have always ignored. This time, though, I deliberately walk over and focus on the receiver. The ringing is constant, beckoning; I can almost hear John's voice whisper, *Pick up the phone, Dawn. Pick up the phone.*

On impulse, I grab the receiver. I am silent.

"Dawn?"

He knows it's me.

"Are you there?"

I still say nothing. Silence.

"Dawn? I, I can hear you breathe, baby."

John's words cut through my very being. They're familiar, they fit, it's me, and I love it . . . and I hate it. Flooding memories cause my body to react, and I taste the chemistry we shared, bittersweet in the back of my throat. "Yeah? I'm here. What?" I'm not going to give in that easily!

"Dawn." His voice is low and sweet, with a faint whimper to it, as it was when my name was dear to him, when he told me it was beautiful. "I'm so sorry, baby. I told your mother I'm sorry. I'm sorry." John sobs, a self-loathing wail, the way he did those times in the bathtub after beatings. "I don't know why I did it. I don't know. It was the drugs. I w, want you back, baby!" He loses his words; his crying catches in his throat. He sounds so frail and weak.

Dawn Schiller

I am quiet a long while, listening to his sobs, checking to see if they are real. "How can I believe you're off the drugs, John?"

"You gotta believe me, baby. I want you back. I want our life back. The way it was in the beginning. I just can't, can't be without you. I don't know what to do. I'm so sorry!" I can hear him pull away for a second and blow his nose.

"I gotta go, John. Is Thor okay?"

He clears his throat. "Okay, I understand, baby. You have every right to be mad at me. I fucked up, I know. But it's the dope. It's the fucking dope. I'm quitting that shit!"

"Tell Thor I love him. I gotta go." I hang up. I didn't like the tone his voice was taking. I've heard this shit before.

Berrrrring! Berrrrring!

"Yes?" I know it is him.

"I forgot to tell you. Baby? Dawn . . . I love you," he breathes, sounding lonely and sad.

"Yeah," I whisper and gently place the receiver back on the wall.

❧

John's apologies are getting to me, and as much as I've resisted, I begin to anticipate his calls. Sometimes I answer, and sometimes I don't. I am enjoying the control I have for a change and a chance to vent some of my anger. In the months to follow, John times his phone calls for the late evenings. He has discovered from my sister what my work hours are and knows when I'll be home. He also knows that my family will be asleep by then.

So I answer and allow him to speak to me of happier days and take me down his dream road of loving memories. Time is taking the sting out of the horridness of our most recent past. Reminiscing about our love, we slip into soft whispers and knowing silences, relishing the sound of each other's breath again.

362

We fantasize that those days have never left us, and we live in the past via telephone wire.

"Dawn. I want it back . . . back to the way it was in the beginning. I want to get out of here, out of LA."

"But where are you going to go?"

"I don't know. Anywhere. Somewhere. Somewhere . . . with you?"

I don't answer.

"Dawn. Dawn, you're so beautiful . . . I miss you so much."

I hear an odd popping noise in the background, and my skin prickles. "What's that?" I ask, suspicious.

"What . . . uh, nothing. It was Thor. Here. Do you want to talk to him?"

A tiny breath sniffs the receiver and I soften, crooning his name to hear his voice. "Thor. Hi, boy. Oh, I miss you." A faint whining sounds through the phone line and then a yip. John is laughing in the background, and I ache for the laughter we once had.

"It was the drugs before, baby. It wasn't me."

"I know."

"I just want to start over—you and me and Thor. Somewhere new."

"What about Sharon?"

"Sharon too."

I think for a moment, trying to picture how John can possibly make it better with Sharon. Then my mind shuts down; the shaping image too painful to visualize. "I gotta go, John."

He pulls in an injured breath. "I love you, Dawn."

"I love you too, John."

Falling into a pattern of a long-distance relationship, John and I speak regularly. I look forward to telling him about my day at the convalescent hospital, the way we used to share our news with Sharon. His days, he lets me know, are dedicated to getting healthy and clearing up his prior arrest for stealing the computer at the Marina.

He wouldn't be able to call me every night if he's still on drugs, I rationalize. It has been over five months already, and he's only missed calling a few times. I've even heard the pattering and barking of John L, Pokie, and Thor, so I think, *Oh, good. He's at Sharon's. He must be telling the truth.*

I'm still not comfortable telling my family the whole story of abuse. I am ashamed, and forgetting seems less painful. But the more John sounds like his old self, the more I want to have those moments of earlier times again. I believe, finally, in his sincerity and allow myself to enter into conversations about a future together.

On an almost summer evening, John calls, barely able to contain his excitement.

"Dawn, baby! The best thing has happened!"

"What?"

"There's a big job coming up . . . and it will take care of everything! But . . . but I need you here with me."

"Why?"

"So we can take off together as soon as it's done. We can start over again. Go anywhere . . . the Grand Canyon, maybe? Anywhere you want."

"Really?"

"Yeah! It's big, baby! Real big. We'll be set. I hate this fucking place. I hate these fucking people and their fucking drugs. I just want you back, baby. I just want to start over with you again . . . like it was in the beginning."

"Oh, John, I want that too. Really, I do. But . . . but you gotta . . . gotta promise me—*promise*—no more hitting! No more streets. No, no more . . . abuse, John!"

"I promise, baby. I promise. No more of any of that. I'm so sorry. It was the fucking drugs. I hate the drugs. I just want a new life with you."

"Yes."

"Huh? What?"

"Yes. I'll come back. But just until your job is over. Then we have to leave. I don't want to be there anymore, John. I can't." I stifle a cry. "Is Sharon coming?"

"Yeah? Okay, when? Baby, you won't be sorry. We'll start over, I promise, and leave all this shit behind."

"And Sharon?"

"Yes, baby. I'll ask her. I'll tell her you're coming back and that we can get out of here. This is gonna be *it*, baby. Finally, finally, we can get out of all this shit!"

I have softened. I miss him—the good times and the love we once shared. I miss Sharon and Thor. Grasping onto hope, I book a flight and quit my job. No one in my family is surprised, but not everyone is happy about it. When my mother has spoken to John, he's been polite and sweet. Doing what he does best, he's charmed her. Terry wants to believe the drugs are gone as well. After all, he was so nice before; cocaine has to be to blame. My brother, Wayne, says nothing and slips wordlessly into the background. Looking sad and dejected, he acts like he did when we parted in Carol City, except this time he doesn't say good-bye.

But I am still crippled; I am still not whole. In my head I hear that fearful voice that says, *He's all I know,* and I say yes. Again, for the sake of love, I say yes to him.

❧

My plane touches down at Burbank Airport in the last week of June in 1981. I replay the parting words of my mother as she sees me off at the airport. *"Arr you sure you vahnt to do dis, Dawn?"*

"He promised, Mom. I believe him."

"Vell, eff you need something, call me." She sighs heavily. *"I luff you, Dawn."*

"I love you too, Mom."

She is still helpless. A blue-collar worker all her life, she has limited resources. She's watched her young daughter leave, get caught up with a porn star and his wife, and run for her life from that same man old enough to be her father. Every step of the way, Mom has been powerless, except to pray. She has prayer, and like Grandma and Aunt Ella in the days in New Jersey so many years ago, she always prays for her children.

John is waiting at the baggage claim. I spot him right away, and my heart pounds. Shyly happy to see him, I walk a bit faster. He is standing with his hands in his pockets, looking fidgety and nervous. As I get closer, I notice how tired and gaunt he is. I keep my pace, getting closer, willing my heart to stay in my chest, and then my smile fades. John sees my reaction and turns his head away.

"Hey, baby!" He bends down to lift me up to him. "Mmm-mmm. I missed you so much! Let's get out of here." He gives me a big squeeze and kisses me on my lips . . . but he is unfocused. The conveyor belt rotates, the first of the passengers' bags roll out, and John stands watching. He circles one arm around me, holding me close.

"That's mine," I tell him, pointing to the green duffel bag.

John makes a quick, paranoid sweep of the area and picks up my bag and another unfamiliar suitcase next to it. "Come on." He pulls me toward the exit.

"John, that's . . ."

"Shhh. Let's go."

My heart sinks as I let him lead me out to the waiting Malibu. *My God! He lied! He's high!*

The Malibu is waiting, more faded and dirty than I remember. He quickly flings the two bags into the trunk and revs it up. Thor is in the front seat, happily jumping like a Mexican bean in my lap.

Then when John gets in, he instantly crouches low, shying away from him. I hold his frail and shaking figure close to my heart, letting him know I will protect him, and I decide to stay quiet.

Sensing I know he's high, John acts nervous. He reaches over to hold my hand, his palm sweaty and rough. "I love you," he says; his speech is awkward and broken like the sound of flipping through radio stations.

"I love you too." My words are like cardboard and taste stiff in my mouth; my stomach does flip-flops inside of me. *Oh, please don't let this all be bullshit. Please,* I pray to whoever will listen and painfully think about the safe and warm home I have just given up . . . for this!

Checking into a run-down motel on Hollywood Boulevard, John pays for a couple of nights. Saddened and shocked, I watch him begin his old ritual: locking the door, putting the desk chair in front of it, looking out the windows, and checking the bathroom. I know the pipe is next as he sits on the edge of the bed and pops open his briefcase.

What do I say? I ask myself, feeling guarded and at a loss for words. *He lied to me!* I want to cry, but my body won't connect the thought with the action.

"Are you okay, baby?" John peeks over at me warily. He knows what I am thinking.

"Yeah, sure." I shrug, teetering on the edge of fear.

He brings out the pipe and taps out the last of the crumbs from the bottom of the film canister. Melting the drugs down, he hesitates for a moment and then sucks in the thick smoke. Closing his eyes, he holds his breath.

At a moment when he can't get angry, I speak up. "John, I

haven't done anything since I've been gone . . . just alcohol."

His eyes open; he chokes a little and nods. The acrid smoke blows in my face, and John falls back on the pillows for a few moments, letting the freebase pump through his body. "I know, baby," he finally answers. "It's just a little. To celebrate your coming back." He pulls himself up, lights the 151-soaked cotton ball, and cooks the pipe once again. Leaning into me, he holds the stem to my mouth and, with his paralyzing blue stare, looks deep into my eyes, freezing me to the spot. "Here, baby. Welcome home." He flares his nostrils and smiles. "Here—suck!"

I curse myself for being here. I dread falling back into the nightmare I thought I had escaped but swallow and do as he asks, refusing to believe that coming back was a mistake. My mind's in turmoil. The conflict sears my soul, and I can't think too much. *This doesn't mean our plans are over. We're still getting out of here,* I tell myself, denying his lies. Then the drugs take over, and I fall into his seductive embrace again, into his mouth again, as we passionately and euphorically taste each other one more time.

The late afternoon summer sun burns streaks through the holes of the shabby drapes. John and I slowly stretch out of bed, laughing at Thor's playful bathroom dance.

"Just a minute, just a minute." John smiles, pulling on his pants. "Let's go get something to eat, huh, Thor? Kentucky Fried Chicken okay with you, baby?"

"Sure. I'm starved."

John counts out a small amount of cash, grabs Thor, and leans in for a sensual kiss. "Come lock the door, baby. I'll be right back."

The second-story room we rented is particularly tiny, damaged, and filthy. Watching John descend the stairs, I notice the garbage, bums, and loiterers crowding the street below . . . even in broad daylight. *Wow. This place is in the thick of things,* I think. I know what kind of street this is; a lump grows in my throat that threatens to cut off my air supply, and I get panicky. *Calm down, Dawn. It's gonna be all right. We'll be out of here soon.* Quickly I lock and chain the door, not wanting anyone to see me, and I count the minutes till John's return.

Evening falls. The clock ticks nearer to midnight. John and I are lounging around watching television and cuddling. Something distracts him, some kind of internal clock, and he gets up to look out the window. Sensing the time is right, he slowly and ritually dresses and packs his briefcase. In the bathroom he fills the sink with cold water and dunks his head. Shaking his wet curls like a dog after a bath, he sprays wet drops across the walls and tiles. His reflection in the mirror freezes him for several long moments. "Hmm," he grunts. He checks his pockets once, twice, three times . . . stops, looks at me, and draws in a deep breath. "This is it, baby. I love you!"

I reach up to give him a hug. "I love you too, John. Be careful." As old words roll off my tongue automatically, the familiarity of seeing him off on a run makes my skin crawl. *But this is different,* I remind myself again. *This is the last time.*

"If everything goes right, baby, we'll be out of here by this time next week." He is shaking a little as he squeezes me tightly for a long embrace and a kiss. He stares deep into my eyes, traces my lips with his thumb . . . like the old days. "I love you, baby. I'll be back by morning."

The Malibu revs up in the lot below the window for a good ten minutes. I can see John fussing repeatedly with the rearview mirror and visor. Finally he rolls out onto Hollywood Boulevard . . . like the old days.

Bang, bang, bang! "Hello, miss!" The motel manager is at the door.

"Yes?" The chain pulls tightly as I unlock the door.

"Checkout time! Checkout!"

"Um, yeah, okay. Um, he's . . . um, my boyfriend isn't back yet. Can I wait for him a little while longer?"

"I can't do that, miss. I'll get in trouble."

"Please! I don't have any money. He's coming right back!"

He thinks for a moment. "Okay. You got till one o'clock! That's all I can do!"

"Thanks."

Holding Thor in my arms, I wait nervously on the bed, my green Army duffel bag packed and ready at my feet. As every minute of the clock ticks excruciatingly by, I will each noise outside to be John's approaching Chevy. Shadows move behind the thin drapes; the maid and her cleaning cart make me more and more anxious as they wheel closer to my door.

Boom, boom, boom! "Housekeeping!"

I know my time is up. "Coming!" I call. With every minute dragging into two or three more, I pick up my bag and walk outside. *Where is he? Oh God, no. He left me! Where do I go? What am I supposed to do now?* I panic. Like something forgotten, discarded, I slowly step out of the boundaries of the motel toward a small cement ledge near the sidewalk and flop down.

In the bright afternoon light, the people on the street take notice. Young men with gold chains strut by, again and again, whistling and making comments under their breath. I look away, clutching Thor close to my chest, and can't help the flood of tears that drenches my cheeks. I can't think. *Where is he? Why hasn't he come back? Why did I leave Oregon?*

A teenage boy looking like a pimp in his white suit and gold chains has been staring at me from across the street. Making a beeline in my direction, he wants to strike up a conversation; I can tell. I hook my foot around my duffel bag and huddle further into myself, wrapping into the safety of my mental walls. *Please don't let him talk to me.*

A flood of despair rains down from every inch of the afternoon sky. Drenched with disbelief that I am back here . . . to this, I break down and weep hysterically.

With no thought of what to do next, I weep uncontrollably, sobs heaving and shaking me down to my bones. I have given up. I think about the warm bed at my mother's house, my family, Grandma's rocking chair, and the new friends I made at work and wish with all my heart I could erase the last couple of days. I give in to the despair of being totally lost, abandoned, and terrified for my safety. I weep and weep and weep.

"Miss? Miss? Are you all right?" A female voice is louder now. "Miss! Do you need help?"

I lift my head. Through a veil of tears, I notice a plain, short-haired, stocky, slightly overweight woman calling down to me from the window of her white Volkswagen van. I wipe my face and nod. "My, my boyfriend . . . didn't come back and, and I got kicked out." My tears rush out again.

"Do you need a ride somewhere? I'm safe. I promise. I run a Christian youth group. Can I take you somewhere? Somewhere safe?" She tilts her head up and down the street.

"Mm, hmm. Yeah! Thanks." She looks kind, but I'm nervous. Through my blurred tears, I can see a few others seated in the back of her van. I gain my composure and quickly jump through the already open door. *God, I hope she is real.*

"My name is Sally."

"I'm Dawn." I don't offer any more information.

"So where do you want to go?"

"My mom's in Oregon . . . The Glendale bus station, I guess."

"Do you have a ticket?"

"No. My boyfriend . . . he left me. He was supposed to be back before checkout, but he . . . well, didn't make it."

"Do you need a place to stay for a while?"

I look at her, suspicious of the offer. "What do you mean?"

"Well, I run a Christian youth group," she repeats, "and we hire out to help with odd jobs for the elderly. We got extra work if you want to earn money for a bus ticket. You can crash at my place till you do. I assure you it is perfectly legitimate and I'm safe. Really!" She smiles, seeing my cautiousness. "Just ask these guys. They work with me every day. I'm picking them up for a job." She points to the young, paint-splattered men in the back row of the van.

"Yeah, she's cool. She's kind of a missionary. Sally's been running the youth group for over a year. You're okay, girl. You got lucky. This is no place to be left on the street."

"Yeah . . . sure. Sounds all right. Thanks." I relax and let out a long, steady breath—so much that even my bones feel deflated. I let my mind adjust to the sharp change of my new environment, and I feel as though I'm being wrapped in a soft, warm blanket, my tears wiped dry.

Where is John? I worry.

Sally smiles and turns up the Christian tunes on the radio. "Let's get to work! Hope you know how to paint." She hums, content, like a mother bird blessing her nest with her song.

***

The second day with Sally is ending, and I am exhausted. I joined her and her crew on their painting job to have a safe place to stay while I save money to go back to Oregon, but secretly I am hoping to hear from John. Sally lives on the second floor of a plain, two-story apartment complex adjacent to a wide, busy street in Studio City. After my long afternoon of painting the day before, Sally did as she promised and brought me to her apartment to let me crash on her couch for the night.

"Can I use the phone please? I'd like to try to call my boy-friend's answering service. In case he's in trouble or something . . ."

"Uh, yeah . . . you sure about that, Dawn? I thought you said he left you."

"Yeah, but I don't know why! I've just returned from Oregon. We got back together and he was only going . . ." I let my voice trail off. "He was supposed to come right back. He's never let me get kicked out of a place before. I'm worried. Something's wrong!"

Sally sighs. "Well, if you really think you should, the phone's over there."

I leave several messages for John in the evening, letting him know where I am, and again the next morning. In the past, some-times John has left me a message with the operator at his answering service, but nothing is waiting this time. By late afternoon the next day, there still has been no word. Tired from the day's physi-cal work, Sally and I grab some takeout.

Sally is a true Pentecostal Christian and speaks passionately of the Bible and the perils of Satan. I don't feel I fit in with that way of thinking, but think she will not like me if I don't pay attention. Politely but distantly, I listen as she drones on about her religion, never connecting any of it with me. The Bible is confusing, and religion's Satan scares me worse than what I already know. The phone rings.

Sally answers. "It's for you, Dawn. He says his name is John."

"That's him! That's my boyfriend!"

"Hello! John? Where have you been? I got kicked out, John!" My voice cracks. "I'm at this nice lady's house in Studio City. I've been painting houses with her, and she let me stay. Okay. You got the address. Are you okay? Yeah, he's fine. Hurry. I love you too."

"I take it that was him." Sally looks down her nose at me.

"Yeah! He's coming to pick me up. He says to say thank you."

John arrives a few hours after calling, much later than expected. It is well past dark and, thinking he may not even show up, Sally has already settled in for the night. But I have been restless and worried. There's a tapping at the door just as we've turned out the lights, and Thor starts barking. I throw off my covers and run to look through the peephole. Sally is up, following closely behind.

"John!" I whisper with relief. "Come in. Sally, this is my boyfriend, John."

"Hello there!" he says with a grin as wide as the state of California. It is dark, but he pulls off a pair of mirrored sunglasses and slides them up over his curls. "I'm John. John Holmes." He reaches out forcefully for a handshake.

"Well, uh, hi. Shh! Let's keep our voices down please. Come on in." Sally is nervous the neighbors will hear. "I found Dawn sitting in front of that motel in Hollywood. She had been kicked out with no place to go. So I let her stay here."

"Yes. I know. Thank you. Uh, thank you so much. I was, uh, delayed beyond my control and I, uh . . ." John's eyes are red, and his head is twitching. Reaching into his pocket, he pulls out a huge wad of cash, peeling a hundred off the top. "Here, uh, ma'am," he drawls in his John Wayne impression. "Here's for taking care of my girl. I, uh, appreciate that." John winks at her as though she is special.

Sally welcomes the money and blushes. "Well, uh, I can't . . ."

"No. No. I insist." He flirts with her harder, in his sexy porn style. "Uh, do you mind if we use your bathroom? We have to talk."

John doesn't wait for a response. Placing his sunglasses back on his face, he smiles his grinchy grin and drags me down the hallway with him. "Baby, baby!" He brings his lips to my ear, still grinning from the other side of his face. He locks the bathroom door behind us.

"Where were you, John? I got kicked out! The guy wouldn't let me stay! Are you all right? Is everything okay?" I have seen the money and can tell he is really high but in a very good mood.

"Fuck that asshole. He coulda made himself a bundle. Wait. Look at this!" John opens his briefcase. Taking up nearly the entire bottom of the case is the cutoff corner of a black plastic garbage bag stuffed full with the largest brick-sized block of cocaine I have ever seen.

"Whoa! Oh my God! Is that . . . the deal?"

"You got it, baby. This is it! We are outta here, and this is our ticket!" He is as giddy as a child on Christmas morning.

I can only stare. My thoughts are mixed with fear and excitement as John reaches in and presses me into a long, deep kiss. "I want you," he breathes hotly into my neck. Then, opening up the bag, he stops to admire his score, picks up a tarot card of the devil that is floating among the wreckage of his briefcase, and lays out four fat, thick lines on the back of a magazine from a shelf under the sink.

Snnnnuffffff. Snnnuffffff. His head snaps back. "Here." He coughs as he holds a cutoff red-and-white striped straw under my nose.

Strangely mesmerized, I pull my gaze away from the ominous, dark-horned tarot and take my turn inhaling the bitter, white powder. John doesn't let the terrible burn stop him from his raw, impulsive urge. Instantly he pulls his clothes off and desperately strips mine away in turn. He seals his tall frame, vacuumlike, onto my small, bony form. Our bodies turn instantly hot, reeling, on fire. We're unable to hear anything but each other's heavy breathing and frantically pounding hearts—and unable to really feel, numb because of the drug.

"Hey. Are you two okay?" a woman's voice calls from outside the door. "I need to use the bathroom."

John starts giggling. "Yeah. Okay. Just a minute." Quickly we put on our clothes and open the door. A different woman waits in the hallway.

"Hi. I'm Pam, Sally's sister!" She introduces herself flirtatiously to John. She is much slimmer than Sally, and she wears makeup and thick perfume. Sally is standing behind her, nodding acknowledgement.

"Oh." *Sniff.* "Hi! Uh, sorry! Uh, we'll be out of your way in just a minute." John looks her slender figure up and down and decides she is cool. "Uh, you two don't happen to want a wake-up call, now, do you?"

Pam's eyes bug out. She watches John lay down two large lines with the very same tarot card, number thirteen, the devil. "Sure!" Pam is excited. Sally declines. I gather Thor to wait for John to follow. He never emerges.

Hours pass. The couch, a velour explosion of multicolored flowers, is a quiet place I wait holding Thor and chewing my fingernails. Immobilized by the coke that filters through my system, my mind stays blank, unable to ask questions like *why?* or *how?* I am in another world, detached, and the fact that John is still in the bathroom with Pam just doesn't matter to me.

Sally brews some coffee and paces the kitchen, intermittently storming down the hall to coax her sister out of the bathroom. She doesn't like this one bit, and she is getting impatient and snappy.

"Can you go check on them?" she asks. She is antsy, the edge of her worry unraveling and fraying like a snag in a wool sweater.

I break out of my private head space. "John. John. What's going on?" My tapping is featherlike, barely making a sound.

The knob turns; the door pushes ajar. John is sitting on the toilet with his briefcase on his lap, rummaging through the assortment of junk that floats at the bottom. The garbage bag is no longer there; I assume he stashed it somewhere else. Pam is on the floor leaning against the tub, leafing through the magazine used earlier as a table for the cocaine. They are both acting nonchalant—too much so—and I can tell they're extremely high.

"John. What are you doing? Sally is getting mad. We need to get out of here."

Pam's clothes are slightly disheveled and the side of John's neck has a cluster of red blotches.

"Oh, uh, yeah, baby, uh, sure . . . I, uh . . ." His mind drifts from the massive amount of raw drugs that swirl inside his head, and he focuses on some stray topic, as if I'm not there.

"John?"

"Huh? Oh yeah. I'll be right out, babe." He flashes me a pasty, dry grin that looks like a discarded Mardi Gras mask. Pam stays glued to the magazine, unnatural and mannequinlike.

"He said he was coming right out." I tell Sally the news, the bathroom announcement, and resume my spot on the couch.

Mumbling something under her breath, she stomps away to her room.

✦

The sun makes brighter and brighter patches on the beige shag carpet, marking the end of a rigid night with no sleep. The coke is wearing off, and my body aches from the cramping tension in my limbs even though I lie on the couch trying to sleep. Sally is up and in the kitchen again. True fatigue sets in now that the many hours of the night have passed without rest, and my mouth, sticky and dry, calls out for water. Exhausted, I drag myself up to talk to Sally.

"Hi."

"You need to get your boyfriend out of my bathroom!" She is furious.

"Where's your sister?" I ask, not liking the accusation in her voice.

"Get him!"

Almost as if John has heard her, he saunters into the living room stretching, yawning loudly, and smiling. "Good morning!" he bellows. "Anybody want some breakfast?" Briefcase in hand and face washed, he tries to diffuse Sally's anger. "What can I get ya then. Sweet rolls? Orange juice? How 'bout you, babe? Come on. Let's go get something to eat."

"Sure," I say flatly, but I'm seething with anger. Still, I'm relieved to see him out of the bathroom. We head out the door as Sally marches back to finally have a private word with her sister.

✦

"Back! Get back, ye Satan!" Sally is screaming at the top of her lungs off the balcony of her stucco apartment complex. Marching, soldierlike, back and forth, mumbling, singing, waving a massive white flag that bears a red cross and crown as her staff of protection.

"In the name of Jesus, I cast you *out!*"

"What the f—?" John and I stare, our jaws dropped.

Grocery bags in hand, I call up to her. "Sally? Sally?"

"I know who you are! I saw that tarot card! Be gone, Satan!" She is in a religious frenzy; she breaks out singing "Onward, Christian Soldiers." Shrill and thunderous, she drowns us out.

"You gotta be kidding!" John almost laughs, unbelieving, then stops himself. I remember the devil card and her sister, clothes rumpled, in the bathroom. Sally is very serious.

"Okay, Sally, please! Just let me get my dog and my stuff, okay? I'm coming up, okay? Please just let me have my dog."

Sally stops marching and points the flag out in front of her like a shield. "Meet me at the elevator!"

In the lobby, amid passersby and gawking tenants, John and I wait as the solid elevator doors roll open. Sally rushes forward, thrusts my duffel bag and a shivering Thor into my waiting arms, her face sweaty and aflame from her hollering and singing. She brushes imaginary cobwebs from her arms and legs, spitting and cursing, calling on protective Bible verses to purify her tainted spirit. Incredulous and emotionally wounded, I am speechless. Feeling scared that I have lost a friend, I shake my head while the doors close to hide her accusing face.

"Oh my God! Was that weird or what?" John tries to deflect my attention from his role in the bathroom scene and to gain my forgiveness.

I am hurt. Sally took me in when I was on the street; I never wanted to make her feel afraid.

"Can you believe her, babe? Thank gawd I got you out of there."

John always has a way of shifting the blame. It confuses me when he fast-talks, and I know it's useless to argue.

"I thought she was going to keep Thor! That was scary!"

We are tired and hungry. The effects of the coke have worn off enough that we're in the mood to get some rest. We travel back into Hollywood feeling like vampires whose skin will burst into flame by the sun. John pulls into another run-down motel and checks us in, paying for a full week in advance this time. We eat noisily, unwrapping fish and chips from the Long John Silver's down the road, smoke a cigarette, and draw the drapes to block out the sun. "Let's get some rest, baby." John gets naked and pulls me tight. "Tonight's the night! The big one!"

I know he means he is going to sell the coke. I know that is where the money for our getaway will come from. So when we wake around dusk that evening on the last day of June, few words are spoken. John throws away the paraphernalia and puts the money in his boot and the coke in his briefcase. His attitude is all business as I hand him his jacket and pack of True Blues. The drug is only a commodity now, not for consumption. The *big one!* This is to be our new beginning . . . fresh and clean.

The walls of my motel room move like willowy ghosts from the shadows of the headlights of parking cars. The entire night, John is gone. My sleep is restless and stiff, and when I finally doze off, nightmares jolt me awake. Thor is spooked too, his ears perked as he listens to the noises and movements outside, anxious to hear the familiar engine *chug* of the Malibu. The streets are damp, heavy with fog and eeriness. The darkness is an ominous and lurking thing. I jump up to look out the window at every noise. Once morning comes, I worry once again.

Light fills the horizon in pink and gray tones even as the sun rises. The marine layer still cloaks the sky. I hear the unmistakable popping of the Chevy's engine as John pulls into the parking space out front.

"He's here!" My heart races as I pull the curtain back.

John is still inside the Malibu, his head laid back against the headrest. Stiff and slow, he gets out of the car and takes a sweeping look around. His shoulders slumped, his skin pasty and pale, he circles around to the trunk, opens it, and peers inside. He seems to be searching for something but comes up empty-handed. He drops the trunk lid closed and limps up to the door of our room.

Oh no. I run to the door and unlock it. John's eyes, bloodshot and blank, don't acknowledge me. He walks by zombielike, the living dead. *He's wearing different clothes,* I register. In slow motion he drops down on the bed, hesitates, then digs in his pockets for some change.

"Can you go get me a Coke?" His words come out weak and emotionless.

"What happened, John?"

"Hmm? Nothing . . . baby, please?"

I disappear and get his soda. He sounds so hurt and lost. I want to comfort him.

Still frozen in the same slumped position on the edge of the bed, he digs deeper in his pockets and downs a few ten-milligram Valiums he has wrapped in cigarette cellophane. *Where's his briefcase?* I wonder, feeling uneasy. Sapped of all his energy, he stands unsteadily. His clothes drop at his feet, and he crawls under the covers. As I cover him with the blanket, words stick in my throat when I see his arms and neck streaked with deep red scratches and marks. Thor rolls around on the bed, kicking and playing, trying to get John's attention, but John ignores him and turns his back, cold, like a deathly shroud.

"John? Are you okay?" I ask as I snuggle in next to him. He offers nothing. *He's different,* I think. *Something's changed . . . broken inside of him.* Devoid of spirit, a shell, empty and hollow, he lies pale and still, as if he were lying in his own coffin, and falls asleep.

❧

John is restless, tossing and turning throughout the night, kicking and pushing me to all corners of the bed. He groans and whimpers muffled screams, squeals, makes unnatural grunting noises like a deaf-mute calling for help. Sweat soaks his skin, drenching the sheets and my own nightshirt. His nightmare is fierce, a battle . . . for his life.

"Blood! Blood!" He thrashes side to side as if he wants to run away. "There's so much blood!"

"What, John?" I try whispering into his ear, but he is deep in his terror and moans and tosses on his side. John quiets for a moment, sprawled over the entire bed. Thor and I can't sleep and get up to pee. Daylight touches the curtains in a soft, glowing halo, and I turn on the television bolted to the wall at the foot of the bed. I light a cigarette and turn the volume low. A five o'clock news flash plays across the screen:

"Four bodies were found bludgeoned to death on Wonderland Avenue this morning in the Hollywood Hills with one survivor. Stay tuned for news at five."

My head snaps up, and I gasp. *That house! That street! I know that place. That's John's connection! Oh no. God!* I hold my breath for ten full minutes, it seems, afraid to exhale. Every ounce of my being knows undoubtedly: *This is bad.* The little things are adding up in my head: John's return with different clothes, his missing briefcase, the red marks on his arms and neck, and most especially the lifeless way he acts—then the dreams. I start to get scared that something has gone very wrong with the sale of the coke. I swallow hard. It is five o'clock.

On the news, police are gathered outside of the house on

Wonderland Avenue overseeing the removal of mummy sheet-clad bodies from the three-story home and loading them into a coroner's van. A reporter, somber outside with a microphone in hand, recounts the gory details asking for anyone with any information to call the police.

A slight movement behind me makes me jump. John is up. Leaning against the faux wood headboard, he lights a cigarette.

"John. Look! It's that house! They found dead bodies at that house! The one you go to all the time!"

John doesn't say a thing but keeps an icy stare straight ahead. I fix my own disbelieving gaze on the headlines again.

"John? Isn't that the place?"

"Shhh!" He sits up closer to listen.

"Neighbors reported hearing noises in the early hours this morning, July first, but dismissed them as primal screams common to the residents of 8763 Wonderland Avenue. Reportedly, there is one survivor in critical condition."

Oh God! I've been in front of that house. Many times . . . I sat right there. I note the spot where the news crew is parked. *This is really bad.*

At the end of the broadcast, John hops up and spins through the channels, until he finds another station headlining the murders. He watches, glued intently to the screen.

"John? You had a dream," I tell him, fighting the sinking feeling in my gut.

"Huh? What?"

"A dream. A nightmare. When you were sleeping."

His face drains pale, and his eyes bulge like a hungry bulldog's.

"You were screaming, 'Blood! Blood! So much blood!'" I imitate the pitch of his voice.

He jumps in quickly, "Oh, I, uh, the trunk . . . the trunk of the car. I was lifting the trunk and hit my nose. Gave myself a nosebleed." His story babbles out fast and awkward. It is too much information, a blatant lie. The hair on my skin rises, warning me to not press the issue . . . about anything. John lights one cigarette after the other; the blue haze floats heavy and thick on the filtered sunlight. He checks every window and door, becoming more paranoid and twitchy as news channel after news channel blasts the "four on the floor" murders, the "Wonderland killings."

For a few days, we lie low. John's demeanor leaves no room for discussion. The cocaine is gone. The money is gone. I don't want to know what else he knows. *If I don't ask, it won't be real.* I try to bend reality, but the truth is biting at our heels, relentless, like a rabid Rottweiler. Too many questions creep their way into my thoughts. Big questions like *Who did this?* and *Are they coming for us?* I wonder also if John had anything to do with it. My stomach curls and skin crawls as I remember John's ranting about the Wonderland gang: "I hate those motherfuckers in there. I've met some shitheads in my life, but those assholes . . . they're fucking scum."

It is too late to admonish myself for coming back. I am here, and there's nothing I can do to change that, but I have no hope or clue as to what to do next. I wait for John's backup plan, his ace in the hole; I wait to hear from him that things aren't that bad—but the words never come.

John is empty inside, struggling to regroup, and has nothing comforting to say.

It is obvious to me that we'll have to do something soon, but not just yet. I want to leave—run from LA anyway, like we planned. "We can find jobs in another state, John. We don't need money yet. Let's just go."

But he wants to keep his ear to the ground instead. He needs to find out how deep this rabbit hole goes. "We can't. They'll find us." John rips the skin off the side of his fingernail.

"Who are *they,* John?"

"Shhh. Stop!" The horror in his eyes is unmistakable, and his face contorts as if to say, *You know damn well who.* Then I realize he has to stay loyal to Eddie.

We eat fast food from the local joints, paying with the small amount of cash John left me before the murders. He dashes outside, incognito, his shirt wrapped around his head, dark glasses covering his eyes, ducking behind cars and nasty brown Dumpsters, while I guard the door.

The room stays dark; our only light, the changing greenish glow from the television, on constantly those few days without sound. We turn the volume up to be barely audible when flashes of the "four on the floor" air on the hour, and we become more attentive to the bumps and bangs on the streets outside.

On the afternoon of July fourth, it is muggy and hot and we sit naked on the bed in the harsh glare of the silent screen on the wall. Some time has gone by, and we are more relaxed, the strained edge of tension having eased a bit with the passing days. Thor snuggles warmly between John's legs beneath the sheets, while I face him, brushing off an emery board to do his nails. We wait for the ten o'clock news to come on. My wet hair hangs loosely down my back; it's the only way I can cool myself in this stifling summer heat. John's eyes are glued to the soundless television. Our senses are alert to every detail of our surroundings. There is not a sound, except the steady *shhicckk, shhicckk, shhicckk* of the rough file against John's nails.

BLAM! An explosion rocks our room.

"A shot!" I can feel my skin split and my ears crack. I leap full force into John's lap and grab at his chest. *"We're dead!"* My eyes squeeze shut, my breath immobile, as I wait for a bullet to penetrate my flesh.

"Freeze!"

Clutching to John's slippery skin, I squint and sneak a quick look. In the place where our door once stood several bulletproof-vested police officers are poised and aiming their nine millimeters at our heads.

"We mean it, Johnny! Don't move! You either, young lady! Dawn, is it? Don't move. Both of you or . . . we'll shoot!"

Boom . . . boom . . . boom . . . boom . . . boom! The shots are like thunder ripping through my head. All sound disappears except the steady, terrified pounding of my heart.

CHAPTER SIXTEEN
Nothing up His Sleeve

The interrogation room in the downtown Los Angeles Police Department is a small, dirty-beige, cement block square with a bare wooden table and a few chairs in the center. A two-way mirror runs the length of the wall next to the entrance, reminding me that I am being watched.

Wearing a pair of Levi's jeans and one of John's oversized shirts, I shiver from the cool air-conditioning and the ripples of diminishing adrenaline exiting my system. My hands are trembling, folded on the table, as I wait for someone to come in and book me into jail. My thoughts surge at me, relentless, and I can't escape the exploding flashbacks of our arrest.

⚜

Blurred faces, guns, and uniforms draped with bulletproof vests race toward us from either side of the bed. There is chaos, confusion—our motel room door is shattered, flattened in the middle of the carpet, the frame a wooden, splintered mess. Naked and frozen with fear, John and I are shuffled around puppetlike as the dozen or so officers carefully and methodically separate us.

They take John into the bathroom first to search and dress him. "Do you have anything on you you'd like to tell us about? Drugs, weapons—anything?"

"No, uh, no. Nothing," he tells them, his arms in the air. He is nervously polite, trying to control his jerky body movements.

John came back from the big run empty-handed—not even a crumb—except for the Valium. I think he won't have anything on him, but I wonder if he saw Sharon before he came back to the motel somehow.

Two female officers step up to surround me. "Can you step into the bathroom with us, ma'am? We need to search you."

They guide me into the bathroom. One of the officers brushes her hand under my hair and between my legs, gives the all clear, and hands me my clothes.

"My dog? Where's my Chihuahua, Thor? He's scared. Let me get him. Please."

A small cage appears from another officer at the door. "Call him out, ma'am. Don't touch him; just call him out."

Thor is under the bed, frightened, shaking fiercely, his face appealing to me for help. But I'm not allowed to comfort him, only to call to him for a uniformed stranger to put him in a cage.

Amidst a bustling crowd of plainclothes and uniformed detectives and officers, John is taken out in handcuffs. He stalls for a moment at the door, and we lock eyes. For that split second, he looks as if he wants to cry. I do. What did you do, John? What did you do?

Like a sad-faced clown on a velvet background, John scrunches up his face anxiously. "I love you," he mouths as he is escorted out in the baking afternoon heat to a waiting police car. Thor and I follow separately.

Left alone in the small, sterile room for hours, I hear the half-glass, half-metal door finally open with a heavy *creak-thud* that echoes in the tiny space. Two plainclothes men step up, pull out a chair, and take a seat at the opposite side of the table.

"Hello, Dawn." The first one introduces himself. He is of average height, has a round face, a brown receding hairline, and a grim expression. "I'm Tom. Tom Lange . . . and this is my associate Frank Tomlinson." There's a pause. "Do you know why we're here?" He glares at me, a serious, dark, mud-eyed stare.

"No." My gut aches. Stabbing pains like a thousand tiny knives pierce through my psyche. So many images race through my brain, but I know. I know this is about the people at Wonderland. Still, I stay quiet.

"This is very serious, Dawn. Very, very serious." He pauses again. I nod.

"You're John's girlfriend, right? How long have you two been together?"

"Um . . . five years."

He clears his throat and raises an eyebrow. "How old are you?"

"Twenty."

Frank Tomlinson, a younger, fuller-haired version of Lange, shakes his head.

"Well . . . maybe we can ask you a few questions. Do you mind looking at some photos also?"

"Sure."

Detectives Lange and Tomlinson are stone-faced, cold, seasoned interrogators. They watch me—my face, my movements—for any reaction or clue that can give them a lead. They divulge nothing, not letting on why I am being held, and lay down a random assortment of pictures. Lange flips through the stack. They are people I don't recognize in front of the house on Wonderland—a place I do recognize. Then there is a picture of Eddie Nash, and I feel sick.

"Do any of these people look familiar?"

"No," I lie, trying to shake my head believably.

"Where have you been this last week?"

The brick of cocaine in John's briefcase, Sally's house, and the motel before John left for his big deal scorch their way into my memory. *Oh God, they want me to rat John out. I can't say anything.*

"In the motel." My words are small, insignificant.

"With John?"

"Yes."

"Was John with you the whole time?"

"Well, uh, mostly. He went out to get food and stuff." I try to skirt the truth.

"Do you know *why* you're here, Dawn?" Lange slams his palms down on the desk.

"No."

"Murder!"

Hot sweat pushes its way through the cold pores of my skin; I swallow hard and look up at Tom Lange, pleading. "Murder? I . . ."

"John's in big trouble this time. He's not going to get out of this one that easy!"

"Who—?"

Detective Lange cuts me off. "All right, Dawn. That's all we got for you for now."

"John?"

"Oh, ha, Johnny boy? He's not going anywhere. Naw, naw, naw. He's gonna be around for a *long* time." They push the wooden chairs back under the table, a long scraping noise that runs through my spine.

I bite my tongue. In my mind I remember the contorted look and fear in John's eyes as he was being hauled off. I know he is scared. "My dog, Thor . . . Is he okay?"

"Ha! Yeah. He's all right. Cute little fellow—knows just whose locker to piss on too." Detective Tomlinson chuckles. During his short stay, Thor has become a mini-celebrity with the officers at the station. I try to smile. "Do you have anywhere to go?"

"No. Well . . . only one place . . . maybe . . . to Sharon's."

"Sharon Holmes'?" He thinks for a moment. "Yeah. John mentioned that. Let's see if we can get you and your dog a ride, then."

A uniformed officer brings Thor into the interrogation room. Panting for breath and scratching to get out of the cage, he wags his tail and frantically spins in circles when he sees me.

"All right. You're free to go. We can give you a ride, if you like." Detective Tomlinson motions for me to follow him.

Thor compulsively licks my arm and makes whiny grunting noises. I stroke his trembling, now-graying brown coat, tuck him under my oversized shirt, and exhale a heavy sigh. "It's been a long time. I hope Sharon lets us in, boy," I whisper into his furry little ear.

❧

Harsh sunlight spills into the patrol car on the drive to Glendale the day after the Fourth of July. There were no fireworks or celebration at the precinct. In fact, there has been no celebration of anything for me in a long time. Tomlinson and the uniformed officer make some kind of political joke that I don't understand, but I'm only drifting in and out of their conversation anyway. I'm feeling the quiet familiar streets of my past welcome me back. *It's Sunday. Sharon will be home.*

We pull up to the cottages, as I've done a thousand times before, and I steel myself. Tomlinson watches from the sidewalk as I hesitantly approach the porch of Sharon's now-peeling, faded house, and I knock. *What if she doesn't answer like that night with the hitchhiker?* For a split second, that horrible evening sends a haunting shiver through my soul.

The dogs are barking furiously. Thor wiggles wildly in my arms and yips. "All right! All right!" Sharon's lilting voice tries to calm them. Her dark gaze peeks quickly through the lace curtains, piercing me straight in the eye like a brown bullet, then disappears. Uncertain as to what she might do, I start to pray, imagining her disapproving, reluctant expression behind the door. The dead bolt clicks, and the knob turns.

"Hi." I clutch Thor, now squirming, and wish he'd be still.

"Helloooo?" she drawls as if to say, *This should be interesting.*

It takes me a few seconds to find my bearings and the right words. "Sharon. We were arrested . . . John and I. They kept him . . . the police . . . they brought me here. I, I have nowhere else to go."

"What . . . ? Come in." She sounds unhappy yet resigned.

I wave to Detective Tomlinson and step in.

"I thought you were in Oregon, Dawn." Sharon lights a cigarette and squints through the rising smoke.

"I was. I was there for five months. I worked as a CNA again. But . . . well . . ." I trail off, hating what I'm about to say. "John talked me into coming back and . . . you know . . . I came back." The words are hollow. I have nothing to say that will make my actions seem reasonable. Nothing to offer that makes sense . . . other than . . . I love him . . . But that all-consuming first love is really just an aching, confused memory—one that, despite the pain, I've been hoping to bring back to life for a couple years now. That's why I came back—because the love is supposed to come back. *But she knows all this,* I think.

Sharon stubs out her cigarette and lights another. "What happened?"

"I don't know, Sharon. The police busted down the door. There were guns pointed at us. First I thought a bomb went off and we were dead! They took us into the station and kept me in a room for hours, asking questions about people. They said it was about murder!"

She watches me intently through the acrid haze of her smoke. "All right. Well . . ." She sighs deeply. "Did they say he did it?"

I am shocked at her question. "No! They didn't. They only said it was about murders. They showed me pictures of people I didn't know and the house where they found the bodies bludgeoned a few days ago." My voice is shaking. I don't want to tell her I've been at that house, or about Eddie.

"What bodies? Where?"

"On Wonderland. It's been all over the news." I motion for her to turn on the television.

"Wait. Wait." Sharon's hands shoot up to her temples, and her thumbs rub circles hard into her scalp. She shakes her head to regroup. "Wait. Okay. Let's see. First things first: when's the last time you've eaten?"

"Uh, I don't know. Since before we were arrested, I guess."

"All right. You find the news, and I'll get you something to eat."

The rest of the day we are glued to the television and the head-lining murders. We're interrupted only by the dogs, John L and Pokie, who obliviously play tug-of-war with an old sock while Thor barks and nips at their heels. There isn't any news of John's arrest yet, and we can only speculate why. Sharon pulls out one of my nightgowns that she has packed in a corner dresser of my old room, and we change. The evening falls somberly, not much more said between us, cigarettes and a dim sense of routine from our past keeping us sane.

It is late; the stress is exhausting. Sharon digs into her stash of Valium from the bathroom drawer for us to get some sleep. We decide to make a last surf through the channels for the eleven o'clock news. The phone rings. We jump. *John*.

Sharon walks stiffly over to the small wooden telephone table and lifts the handle of the red rotary phone. "Hello? Yes." There is a pause. "Hi. Uh-huh. Uh-huh. Now calm down . . . I don't have that kind of money, John! Yes, she's here. Just a minute." Sharon hands me the phone, her face drawn and worried.

"Hello."

"Baby. Listen, please. You two gotta help me!"

"Okay, John. How?"

"Listen. I'm in jail, and I only got a minute. Someone just threatened to kill me! *You have to get me out!*"

"John. I don't have any money. What . . . ?"

"Can't you and Sharon scrape something up? Sell something? I don't know . . . Just do it. If I'm in here much longer, *I'll die!*"

"Okay. I'll ask . . ."

"I gotta go, baby. Baby, please . . . I love you!"

"I love you too, John."

Click.

Sharon lets out an audible sigh as I hang up the phone. Snapping open her needlepoint cigarette case, she lights another and sits down to think.

"He says he's going to be killed if we don't do something!"

"He told me. I don't know what he expects us to do about it. He's already stolen everything of value I have. Everything of Grandma's—her china, her silver—and I'll be damned if he thinks I'm going to my parents or anyone else again for a loan!"

I don't know about Sharon's things being missing, but I know John is a thief. My jewelry, missing items from Michelle's, the suitcase at the airport . . . I recall a time I heard the dogs in the background when John was on the phone with me in Oregon. Still, I feel as if we have to do something. "He sounds scared, Sharon." I'm out on a limb. "I believe him. There are bad people out there."

"I know, but . . ." Her tone softens. "There's nothing I can do."

"Me either." We don't speak for a long while, both of us chain-smoking as if each cigarette might bring a fresh idea, but no solution comes.

"Well," she says, finally giving in to emotional exhaustion. "We might as well go to bed."

❧

I wake the next day to Sharon's voice on the phone as she calls in sick to work. "Family emergency." Her words, starchy, cardboard-like, clear some time off with the doctor's office.

"Morning." I shuffle out of my old bedroom with mixed feelings of comfort from my things that still adorn the walls, but also pain from the memories of my attempted suicide and the bitter last days here. "Any news from John?"

"Nope. Nada." Sharon's tone is controlled and even. "Fresh strawberries in the fridge. Cream on the top shelf."

I dole out a bowl for each of us with lots of sugar, and we sit down with the dogs to methodically peruse the daily news flashes. We jump every time the phone rings, thinking it is John or news of something worse. We pass the time playing rummy and catching up with each other's lives.

"David, Karen, and Jamie moved away about six months ago. Thank God!" Sounding a little like her old self, Sharon exhales a blast of smoke with relief. "That's the only good news I've had in a while."

I laugh, enjoying for a moment some lightheartedness of the past, and I play a good bluff game of cards. "Are you all right, Sharon?" I finally ask. I feel a sense of heaviness from her that parallels mine. We haven't spoken in a long time. I remember so many things John told me about how she didn't care about me anymore and then, on the phone with him in Oregon, about her willingness to try and start over together with the promise of no drugs. My affection for her is real, and in my mind we are all supposed to have a fresh start . . . together. *He said Sharon too!* I remind myself of our conversations when he begged me to come back to LA, and I wonder if she knows this was going to be his last big deal . . . for us.

"I'm fine." Her high-pitched tone strains as it always does when she has to talk about her feelings. "Like I've always told you, Dawn, the best you can do is to take all the garbage from life, stick it in a box, and put it away in a closet—somewhere where you don't have to look at it—and get on with things."

"Like organizing?"

"Exactly. I've been fine. Trust me."

Sensitive to Sharon's personality, I leave it at that and, as usual, we don't speak anymore of such things, instead playing cards until bedtime. We go to sleep with no further word from John.

Tuesday morning is scorching. The finches in their bamboo cage by the window sing loudly with the sun's praise, sweetly unaware of our troubles. It's been nearly one week since the murders, and three days of waiting for any word. It arrives around noon.

The phone rings. Sharon stops dead in her tracks, takes a deep breath, and calmly walks over to the telephone. "Yes? Okay? That's fine. Just a minute." She puts her hand over the receiver and speaks directly to me. "Do you mind speaking to Detective Lange again?"

"No. Sure."

"That's fine. No problem. Good-bye." She hangs up. "Well . . . Tom Lange will be here in about half an hour. He has something important he would like to speak to the both of us about. It has to do with John . . . of course." I can't tell if she is being sarcastic.

"Is he all right?"

"Yep. He's in protective custody. He got ahold of Big Tom and told him his life's been threatened. Apparently Big Tom got him into protective custody, and now Lange wants to speak to us."

"About what?"

"I don't know." This time she definitely sounds disgusted.

"Sharon?" I ask, deciding to break the rule of silence around the name "Big Tom." "Who exactly is Big Tom, anyway?" After all this time, I know the man's voice, I know he is a friend, but to my knowledge this is the first time he was ever connected to the police.

"He's a vice cop. What did you think?" She looks amazed that I don't know.

"What's that?"

"John's a stool pigeon! Didn't you know?" She sees my confusion. "An informer! Get it? John was arrested before you even got here in New Jersey . . . Point Pleasant, where you were born, interestingly enough. He's been turning people from the porn business in to authorities for years now!"

Sparks of realization ignite inside me as I remember the many times John took Big Tom's calls with urgency. *So Big Tom is helping John.* Then, for the first time, I think that maybe . . . maybe everything will be all right. John has a friend on the side of the law, and he will protect us.

❧

Peeking down the courtyard from the sun-warmed porch, we watch Detective Lange, square and balding, saunter toward the cottage. Casually he looks from side to side, scoping out each cottage window and alleyway. The image of him, cautious, ready to react, proves to us that we are most likely being watched . . . by more than the police. Sharon herds the dogs into the bedroom while I let Lange in.

"Dawn." He nods. "Good to see you again."

"Hi. Come in."

"And you're Sharon? Sharon Holmes, I take it?" He sticks his hand out for a formal handshake.

"Yes. Hi. How are you?"

"Mind if I have a seat?"

"Certainly." Sharon offers a space on the couch.

"Well . . . you both probably know this is about John."

"Is he safe?" I ask, jumping into the conversation.

"He's out of jail, if that's what you mean, and we have him in protective custody. We know he was receiving some threats from the inside."

"Who was threatening him?" Afraid of what I might hear, I hold my breath.

"Well, could be a number of people. We have a pretty good guess, and that's why I'm here." He pauses, wiping the sweat from his head. "We have every reason to believe the two of you may be in real danger."

Our bodies lean in his direction like metal drawn to a magnet as we give him our undivided attention.

"Like I said, John is being held in protective custody. He has disclosed to us that he is willing to turn over certain information in exchange for entrance into the Witness Protection Program. John has also indicated that this is something he would be willing to do . . . well . . . only if . . ." He clears his throat. "Only if he speaks to the two of you first."

"You mean speak to him . . . over the phone? Or . . . ?" Sharon asks.

"No. I'm here to ask you if you would be willing to meet with John."

"When? Now?"

"Yes. Myself and my partner are ready to take you to him right away."

He has someone waiting outside, I think. *This is real.* I look at Sharon and wait for her to answer for us. I think she must want to go see him as badly as I do.

Deep in thought, she stares at her foot on the green vinyl stool.

"Sharon?" I prompt.

"All right," she answers slowly and meticulously. "For how long, and what about the dogs?"

"So you both agree?"

We nod.

Tom stretches his legs, glances nervously out the window, and asks to use the phone. "I can have your dogs taken wherever you like and, well, as for how long . . . That's up to you and John. But realistically, you should be prepared to be away at least a couple days, maybe longer. It'll depend on how long it will take for all the interviews to be completed."

He picks up the receiver and dials. "Yeah. It's me. Tell him they said yes and we will be on our way as soon as we close things up here. Sure. Hey, John. They told you. Good. Sure. Just a minute." He places his hand over the mouthpiece and holds the phone out for either of us. "He wants to talk to you two."

Sharon doesn't budge, so I grab the phone first. "John. Are you okay?"

"Dawn? Oh, baby, I'm so glad you're coming. You're coming, right? And Sharon?"

"Yeah, Sharon's coming too."

"Good. Listen, baby." I can hear him press his mouth over the receiver and whisper. "Say as little as possible. Everything is being tapped. I need you to do me a favor. Please? When you pack your things, go into my office, and in the top file cabinet drawer are my papers."

"Uh-huh." My God! He wants me to sneak him some drugs.

"Can you bring me my papers, baby? You know—my important papers. You got that?" His voice changes, becoming louder and more formal. "Very important, okay? Wrap them up like I showed ya, and they'll be fine. Thanks, baby. I love you."

"Sure, John. Love you too."

"Baby? Is Sharon there?"

"Yeah. Just a sec." I look at Sharon, who still sits like stone.

"He wants to talk to you."

Sharon snaps out of her daze, pulls her glasses off, and rubs her eyes hard as if to erase the next moments in time. "Hello. Yes. Okay. Love you too. Good-bye." I figure he told her the phones were tapped and kept it short.

"Well. Let's get this over with."

❧

The looming shape of the Bonaventure Hotel in downtown Los Angeles towers dark and gray above our heads as we approach the curved and mirrored exterior. Sharon and I are impassive in the backseat of the undercover car and barely make a sound. I am biting my already worn-down fingernails; Sharon, hands neatly placed in her lap, twiddles her thumbs.

True to his word, Tom Lange has arranged everything expediently. The dogs are boarded with our vet, and the house is locked up and kept on a twenty-four-hour guard. Two sets of officers are stationed downtown to watch both the hotel entrances and the streets outside for any unusual activity or excess drivers-by.

We arrive at the main entrance, met by plainclothes officers who instantly surround us and head to the main lobby. Their height and width block my view of the lobby and keep us hidden. Whisked to the twenty-second floor, swiftly and undercover in the see-through tube elevator, we are hurried out to an unassuming suite nearby. *They're even blocking us from the windows,* I think. *Is there a sniper?*

The room is bustling, swarming with officers of every shape and size pressing black boxy walkie-talkies to their mouths. A drug-sniffing German shepherd yanks at his leash to smell us as we enter. At the end of the king-sized bed, an oblong foldout table is propped with two more detectives waiting to search our bags. The room is the hub for this covert operation—"Operation John Holmes"—and everything moves smoothly, like a well-oiled machine. No time to ask questions.

"We will need you to step into the bathroom for a moment, please. We need to search you before we let you in to see John." A female officer appears to ask me and to steer me into the bathroom before I can even answer.

"Uh, no. Sure," I mumble. *Oh shit. I hope they don't find the pot I hid for John in the baby powder.* I've found his "important papers"—the stash he begged me for on the phone, exactly where he told me—and I hope Big Tom will let it slide, knowing how badly John needs it to calm his nerves.

Smoothing down her shirt, Sharon steps out of the bathroom next, and we are asked if we have anything in our bags to tell them about. "Nope. Nothing."

"Hello, Sharon." A brown-haired man approaches us from the table near the balcony. "How have you been?"

"Tom. Hi. Well, could be better . . . you know," Sharon addresses the husky man in a familiar tone.

"And this must be Dawn. I'd recognize your voice anywhere," he says, shaking my hand in turn.

Sharon sees my bewilderment. "Dawn. This is Tom. Big Tom."

"Oh. Hi. Nice to meet you finally." A tiny sense of calm sparks in me as I realize this longtime friend is here—someone John worked with on the right side of the law.

Another man approaches and stretches out his hand to introduce himself.

"And this is Bob . . . Bob Sousa. Another lead investigator on this case," Big Tom announces.

"Hi, uh, nice to meet you two. We're real glad you're both here. If everything works out, John will be helping us . . . and a lot of other people." His speech ends abruptly, and like a good detective he stops himself from going any further. "Well. Shall we?"

He takes hold of the knob of a door connecting the room to the next, taps, and pushes it open. "Company's here, John."

A flurry of officers buzzes around and clears an opening that reveals John, pale and sick-looking in a borrowed tan suit jacket and jeans, sitting on the end of a king-sized bed. "Hey, baby. You guys made it." He stands up and comes toward us with his arms outstretched. He smiles nervously, relieved and apprehensive, eyes darting back and forth between Sharon and me, wrapping his arms around us in a group hug. "Oh, I'm so glad you're here. Everything's going to be all right now . . . now that we're together." He kisses both of us on the cheek, squeezing hard. "Here. Let me take your bags. Do you want something to eat?" Like servants waiting for his command, John motions erratically for Big Tom to get someone with a menu.

We are confused for a moment. "No, uh. Well—," Sharon says.

"Well, I think I'll leave you all alone for right now to catch up. Don't you think so, John?" Big Tom looks large and awkward, uncomfortable in a fat, choking tie and boxy shoes.

"Oh. Yeah. Sure. Thanks, Tom."

"Right. So if you need anything, John, you know what to do." He signals for everyone to clear the room.

When the door shuts, John rushes up and checks the lock. "Sharon. Dawn. I'm so glad you're here. Did they help you board the dogs and lock the house?" He steps between us anxiously and plants another kiss on each of our cheeks. "Dawn, you made it to Sharon's. I told them to let you go . . . that you didn't know anything. Let's order something to eat. You can have anything you want. Filet mignon, prime rib . . . whatever you like." His behavior is erratic, wild.

"John?" Sharon interrupts. "What's going on?"

"Let's eat first. I have a lot to talk to you two about, but not on an empty stomach. They're paying top dollar to take care of us. We might as well take advantage of it." John's anxiety is extreme, and I take it to mean he's worried we'll be uncomfortable. He herds us over to a round table by the floor-to-ceiling-curtained windows and passes out menus.

"All right. If you say so," Sharon says dryly.

As if we're at a fancy restaurant, each of us orders a high-end dinner, which is delivered promptly by plainclothes officers armed with sawed-off shotguns—the same officers who guard our door constantly. We eat slowly and formally and make small, unfunny comments. John orders a bottle of thirty-year-old Scotch with the meal and passes around small shots to take the edge off the tense situation. From his jacket pocket, John retrieves a Tiparillo and draws in the rich, heavy smoke, offering each of us our own.

"Well. I guess we need to get down to business." Breaking the uncomfortable emptiness in the air, John stands up as a dictator would, cigar in hand, as if he is going to make a speech. "Sharon, I need to talk to you first, uh, in private. Do you mind?" He pulls her chair out for her.

Without a word, Sharon complies. It looks to me as though she has shrunk a size; with tiny steps, she follows John's looming shadow into the bathroom.

The door sharply slams as Sharon returns from the bathroom. "He wants to see you," she says, blandly and without emotion. She beelines over to the large picture window and pulls back the drapes to sit on the ledge overlooking downtown LA.

I watch her stiff, robotic movements and mistake them for resolve. John steps out right behind her, wiping his red-rimmed eyes, and spies her perched at the sill. *This is hard,* I tell myself.

"Dawn?" John reaches out his hand to me and guides me to the bathroom. The room is steamy, the water running in the tub.

"Shhh." He puts his finger to his lips. He pulls his hair back from his forehead and wipes away another tear before taking both my hands in his. "Baby . . ." He clears his throat. "You know this is about the murders on Wonderland, right?"

I look deep into his tired, sunken eyes. "Did you do something, John?"

"No! Listen. I went that night to get the money for us to leave. You know—sell the dope. I stopped to pick up my messages first, and when I got back in the car Diles was waiting. He put a gun to the back of my head!"

"You mean Eddie's bodyguard?" I can feel that night on my skin as if it's happening right now.

"There were other guys in the car too. They forced me, baby." He lets out a sob. "They took everything I had—the dope, the money, my briefcase with my *address book!* Eddie got it, and I couldn't let him find out about you or Sharon . . . our families too. Your mother, my mother . . . And, and they took me and forced me to let them into the house . . . buzz them in . . . and stay . . . and watch as they murdered those people." He is shaking, his hands pulling on my arm, slippery from the steam in the air. "They tried to get away with robbing Nash, baby. Nobody gets away with that shit. No one!" Then the weight of his confession overwhelms him. His shoulders drop; he hides his face in his hands and weeps.

The blood drains from my face. The thick humidity and the shot of Scotch make my head heavy, and my stomach folds over on itself. I reach out to rest my head on John's shoulder.

"The police found my fingerprints, and now they want to blame *me* for the murders!"

Easily I take John's side. "They can't blame you, John. What are you going to do?"

"If I tell everything I know about Nash and . . . well . . . people—we're talking drugs, arson . . . *murder,* baby—they'll give us protection, put us in the Witness Protection Program. You, me, and Sharon. We can start a new life together like we wanted, baby. That's all I ever wanted was to start over. What do you say? Will you come with me? I told them you two had to be safe first, that I'd only do this if you guys said yes!"

"What did Sharon say?"

He looks at me offended, takes a moment. "She already said yes. She's gonna settle the house and meet us later. What do you say, baby? You, me, and Sharon . . . like it was in the beginning. We'll be set up for life and protected. But . . . well, there's one thing."

"What?" I don't blink.

"It's gonna be hard. Eddie's got my address book, and if he thinks I'm still alive, he'll go after Mom—you know, everyone. People will have to think we're dead. The cops will have to give us complete new identities and move us somewhere in the country where no one will find us. They're gonna have to fake our death certificates." He is rambling and takes a deep breath. "It means we can never contact our families again."

"What? Never?" An immediate sense of grief and sadness burns through my heart at the thought of never seeing my family again. *This is cruel. I don't want Eddie after my family because of me.* I'm scared and can't keep my anguish in anymore; I bury my head in his lap.

"I know. I know, babe. This is the hardest thing in the world to ask you. But I need you. Like I needed you to come back from Oregon. I never meant for this to happen. I only wanted to start over again. But this can be our fresh start anyway. We still can have it, baby. But . . . but if you don't . . . I told them I wouldn't do it if either of you said no. It'll be dangerous without protection. But I'd rather be killed on the street than be alone . . . without you. I love you, Dawn!"

In my mind's eye, glimpses of my life with John materialize and crash down hard like a terrible storm into broken pieces of concrete and rubble. All that's left standing in my imagination is

John and I, clinging onto each other in the center of an open, barren field. And like a nightmare that I know is mine, he is all that there is for me. Through swollen, burning eyes I look up at him. "Yes, John. I'll come with you."

He holds my face in his hands and whispers, "I love you," as we rock to and fro on the edge of the bathtub. Wiping my tears and his, he kisses my forehead. "Come on. Let's get some rest." Sharon doesn't look our way as we walk out of the bathroom together. She remains stonelike on the sill of the giant corner window, facing the busy lights from the construction site across the street.

We have a fitful sleep in spite of the Valium Sharon hands out to help us rest. After Sharon and I go to bed, John stays in the bathroom smoking the small amount of pot I snuck in for him. The fan buzzes loudly, and I can smell the pungent skunklike odor drift up from the cracks. I'm nervous John will make the police angry.

Finally he crawls under the covers between us, something he has only done when he, Sharon, and I were in Vegas together, and puts an arm over both of us. As I cuddle into him, I notice Sharon has her back toward him on the other side. This is how she always sleeps, but I think it's cold, considering the emotional decision we've all just made to go undercover together.

At least that's what John told me.

The next morning John is immediately summoned to the adjoining room with Big Tom, Lange, Sousa, and Tomlinson. Everything will be business for him from now on.

Sharon and I pick at our meals and play mindless games of Yahtzee and Scrabble, which we brought from the house, while John meets with the police and higher-ups. Mostly, though, Sharon takes to her usual seat at the window, staring intently at the comings and goings of the busy strangers below.

I say very little and think about the last time I saw my family and if I will be able to tell them good-bye before we leave. *Maybe after a while we can come out of hiding and contact them again.* I flip through channels, falling in and out of sleep on the California king as the heavy dose of Valium still pumps in my veins.

John returns periodically, an armed gunman glued to his side. Guzzling giant swigs from the Scotch bottle, he plants agitated kisses on our cheeks.

There's a commotion in the afternoon on the first day. John and Detective Lange rush into the room and need the keys to the Glendale house in a hurry. "People have access to fake official uniforms—police, security—you know, they might try to get into the house," Lange explains. He sends someone to pick up all of the family's important papers—for our safety. Sharon doesn't argue and hands over the keys, and I take this to mean that everything is going as planned. A real, suffocating panic from the impending danger threatens to steal the breath from my lungs and render me immobile, but the detectives are experts at keeping us calm.

After a long first day of interrogation, John returns. Visibly pale and exhausted. He kicks the door behind him and flips them the bird after the lock turns in the small suite for the night. "Fucking assholes. Sons a bitches. Let's fucking eat." We order lobster and cherries jubilee and again are served by the shotgun armed guards at our door. Sharon takes her cue and passes out the Valium like an evening mint and we escape, thankfully, into a deadened sleep.

Very early Wednesday morning we are given an alert. John and a handful of detectives rush in and unceremoniously pack our things. Big Tom approaches, explaining calmly, while John bounces off the walls, jumpy like a rubber band, continually wiping his hands on his jeans. "Our intelligence understands there are several contracts out on your lives; it's been leaked that John is negotiating for the Witness Protection Program. Our sources are pretty sure he's been located here. We are going to have to move you. We'll do it separately and right away. We would appreciate it if you would allow these officers to assist you in your relocation. It's important that we hurry!"

Instantly we switch to autopilot. The plainclothesman separates us, assigning two guards to each of us. Detectives armed with walkie-talkies and handguns in shoulder straps escort us out one by one in different directions. From the room to the elevator to the lobby, there are groups of cops stationed to check and double-check our status on their radios. The elaborate glass elevator descends; a large, heavy, calloused hand weighs itself on my head, and a matching booming voice orders me to keep low. Every action is like a sharp, swift stroke of a perfectly timed blade. When we hit the street in the harsh light of an overcast day, there is but a minute to notice the onlookers or to be noticed by them.

"Stay down," the officer in charge repeats, holding my head down for the climb into a waiting car. With their hands inside their shoulder holsters, two men on either side lean over me in the backseat, peering up at the hovering skyscrapers of Los Angeles.

What are they doing? Are they protecting me from snipers? I wonder, strangely numb and removed. *This is like scenes from* Hawaii Five-O. *This can't be real.* I worry about Sharon and John. *What's going on in their minds? Are they getting shot at?*

A few blocks away the Biltmore Hotel, a 1920s classy brick building with ornate columns and marble carvings, spreads out over large green parks and taller contemporary skyscrapers. The black undercover car I'm in pulls into a back service entrance, where we meet yet another pair of cops waiting to escort us from the loading dock to the kitchen service elevator.

The eleventh floor of the Biltmore Hotel hosts the presidential suite. Royally decorated, it is used for just that—presidents. I think of the Kennedys and magazine images I remember of the White House in the 1960s. John and Sharon are already settling into the master bedroom when I am ushered in. These are to be our quarters. The kitchen, dining room, smaller bedrooms, and huge sunken living room are arranged for the police and the "important people" John is preparing to meet.

Big Tom returns, all business now. "Settle in and order some lunch. We're pulling together the people we spoke to about John. We'll try to have something for you first thing tomorrow. So use your time wisely and rest up. Should have some news for ya by this afternoon."

John mumbles something in the affirmative and waves him out.

We're all extremely weary and drained, but John looks like he is about to collapse. The thought of having contracts out on our lives is traumatic and, to me, so completely unrealistic I cannot wrap my mind around the thought. The knowledge of how well we are being protected offers some solace, but nothing is appealing except to get this ordeal over with.

Again, Sharon finds her spot immediately on the ledge by the window while I try to find a television show to numb my mind. John chugs down some more Scotch, the bottle already waiting in the room. He orders steak for us even though the thought of food turns our stomachs. Then he orders a side of cognac and Cuban cigars for himself.

Word is passed along to us that John is to talk to the bigwigs in the morning. A shrouded group of influential people will gather in the formal sunken living room at the center of the penthouse suite and record all the sordid details of John's criminal information. *This is really going to happen.* I am convinced. *He has given the police information through Big Tom for years, and Tom is someone who can help John do this . . . and do it right.*

The knock on the door cracks earlier than we want it to. It is time. John is fidgety and busies himself with insignificant things, running in and out of the bathroom, stalling for time.

"Come on, John." Lange stands at the door, his jacket off, the pistol in his shoulder holster on the outside of his dress shirt exposed.

"Okay. Well, this is it." John bends down for a kiss from Sharon and me. "Wish me luck!"

Sharon and I make small talk about the hotel. "This place was built in the early 1920s. Lots of celebrities stayed here . . . politicians, dignitaries . . ." Sharon recites a part of Los Angeles history, a calming exercise for her. I head over to the television and flip through the channels again. News of the murders airs intermittently, and when it seems we can't escape the headlines, we turn the television off.

At lunch John returns with few words and a troubled expression etched on his brow.

"See them?" As the door swings open for John to leave, we catch a glimpse of the men sitting on the couch. "That's John Van de Kamp, the district attorney," she whispers, raising her eyebrows to add severity. The level of John's confession rises to the highest ranks.

❧

The late afternoon sun streaks through the fancy curtains, casting a blinding glare of abstract lines against the walls. John walks in looking thoroughly dejected, Tom Lange close at his heels.

"Well, that's it!" Lange announces angrily.

"That's it? Are we leaving?" I ask, confused.

Sharon's head shoots toward the detective.

"No, I mean pack it up. You're going home in the morning."

"Home. Okay." At first I assume he is speaking about a new undercover home, but by John's slumped shoulders and averted gaze, I surmise that there is something very wrong.

"Johnny here isn't going to give us what we came for, so we're cutting him loose. Let him take his chances on the outside. Gotta couple hours to change your mind, Johnny. You know where we'll be." Lange leaves the room.

Does this mean they could kill us on the streets?

Sharon and I are incredulous, shocked, and speechless. John avoids my question about whether we're leaving. Keeping his distance from me and Sharon, he pops another Valium and crawls under the covers. "I gave them what they wanted. Fuck 'em." He puts his hand over his face to block us out, turns his back, and completely withdraws from any more questions—especially from ours.

❧

Tom Lange drives Sharon and me to Glendale the morning of July 11. John has left to go through an official release process and to pick up the dogs boarded at the kennel. Being out of protective custody with nothing resolved makes me extremely uneasy. Sharon is ever silent, her gaze remaining focused out the back window, and I can only guess that she is scared too.

"What happened?" I ask.

"John didn't give us what he promised, so the deal is off." Irritation rings in his voice.

"Off? But what about the contracts out on us? We'll be killed!"

"I'm sorry. We'll try to protect you as best we can, but we really can't help that much."

"But John gave you the information you wanted," I cry.

"No. He fed us bullshit! We think he's stalling, protecting Eddie Nash . . . and wasting all of our time. Sorry." With nothing more said, Detective Tom Lange drops us off and wishes us good luck.

❧

Drapes drawn, doors locked, we lie low, tiptoeing around corners and startled at every shadow. Sharon, John, and I barely speak to one another. Sharon hides out in the small corner of the kitchen, engaged in mind-numbing tasks. Deep in thought, she does the dishes in long, slow, soapy strokes.

John confronts her briefly by the kitchen sink and they exchange short, heavy whispers. Sharon slips past John. With an uncomfortable, anguished expression twisting her normally statuelike dark features, she grabs her purse and leaves for a "quick errand."

The once impounded Malibu is parked next to the cottage camouflaged beneath the shadow of the giant magnolia tree. I try to calm the excitement of the dogs, the dancing of their toenails like falling rain on a tin roof, hollow and depressed. Sharon returns balancing her heavy purse and plain brown paper grocery bags. Frantically John unpacks them, lining up several spray paint cans in a long row on the varnished counter.

"Here. Come on." He hands me a can of spray paint and motions for me to follow. Outside he crouches down on the ground next to the Malibu and pulls me down with him, spraying sloppy streaks of gray primer over the weathered dark blue sides. "Hurry." John nudges my arm. He pops off the cap of rust red paint and sprays wild strokes on the black textured vinyl top, leaving blatant, conspicuous streaks and drips.

It looks like dried blood, I think. *It's a bad sign.* "What are we doing, John?"

"We gotta get out of here . . . and fast. Once they find out I'm out of jail, they'll be looking for us. There are contracts out on us. Get it? Death contracts. So we gotta get out of this state and hide somewhere. Sorry, baby." He squeezes my hand. "Fucking cops."

I know we are going on the run now, not from the police, but from something far worse—evil, looking for us—and we need to run for our lives.

The spray paint cans empty fast. We have covered most of the Chevy's original color. John holds my hand and dashes into the house, keeping close to the bushes and trees. "Pack your things. Only what you need."

Sharon is already in the bedroom rolling John's clothes into tight, neat bundles in plastic garbage bags.

"Sharon, come on," he calls. "We need to get this done."

Like many times in their relationship, it seems Sharon simply obeys John's barking orders, but she already knows what *this* means. I watch her actions to determine what will happen next. She removes an old, white tablecloth from a kitchen drawer and drapes it around John's shoulders. With scissors that appear out of nowhere, she snips at his shaggy curls, hacking and trimming a hair's breadth from his scalp. I think of her nurse's training, all the times she cleaned a wound or wrapped a bandage, and I picture her in an operating room performing surgery.

"Here. You can have the honor of doing that." She nods to a box of jet-black hair dye on the counter.

Darkness falls; the crickets are screeching loudly outside. I wish they would quiet down so I can hear any other noises—unfamiliar noises—from the courtyard outside.

John packs the still wet car as his cropped black hair dries. Accidental drips of jet-black dye stain his forehead, and a long one runs down his cheek. The newly acquired short, dark dome of hair shadows his features and dulls the blue of his eyes to gray. He hands me Thor, wrapped in a blanket Sharon has warmed in the dryer, and asks me to meet him in the car. He takes one last look behind him, and I do as I'm told.

John and Sharon whisper privately for only a few short, hurried minutes. Their bodies are rigid, and Sharon keeps her head turned away from John.

John whips around and instantly appears in the driver's seat. "Ready, baby? Well . . . we're finally getting out of here!" He smiles a shaded reaper's grin.

"What's Sharon doing?"

"She's gonna meet us, baby. Don't worry. She's gonna catch up to us soon."

The Safeway parking lot a few blocks away is garbage-strewn, dark, and nearly deserted, except for the homeless man guarding his shopping cart full of cans. Within minutes Sharon pulls up in her aunt's pale green Valiant. John jumps out of the car to meet her. A white envelope exchanges hands, and he reaches over to wrap his arms around her five-foot-two frame. She is stiff, arms to her side; then she awkwardly breaks free.

Sliding quickly past him, she heads over to my lonely silhouette in the passenger seat.

"Hi." I show her a brave smile.

"Hi . . . Well . . . this is it." She hesitates. Time is frozen for a minute, like the low, gathering fog, as her brown eyes bore intensely into mine. "I love you, Dawn," she blurts with a heave of her shoulders, and she reaches in to give me a warm hug.

"I love you too, Sharon. It'll be okay," I reassure her.

"I know. Well, good-bye. Take care of him."

"I will, Sharon. I will. We'll see you soon."

John swoops in to hold Sharon's reluctant small frame once again before she turns away and drives off, profile unflinching, eyes straight ahead.

"John? When will she be coming?" I ask once again.

"Soon, baby. As soon as we get settled, we'll let her know where we are and she'll meet us. She needs to close up the house anyway."

"Yeah." I believe John, so I don't question it. I am anxious to be on the way out of LA and to safety.

⁂

Driving through the vibrantly lit streets, I recognize Hollywood. "Where are we going, John?" An uneasy feeling churns in my gut.

"Gotta make one more stop before we go." He flashes me that unsettling grin again.

"No. John. No! We don't need to stop anywhere! Let's just go. Please. We don't need anything." I panic. *Please don't let him stop for drugs.*

"Yes, we do, baby. We need money! Sharon didn't give us enough! Five hundred dollars? How far are we going to get on that? Not far. We need more, baby. Just one more stop. Besides . . . he *owes* me." His jaw clenches, and he grips the steering wheel till his knuckles whiten.

"Who owes you?"

"Eddie."

"Oh my God, John! No! He's gonna kill you! That's the last

place we should go!"

John's face drains visibly pale in the dark interior of the car, and his voice lowers to a gravelly mumble. "I know . . . but . . . I got a plan."

"Plan? What kind of plan, John? He's got contracts on you! He wants to kill you!"

"I know; I know. But listen! I need you to back me on this. He knows by now that I didn't rat him out, that I didn't give the police any incriminating evidence."

"Yeah! And he's gonna make sure you don't either, John! He'll shoot you!"

"No. Listen! Not if I bluff him."

"Bluff him? How?"

"Now listen. Here's the plan. I'm gonna ask him for a couple thousand dollars. I know he's got that much handy. I'm gonna tell him that if I'm not back in half an hour, that I have someone holding three letters. These letters . . . addressed to Van de Kamp, Lange, and the Los Angeles Police Department, have enough evidence—I mean *everything*—to put him away for life. They'll be dropped in the mail if I'm not back in half an hour."

"Oh my God, John! He's not going to do this. He's gonna kill you. Let's just go now! Please!"

"No! He owes me for saving his ass, and he knows it. I didn't rat on him—and now, by leaving town, I'm saving his ass again! Besides, I got the letters and you. He knows I got you for proof!"

I can't believe this. John is playing this like a bluff on a bum poker hand with absolutely nothing up his sleeve.

We pull into the DuPar's Coffee Shop parking lot at the bottom of Ventura and Laurel Canyon. John throws the car in park. His hands run habitually through his hair, and he remembers suddenly it has been cut off and is black now. He checks to see if his hand is stained and, trying to muster some kind of confidence, lets out a long breath.

Inside, he guides me to an orange checkered booth near the pay phone.

"Order us some coffee, babe. I'm gonna make a call."

I sit trembling, convinced this is a deadly idea, until John returns from the phone. *Please don't let this happen,* I pray.

"Well, what did he say?"

"He said to come up." He stirs cream and sugar into his coffee, then takes a giant gulp, draining the entire cup. "I'll be back in no more than half an hour. But if an hour goes by . . . call the police." He bends to give me a hard kiss on the lips. "I love you, Dawn. Wish me luck."

The hands on the clock move painfully slowly. With dread, I watch every second tick by. *Eddie will be more pissed off than grateful!* I yell in my head to no one. *What is he thinking?* Suspicious eyes keep track of me as I nurse my coffee and jump at every movement and noise. The thirty minutes have passed. John has not returned. Thirty-five minutes pass . . . no sign. Then forty minutes . . . forty-five . . . and a battered-looking John returns. Shaking, he slides into the booth across from me and holds my hands.

"John? What happened?" I grip his hands hard to hold him still.

He can't speak at first and raises a finger signaling me to give him a minute to gain his composure. "He made me get on my knees," John finally hisses, then swallows half a cup of coffee hard.

"Did you tell him about the letters?"

"Diles was there. He had him hold a gun to my head. Asked why he shouldn't just kill me—*and* my family. He asked me why he should believe I didn't tell the cops anything. 'Why should I trust you?' he asked me."

"What did you say?"

"I said, 'If I'm not back in exactly thirty minutes, the letters will be dropped in the mail.' He didn't believe me. He made me beg—beg him not to put a bullet through my head. And then . . . he let me go."

"Are you all right? Did he give you the money?"

John's eyelids crease as if he will cry. "He said he would think about it. He said to come back in an hour and check the mailbox."

"Oh my God. We can't go back! No! No! Let's just leave, John. Don't go. A bomb, a sniper—something—will be waiting, but it won't be the money. Don't believe him!" Fear consumes me like millions of bees stinging my skin. Eddie is mad. I want to run as fast as I can, as far as I can, and never come back.

"No, baby. We have to. We just don't have enough money, and—and I think he's gonna do it. Finish your coffee. We gotta get out of here."

We drive around for an eternity in our newly painted car. After circling Studio City several nerve-racking times, John finally winds up the steep road to Laurel Canyon toward Eddie's.

Is this to be our death ride? I wonder in despair. My gut twists in knots, and I cannot comprehend that I am in a car driving up to the home of the drug lord who has contracts out on our lives. I get down low out of habit as we approach Eddie Nash's house on Dona Lola Drive.

Listening intently, I hear every footstep John's boots make up the brick walkway, then the creaking of the mailbox opening and closing shut. I hunch my shoulders down, bracing myself for a blast or gunshot, but instead hear the heavy thud of John's footsteps running back to the car.

At the bottom of the Canyon road, he rips open the end of an envelope with his teeth and looks inside. "Fucking bastard!" He flings the shredded envelope to the floor.

"What?"

"He only gave me half! Son of a bitch!" John's fist hits the steering wheel, and veins bulge in his neck as he punches on the gas pedal, peeling onto the freeway to head out of town.

Half. That's Eddie's thing, isn't it? The understanding leaves a bad taste in my mouth. But with every mile farther and farther from this wretched place, this place of broken dreams and pain, I feel lighter and less oppressed. John reaches over to hold my hand tightly as we near the desert . . . and our new beginning.

CHAPTER SEVENTEEN
No!

From behind the shadowy ridge of hills in the east, the desert sun rises, magical hues of pink and gray thrown across a barren desert highway. Memories of the wonder I had in my heart when I traveled cross-country with my dad to California almost six years ago entertain the silent hours as the miles slip behind us.

I lift my head from John's lap to look at him and smile.

"Hey, baby. Sleep good?" His voice is like a soft, sweet song in my ear.

"Mmmm. Where are we?"

"Almost to Vegas." He brushes my hair from my face.

"Where are we headed, John?"

"Montana. We'll go to my sister Anne's in Billings. She'll let us hang out for a while till we can figure something out. If we like it enough, we might even settle down there."

"Yeah. That sounds good." I snuggle up next to him and rest my head on his shoulder. Spinning the dials on the radio, John finds only country music and then shuts it off, content to listen to the engine whirr through the desolate plains. Thor's warm, four-pound body fits perfectly in the crease of my leg under the scratchy, orange polyester comforter.

The moment is peaceful for once. We're alone in the desert,

419

secure in the thought of leaving the city. It's just John and I and the fading stars.

WHAM! A large feathered bird smacks the windshield dead-on.

"What was that?"

Color drains from John's face. It's as if he has seen a ghost.

"What, John? What is it?"

He swallows. "A hawk." His tone is low and sad.

"Wow! That was huge!"

"It's bad."

"What do you mean 'bad'?"

"It's a bad omen for a hunter to kill a hawk . . . real bad." John squeezes my hand, and I tense with the familiar apprehension of dread at the prophecy that fell from the sky. Now the fear of an unknown future is real again and as big as the sharpening outline of the mountains in the distance. I am afraid.

Gripping my hand tightly enough to crush my knuckles painfully into each other, John summons the strength to face the road ahead.

❦

The car's reduced speed and the stifling heat wake me. The parking lot at the Las Vegas Stardust Hotel is sporadically lined with cars, the air a blast of hot oven wind.

"Shhh. Take Thor for a pee, will ya?" John asks before I have a chance to say anything.

"What are you doing, John?" I ask, annoyed at seeing the casino.

"Just fifteen minutes, baby. I just want to place one bet on aught double aught. You know, and my lucky numbers . . . to see if we can double our money."

John is already out the door before I can argue. "Hurry up, John. I got a bad feeling here. This place is too public."

He blows me a kiss for luck and walks off, yanking at the back of his jeans, smoothing his wrinkled T-shirt.

After watering Thor, I kick back on the shaded backseat, my feet sticking out the window as I pick at a leftover glazed dough-nut. The sun glares off the parked cars, and each minute that ticks by grows hotter.

Abruptly, a quickly moving figure rushes toward me through the bright glare of the sun. It is John. Shirt collar pulled up to his ears and head ducked down, he slides into the driver's seat. "Get down," he orders.

"What is it?"

In swift movements, he turns the ignition and slides the gear arm into reverse. A trail of dust gathers behind him.

"John? What?"

"A hit man."

"Eddie's?"

"No!" He is visibly trembling, his hand fumbling on the dash-board for a cigarette.

"Did he see you?"

John ignores me, pulls in a lungful of smoke, and steps on the gas.

Get out of here. Get out of here. Get out of here, I think, real danger suffocating me like the terrible desert heat. It is what the police told us. There are many . . . many contracts out on us. They are everywhere.

Then I remember the hawk.

It is good to be out of Nevada. After crossing through the red colors of Utah, we hit the plains of Wyoming and head up to Montana with a detour at the Little Bighorn Battlefield National Monument. John wants to stop and walk through the gravestones that mark Custer's last stand. Cowboy drips out of him in the way he talks and walks. It's as if he has changed into a favorite old pair of jeans, and I remember how much he loves John Wayne.

It is beautiful—the countryside of America—and it has a calming effect, one that irons out the static of our fear. Soon we are laughing and playing around as we did in the old days. With no drugs around, John is his old lighthearted self. It's the first time in so many years that I feel kind of happy again.

Billings, Montana, seems like a town with ancient history. Redbrick buildings line either side of downtown, and the trees grow thick and tall. With plenty of space and light, their branches stretch up to the sky in bountiful twists and curls.

John's sister, Anne, lives in an older, one-bedroom brown-stone. When we arrive, she welcomes us at the door in her faded pocket housecoat.

John slides into a down-home country accent, a little more childlike than his John Wayne drawl. He and his sister laugh and joke and genuinely enjoy each other's company.

Anne is a plain, pear-shaped woman in her late thirties with long mousy-brown hair parted down the middle, reminding me of the style John likes me to wear. I can see a resemblance to her mother in the long oval shape of her face and her small brown eyes. Soft-spoken and shy, she doesn't mention Mary except to ask John if he has talked to her since he left California. John pretends not to hear her question. She offers us the pullout couch to sleep on for as long as we are in town.

John doesn't tell Anne the full story of what happened to us in LA. I don't think she wants to know. I'm burning with curiosity about what her mother may have told her about me, but I don't ask.

Our lives are simple again for the first time after so long. John and I are romantic, taking lazy summer walks, holding hands under the full shade of the trees, and browsing through antique and secondhand stores. Our meals are filled with laughter, fried chicken, beans, and a sense of home, making it easy to forget the terror of the past, until . . .

When the phone rings incessantly all day about a month into our stay, I get frantic. Anne is at work, and John and I have made a pact that while we're in her house we will never answer the phone. We don't want to give away our whereabouts, just in case. The continuous, foreboding ringing unnerves us, though.

As soon as Anne walks through the door, the phone shrills predictably again. She sees the fear on our faces, sets her grocery bags on the floor, and takes a resolved step to the phone.

"It's Mom," she says to John. A doe-eyed blank expression pales her summer tan. "She needs to talk to you."

The call is brief. John doesn't want to be on the telephone line for any length of time in case it's tapped. He rakes his fingers through his hair, nervously setting his survival mode thinking into motion, and begins in a monotone: "The FBI was at my family's in Ohio this morning. There's a warrant out for both of us, and we're on the FBI's most wanted list. The FBI is involved because we crossed state lines. First they wanted me for failure to appear in court for the stolen computer in Huntington Beach, but now they want to charge me for the murders again." He doesn't blink. "We're considered armed and drug-crazed."

Nobody looks at each other for a long time, not wanting to project any negative energy to jinx us. *We have no drugs. We have no weapons. We aren't like that. I'm not like that*, I think. *I just want to get away and start over with my boyfriend.*

John doesn't mention why they want me too, but I remember the warnings of Detectives Lange and Tomlinson while we were in protective custody. *They'll be after you as long as you're with him, Dawn.* Instantly I worry about my family in Oregon. A dull awareness of anger toward John surfaces in my consciousness, suppressed over and over again almost like swallowing a surge of bile, for putting me in this situation. Again, I swallow the bitter taste back down. This is too much. Bewildered, I look at John, pleading once again for him to tell me what we should do next.

"We gotta leave. Right now!"

I know he is right and, without letting in any more emotions, zombielike, I gather and pack our things in just a few short minutes while John busies negotiating with Anne to borrow some money.

"Where will you go?" she asks him.

"Florida. Dawn is from Florida, and it's far enough away from California. I think we'll be safe." John knows his sister won't tell the cops about us, not for a while at least. His family wants him safe, of course, but they have no idea what that could cost them and I can imagine that they won't protect him for long. Anne only nods at her brother, watching him change from that down-home good guy she grew up with in rural Ohio to an FBI fugitive, and she says good-bye. We leave our monthlong reprieve and, like a movie in fast-forward, escape from a rapidly approaching past to enter another looming, unsure future.

⚶⚶

The highway reaches out endlessly before us, and John's foot hits the gas as if he's attempting to catch up with it. We are now in a mad rush to get out of Montana, where we know the authorities will be coming for us next. John's focus is straight ahead, his speed lightning fast. The landscape is an elongated blur—seventy-five, eighty, eight-five. The Malibu strains with a constant high-pitched pinging noise, leaving miles of blessed freedom between us—until the red and blue lights of a highway patrol car blink haphazard signals for us to pull over.

"We're caught!" I choke, feeling as if I have tripped just before the finish line in the 600-yard race.

"Shhh! Just stay calm and let me handle this." John gathers his composure.

"Afternoon. Driver's license, registration, please." The officer's voice booms with authority.

John slips into his down-home friendly persona again, letting the officer know he is cooperative and unaware of why he has been pulled over.

"The speed limit on Montana rural highways is fifty-five, Mr. Holmes. This isn't California, you know."

"Oh, it is? Why, no, sir. I didn't know that, sir. It's seventy-five in California and I, uh, thought . . ."

"What's your business here in Montana, sir?"

"My sister lives in Billings. We were visiting for a few weeks. Summer vacation, you know, and now we're headed home." John tries to keep his story simple and close to the truth.

"I'll be right back." The officer walks back to run John's license and car tags.

Every second we wait for the patrolman to return, John rhythmically digs his thumb into my palm enough to peel the skin off and, although I feel the pain, I don't stop him. The sweat from my brow drips pearl-sized beads down my cheeks and rolls cool between my breasts. I look over at John and panic at the sight of his blond roots pushing out from underneath the dark hair dye, and I envision us sent back to California in handcuffs. I know the warrants for our arrest will show up on the police screen somehow. When the cop slowly, carefully returns to our car, checking out the paint job, I am positive he is taking us in.

"Well, uh, Mr. Holmes. I'm not finding any priors . . . so I'm gonna let you off with a warning this time. From now on, keep to the speed limit and make sure you get this young lady home safely." He throws a smile my way.

I can't believe our luck. I smile—a plastic, phony, innocent grin.

"Why, uh, yes, sir. I promise. Sorry 'bout that." John's hillbilly tone is thick with appreciation. We wait for the officer to drive off ahead of us, pretending to let Thor out on the side of the road to pee. John waves, releasing his long-held breath. "That was close . . . real close!" John whispers without moving his lips.

Why John's name didn't come up when the officer radioed it in, I don't know, but we learn from the stroke of luck. We are on the run from the law now. Not only the law, but the FBI . . . and this had been a narrow escape. John won't make the mistake of bringing attention to himself again. Not for driving, anyway.

※

Florida. We are headed for Florida. Back to the East Coast and orange trees. "What do you want to see, baby? The Grand Canyon? Arizona?" Acting silly and goofy, John tries to get me to smile and relax.

"Sure, John. Can we see the whole thing?" I ask, loosening up a little. I remember the short stop I took with my father on the way to California over five years ago.

"Yeah, baby. Come on. Cheer up. We did it. It's you and me again. Like we wanted." He kisses my hand for reassurance.

I warm up to John's charm, as I always do, and we saunter through Arizona like common tourists. Walking arm in arm and acting like sweethearts again, we gawk with the crowds at the Grand Canyon, walk the edge of the Meteor Crater near Flagstaff, and feel the age of the earth in the Petrified Forest.

We flit in and out of carefree moments, talking about the kind of home we would like to settle into and how long it might take for Sharon to meet up with us. We do it partially because it separates us from the severity of our situation, making it easier to cope, and partially because it reminds us that once upon a time we were happy.

Time and distance are our friends these days. Once out of the Southwest, we hurry through Texas and Oklahoma, paranoid on a different level to be stopped in these fanatically religious states.

Then we drift through Louisiana, Mississippi, and Alabama via rural highways. Spanish moss and mist in the evening hours make the scenery haunting. We hold hands and picture ourselves in Civil War garb rocking on the porch of an old plantation.

We are in Alabama, off a weathered side road, when John becomes fidgety again. We are running out of money, and he is doing his best to not let me know how low our finances have become. Checking into another unassuming cheap motel, we look forward to finally arriving in Florida the next day. Without warning, John makes the decision to take a walk by himself just after dark and slips on a pair of dark leather gloves. "Keep an eye out the window for me, baby. And shut the lights out if you see someone coming."

It catches me off guard. "John . . . why?"

"Now, baby. You know I'm doing this for us, right? I just need to make sure we have enough to make it to Florida. Now be a good girl."

John doesn't give me a moment to argue, gingerly turning the doorknob so no one will hear. I jump up to be his lookout, as I've been told, hating John's return to his old behavior. In a few minutes he returns, his jacket stuffed with the contents of a suitcase he has pillaged from the back of another parked car. *He must have scoped out the car beforehand,* I think, noting how fast and precise he has been. And with that thought, flashes come of some of the last motels we've stayed in. *Was he stealing back then as well?* It seems possible, but I quash the thought anyway.

John pulls out some cash, loose change, and a watch, dumping them on the bed. Then, ever so gently, from under his arm he retrieves a .38 caliber pistol.

I grab Thor and slip him under my sweater, squeezing him close to my chest as if to comfort a horrible ache in my soul. I keep an eye on John as he empties the chamber over the bed and counts the bullets. *Now we really are armed like they think we are!* I shudder at how the FBI made this deadly prediction.

Collins Avenue runs the length of a small strip of land that separates North Miami from the Atlantic Ocean, and is the main road on my favorite beach, Haulover. We used to beg our mother to take us to Haulover Beach on weekends when we lived in Carol City. Then when we got older, we'd hang out there with our girlfriends. There is a single wooden pier jutting over the ocean with an ice cream shack and miles and miles of sun-filled sand, a getaway from the gang fights of our neighborhood streets. It is here that I think John and I might find refuge, if for no other reason than that I remembered feeling safe here years before.

We enter the parking lot of the Fountainhead Hotel, a 1950s, two-story transition hotel that stretches from Collins Avenue to the beach. A life-size figure of a mermaid-haired female bust is bound to the bow of a ship. The Malibu, on its last leg, chugs and spits into an empty space in the lot.

John's long legs extend one by one, stiff and weary, as he leaves to check us in. I keep Thor out of sight.

In a burst of laughter, John swaggers out of the lobby, flanked by a queen-sized redhead and a lanky, dark-haired man. "Hey, babe. This is Big Rosie and her husband, Tom. They run the place. They love Chihuahuas and wanna take a look at Thor." He reaches in to pass Thor to Big Rosie by the scruff of his neck.

"Hi there!" Big Rosie booms, holding out her hand to me. "You must be Dawn."

"Yeah. Hi! You like Chihuahuas?"

"Oh God, yes. I was raised with 'em. My parents just lost Tiny, a little fawn-colored one they've had since I was a kid. They're devastated."

"I can imagine. I don't know what I'd do without him. They're the best dogs."

"Yeah. Tough little guys and loyal too. They'll stand up to anything to protect ya."

"I know," I say, remembering . . .

Thor takes an immediate liking to Big Rosie, quivering as she coos his name and reaches out to steal a kiss. "Yeah, we don't got a problem with small dogs like this here. We get all kinds of things; I just like to know about it first. Just make sure you take him out to pee, and everything will be fine." She hands him back with a grin that matches her size.

"Thanks."

"All right, we'll let you two get settled in. Italian Joe serves dinner at the snack shop around five. He makes the best meatball subs on Collins Avenue. Don't wanna miss it." They head back into the front office, and I feel as if I've run into old friends.

John is smiling from ear to ear. "Come on, baby. Let's get unpacked."

※

The first week of rent, John pays with what little cash we have left. We'll both have to look for work. Our registered identities are John and Dawn Evans, a newly married couple who have been sweethearts for years. Big Rosie is warm, loud, smart, and genuine. She has been running the Fountainhead for several years now and is proud of the fact that she can maintain a place that is affordable enough to help people get on their feet. It's this line of thinking that causes her to take notice of our desperate financial situation. When John approaches her to do odd jobs for room rent, she's already made a plan.

"Well, my husband is actually the official handyman here, John, but he might need extra help with a few things. You'll need to talk to him. Now, I could use someone to be my housekeeper. I've been doing it, but I can't do everything. If Dawn's interested, tell her to come see me." John can't wait to give me the news, and soon I'm employed full-time—housekeeping in trade for rent, including a few extra dollars under the table.

We set up home in a fairly large room on the second floor near the back stairs, which lead to the enclosed pool and Italian Joe's Snack Shop. On the other side of the pool fence is an enticing stretch of public beach, white sands rolling straight into the refreshing crystal turquoise of the Atlantic Ocean.

It is nearing the end of a hot August, and it's been almost six weeks since we left Los Angeles. I allow myself to fall into a safe intimacy with the humidity and the heat of southern Florida, where the people don't seem to recognize John for his porn image. We are the nice, likeable couple in love, and it's not long before we're introduced to the other live-in residents at the Fountainhead. We often gather at Italian Joe's Snack Shop at the pool for dinner, lingering evening meals where Joe dishes out special sausage dishes to the tenants for a deal. We eat with Louise, a stripper with a lisp who's waiting for a divorce settlement, her five-year-old daughter, Heather, and Big Rosie and her husband. Armand, a dark-skinned Cuban male stripper, joins us on his nights off.

We couldn't have found a better place to hide out from the law. Accepted and liked, John and I fit in perfectly with the misfits in residence here and nobody asks any questions about a subject they aren't willing to ask about directly. The blond regrowth of John's hair is obvious but never mentioned. Big Rosie makes a side comment about how tough it is for an older man to keep looking good for his younger bride, and I figure she feels sorry for John for dyeing his hair to impress me.

The weeks slip by with the comfortable feeling that we have blended into this place that feels a world apart from the chaos lurking on the outside. The worry that someone will find us to fulfill an underground contract diminishes.

Many an evening John amuses the gang at Joe's with his animated jokes and charm. They are impressed, and the attention feeds John's ego. He is the star of the show, and I laugh along with our new neighbors. The people here have all the familiarity of the neighbors at the courtyard back in Glendale . . . before the drugs and the beatings.

Like a firefly restlessly, rapidly moving, a touch of affection flitters back between John and me. He writes me love notes and poetry again and lingers with me on long, romantic strolls down the beach while Thor bounces near our heels. John dabbles in drawing again, often sitting in a chair by the pool sketching me intently as I talk to people at the snack shop or watch television in our room. Beautiful profiles and warm, tender moments with Thor flow onto his artist's pad, and he signs each picture gallantly in his old, unique style. Here, it seems the world is allowing us to make a niche for ourselves again, a refuge from those who hunt us.

I clean rooms once a week for the residents. After every overnight guest, I sneak spare towels from my maid's cart to our new friends, which earns me extra tip money. I don't mind working hard scrubbing bathtubs and sinks. It is trivial enough and keeps my mind from worrying.

Big Rosie and Tom help us further by giving John as much side work as they can, and he stashes any extra money to buy me small gifts. The west side of Collins Avenue is filled with a mix of coffeehouses, shell and rock shops, and seedier non-ocean-view X-rated motels. Collins Avenue's massive four-lane stretch is busy in the daytime and busier at night. John holds my hand to dodge traffic so we can wander the gem and rock shops to browse through piles of lapis lazuli, malachite, and quartz in search of just the right piece.

"Oh! Look at this!" I hold up a bloodred necklace. "It's beautiful, John!" Polished beads of garnet spread the light into an intricate, fractured spray of burgundy.

"Here. Let's try it on, baby." He gingerly places them around my neck and steps back admiringly. "Oh! Nice. Here—for you!"

"John. Really?" I gasp.

"Your birthstone, Dawn. I have to. It's the perfect piece!" He digs in his pocket to pay the storekeeper with every dime of the extra cash. "Nothing's too good for my girl!" His nostrils flare with the fierce pride of ownership. But it is to be a false pride.

<hr>

Come October, John finds an outside job on the construction site of a large four-star hotel about a mile north on the beach. He gives his employer a fake name and makes up lies about losing his Social Security card. Hired as a minimum wage laborer, he begins every day early and ends late.

Somehow, for the first month or so, he arranges to borrow money from fellow workers, weaving stories about paying them back as soon as management straightens out his paycheck. The guys figure he earns the money when he works with them; after all, he's a nice guy, so they think he has to be good for it.

John plays his bluff at the job like an addiction for as long as he can, banking on the odds that something else will come up in the meantime, before the obvious lie catches up to him. His mood is still happy and sweet, and he and I take it to mean that landing this job is a good omen.

I feel as if our roles are on level ground with each other; it's a place I've never experienced with John, and I find a sense of strength in it. He makes his own lunch the night before work. In the mornings he wakes himself, setting the alarm to wake me later. He kisses me good-bye tenderly every morning, as if it might be the last time, before walking out the door for work. At night when he returns more tired and drawn than usual, he keeps our dinner visits at Joe's brief so we can cuddle in front of the television and fall asleep in each other's arms.

It is subtle at first, John's mild detachment from meals and conversation. The change goes relatively unnoticed by everyone, except me. But his excuse of being too tired makes sense, diminishing my alarm. Like a slow-starting avalanche, his need for more privacy builds up to irritability and then sleepless nights. John is changing again.

Is he beginning to crack from the pressure of being on the run? I guess it's catching up to him. I hope no one will notice and try to cover for him when people notice he isn't his friendly self. "He's fine. He's just tired. They're working him too hard over there," I tell Big Rosie and the gang. It doesn't help that people are beginning to get suspicious of his stories at work too. John is running out of ideas, feeling trapped, and I think about the possibility of having to move somewhere else. I hate to lose the small corner of comfort we have etched out here.

It is Big Rosie with her no messing around personality who approaches me to say that John might be on drugs. I don't know when I suspected it; too many other excuses have clouded my vision.

Big Rosie brings it out into the open with me. "He's asking all kinds of questions about where you've been all day and if Tom and I have seen you with anyone else. He's being weird. Then he acts like we're lying!" She shakes her head, demonstrating that she doesn't like this change one bit. "I'm worried about you both, Dawn. You don't think he's using anything, do you?"

It can only be one thing, my gut screams. *He must be doing drugs! Not a lot, 'cause it's not full-blown,* I rationalize. *He's still managing.* I can't figure out where he's getting the drugs, but I'm becoming scared. *Just ride this through, Dawn. He won't do anything here.*

Everybody knows us, and we see each other every day. I assess the situation around me in an unconscious act of self-preservation.

Distance grows between us again. He doesn't sleep at night but stays up listening to the noises outside our door. John is so paranoid that I find it hard to say or do anything right. The sound of walking on eggshells plays on repeat in my mind like the lyrics to an old song I know by heart.

The other locals notice as well. I keep making excuses. "He's worried about money. They're having trouble with his paychecks." Offering to help, Armand the male stripper pays me extra to clean his room an extra day a week, and Louise hires me to babysit her five-year-old till she gets home from her shift around two in the morning. It earns us extra money and affords me time away from John's brooding, but it also allows him all the more reason to distrust me.

November has begun, and John's depressive mood swings are disturbingly obvious to everyone now. He stops speaking to most people, refuses to eat, and holes up in our room complaining about the jerks at work. He goes to work regardless of whether he has slept or eaten, and he returns home each night bleary-eyed and reclusive. Then, one evening near Thanksgiving, John snaps and breaks his promise—the one that means everything to me—and crosses that invisible line into insanity again . . . the likes of which I haven't seen since before the murders.

Slipping into our room after a night of babysitting, I turn to close the door quietly so I won't wake him. *Something's not right,* I think, noticing Thor isn't dancing at the door to greet me. "John?" I call into the darkness.

"Where have you been?" The terrible, low tone of his voice

reaches ominously from behind the door.

Startled, I jump. "Oh! John? Is that you?"

"Who've you been fucking?"

"What?"

Quickly his hand lands over my mouth, and he shoves me up against the wall. "Don't give me that shit, bitch. I know you're out fucking someone!" he whispers harshly, his breath like fire in my ear.

I don't fight. I hold still. Disjointed emotions barrage my thoughts and, of all things, I irrationally panic that our new friends will hear us. Beneath his weight, I shake my head feverishly.

John's voice, thick and heavy, orders me to be quiet. Then with eerie, precise movements, he pulls my hands up and behind my back, rendering me paralyzed. *No. Not again.* My internal alarm clangs. Shattered images of my life here at the Fountainhead play behind my eyes squeezed shut and splinter at my feet, a useless pile of a thousand pieces.

I can feel John's rage grow from his body, and I snap into autopilot, shrinking into the size of a pea, smaller even, cutting off all external connections with my thoughts and feelings. *I can't let anything in. It's the only safe place to go.* John's other palm, rough and calloused, clasps firmly over my mouth. The smell of concrete and sweat infuse my nostrils, and I want to vomit.

He throws me to the bed. The sound of my clothes being torn from my body seems distant until I feel the breeze of John's movements across my bare breasts. With his one free hand, he twists my legs into contorted mannequinlike poses and cruelly rapes me, ranting accusations of my cheating as he slams his power ruthlessly down.

Afterward, I lie frozen, my insides lifeless as I shake, wrapped tightly in his steel-like grip long after he has finished. Racked with pain and desolate grief, I feel the tears pour silently down the side of my face and into a puddle on the stained bedspread. My soul, tortured and frail, howls in ghostly silence to anyone who cares.

No! Why? He can't be this person again! This can't be happening!
Every ounce of my being screams at my emotional crash into reality.
Denial takes its time coming, arriving slowly with the sunrise, like a
thin, worn blanket, allowing me to disappear into a shivering sleep.

John doesn't go to work the next day, and I don't move from the bed.
The phone incessantly rings and rings. My guess is it's Big Rosie
calling to find out why I haven't shown up for work. Neither of us
answers, and within the hour there comes a pounding at the door.

"Answer it!" John hisses as he slips into the bathroom.

I wrap the covers around me and hobble to check the peephole. Big Rosie glares back at me. I crack the door open. "Hi.
Uh, sorry. I'm sick."

"Where's John?"

Shame-filled and guilt-laden, I stare blankly right through her
burning gaze. "Oh, uh, in the bathroom." I know she's aware of
his car parked in the lot.

She scrutinizes my body and steps back. "You okay?"

"Mmmm. Yeah, I'm okay. Just a little sick. I'll be better
tomorrow." I hide my eyes from the glaring morning light. I want
to somehow give her a secret signal to ask her to watch out for me,
to check on me tomorrow for my safety. I want John to hear me
say it too, so he will think twice about hurting me. I am afraid for
my life now . . . again. I fear that if anything happens to me, he
can easily blame it on one of the hit men. He can get away with
murdering me, maybe, as I start to think he is getting away with
the murders on Wonderland.

"We need more money. We can't get out of here unless we get more money!" Like a caged animal, he paces the room wildly. Like a broken record, John says what I know he will: "You gotta go to work. We need more money fast. I think somebody recognized me the other day. We need to get out of here."

"I do work, John!" His next words ring in my ears before he even speaks them, and my lip curls.

"You know what I mean," he snarls back, leaping on top of me. His weight presses heavily above me, his backhand smacking across my head. "Not this piddley shit . . . cleaning rooms . . . babysitting!" He pauses. "The beach! You need to be making fast money on the beach! Do you want them to catch up to us and kill us? They're looking for you too! What? Do you think they forgot about you? You're on at least eight hit lists, baby, just like me. And that kind of shit don't go away . . . unless *you* go away! Get it?" His face hovers over mine, red, puffy, and cigarette stale.

"Stop it! No! I can't, John!" I'm hysterical, trying to squirm free.

"You'll do it. You know why? 'Cause if you don't, they'll get you! The shit's coming down, and if we don't get out now . . . that'll be the end of me . . . and you!" He pushes up off of me and wipes the sweat from his face with his sleeve. "Now get up!" He yanks me to my feet, raising his hand in a threat to backhand me again.

"No. Please." I cower and cover my head.

John picks out a pair of cutoff shorts and a bathing suit top for me to wear. He combs my hair and wipes my face with a washcloth from the stack in the bathroom. "Here. Put these on." He hands me a pair of dark sunglasses to hide my red, swollen eyes, takes me by the hand, and escorts me to the beach.

Thinking we are coming down to eat, Italian Joe smiles but looks confused when we walk past him without acknowledging the crowd.

We continue down to the breaking waves of the ocean. The beach is full of afternoon sunbathers. John nods and smiles at several single men, trying to catch his attention. Reaching a large hotel north of us, he lays down a towel and spreads warm suntan oil over my back. Another dark-haired man lays his towel a few feet away, and John addresses him. "Hey there. Sure is a hot one."

The man blushes. "Yeah. Sure is."

John leans into my ear. "See there. There's a guy who looks like he'll pay. He sees you're with me, so you're safe. Take him across the street, where the motel has the X-rated movie sign— you know, near the rock shop—and meet me back here in exactly twenty minutes. Now go!"

John jumps up from the sand and, before he walks away, gives me a shove toward the leering man who has been eyeing me.

A fearful gulp of air sticks in my throat. I touch the gar- net necklace at my neck, thinking sadly, *This really doesn't mean a thing, does it?* As the man approaches nervously and smiles, I tremble, my eyes welling up behind the dark lenses. I pull my lips back in a grimace, imitating a smile.

He pays no attention to my expression, nodding to something over my shoulder. I turn to look. John is nodding back to the man, wearing a crooked grin.

The bathtub water is as hot as I remember it, and I remember all

John's baths before now. Numb, and without a fight, I let John scrub me down while he begs for my forgiveness, tears streaking his face. Then he does it all over again.

My world is rubble at my feet; there is no meaning to anything anymore. I know his perverted ritual is set in motion, and it just doesn't matter. John has reverted to the person he promised he would never be again. I am trapped in his hell, unable even to die. Back in this pitiful place, there is nothing left . . . of my heart, my hopes, my reason for being. Every shred is gone . . . and I just want to crawl under something and disappear forever.

Big Rosie's phone call snaps me out of my stupor the next morning. I roll over to answer the persistent ringing and let her know I'm still feeling ill. *I can't face anyone! They'll know!* I am humiliated, ashamed, and certain that if Rosie—or anyone—looks at me she will know all my ugly secrets.

Rosie sounds understanding. John, she says, stopped by the front desk this morning to say hello on his way to work. "He apologized for the inconvenience yesterday," she says, a questioning lilt to her voice.

God, he's covering his tracks with everyone, I think. *Thank God he's not here.* I thank her and hang up. Curtains drawn, I crawl under the bedsheets and spend the day hidden in the darkness.

John gets home early in the afternoon, and I panic when I hear the key turn in the lock. Burrowing deeper under the covers, I wish myself invisible, not wanting to see or speak to him. He bangs randomly around the room, opening a can of beans to cook on the hot plate, trying to wake me and get my attention as I will myself to sink deeper into the mattress and oblivion.

"Get up!" he finally shouts, ripping the covers off. He has been watching the clock, his temper steadily building. Thor is spooked and jumps down to hide under the bed.

"What? Stop it, John! I don't feel good!" I cry. I know it's a lame attempt to deflect his instructions, but I don't want this kind of life. I have to try to resist.

"Bullshit! Now get up. There's still enough light out for the beach. Let's move!" He is taking complete control, strutting about the room slamming things around, rummaging for my clothes, and talking as if I am a child he's waking up for school. His old, ugly self flames brilliantly in orange-red rage, and I think I'm going to pass out.

"No."

John's head snaps to attention and his eyes bore into mine. "What did you say?" he asks menacingly.

Eyeing the unchained door, I brace myself. "No, John. I'm not going anywhere!" My voice is more defiant than my nerve, but I can feel a charge of rebellion.

Whoosh! He lunges for my throat.

I run for the door. It swings open wide, hitting John in the face, and gives me a fractured moment to make it to the stairs. He is running after me full force, and I scream at the top of my lungs, sprinting toward Italian Joe's for safety. "Help! Help!" He's seconds behind. "No! John! Stop!" I yell, hoping someone will intervene. I make it to the fence by the pool, crashing through the metal gate. Then, in direct view of the dinnertime crowd, John, relentless, catches up to me. In his outstretched hand, he manages to grab my hair and yank me down onto the cement by the deep end of the pool, brutally pounding on my body and face with his fists.

The looks on the faces of the dinnertime crowd at Joe's is shock and horror—disbelief—but no one moves a muscle.

John's strength fades as his adrenaline pours out into his raging fists, and his anger subsides. As if he realizes everyone is watching, he pulls me up and drags me behind him back up the stairs to our room. He locks the door securely behind him, peeks out from behind the curtains, and falls to his knees. "Baby, oh baby, I'm so sorry!" he heaves, sweaty grime caked in the creases of his brow. "Please, please forgive me." He reaches for my arm, pleading.

Cringing at his pitiful attempt to touch me, I can't look at him. My face and cheek are swollen. A goose egg swells on my forehead, and my lip is bruised and numb.

Desperately, he pulls me into his lap. Clumps of my hair sticks to his arm, and I let him rest his head on my chest and sob.

He has that scared look again. Like a lost little boy, I think. I give in and rest my arms around his sobbing frame, a broken man, until we fall asleep in each other's arms . . . for the last time.

⌘

The alarm goes off at six in the morning. John is up to make coffee. Letting me sleep, he tiptoes into the bathroom to get ready for work. Stretching in a half sleep, I feel my head throb and re-member the night before. I watch him as he dresses and finishes his morning coffee. He crosses over to the bed and sits on the bed next to me.

"Good morning, Dawn," John whispers, stroking my hair and face. He waits for a long time, just staring. In my waking thoughts, I remember all the times he lovingly woke me in the past, brushing my hair from my face, telling me I was beautiful. "Sleep in. Okay, baby?" I give a small nod, feeling the pain in my face. He gazes a bit longer and then, kneeling down, breathes an "I love you, Dawn." He kisses the bruises on my forehead and lips.

He starts to open the door, then stops. Shoulders slumped and head hanging low, he turns to give me one last look. "See you tonight, sweetheart," he mumbles unconvincingly. Then, looking as if he has lost his best friend, he sadly leaves.

✧

Bang, bang, bang! Bang, bang, bang! The door shakes at its hinges from the vibration.

"Yeah? Who is it?" I call, alarmed by the intensity of the knocking. I step up to look through the peephole. Big Rosie, Tom, Italian Joe, and Louise press up against the door. "Oh, hey. What's up?" I shyly poke my head out, hiding the "bad" side of my face with the door.

"Are you okay?" Big Rosie barrels into the room.

"Yeah, uh, I'm okay, I guess." I look away, embarrassed that they witnessed John's rage on me last night.

"Pack your things!" she orders.

"What? I, I can't. What about John?"

"What about John?" Rosie snaps. "That asshole! We saw what he did yesterday. He don't deserve you! Now let's go. You're coming with us."

I am stunned at the hurried rush of my friends gathering to rescue me. Overcome, I weep.

Big Rosie sees me crumble and reaches over to hold me as I cry in her thick, freckled arms. "Where, where will I go?"

Rosie rocks me protectively. "Louise's divorce is final, sweetie, and she just got her house back. She needs someone to watch Heather while she's at work. You've already been babysitting, so it's perfect, Dawn. You're gonna be okay."

"He won't find you at my houth, thweetie," Louise lisps, "and no one'ths gonna tell him either."

Tom and Italian Joe stand guard outside while the ladies help me pack. Holding a shaking Thor in my arms, I take one last look around the room. "Just a minute. I need to get one more thing." Lifting the mattress, I pull out the .38 pistol and spare bullets, the one John had stolen in Alabama. "I'll take this, just in case." I shudder as everyone looks on. I am afraid . . . but it's different this time. This time I am not worried about John; I am afraid for myself.

What have you done? my mind asks him. *I gave you my love and my loyalty and you . . . you gave me . . . this.* I steal a fleeting glance at the room I have called home—my last home with John—and without a tear, I turn and flee.

꧁ꕥ꧂

Louise and Heather are singing in the front seat of her brown-paneled station wagon. They are happy. At least Louise is. She has been going through a rough divorce and finally pulled through victorious for her and Heather, according to her. Everything is working out perfectly in her eyes. Her house, my needing a safe place to stay—things couldn't be better.

But I am depressed and still not fully comprehending that I am getting away from John. *Why am I acting like this?* I wonder. *Why do I still care about someone who hurt me so much?* I know it's because I never wanted to give up on love; I keep hoping there is still some good inside of him. In truth, I'm clinging to just a memory of something good. It has always hurt too badly to give up on what could have been.

"Hey, come on. Cheer up!" Louise sings.

I force a smile and tap my foot to the beat of an ABBA song, drifting in and out of thoughts of my last moments with John.

꧁ꕥ꧂

At Louise's place, a house sunk deep in the suburbs of North Miami, I feel safe right away. *He'll have a hard time finding me here,* I think because I know he will look for me. I know he is scared I will get him caught by either the police or . . . Eddie.

It is Thanksgiving week; since Louise is working, we won't celebrate with a turkey, but it is a celebration anyway. I will get to call my family.

Mom sounds shocked when she hears my voice.

"Some people helped me get away from John, Mom. He hit me again and, well, I'm in a safe place now, and I'm working. I'll try to make enough to get back . . . if that's okay."

"Yah. Okay. You sure? Yah, da police vas here looking for you. They told us people were out to kill you, Dawn. They said the whole family vas in danger. Stay away from him, Dawn. He's bad news."

"I know, Mom. I'm sorry. I have help this time, Mom."

"Vell." She sighs. "Vaht number can I call you back, den? So I can call you."

I don't blame her for not acting overjoyed. My God, my family thinks they could be killed too!

Mom calls me every evening, and it feels good to hear her voice. I don't give her my address yet, just in case, but I look forward to her calls. When the phone rings, I race Heather to answer it. A week has passed since I left the Fountainhead and John . . . and I am feeling good again. I am in touch with my family and getting on my feet. The phone rings early that evening and, as usual, I am eager to talk to Mom. "Hello." I am out of breath from dancing with Heather.

"Dawn?"

It's John. My heart freezes. "Yeah?" I keep my anger down.

"Listen. Please, Dawn, don't hang up. I promised Rosie I wouldn't force you to do anything you didn't want to do. She didn't want to give me your number, but I, well, kinda promised I just wanted to talk to you."

"Yeah?" I know he wants more than just to talk, and I feel my heart rate rise.

"Baby. How have you been?"

"Fine, John." I am determined not to fall for any of his sob story ploys. Not this time. I brace myself.

"Good. Good." A long silence passes. He is crying. It's unmistakable. The low hiss of emotional pain releases into the air. He clears his throat and continues. "Baby? Dawn? I know you don't want to hear this, but . . . I'm sorry. I'm really, really sorry. I know I fucked up. I know this time it's for good. I know that. I don't deserve you, baby. I fucked up." His crying is loud now, and he makes no effort to hide it.

"Yeah," I acknowledge, feeling the tug at my sympathy. *Don't, Dawn. Don't give in. He's full of shit!* I reinforce my willpower with memories of his lies and abuse.

"I just want to ask you one thing."

"I can't, John. I just can't—"

"No. No. Baby, wait, listen. Just one last favor, and I promise you . . . I'll never ask you for anything ever again!"

I don't answer.

"Dawn? Are you there?"

"Yeah." I brace myself.

John breaks down sobbing again. "Baby . . . one favor please. I just need to see you, your face . . . one last time. I won't talk to you . . . touch you . . . I just . . . need to see my beautiful Dawn . . . one last time. Please . . . Dawn?"

I picture it . . . in my mind, to kindle that one last romantic moment with him and then be strong enough to walk away. To get close enough to him again to be in his view. I miss him . . . too much . . . and with that knowledge, I know it is impossible. A last meeting with John should never happen, and I need to be strong . . . stronger than surviving the beatings . . . the prostitution . . . the arrests . . . strong from my heart, to turn my back on this terrible love that owns me. I know that it has to be really over . . .

for good this time. We are never to go back to the beginning, the good times—anything.

The phone line is as still as death. I take a deep breath and brace myself. "No, John."

"What?" He sounds truly surprised, not expecting defiance from me, the one person who has always been his personal puppet.

"I said no, John." The words feel like perfect freedom—a crack in the agonizingly heavy chains that, for years, have burdened my heart and crippled my life. I say nothing more, expecting him to fly into a rage.

"Well, can you think about it?" There's an edge to his voice that I don't like as he swallows his pride.

My heart beats like thunder. I hold the receiver away from my ear. I have never meant anything as much as this, as I do right now—and gently, like a soft kiss good-bye, I hang up.

* * *

True freedom—I feel true inner freedom. There is nothing I want from John anymore. I am sure of this. All I want is to get away and wipe his name completely from mine. It is almost December, and I look back on my years with him with shame and terrible regret. I have nothing good to salvage—not even any fantasy— and I want to forget him. All of him.

Everything seems to happen quickly from this moment. Mom calls at her regular time, but I am a bit more hesitant to answer the phone.

If John managed to get my number from Rosie, he might find out my whereabouts as well. I want to get away—far away—somehow.

A few worrisome days pass. Then a welcome call comes from my brother with news to cheer me up. "Hey. How's it going?" His voice is warm and friendly.

"Hey. Good. Well, better. I got away from John. Did Mom

tell you?" I am excited. It's so good to speak to him again . . . without John.

"Yeah. I heard. Cool."

"So what are you up to, man? How's Oregon?"

"I'm not in Oregon."

"You're not? Where are you?"

"Florida," he says flatly, then adds, "Carol City."

"You are? What are you doing down here?" I can't believe my luck, and my eyes well up a bit. The thought of my brother being so close has me hopping, excited.

"Aww, you know. Hanging out with old friends. The Taylors from our old block . . . that kind of thing."

"Well, you have to come see me! I'm not far . . . in North Miami. Wow! This is great! But, uh, how did you get here?"

"I got a rental car. Me and my friend, we drove." His tone stays even.

"Drove!" Something strikes me as odd, and I worry he's involved with something illegal. "Really?"

"Yeah. Don't worry. It's cool."

"All right." I dismiss any concern and focus on seeing him.

"So, uh, what's your address? So I can come by . . . maybe, uh, tomorrow?"

"Tomorrow! Wow! Sure. I'm off tomorrow. We can hang out! I'm so glad to hear from you, Wayne. You can't believe how good this makes me feel."

"I know," he says in a whisper. "Me too."

⁂

The next day my excitement has me jumping to the window every time a car passes. I have visions of leaving for Oregon with my brother. When the plain, white rental car pulls up around noon, I

447

run out to greet Wayne with open arms.

"Hey! Oh, I'm so glad to see you. Come in. Come in."

Sitting in the driver's seat, he says, "No, uh. I only got a little bit of time . . . uh, before I have to turn the car back in." He seems a little disjointed, yanking on the visor, adjusting the rearview mirror.

Looking up into his warm hazel-brown eyes, I notice them glaze over with compassion for me. It's good to see him again. I marvel at how much he has grown. Six months ago, in Oregon, he was sixteen and almost six feet tall. Now he has filled out even more. *God, he just turned seventeen,* I think, amazed at how much time has passed, *and he's becoming a young man . . . a mature one at that.*

"All right. So what do you want to do?"

"I thought we could go someplace. You know, someplace like a park or something . . . to catch up. I got a six-pack in the backseat and, uh, I haven't seen you in a while and thought it would be cool if we just kicked back and talked."

"Yeah. Sure. A park? That's cool. I don't know where any park is around here."

"I do. Remember, Mom and I moved to North Miami . . . after you went to California. There's a park a couple blocks away. Get in."

"Yeah, that's right. You did. All right. I guess that'd be okay. Just a minute; I need to get my bag."

I run to the house and grab Thor and my purse. Then the strangest sense of unease envelops me. *I'd better bring the gun,* I think, reacting to my fear, *just in case.* I stuff it in the bag and worry for a second about being out in the open, a target with a contract on my life.

The ride is short, just as Wayne promised. I find myself gushing with a very brief, edited version of what happened with John and me since I've last seen Wayne in Oregon. I tell him about being arrested for the murders, protective custody, our run and, finally, John's fall back into abuse. Many of the details are left to silence, experiences without words, as Wayne turns a corner onto a lush, tree-lined road.

"Here it is."

"What? Already? That was fast."

He remains silent. Driving overly slowly, he looks from side to side, searching.

The hair rises on the back of my neck. *What's going on?* I think, feeling my throat constrict. I can hardly breathe.

Wayne pulls in next to a small lake at a parking clearance. He places his hand on my knee, then turns to look me in the eyes. "Dawn, I have something I gotta tell you."

"What?" I feel the world become slow motion, surreal.

"Well, uh . . . I'm not here to just catch up with you, and I didn't rent this car with a friend."

"What?" My chest seizes with dread and pain as I wait for his bomb to drop.

"Well, the police sent me."

"The police!" I scream. "What do you mean, 'the police'? I don't see the police! Where are they?"

"I know; I know. Just wait. Listen." His tone is pleading. "They just want to talk to you, Dawn. They don't want you . . . they want John!"

"No!" I panic and open the car door to run.

"Wait! Dawn. No!" He grabs my arm and shoots his hand up to signal the men hidden in inconspicuous cars surrounding us to stay back. Wayne puts the car in park and jumps out to stop several approaching dark-suited men. "Wait a minute. I need to talk to her. Just give us a few minutes alone. Please!" The men signal an okay, and Wayne circles the car to escort me out onto the parking lot. "Come on, Dawn. Come with me. Let's just talk . . . here . . . by the water."

I feel trapped, betrayed. Seconds are frozen in place. I let him guide me to the edge of the lake and hold me in his arms. "I can't do this, Wayne. Not the police. I can't." I am sobbing now. "I've always promised him I'd be loyal . . . that way . . . I'm not a rat. I didn't tell the police anything when we were arrested in LA." It sounds strange to explain my reasons out loud, but it means my integrity to me. "He'll be mad . . . and, well . . . I just can't! There are contracts out!"

"I love you, Dawn. And . . . and . . . I can't tell you how bad John is for you. He's one of the most selfish assholes there is. People are looking to kill you for him. That's not love!" He is fuming with anger now. "Promised him! Ha! He don't care about no one but himself, Dawn. He's drug you all this way, 'cause he knows you love him . . . and he don't deserve your love! You've been too good to him." He hugs me again. "I don't want anything to happen to you, Dawn. The cops don't want anything to happen to you. And if John stays free, there will still be contracts out—not only for him, but for you too!"

My tears are too much. I wipe a flood from my cheeks and nod. "Yeah. I'm scared of that too, Wayne. I'm scared someone's gonna come after me just to find him. I, I even took his gun . . . to protect myself." I pat the side of the handbag glued to my side. "But I don't want to be the one to turn him in."

"Yeah, I know. I'd do the same thing. Just talk to them, Dawn. See what they have to say."

I'm torn up inside; the conflict is excruciating. Instinct tells me to protect John, but I know I have no choice really. The thought that maybe this is the best thing for both of us keeps me sane. "Yeah. Okay."

Wayne hugs me tightly. "I love you, Dawn. You're doing the right thing." He walks me over to the waiting police, who have been huddled in small groups and hovering around my brother's rental car.

"Ms. Schiller." Tom Lange reaches his hand out to shake

mine. "Remember me? From Los Angeles . . . and my partner, Frank Tomlinson? And this is a local Dade County detective. We're here to help you."

Sniffling and wiping my wet cheeks, I acknowledge the three of them.

"You already know, well, uh, we've been looking for you and John. John really, of course. We've been trying to find you both . . . to get you off the street . . . to protect you."

"I'm not with John anymore!" I snap.

"Yeah. We know. We're glad for you but, you see, there are a lot of those, well, contracts out for the both of you and, well, if we have John . . . those contracts will go away . . . disappear. You can go on with your life, stop looking over your shoulder. You, your family—anybody you come in contact with—will be safe again. Right now, things are very dangerous."

"So you want me to tell you where he is? Rat on him?"

"Uh, yeah. That's about it. If you want to call it that. You're the only one who knows."

"I left him because he . . . well . . . he started hurting me again . . . and making me, uh . . . But I never wanted to rat on him! I just want you to know that I never wanted to do this. I just have to get away from him . . . get my life back!" My sobbing is wild, punctuated by hysterical gasps for air.

The group of detectives bob their heads in acknowledgement and shift their weight, uncomfortably helpless with my pain. "Certainly, we understand, Dawn. John's made some bad choices, and he's taken you with him. This has got to be hard . . . but . . . well, he's probably going to be safer with us than he is on the streets . . . and the sooner that happens, the safer you'll be."

They are right, and I know it. This is the best I can hope for, for both of us. My body folds, my tension expels like a gasp of air released from an overstressed tire, and I surrender to their reasoning. What choice do I have? Overcome with shaking, I reach a jittery hand to the purse dangling at my hip and flop down hard on the asphalt pavement of the parking lot. I dig deep into the bottom of the bag, my hand searching for one of the business cards from the Fountainhead Hotel. "He's not armed either, you know?"

"We understand. He's going to be safer with—"

"'Cause I got his gun." I pull out the .38 and lay it on the warm blacktop to get a better view of the bottom contents of my bag and the number to the hotel.

Instantly the three officers react, grab the concealed weapons in their shoulder holsters, and brace themselves for the unexpected. The air freezes with thick tension. I realize what I've done and halt. *Are they going to shoot me?* But then I continue searching anyway. I don't really care.

Shuffling uncomfortably, Tomlinson grimaces. He doesn't like this one bit. Lange signals him to stay cool. "All right . . ." His tone rings with a cautious key. They keep a sharp eye on the exposed pistol and my nervous, jerky hands, impatient for me to retrieve the address.

"Here it is." I stand up, leaving my things on the ground. Hesitantly, I hold the Fountainhead's logo card out to Lange. "Can you do me a favor?" I ask, feeling a rush of sadness and tears wash over me again.

"Sure. If it's within our scope of power, we'd be happy to."

"When you get him, call me and let me know that he's okay . . . that, you know, everything went all right."

"Yeah. We can do that. I'll make sure someone calls you right after we apprehend, uh . . . take him into custody."

I cringe at his words.

"Again, we know this is very hard for you, Dawn, but really it is the safest place he can be right now . . . and the safest thing for you."

"Sure." I turn away, hollow and empty, and find my brother's eyes, blinking in the bright sun. As I gather my things, the officers thank me. My gun no longer concerns them. On a parting note, each detective offers me his business card. Lange has written a note on the back: "If you ever need anything, just call."

I place the cards carefully in my wallet, just in case I will need them one day, and let my brother take me back to Louise's. He has to get the car back and catch his return flight to Oregon. "You did the right thing, Dawn," he says as he hugs me good-bye.

The police's stakeout of my family is over.

⁂

The call rings through to Louise's the next afternoon. It is Detective Lange. "Just wanted to let you know we got him. I promised you someone would call, and I thought I'd be the one."

"Yeah."

"He was there, unarmed, just like you told us." He lets out a bit of a chuckle. "He acted like he was expecting us . . . even invited us in to sit and have coffee. He asked if you were okay, but we didn't tell him we talked to you. Thought it would be better. You know . . ."

Silent tears stain my blouse, and I sniff. "So, so, he's okay?" I don't want to know any more than this. He is safe, and what happens after this is up to him. My relationship with John needs to be done with this one last question.

"Yeah. If you ask me, he was relieved. He left on the plane with Detectives Tomlinson and Blake this morning. Everything went smooth as silk." There's a long, awkward pause. "Again, Dawn, if you ever need anything, you got my number."

"Yeah. I do. Thanks."

I can't think about much in the next days. I'm still digesting the events of my brother's visit. It hurts that he left so quickly too, a result of police timing. It was a cold and heartless maneuver to get what they wanted. They had to do it, I know, but still I wish it didn't have to happen with my family . . . and I miss my brother. I have to accept the way things turned out, as hard as it is. It's the best that could have happened all around. I am glad for that. Mom keeps the calls coming to make sure I'm okay, but I'm not in the mood to talk much anymore. And when the newspapers expose the details of John's arrest, I want to disappear from the world's radar completely.

At the end of the first week of December and days after John's arrest, another fated call rings for me at the suburban house. Louise is home and hands me the phone. "It's a man," she whispers with an anguished look.

It might be the police again. "Hello?"

"Dawn. That you?"

"Yeah. Who's this? Dad?"

"Of course it's Dad. Who'd you think? Oh. Yeah, never mind. I guess you got a few reasons to be worried."

"Yeah. You heard? How'd you get my number?"

"How else? Ha. Your mother."

I'm not sure what to say. The last time I saw Dad was when he stopped by to visit me in Glendale a couple years after he took off with Pen Ci. They were no longer together. She had taken the green stone and its secrets and left him. Dad spent time doing what he loved to do afterward—backpacking across Southeast Asia. He tried to visit me once, almost two years ago now, between Kathmandu and Bombay, but John kicked him out and accused him of stealing from tenants in the court, as I stood by . . . helpless. He left furious and cursing John's name.

"Naw. Now listen. It's the funniest thing, really. I go to, uh, ahem, sit on the pot first thing in the morning like I always do. I sit down . . . open the paper, and what do I see but *John Holmes arrested on Miami Beach!*" He lets a cynical laugh escape. "First thing I think about is—where is Dawn? So I call your mother."

"No way." I snicker at the way he is telling the story. "Yeah, things have been pretty crazy, Dad."

"Yeah. That's what I thought. So, uh, where are ya, Dawn? Close by or what? I'm in Pompano. You know where that is?"

"Pompano! You're here? That's only a couple of towns away! I'm in North Miami. But, uh, I don't drive, Dad."

"Yeah, well. I can pick you up. Besides, I wanna hear the whole story. That asshole. I'm glad he finally got . . . Glad you're finally away from him, Dawn. Motherfucker."

"Me too, Dad. Me too."

"So I gotta let you in on what's going on with me first, Dawn. I'm married again, and we have a baby girl. Alicia. She's nine months old and, well, we're quiet, you know, married folk."

"Really? Sounds cool, Dad. I can't wait to meet them . . ."

I hang up feeling like God has dropped a miracle from the sky. I'm amazed at how welcoming Dad seems. *Sounds like the same ol' Dad!*

Dad picks Thor and me up a few hours later, driving straight back to his house in Pompano. He is not too thrilled about my little dog but puts up with him. I'm happy to see he is still cancer-free. The only visible reconstructive surgery on his face is how he wants it—minimal. He has no tolerance for doctors and is satisfied that the flap of skin from his forehead that twists to cover the place where the gaping hole once was gives him a handsome, rugged edge.

Kathleen, Dad's new wife, is a tall and slender young woman with brown hair and eyes. Stunningly, she is only two years older than me. One look at each other and we know we will be instant friends, nothing like a stepfamily. Alicia, a blonde little cutie, tumbles and bounces on the living room floor till Kathleen calls us in for dinner.

The four of us settle down to our meal, quietly comprehending the queer newness of our relationship to each other. Dad opens a couple of beers, passes one down in front of me, and hands me half a quaalude. "Now. I want to know everything, Dawn. Don't leave nothing out. We got all night."

I take a long, hard swig of my beer and find myself stuck, unwilling to spew the garbage that has tainted me since I last saw Dad. I reach down deep inside me and gather the reserve of my strength. "Okay, well, here it goes . . ."

By the end of the hair-raising tale, my heart is banging against my chest from the adrenaline of the memories that feel like yesterday's. I am sick to my stomach. Dad stares off into the distance as I recount the details of my history with John. He gets up only to replenish the beer when we run dry and to offer me another "halfie" of the quaalude.

I decline. "I think I'm gonna puke, Dad." My head spins violently in sparks and blurs.

"'Kay. Bathroom's over there. Come on. I'll help ya." He walks me to the toilet.

I kneel before the stark whiteness of the porcelain pit to heave and retch my guts up . . . purging the darkness, the pain, the horror and filth . . . John.

"Well, get it out, Dawn. It's all over now." He holds my hair back lovingly. "I'm glad you're out of all that shit, Dawn. Really. Get yourself cleaned up, and come back in. I got some stuff to talk to you about."

Back at the table, I sit drained and pale. Kathleen has put Alicia to bed and brings me a cold, wet towel for my head. Dad is sipping another beer and opens one for me.

I think I'm going to puke again. "I can't, Dad. No more."

"All right, babe." He takes a moment to gather his thoughts, tapping his fingernails on the shiny, polished wood. "Listen. I wanna ask you something. Kathleen and I are leaving the end of the week to go to Belize, then Thailand. We're looking to buy a beach resort. You know, income property."

"Oh, that's nice," I lie, my hopes of finding refuge sinking.

"So, well? You wanna come with us or what?"

This doesn't seem right. Did Dad just ask me to leave the country with him? It sounds like a dream . . . a dream I don't dare think too hard about . . . that might come true. "Yes! Are you kidding? Of course I do!"

Kathleen, who has been sitting quietly with us at the table throughout the retelling of my ordeal, gives me a friendly smile. "You can help with the baby!"

"All right. That's it then. You gotta get all your things to-gether real quick like." I can see Dad mentally making the plans, as he did back in Carol City while playing solitaire. "What about your dog?"

"Thor!" I gasp, knowing he can't come with us. My little hero's chocolate head rises up from my lap. A wag of his tail asks silently if I'm all right. My faithful companion. *Not my Thor!*

"Well, I know he's your pet, Dawn, and I'm sorry, but you can't take dogs to foreign countries. Nothing we can do about that."

The tearing of my heart is killing me, but I know Dad is right. I have to let go. I know leaving the country is the only chance I have to start fresh and make sure John, and anyone connected with him, will never track me down. I look down at Thor's little face, with those pleading eyes, and rub his ears and neck. As I squeeze him tight, he shivers. *He can sense when something scary is about to happen. John taught him that.* Memories flood my mind of how brave and loyal he has been to me in the most terrible times. My friend, my angel to the very end. *He deserves better. He deserves to not be scared all the time too.* I beat myself up inside for not being able to take him with me.

Big Rosie . . . Her face appears clearly in my mind's view. *Her parents . . .* I wrap Thor's soft, familiar frame in a vision of a warm bed near a fire and see him happy and content.

"I know somebody." I weep. "They'll be good to him. Won't they, boy?" I look into his graying reddish eyes. And for a moment, he stops his shivering and sweetly blinks. *He knows!* I think.

"I'll ask a lady, a friend—Big Rosie—if her parents would like to adopt him. She loves him, and they'll take good care of him." I kiss his head and cry some more, rocking him in my arms, knowing this will be one of our last days together. It will have to be.

And it is.

CHAPTER EIGHTEEN
War and Peace

Sitting in the booth of Clancy's Clam Broiler in Glendale, I am filled with nostalgia mixed with nervous anticipation as I keep a watchful eye on the lobster tank near the entrance. Fidgeting with my napkin and place setting, I wait for Sharon to meet me for lunch. It is April of 1988, almost seven years since we last spoke—that day in the Safeway parking lot. When we said good-bye. When I thought somehow she would meet up with John and me.

The stained-glass door swings open, and a small, neat frame steps inside. I recognize her right away. In her impeccably tailored navy blue gabardine suit and matching navy shoes, she instantly scans the dining room. She turns in my direction, and we lock eyes. I draw a deep breath and stand to greet her.

"Sharon? Hi. It's me . . . Dawn." I tentatively hold my arms out for a hug.

Swiftly she inspects me up and down, gives a short nod as if to acknowledge that I am really Dawn, and steps toward my out-stretched arms. "Hi!" she gushes clumsily, and then reaches in for a steel-like embrace.

We stand awkwardly for several moments, holding one another, absorbing the reality of being in each other's presence again. Sharon's strong nurse's fingers hold my shoulders in a viselike grip, and I feel her take in a deep breath—a sigh maybe, or a silent cry. "I knew you'd return," she says, gaining her composure and stepping back to look me over again.

"Your hair!" I comment, fumbling for something to say. Sharon's hair no longer hangs down her back; it is cut short—very short—and is nearly solid white.

"Like it?" She smiles. "I love it. Cut it off as soon as the divorce was final. In celebration! Freedom!" She runs her fingers through it, fluffing the white strands in different directions. "Wash and wear too!"

"Yeah. It looks good. I'm just not used to seeing you like this is all." I am instantly conscious of the extremely long mane of golden brown hair that flows down my back past my hips. "Hey! In Asia, this is still the style," I dismiss jokingly, flipping at the tendrils behind me.

"That's fine. It's not for everybody. This is something I had to do. You know?"

I nod somberly. I know. "Let's sit down." I motion in the direction of my table, realizing we are still blocking the door. "Here. I have a booth."

We settle in uneasily. My heart races in my chest; my palms sweat. I resume folding my already well-creased napkin and rummage through my brain for the next "right" thing to say. I have no idea if she will stay friendly or get distant and cold, and I realize I am still afraid of what she thinks of me.

So . . . I think. *I knew she and John got divorced because of the articles I read in the* Los Angeles Times, *but how? When?* I can only guess, and I guess the worst. My stomach does a summersault. *But she's sitting here. We're sitting here. And we're okay! And John . . . well, John is gone now.*

"How long have you been in town? You mentioned something about Asia." Sharon breaks the ice.

A waitress appears, interrupting us, and we each order an iced tea to be polite.

I have no appetite and take the moment to pull in a deep breath and gather my thoughts. "Southeast Asia. Thailand mostly . . . with my father." The words seem to come out on their own. I don't want to give much detail. "He opened a hotel on an island in the south—Phuket Island—back in early 1982. But that was after, well, John was arrested in Miami."

I lower my head. "So he's dead? AIDS?" I let the reality of the words linger in the air. The *Los Angeles Times* splashed the news on the front page less than two weeks after they reported his admittance into the VA hospital with the disease. "Just doesn't seem real . . ."

"Yup. Died fittingly on the thirteenth, if you ask me," Sharon replies, her words cutting swiftly.

I lift my head to check her face, to detect any sign of concern or grief, but there isn't any. "Yeah. Strange how thirteen was his lucky number too . . ." The hair on my arms rises in gooseflesh. Then, shaking it off, I let out a short laugh at the irony and think very hard about how to stay delicate with what I want to say next.

"He beat me, Sharon." I decide to come right to the point. Breaking the terrible wall of silence between us about the abuse is something I've been waiting years to do. "He sold me on the streets . . . sold me to . . . you know . . . to people . . . Eddie Nash . . . for drugs. Then he beat me afterward. He was ruthless and cruel . . . beat my face . . . gave me more black eyes than I can count . . . broke my ribs."

My throat constricts and, although I feel my soul erupting, I can barely choke out the words. "I came back to LA to work, but mostly to find *him*. To tell him I made it . . . in spite of him. And show him . . . to his face . . . how much better I became. Better than he ever said I would be! Better than he ever treated me . . . especially in the end."

I stop myself, realizing I am sinking too deep into my

emotions, and try again to shake off the pain. I feel the crushing anguish of John and the memories of the risks I took believing I was nothing, not worth living . . . lost, self-destructive, drinking myself into oblivion . . . alone in Southeast Asia . . . so alone.

The list of John's offenses goes on and I know I'm not through it all, but finally I am ready to face him, the angry beast who left me with such terrible scars. After these many years, I've come back to confront him . . . but it seems, it wasn't meant to be.

As Sharon listens to my story, her eyes grow large, then soften. She nods. "Yes, I kinda figured as much." Her head lowers, and she stares hard into her lap. "I went to see him in jail . . . after he was extradited." Her expression hardens, and she looks up, staring somewhere beyond me. "Another bit of poetic justice," she continues smugly. "John was jailed between the Hillside Stranglers, the Trash Bag Murderer, and the Skid Row Slasher. Right where he belonged, if you ask me."

I gape at her, disbelieving. *How bizarre,* I think, flashing back on my bike ride past the Hillside Strangler victim's house, not knowing that Angelo Buono, one of the stranglers, was living on the street. "Did he ask you about me?"

She snaps to. "I asked him where you were. What happened to you? All he told me was not to talk to you, that you had taken off with some people you met in the hotel in Miami and turned state's evidence."

"Turned state's evidence! It was more like a sting operation, a setup, in a North Miami park, where I had no choice but to turn him in. The cops even sent my brother down from Oregon— awarded him a plaque of honor for bringing me to them. They told me my family was in danger, Sharon . . . that the best thing to do, for him and for me, was to tell them where he was. And those people saved my life! He was so crazed he would have eventually killed me, Sharon. If they hadn't helped me get away, I'd be dead right now. He made a mistake—one he'd been so careful not to make. He never hit me in front of anyone before, and he messed up when he beat me in front of those people. People who cared about me and weren't afraid of him!" My anger burns again as I recall the day of my liberation from John. I force the familiar pent-up rage back down. A fiery ball of fury, as great as the scorching sun, is the burden I've carried with me since I last saw him.

Sharon shifts her fork and spoon nervously around the table. A thin line of perspiration on her upper lip glistens from the light's reflection as she swallows a hard gulp of air. "I know he went looking for you when he got out." She finally opens up. Her brow is damp with sweat. "And I thought, well, since I hadn't heard from him after I stopped going to see him in jail and I hadn't heard from you . . . that . . . maybe he found you again."

"No. Ha! He didn't find me. It turns out, right after those people helped me to a safe house, my father, who out of the blue was maybe thirty miles away, read about John's arrest in Miami and came and got me."

Sharon's gaze drifts past me again, and her eyes cast shadows as if her memory plays a scene from the past. "I'll never forgive him," she says gravely after a long pause. Then, staring me straight in the eye, she continues, "He crossed the ultimate line with me." Shadows dance wildly in her stare. "I'm a nurse. I've devoted my life to healing. I am a nurturer. I can do nothing else and feel there is no other way than to have the greatest respect for human life." Her eyes lock fiercely with mine. "He came to me that night of the murders—to the house." Her lips curl in disgust. "He was covered in blood, gray matter—brains and bone . . ." She clears her throat loudly. "At first, I thought it was his . . . that he had been in an accident. He was crying . . . like he was hurt. He asked me to draw him a bath . . . I should have known . . . the bathtub . . . his favorite confessional!"

I don't blink, clinging onto her every word. I picture myself in the bathroom in Sharon's place, watching him, waiting for him to speak first, as she did the many times I saw her interact with him in the past. *A nurturer.* I visualize her letter to me after my attempted suicide.

"You must promise me you will never repeat this!" she insists, leaning in to me. Her tongue thrusts out as if to wipe a bad taste from her mouth as her expression falls. Replaying the repulsive scene in her head, she presses on. "He said they were *scum.* That they deserved it; that they were lowlifes and didn't deserve to live!" Her face goes pale, and she pauses again.

"What did you say to him, Sharon?" I breathe.

"I asked him, 'who?' Who was he talking about and what did he mean, 'didn't deserve to live'? That's when he told me Eddie had sent his thugs to the house on Wonderland. He said Eddie had his black book and that he threatened to kill everyone in it, including you . . . me . . . his mother, Mary! He said that it was either them . . . or him and everyone he loved. He said they were dirt . . . to screw them!"

She swallows hard and lowers her head. "I told him, 'But they were your friends, John. How could you?' I told him to get out! Get out and never come back! How dare he expose me to such filth?"

Shifting uncomfortably in the booth, I ask no more questions. As I mull over her revelation to me, it fits like a missing piece of a puzzle I've almost given up on completing. Sharon is shaking, visibly unnerved at the recollection of the horror of that morning. I sense that this is the first and only time she has ever told anyone—ever gotten it off her chest—and that somehow, in doing so, she can find some peace from the memory of such betrayal. But I also sense she has more to reveal.

"Do you think that maybe he really was trying to protect us, Sharon?"

"Maybe," she answers. "And himself, of course."

I nod. "Well, that explains why he showed up at the motel cleaned up then." I purposely avoid mentioning the Valium he took to sleep that night.

"Uh-huh. He took his bloody clothes rolled up in a paper sack when he left at dawn, and later, he told me he dropped them in different Dumpsters along Glendale and Hollywood on his way to pick up the car that got left near his answering service."

My mind pictures him slinking in the early morning hours through the streets of Hollywood, frantically trying to cover his tracks. I stop . . . and let the image fade to black. *Too much,* I think, allowing my brain to rest unfocused for a short time. "He told me you said yes," I blurt before I can understand why. "Yes, that you would go into the Witness Protection Program with us. That you were just going to close up the house and meet us . . . later . . . when it was safe. He kept on telling me that . . . the whole time we were running . . . all the way to Florida!"

Sharon's eyes grow large with disbelief. "I told him *no!* I told him again, how *dare* he ask me to leave my family . . . for him! I said I would stay undercover in downtown LA while he turned over evidence to the police, but after that . . . well, he was on his own!"

My gut twists, knots in a ball. *So . . . that was a lie too,* I think, stunned for a moment. *Wow . . . ha . . . amazing. That's one I still believed.*

"I believed him, Sharon," I tell her flatly.

Sharon shakes her head slowly. I can see in her face that she's picturing me waiting for her all that time. "I . . . I'm sorry. I thought you knew."

"Yeah. Ha. I can understand that!" I feel like a fool.

Sharon appears anxious, her mind seemingly triggered by something even more disturbing. Her eyes dart wildly about the restaurant. From the main door to the lobster tank, from the waitress station to the bathroom exit. Perspiration glistens on her forehead, and her hair is damp as if she has stepped out of a steamy bath. She wipes her palms dry on her navy pants. "All right, Dawn. I'm going to tell you something now that I have not repeated to anyone since July of 1981 when it happened. After I tell you, I never want to talk about it again. You can take it how you want, but I don't ever want you to breathe another word. Am I clear?"

"Okay. I understand." My hands are curled into fists of tension; my body is tight, immobile. I prepare myself to hear what Sharon has to say next, as if I'm about to be pounced on by a lion.

"Okay. Good. Well . . . here it goes." She clears her throat and continues. "That night when you and John left and we said good-bye in the Safeway parking lot . . . well . . . I went home to finish packing up the house. Not to meet up with you and John, but to close everything up. I knew it wasn't safe there anymore . . . because of John and Eddie and, well, how John lied to the police. I was going to Oxnard to stay with my parents. Anyway, I was in the bathroom, finishing my bath and packing. The dogs were in there with me. They had been boarded for three days and didn't want to leave my side . . . you know." Sharon's mouth is parched; I can hear her tongue stick to the roof of her mouth. She takes a long drink of her iced tea. "Well . . . I was just stepping out of the bathroom, into the doorway of the kitchen . . . you know . . . when he grabbed me."

"Grabbed you? Oh my God. Who?"

"One of Eddie's thugs . . . who knows . . . a bad man? He was wearing a black ski mask, so I couldn't tell. He grabbed me around my waist and pinned my arms to my side so I couldn't move. He put a knife to my throat and told me to keep quiet."

"Sharon. What did you do?" My voice is a raspy whisper.

"You remember the antique meat hook you and John cleaned up and mounted in the kitchen by the stove?"

"Yes. The one we got from the swap meet."

"Right. Well. We struggled for a while. It was hot, and I was slippery from the bath and managed to pull one of my arms free. I was reaching around for something, anything I could grab to use as a weapon, when my hand found the meat hook."

"No . . ."

"Yes. I took hold of that handle and, as hard as I could, brought it all the way down in front of me for momentum, then swung it straight back with every ounce of strength I had . . ."

"What happened?"

Sharon sits upright confidently. "Severed his spinal cord right at C6-C7. It was instant. Sucker wasn't going to take me out without a fight." She looks impenetrable, like a fortress made of iron daring anyone to challenge her strength.

"Sharon, you're kidding! Then what did he do?"

"Dead. Instantly. He collapsed where we stood. I slipped right out of his arms."

"Sharon!" I'm incredulous, immobile except for my eyes that won't stop blinking in disbelief. "What . . . How . . . ? What did you do with the body? I mean . . . how . . . ?"

"It was a mess. Bled like a stuck pig . . . everywhere. What do you think I did? I made a phone call."

"To who?"

"Big Tom. He . . . well, his guys . . . came and picked the poor sucker up within an hour."

"What did they do with the body? Did they know who it was?"

"I didn't ask. I was told not to worry, to assume it never happened. I thanked them and said that was fine. I never wanted to talk about it again. I just wanted him out of my house. Became another John Doe, I guess . . . and that's that."

For a fleeting moment, I can't believe what Sharon has just revealed. I remember the traumatic fear of a sniper's bullet when John and I were on the run—the sinister feeling I got when John ran into that hit man at the Stardust in Vegas. Somehow, back then, I thought Sharon was safe. *John must have diverted my fear more than I knew.* Then I think about all those years of suffering and beatings I endured at John's hand, how many times I was sure he was trying to kill me—and I realize how, as a consequence of his actions, Sharon was almost killed too.

My childish impression of Sharon, always impervious to John's bad behavior, dissipates and I see her true vulnerability behind her detached armor. She is, as I am, a survivor. "I'm glad you're all right, Sharon. That probably *freaked out* the people who sent this guy after you. You sure gave them something to think about. What else happened? I mean, anyone else come looking for you?"

"Nope. I sent the fear of God through them, though. Imagine finding out your hit man is in the LA morgue with a meat hook in his neck. And John . . . well . . . I told you, I will never forgive him. I vowed as a nurse to never take a life, and *that bastard* took the one piece of identity that meant everything to me. He is the one who didn't deserve to live. He was the scum . . . and he is right where he belongs."

"Sharon, it was self-defense. You had no choice." I attempt to console her, but she doesn't respond. "Well, it doesn't matter anymore anyway, does it? He's dead now, and that's the end of it." I envision John in the hospital bed, thin and ravaged with the symptoms of AIDS, and I wonder if his family, his mother, was really there when he died, as I read in the newspapers. I wonder also if his mother prayed for him. *That would have been a blessing,* I think, warmed by my kindled faith in God that began in Asia. I feel an unexpected stab of sadness and pity imagining John's last breaths on earth and am torn again by the anger that festers inside me.

My thoughts shift suddenly back to Sharon, and I remember another piece of information I read in the paper. "I understand that he was remarried. Is that true?"

"If you want to call it that. Misty Dawn? Ah-hem! It was the closest thing he could get to you. I'm sure of it!" Sharon raises her eyebrows and dons a sly grin. "I have no doubt why he needed to get married before he died."

"What do you mean?"

"He had to have somebody there to make sure . . . well, ah-hem

. . . you know . . . that *it* was still intact!" She looks away, her face in a frozen smirk, to stifle a belly laugh. "You remember, don't you? He was *deathly* afraid someone would cut it off . . . as a trophy or something!"

"Yes . . . I remember," I reply. "He made me promise him never to let anyone remove it from his body. He was insane over the thought that someone might mount his fame and glory on their wall or something. Too bizarre!" Such insanity surrounded John. I'm repulsed that my youth was consumed by him.

I shake my head, and my mind focuses on the years, countless days and nights, after I ran from him.

In Asia, sitting in my small ta-ta-mi mat apartment in Tokyo, I am obsessed with visions of violent rage, hell bent on revenge. I hate him because the angry, mean days of him were open wounds and all I could remember. For years, any mention or memory of his name or face has triggered my anger anew, sending piercing daggers of death from every inch of my being out into the universe to impale my image of him.

I have pictured myself many times, like a Samurai . . . standing between John's legs brandishing a gleaming steel sword while he lies helpless beneath me. "Afraid were you?" I say to him. "Afraid someone might cut it off? I promised you I would never let that happen. Now what do you think?" Oh, how I wish to see him squirm. I relish the fear in his eyes. "So, do you trust me now? Like I trusted you? Did you keep your promise to never hurt me, John?" I raise the blade high above my head and come down swiftly toward his nether regions. "Heeiiiii-ya!" I scream at the top of my lungs into a blackness that, thank God, won't let me go any farther.

I snap out of my bitter fantasy and think for a moment that I'll tell Sharon about my fierce visions of vengeance. I stop . . . and change my mind. "I was really mad at him, Sharon. Mad for years. He took away my innocence, my trust . . . my heart!" Tears form in the corners of my eyes. "How could he?" Now a sense of self over-whelms me. "I survived him, Sharon, and survived a dangerous, lonely life after him. I struggled in Southeast Asia. My dad was there, but he wasn't a lot of help. He made promises he didn't keep and, well, let's just say he gave me bad advice . . . and basically left me on my own. I managed, though—drank a lot of alcohol to get through it. But I did some amazing things too. I climbed Mount Fuji and sailed down the Malacca Straights in a monsoon. I speak Thai and Japanese well enough to travel comfortably among the locals. In Japan, well, some terrible things happened and I almost lost myself, but I found a connection with God and learned how to pray. Now, that saved me!" I stop myself, noticing the uncomfortable squint in Sharon's face and remember how angry she has always been with God. "I have a certificate in gemology, Sharon! It's not a big deal, but it's an education!" Waves of raw emotion spill out as the floodgates of the last six years are released.

"Well, I always told you you had a brain." She smiles kindly.

My heart is still audibly pounding as I exhale. "He never wanted me to grow up, did he, Sharon?"

"No. He was already threatened by you before you even turned eighteen!"

I shudder and look away. "Why?"

"He didn't want to lose you . . . so he had to keep you . . . ah-hem . . . below his level."

I know she is right. Then in a softer tone, I whisper, "I'm better than that, Sharon. I'm simply better."

"Yes, you are. We both are."

"Yeah." I'm worn out . . . tired of these memories that beat me down. "It hurt too much to hate him, Sharon. I had to do something. I was going crazy. It was while I lived in Japan that I was at my lowest. My insides were tearing me up. All those horrible memories haunted me. I almost couldn't go on; I got so depressed. Then . . . I can't explain it, but finally something lifted. The pain, that suffocating burden broke . . . kinda like a fever would . . . and my poetry came back to me again."

"Well, they say that writing helps the healing process, and

poetry is even better. You can't blame yourself, Dawn. You reacted like any abused person would."

"Yeah. I know. Ha! Well, if life is poetry, then this is my poem." I laugh at the irony because I know my poems are scary, not joy-filled lyrics of love and light.

We are silent then. The bustling of the restaurant's lunch crowd glides on around us, customers being seated, glasses clinking. I focus on John again, the time that has gone by since we last saw each other. I think about the conflict of my emotions toward John—loving him, hating him. The realization that now I will *really* never see him again hits me, and then I remember . . . the bus stop a few days ago . . .

Compassion fills me like a warm breeze as I recall the robin's-egg blue of the sky that stands out in contrast to the large wooden crucifix of Saint Anthony's on Third Street. I step off of the bus at my regular stop the morning of March 13, 1988. The sun is bright with barely a cloud for shade. Without warning, I hear the calling of my name, clear and sharp: "Dawn."

I whip around to look toward the church—up in the direction of the voice. It is John's voice . . . and distinctly he calls my name again. In the sky, directly above where I am waiting and staring, frozen to the sidewalk, is only the crucifix jutting up from the pointed steeple of the church. He's not alive anymore, I whisper to myself. He is not on this earth. A flock of small sparrows darts up and to the right, and as an airplane's thin streak of white smoke passes by, John's voice cries out in a tone that can only be the pouring out of someone's last words to earth: "Forgive me?"

John?

"Dawn." The vibration of my name triggers every cell's full attention. "Forgive me, Dawn? I'm sorry."

The words catch in my heart. A sudden memory of the affection I felt between us envelops me, and I am overcome with the deepest sadness.

"I'm sorry," his voice pleads again. Then—with those words—it

is as if a veil of confusion lifts from me and I understand. I recognize the heaviness, the viselike pressure of pain and sorrow he carried these last several years. His suffering seems to sear through me, and I take on his identity for that moment, a vision of crippling remorse that tears at his soul and leaves him paralyzed with overwhelming helplessness. I see that his life had been consumed by fear, a tireless weight that finally drowned him . . . and now in death his bondage is ended and he is ready to move on.

Whether this is an illusion or real, to me there is no question what my response will be. No throat-clutching anger or old pain to halt me . . . Yes, John. I forgive you . . .

As suddenly as it appeared, the presence is gone.

Blares and whirrs of the nearby traffic on Third Street bring me back into the moment, and numbly I continue to my apartment in a daze about what has just happened.

At the door to greet me, my roommate has the Los Angeles Times *in hand. "I'm sorry," he tells me, pointing to the headlines. I know what he is about to say. "John passed away this morning."*

"I know," I tell him, and he hugs me as I melt into his body and cry.

Sharon is stirring her tea compulsively after the long bout of silence between us. Awkward about wanting to share my experience, I decide to be brief. "He came to me at my bus stop on the day that he died, Sharon. Well . . . it was his voice, really." I blush a little and continue. "He asked me to forgive him. And, well . . . I said yes."

Sharon stops clanking her tea glass, and her face drains ghostly white. "He came to me too," she says grimly. "But not like that!" She looks appalled.

"He did?"

Scooting straight up in her seat, she flattens her napkin tightly on her lap. "I couldn't sleep . . . ," she begins. "You remember how solidly I usually sleep?"

"Uh-huh." I nod.

"Well, that night was different. I hadn't thought of him for a while, not other than briefly, but for some reason that night I couldn't get him out of my head. I knew then it was going to be a rough night. I finally started to fall asleep around midnight when I distinctly heard screaming . . . an agonizing, pitiful scream. I sat bolt upright, scared to death! The screaming came from the closet and got closer . . . the most god-awful noise you'd ever want to hear. It was John. He came wailing from out of the closet, past the foot of the bed, toward the door to the hallway. There . . . was another door there instead. Not the bedroom door, but a large, round, vaultlike door." She wipes the accumulating beads of sweat from her brow. "Wailing piteously, John was pulled through this door. And then it slammed shut."

My heart is pounding. "Did he say anything to you?" I ask, horrified.

"Nope. Didn't look at me either. Just crossed through the room . . . screaming. I'll never forget that sound as long as I live." She looks weary. "When I checked the clock . . . it was exactly one in the morning. Later, when I read the paper, I found out that was the exact time he died."

"My God, Sharon!"

"I know. Well, there is no doubt to me where he is now. Hell. He made his bed, if you ask me . . ."

I swallow a gulp of air hard, picturing her sinister bedroom vision, and I shudder. How horrible . . . how sad. Can something like that be possible? Sitting still for a few moments, I shake the disturbing images off my psyche. John's voice and presence were too real to me, too strong and sudden; I cannot deny it. What Sharon saw was her vision, not mine . . . and I'm glad. I don't want to be caged by my hatred anymore. *It's sad that she is so inflexible and hard still. And John . . . he could have been so much more,* I think. *But instead . . . It's just a pity.*

"Well, enough about him," Sharon interrupts, intentionally

changing the somber mood. "That's not all I came here for. I need to give you something." She retrieves a package wrapped in bunny paper that she carried in with her under her arm. "Happy Easter!"

"Sharon! No. Really?"

"Well, Easter is coming up and, anyway, I decided we needed to celebrate." Her smile beams with anticipation, and a nostalgic sense of old *home* startles me. I reach over to open the card.

Dear Dawn,

For these many years I have thought about you, wondering if you were safe, knowing that one day we would see each other again. I've had this on my wall since the day you left to remind me of you, and today I happily return it. We have survived some of the hardest times any person should have to endure and now it is time to enjoy each other in better days. I'm so glad to have you back in my life.

I love you,
Sharon

Unsure of how I feel, I don't speak. Gingerly I peel the paper back from her gift to me. There, packaged ever so carefully, is my favorite signed and dated Stewart Moskowitz lithograph of comical penguins following a "trojan duck." It is a gift originally from John and Sharon, given in what I call the good times. "I thought John destroyed this."

"Nope. Not that."

I stare at her dark-rimmed glasses and then into her brown eyes, and a well of emotion comes to me from across the table. I am touched. "I'm sorry, Sharon," I say with a burning need to clear my conscience. "I . . . John always . . . I thought you, well, knew. I'm . . . so sorry."

"No!" She breathes a deep sigh. *"I'm* sorry. I never thought he would stoop so low. To me . . . I just couldn't imagine it. I should have known . . . but, I . . . it was something I couldn't look at. It's me who should apologize. You were just a kid. I only, well, again never thought he could . . ." Her words fade.

In my heart, I know she was aware of John's inappropriateness with me—all along. But I know Sharon is doing the best she can to turn past mistakes around for the better . . . and so am I.

❧

I try to remember, for the book's sake, as much of the abuse as I can stomach. Several of the details are left dark and impenetrable for many self-preserving reasons. My throat constricts when I close my eyes and picture myself back there, and I feel frustrated. Many days, the need comes over me to hike up the mountains behind my house for solace. There is a trail I take in the summer months, and right now I can't resist.

I bring my daughter to a friend's, throw on my hiking clothes, and head up the path. My heart begins to beat louder as I make my

475

way up. I can't stop asking myself, *Why? Why am I bringing myself to remember such terrible memories?* I cannot remember my reasons for beginning to write my story with John. I know they were good reasons, but somehow I cannot recall any of them.

I begin to chant, "God's will, not mine. God's will, not mine," as I steadily climb to the top of Table Mountain.

The top is my reward. I am breathless, and my mind is clear. Everything is beautiful, and all is right with the world.

I still cannot put words to why I began to write this, but I know I am right where I am supposed to be and I say a prayer out loud, out into the sky and the wind, for strength.

EPILOGUE

Who would have thought that twenty-two years later, Hollywood would make a movie called *Wonderland*? But I'm not Alice, even though I fell into a world I could never have imagined. I am Dawn. For all my wishing, it seems I was never able to wipe John's name from mine after all, but it doesn't matter.

As with all stories, this one has as perfect an ending as you can get. And, despite all its pain and sorrow, it is simply a true story—and nothing is better than real life . . . if we listen.

ACKNOWLEDGMENTS

To GOD . . . for my life.

To Maria Morris, the mother of my heart, for encouragement, reading my early chapters, and grading me in the loving way only a fourth grade teacher could.

To Val Kilmer for launching this book by asking for my chronology and then praising my writing. For keeping a special place on his office shelf marked "Dawn's Book."

To Linda Pereira—songbird, rooster, lioness, and angel—who praised me for my courage, disarmed those who spoke against me, and called me every day to make sure I hadn't given up.

To Rhea Sampson, the Angel Lady, who kept my spirits up by sharing the words of the Angels.

To my brother, Wayne, and my sister, Terry, for the many tears we shared back then and to the healing that still needs to happen.

To my mother, Edda, for teaching me strength.

To my father, Wayne, for serving his country.

To Paula Lucas, my friend and supporter.

To my counselors and support groups who brought me out of the dark.

To the Blue Mountain Writers (BMW) and all my writing mentors.

To everyone who supported and believed in me.

RESOURCES

Adult Survivors of Child Abuse
www.ascasupport.org
The Morris Center
PO Box 14477
San Francisco, CA 94114
info@ascasupport.org

Ahava Kids
www.ahavakids.org
PO Box 498
Old Saybrook, CT 06475
Toll free: 1-877-416-
0050
1-860-760-0370
info@ahavakids.org

American Professional Society
on the Abuse of Children
www.apsac.org
350 Poplar Ave.
Elmhurst, IL 60126
1-877-402-7722
apsac@apsac.org

Covenant House Florida
www.covenanthousefl.org
5931 E. Colonial Dr.
Orlando, FL 32807
1-407-482-0404
733 Breakers Ave.
Ft. Lauderdale, FL 33304
1-954-561-5559

End Violence Against Women
International
www.evawintl.org
PO Box 33
Addy, WA 99101
1-509-684-9800
info@evawintl.org

FAIR Fund, Inc.
www.fairfund.org
PO Box 21656
Washington, DC 20009
1-202-265-1505
info@fairfund.org

Family Violence Prevention
Fund
www.endabuse.org
383 Rhode Island St., Ste. #304
San Francisco, CA 94103
1-415-252-8900
info@endabuse.org

Girls Educational & Mentoring
Services
www.gems-girls.org
1-212-926-8089

RESOURCES

Love Is Respect.Org
National Teen Dating
Abuse Helpline
www.loveisrespect.org
1-866-331-9474
TTY 1-866-331-8453

National Center for Missing
& Exploited Children
www.missingkids.com
Charles B. Wang International
Children's Building
699 Prince St.
Alexandria, VA 22314
Hotline: 1-800-THE-LOST
(1-800-843-5678)
General: 1-703-224-2150

National Coalition Against
Domestic Violence
www.ncadv.org
1120 Lincoln Street, Ste. 1603
Denver, CO 80203
1-303-839-1852
mainoffice@ncadv.org

National Criminal Justice
Reference Service
www.ncjrs.gov
PO Box 6000
Rockville, MD 20849-6000
1-800-851-3420

National Domestic
Violence Hotline
www.ndvh.org
1-800-799-7233 (SAFE)
TTY 1-800-787-3224

National Human Trafficking
Resource Center
nhtrc.polarisproject.org
1-888-373-7888

National Network to End
Domestic Violence
www.nnedv.org
2001 S St. NW, Ste. 400
Washington, DC 20009
1-202-543-5566

National Organization for
Victim Assistance
www.trynova.org
510 King St., Ste. 424
Alexandria, VA 22314
Hotline: 1-800-TRY-NOVA
(1-800-879-6682)
General: 1-703-535-NOVA (6682)